Jane in Love

Jane
in
Love

A Novel

RACHEL GIVNEY

WM
WILLIAM MORROW
An Imprint of HarperCollinsPublishers

JANE IN LOVE. Copyright © 2020 by Rachel Givney. All rights reserved. Printed in the United States of America. No part of this book may be used or reproduced in any manner whatsoever without written permission except in the case of brief quotations embodied in critical articles and reviews. For information, address HarperCollins Publishers, 195 Broadway, New York, NY 10007.

HarperCollins books may be purchased for educational, business, or sales promotional use. For information, please email the Special Markets Department at SPsales@harpercollins.com.

Originally published in Australia in 2020 by Penguin Australia.

FIRST U.S. EDITION

Designed by Diahann Sturge

Part opener book illustration © Gruffi / Shutterstock, Inc.
Part and chapter opener feather © aksol / Shutterstock, Inc.

Library of Congress Cataloging-in-Publication Data has been applied for.

ISBN 978-0-06-301908-9

20 21 22 23 24   LSC   10 9 8 7 6 5 4 3 2 1

All geniuses born women are lost to the public good.

—Stendhal

Jane in Love

Chapter One

As Jane climbed over a hedge and landed in a pool of mud, some of which flew upward and came to rest on her boots, gown, and face, she paused for a moment, pondering whether behavior like this might be the reason she struggled to find a husband.

The fact that she was wandering through some farmer's turnip paddock at eight o'clock in the morning did not alone make Jane consider ineligibility for marriage to be her greatest talent. As she leapt over a stone fence and into another field—less of a field, in fairness, and more of a quagmire (Why did she always end up in the dirtiest fields in England? Did mud seduce her?)— she compiled a list of all the ways in which her character could be considered unmarriageable.

She preferred a good book to an assembly and liked to wander the countryside alone for hours. The neighbors all agreed these were suspicious traits for a woman to possess. Jane also destroyed hairstyles at the same rate she muddied dresses. Her fawn curls, commanded into a Grecian knot on the crown of her head by her mother earlier that morning, now rested below her left ear in a disappointed bundle. These facts alone ruled her from contention for any prospective husband.

But as well as the scandalous affectations of reading, walking, and hairstyle-assassinating, Jane possessed one marriage-deterring peccadillo that put all the others to shame.

She wrote things.

Not letters and poems, though she had talent for both. Novels were Jane's canvas. A germ of a story would come to her, in the woods or during an assembly, and she'd toil and rage to tease the seed from its pod. She'd walk around in a funk, unable to put her mind to any other task until she wrote it all down: until sisters were reunited, villains dispatched, lovers married. Once finished, she'd drop her quill and fall asleep with an empty head, her voice added to the dream of the world. She'd wake the next morning with a new idea bothering her, and the toil would begin once more, its importance for her on par with breathing.

As an accomplishment, writing did not equal embroidery or watercolor, but at least it displayed neat handwriting. This had once endeared her to her family. She also told crude and diverting stories, of which everyone approved, and which were as pleasant a way to pass the time before dinner as any. But as each year passed and she remained unmarried, the habit went from a harmless folly to the culprit for her failure in life; ladies did not write books.

No one published Jane's work. When she was nineteen, her papa, filled with fatherly pride, sent one of her novels to the publisher Thomas Cadell in London, even offering to cover the costs of printing himself. The family waited with joyous anticipation at the prospect of seeing the Austen name in print, and after several weeks, the letter was answered by Cadell: "declined by return of post." The quality of Jane's writing did not even deserve a written rejection. George Austen never approached a publisher again, and Jane hid the manuscript under the floorboards of her room.

But despite the rebuff and declaration that her talent did not exist, Jane found herself unable to stop writing. Lady writers did exist, but as oddities, outcasts, and degenerates. Ann Radcliffe, Jane's idol, published five novels, but people knew her more for being barren. With stories such as these the guide to what the future might hold for Jane, her mother declared one Tuesday afternoon that if she ever caught Jane writing anything but a shopping list again, she would set it on fire.

From that day on, Jane wrote in secret. She kept up her hobby, concealing it from the world. She scratched her thoughts onto scraps of paper in the woods, then collated everything later while Mama was out of the house.

JANE HAD WALKED the woods and groves above Bath for the past hour, ruminating on these topics. She did so for a specific reason: Mr. Charles Withers, a young gentleman, and his father would come to the house in less than an hour to call upon Jane.

Jane had never met Mr. Withers before, but she understood the importance of his call. It had once felt as though a new gentleman visited the house every other week to inquire after Jane. That was when she was twenty. She had now reached twenty-eight, and no man had called on her in seven months. She was resigned to the fact that one might never call on her again.

Jane needed a husband for two reasons. First, if she did not acquire one, she would become a spinster and then perish, as her mama informed her daily. Jane held the grand title of the second-oldest unmarried woman in the West Country, besides her own dear sister, and Cassandra only remained single because her fiancé had passed away. Jane had no such excuse. The older she grew, the more piteous looks she collected from friends and family, and pity induced few men into marriage. If she reached thirty years of age, still unwed, all would be lost.

Jane's second reason for marriage involved her finances. Once her parents exited God's earth, her father's meager assets would pass to his eldest son, James, and Jane would fall upon the fiduciary mercy of her brothers: the rich ones who did not care for her and the poor ones who did. Alternatively, she could earn her own income by selling flowers, washing clothes, or becoming a pirate.

A third reason existed for Jane wanting a husband: more of an idle want than a reason, a feeling of such silliness she dared not mention it to anyone.

It was love.

But as she reminded herself daily, love was a luxury for a woman in her position, and whenever this third item returned to her mind—persistent little annoyance that it was—she pushed it out of her brain. It did no one good to mull over wishes.

She pushed it away again now as she leapt over a boxwood hedge and into the next field. The mud splatter now reached above her middle, while a piece of hedge rested in her hair. She performed an excellent impression of a speckled egg. Measures needed to be taken to ensure the best possible chance of securing this Mr. Withers as her husband. Nothing could be done about her poverty or age, but if she could conceal her true nature, at least for an hour, she might have a small chance.

Jane fetched a quill and a scrap of paper from her pocket and compiled a list.

Silence appeared to be an excellent tactic. She wrote that down.

Her cleverness disquieted. If forced to communicate, she'd restrict her comments to the weather or, better still, perform feminine noises in his general direction.

Smiling was also a virtue in this environ. When she was thinking, her face tended to fix itself in a scowl. Ahh. She added *no thinking* to her list.

With her directives complete, she placed the scrap of paper in her pocket and left the fields of Somerset. She sighted the spires of St. Swithin's church and returned to the edge of Bath, already late. As she stepped onto the cobblestones, Jane spotted the back of an old man with white hair. "Papa, what business have you in this part of town?" she asked, pushing the paper further into her pocket.

Her father turned, his blue eyes shining. "I was sampling the fine Somerset air," he said. "I must have lost my way. Will you escort an old man back to his house?"

"With pleasure," she replied, taking his arm and patting it. Years of preaching in freezing churches had ruined his spine—he could not walk more than fifty yards without cursing—so Jane knew he had not been taking a stroll, but had come to find her, probably to make sure she did not deteriorate in a field somewhere.

He did not rush her or say anything about their upcoming appointment with Mr. Withers. Her father's age surpassed seventy, but he remained as handsome as in his portrait as a young parson. His long white hair was tied back with a ribbon of duck-egg blue that Jane had bought for him on a trip to Kent. He rarely wore it, claiming it too nice to spoil with everyday wear, and Jane was hurt more than she let on. But he wore the ribbon now. Jane sensed he did it to win her favor that morning, and he succeeded.

As Jane and her father made their way back to the house, they passed the Pump Room on Stall Street. Giant honeystone columns soared into the air at the grand building's entrance, welcoming people as though they were entering a Grecian temple. A woman cloaked in an emerald pelisse paused before them and turned her head up at the building's facade with reverence, as though she was sending up a prayer. Jane scowled. Performances like this happened often in Bath, for the Pump Room was indeed a church, deserving of worship. Aside from the tea-taking, sacred water–imbibing, and intrigue that went on there, some of the most spectacular marriage contracts in England had been agreed in its assembly room. Jane never went inside; as a single woman, rapidly aging, she would be welcomed by its guests with the same reception they might offer a leper.

Jane did not entirely love the town she lived in. Her parents had moved there upon her father's retirement from the church, uprooting their comfortable life in a country parsonage in Hampshire. Jane's parents claimed the benefits to her father's health had prompted the move west—every neighbor and newspaper raved about the healing properties of Bath's spa waters—but Jane suspected another reason. George and Cassandra Austen had themselves met in Bath, and with two daughters speeding toward spinsterhood, they had relocated their family not to improve Reverend Austen's digestion, but for one last-ditch attempt to marry off their female children. Where else to make these happy events occur but Bath, the marriage capital of England, and the place where Jane's parents themselves had wed. In the move to Somerset Jane observed no changes to her life but one: where green fields and quiet once filled her days, now fog and gossip replaced them.

Still, she could not abhor Bath completely. After all, without its scandal and silly people, its intrigue and nonsense, she might have nothing to write about.

Jane stepped around the woman in the green coat who continued to pray to the Pump Room and avoided her eye. At least Jane was not as odd as she—or so she hoped.

Chapter Two

*O*f all the things that delighted Jane about Bath, her living arrangement pleased her most. The other residents of Sydney House were an assortment of kind people, always ready to relate the misfortunes of the building's inhabitants. One such person, Lady Johnstone, greeted Jane and her father in the foyer.

"You are expecting Mr. Withers of Kent and his son this morning," the woman announced. She wore a long, draped pelisse. If the intention was to advertise her husband's wealth through the amount of fabric required to cover her, Lady Johnstone succeeded. She fiddled with her reticule, fashioned from French silk, which she held at an angle to reflect the light. "Mr. Withers wears a blue coat. The buttons are smaller than I expected. My concern is that you are so late, the gentlemen may have noticed," she counseled, with all the kindness of her heart. Lady Johnstone still powdered her hair, though the style had gone out of fashion twenty years ago, and flecks fell on Jane's arm as the woman spoke.

"Thank you, Lady Johnstone," said the Reverend. "You are kind to us. A pretty bag, madam. Is it new?"

Jane opened her mouth to make a less diplomatic remark, but before she could, her father guided her up the stairs. They entered their own apartment, where Jane quickly changed her gown and washed her face before being set upon by her mother, who dragged Jane and her father into the parlor. "Mr. Withers and his son are already here," Mrs. Austen hissed, as she had a habit of doing when eligible men were around. "They wait in the sitting room."

A breeze blew down the hallway and opened the sitting room door by a crack. Jane crept forward and stole a glance. She inhaled.

"What do you think, Jane?" asked her father.

Jane Withers, thought she. She could scarcely believe the man standing in the sitting room across the hall. The last man who'd come to the door as Jane's intended suitor resembled a boiled egg. From where on God's earth had the matchmaker drummed up this chiseled statue? Mr. Withers's height required him to duck to see through the window. His shoulders protruded from his torso at twice the width of other men's. He smiled when he looked out the window and smiled again when he spoke to his father, who stood next to him in the sitting room. From what Jane observed, he smiled a great deal.

As Mr. Withers turned to point out the window, a singular shard of English sunlight caught every fleck of gold in his chestnut hair. Jane gasped. The angel Gabriel had stepped from his cloud and entered their drawing room.

Then Jane halted the celebratory feeling, replacing it with a more appropriate one of worry. The matchmaker had erred once more. Whereas before she had delivered partners of too low quality, imbeciles and shouters, this time she delivered one too high. Jane calculated the combined worth of her prospective spouse's handsomeness, financial solvency, and station, compared them to her own, and found the totals did not match. This wealthy Adonis, with his pick of women, would not fall for a novel-writing, rapidly aging, dowry-lacking woman.

Jane caught her reflection in the hallway mirror. She'd swapped her muddied boots and field-splattered pelisse for silk slippers and her finest gown, but her best clothes looked like rags compared to the fine wool of Mr. Withers's coat. She gasped at the worst portion of her person. "My hair!" A bird's nest had replaced her mother's Grecian knot.

"Perhaps take the lumpy left bit," said the Reverend in a helpful voice, "and move it northward?" Jane did so.

"You are making it worse," said Mrs. Austen, slapping Jane's hands away. She grabbed Jane's head, removed the piece of hedge, and scraped the hair back into a painful yet decent style. "Let me look at you." Her mother stepped back and studied Jane's overall appearance. She harrumphed with a frown and ran her hand along the thick, solid gold necklace that hung around her neck.

Mrs. Austen came from a wealthier family than Mr. Austen, with distant connections to rank and title, and had upset her relations by marrying a country parson. As the years passed in their quiet parish, her income and station had diminished still until she retained a singular vestige of her old life: a solid-gold locket and chain that shamed the brass trinkets she had acquired during marriage. Purchased in the 1600s for a princely sum by her great-grandmother, a baroness, the necklace had since then grown in value. Mrs. Austen displayed it proudly around her neck and polished it every Sunday with a silk cloth.

She grabbed Jane by the shoulders. "Listen now, Jane. Say beguiling and coquettish things to this man. Do not talk about books or politics or anything else to make him feel stupid. No one marries a clever boots."

Jane bristled; she would have argued had she not explored the theme herself all morning. "Yes, Mama," she said. "I promise to act as silly as possible."

Then her father touched her hand. "It will be all right, Jane."

Jane nodded. With the gravity of the situation communicated, and enough scowling and worrying completed, the trio each took a deep breath and proceeded into the sitting room.

Reverend Austen entered first and greeted Mr. Withers and his son, Charles. Introductions were then made with startling control for the Austens. Even Mrs. Austen was shushed into a modicum of decency by the wealth and handsomeness of the suitor. She waited a full seven minutes before providing a list of her son Edward's houses, filling the space with polite and meaningless chatter, as was her talent.

Jane sighed with gratitude for once at her mother's conversation, for it removed the focus from her. She preoccupied herself with not meeting the young man's eye; the first time Jane allowed him a decent look at her face, he would run a Yorkshire mile. She counted the floorboards instead. But when she finally snuck a glance in his direction, to her great surprise, she found him smiling at her.

"Mr. Withers, I believe you are a naturalist," Mrs. Austen said to the father.

"Indeed, I am," replied Mr. Withers Senior. "Though I am no professional botanist; it is a hobby of mine."

Jane stole another glance at the young man as her mother praised and flattered the older one for his dedication to nature. Could it be? Was Mr. Withers truly smiling at her? He was. Jane commanded her breathing to slow.

"There is a bush of roses in the garden which I cannot identify,"

Mrs. Austen said. "Would you assist me in classifying it?" Mr. Withers Senior replied his assent, and the quintet set forth outside to explore Sydney Gardens. Jane knew the roses her mother referred to were pink Queen Mary's, the standard-issue flower in the limey soil of Bath, and her mother knew this also. While Jane could see her mother's strategies from miles away, evidently the men could not.

"If you will observe, Mr. Withers, I see the bud of a rose by the garden wall," Mrs. Austen said.

"I see no buds, Mrs. Austen," Mr. Withers Senior replied. "We might struggle, for it is March."

The gardens resembled a graveyard of bare earth and sticks, but Jane's mother persisted with her scheme. "Perhaps you are right," Mrs. Austen said. "Will you join me for a closer inspection? Then we may settle the matter."

Mrs. Austen led him and the Reverend away, leaving Jane and her suitor alone, filling Jane with terror. Jane felt grateful for her mother's plotting but now the situation would force her to say something, whereupon she'd ruin everything.

As Jane and Mr. Withers walked up the path in silence, Jane recalled her mother's earlier instructions and strained for something coquettish to say. The weather? It appeared the rain had ceased. She thought of the most flirtatious way to comment on precipitation, perched on the verge of despair, when Charles Withers himself turned his head and smiled. "Have you taken the waters, Miss Jane?" he asked her.

She struggled for a way to reply without speaking. "I have not, sir," she answered at last, defeated into verbalization. He referred to the famous ancient spa waters that bubbled up from the earth's center and collected in a pool in the center of Bath. King

George had drunk the water and been cured of his gout. People flocked from far and wide to imbibe the pool's magical liquid after the miracle. John Baldwin built a grand tearoom, the Pump Room, adjacent to the mystical site so people might drink it in style. The only person Jane knew who'd been inside was Margaret, the Austens' housemaid. After much prodding, Margaret had confessed to paying a week's wages to drink a teaspoon of sulfurous water, which she spat out when her friends turned their backs. She assured Jane it had done her good in the brief time it sat in her mouth.

"Do you know what it is, to take the waters?" Mr. Withers asked. "I have walked around Bath for three days now pretending to know what it means. With the performance gone on for so long, I am too afraid to ask anyone." He adjusted his coat button.

Jane stopped. Did this handsome man make a joke? Jane tested him. "What do you think it means, sir?"

"From what I can gather, one breaks into the Pump Room under the cover of darkness, gathers up as much water as he can carry in his pockets, then runs back out again." He smiled again.

Jane swallowed. "You are modest in professing your ignorance, Mr. Withers. That is precisely how it is done."

"May I take my own water from the bathtub or repossess it from an obliging puddle, or is it only the water from the Pump Room tap that is magical?" he asked.

"I regret the sorcery is limited to the water you must pay for."

"Oh, but I intend to steal it."

"Of course." Jane could not contain a small smile.

"I shall need an accomplice, if you will do me the honor."

So much time had passed since a man last requested Jane's company that she almost missed the invitation. "With pleasure," she said with another smile. She elected to stop smiling then; two sufficed. Any more and she might be accused of having a nice time.

"Tomorrow I have business in Bristol, but perhaps the day after," he said.

Further conversation revealed, to her horror, that he admired *Cecilia,* Jane's favorite book. Jane was worried, for now she enjoyed this man's company, respected his opinions, and shared his mockery of Bath. With his one great defect being the smallness of his coat buttons, Jane had no choice but to like Mr. Withers.

They reunited with their parents and returned to the house. Jane and her mother agreed to attend the Pump Room in two days' time. Charles Withers and his father took their leave with felicity and goodwill and, as the Austens bade them farewell by their gig, Mrs. Austen enjoyed the happy opportunity to wave at Lady Johnstone, who spied at them from behind her sitting room curtain.

Chapter Three

The next morning, a letter arrived for Jane from Cassandra. *My dear Jane,* it read. *It seems so long since we last spoke. I trust I have missed much while I have been away, and Bath misses me as much as I it.*

Her sister made this joke often, for their lives in Bath were duller than their brother James's Sunday sermons. A parade of vapor and nothings filled their time, meeting silly people who stayed for a week and then returned home, never thought of again once they departed Stall Street. However, today Jane did have news. She longed for Cassandra now, but her sister had travelled east twelve days ago to help Edward's wife birth her eighth child. Cassandra had expressed reluctance to leave Jane, observing that Jane may have slumped into one of her fogs, as she did from time to time. But Jane insisted she go, for her own struggles of the mind were ridiculous compared to the safe delivery of a spare Austen heir. Her sister would delight in reading Jane's news.

Jane took a place at the small desk by the drawing room window, where Mr. Withers had stood the day before, and drafted her reply. *My dear Cassandra,* she scratched onto the paper with her father's quill. *Steady the buffs, sweet sister. I have news from Bath.* She dipped the quill, composing a few lines in her head about

Mr. Withers, his coat buttons, Lady Johnstone, but found she could write none. A drop of ink fell from the pen to the page.

Jane felt silly. In the new day, it all appeared a flight of fancy. Mr. Withers had smiled at her and invited her to a public assembly. In her desperate state, her mind had collected these crumbs of regard and transmuted them into true love. He'd likely invited her to the Pump Room out of charity. Jane cursed her daydreams and put the quill down.

"What are you writing, Jane?" her mother asked as she entered the drawing room. "Not a story, I hope." She snatched up Jane's letter and studied it.

"No, Mama," Jane replied.

Jane's mother squinted at the paper. "I maintain my previous decision to incinerate any novels I find. Even now you have Mr. Withers."

"I do not have Mr. Withers, Mama."

Her mother put the page down. "Come now, you may write to your sister later. We are due in town."

As they crossed Pulteney Bridge and headed toward the center of Bath, Jane noticed something strange. Most of the townsfolk usually ignored her or shook their heads when she walked by but today a woman called, "Good morning, Jane!" with a broad smile as they passed. This peculiar salutation preceded a dozen similarly enthusiastic greetings as Jane and her mother continued down the cobblestoned street. By the time they reached the corner, every tradesman's wife and churchgoer in the lane had waved or smiled at her. Mrs. Austen looped her arm through Jane's happily.

"Why is everyone so pleasant, Mama?" Jane asked. "They scare me with their smiles."

"Oh, hush now," said her mother. "They are happy for us."

Jane stopped walking. "Why are they happy, Mama?" Her mother made no remark. "Mama, how many people did you tell of Mr. Withers?"

"Hardly anyone!" her mother cried, waving her hand as though swatting a fly. "What is the problem, in any case? Who conceals such good news?"

"I have only been invited to an assembly."

"What nonsense you speak sometimes," her mother said. She dragged Jane down Stall Street and turned left, where the waves and smiles of half the population of Bath assaulted Jane. She swallowed in panic and was about to berate her mother for her foolish indiscretion when Mrs. Austen halted out in front of Maison Du Bois, a dress shop at the end of Westgate. At first Jane assumed her mother paused there to tie a bootlace, but then she turned to enter the shop.

"Mama. Have you gone mad?" Jane asked. Maison Du Bois sold the most expensive gowns in Bath, if not all of England. Locals never patronized this business; it existed solely for rich Londoners and nobles who shopped there on holiday. The child princess Charlotte had purchased her entire wardrobe there, to the dismay of the privy purse, with every gown, glove, bonnet, and boot shipped exclusively from Paris.

Mrs. Austen walked inside, pulling Jane behind her. It surprised Jane that the door remained unguarded. She expected an armed sentry to stand there, blocking the untitled likes of her and her mother from entering in their soot-stained boots, but they passed through the doors undetected. Once inside, the most beautiful room molested Jane's eyes: white plaster roses adorned the ceiling, polished cornices trimmed with brass blessed every cabinet. A giant oak staircase soared upward into the back of the room, leading to who knew where—heaven, maybe. Glass cabinets held cream scarves of silk and damask, lemon-hued bonnets, peach slippers as light as air, and shawls spun from pure gold. Gowns hung from every surface. It more resembled a patisserie than a dress shop.

"What a dreadful place," Jane said. "This will not do at all."

"This is what the afterlife must be like," Mrs. Austen said in a hushed tone.

A shop hand scowled at them from behind a cabinet. "Are you lost?" He studied them from head to toe and made little attempt to conceal his appraisal.

Jane nodded. "Let's go, Mama," she said. She made for the exit.

Her mother ignored her and turned to the man. "You sell dresses here, sir?"

"As you can see, madam," he said. "Expensive ones."

"Good," she said, with a nod. "We should like to buy one."

"Mama, no!" Jane said.

"Quiet, daughter, or you shall get a slap," Mrs. Austen said.

"Are you aware, madam, this shop once made a hat for Marie Antoinette?" the shop hand said, sniffing at Mrs. Austen.

"Before she lost her head, I suppose," Mrs. Austen said, raising an eyebrow and tilting her head. The tone and the words warmed Jane's heart; her mother used her wit when she wanted to.

The man gasped. "We make and import the finest gowns for the most exclusive commissions."

"I am glad to hear it. Please make one for my daughter." She crossed her arms over her chest. A stalemate ensued where the shop hand refused to move, and Mrs. Austen refused to leave. Finally, the man realized sensibly that Mrs. Austen possessed more stamina for stubbornness than he. He sneered and crouched down to measure Jane with his length of tape.

He proceeded with great ceremony, tutting and clucking and muttering under his breath at the length of Jane's arm and the size of her waist, as though each measurement surprised him, despite Jane's genteel proportions. A more objective person might have even called her figure pretty, or lithe, but not this person with a vested determination to find fault. He emitted a long sigh, then retrieved a single gown on a silk hanger, declaring, "This is all we have in her measurement."

Jane studied the dress and gasped. "Mama" was all she said. Surely a month of skill and love had brought this dress into being. An ivory overdress of silk shrouded a gown of bone-white muslin. The seamstress had embroidered lines of roses into the strips of gold that ran down the dress. Jane discerned the petals and leaves of each flower; she imagined a woman leaning over her table for hundreds of hours in a drafty workshop on the Left Bank, with a tiny needle and delicate thread. Lengths of silk braid were used for its closures, giving it the appearance of a military coat, the detail Jane approved of most. It reminded her of a uniform her brothers Frank and Charles, who were naval officers, might wear when they sailed down the Spanish coastline. Jane ran her hand down the diaphanous fabric. "Such a shade of white," Jane remarked. "I'll soil it in the space of a morning's walk."

"The whiter the dress, the better," the shop man instructed. "One does not walk in this dress; one takes a carriage." He reached to take back the gown.

"See if it fits you," Mrs. Austen said, moving the dress from his reach and offering it to Jane.

Jane protested, feeling she would destroy it with the first touch of her finger, but relented when her mother's expression threatened violence once more. She moved behind a chinoiserie screen and changed.

"Good God," said her mother as she returned.

"What is it, Mama?" said Jane. "Does it fit ill?"

"Jane." Her mother paused, her face making an expression Jane had never witnessed before. "You are beautiful."

Jane scoffed. Her mother had never uttered such sentiments about her. No one had. But when Jane inspected her reflection in the mirror, she went quiet. The bone-white fabric brought out the gold in her fawn eyes. Pink flushed her cheeks. She never dressed this way. She pushed her shoulders back; the dress demanded it.

"How much is it?" her mother asked.

"Twenty pounds," the man replied with a triumphant smile.

Mrs. Austen grabbed her reticule. "We shall take it."

"Mama, no," Jane said. Twenty pounds paid their rent in Sydney House for six months. Mrs. Austen could not own such a sum. Yet she pulled a banknote from her bag and offered it to the man.

"Where did you get this?" Jane asked. She glanced at her mother and noticed a change: her neck, ordinarily adorned with heavy gold, now lay bare. "Mama! Where is the baroness's necklace?" The white skin of her mother's neck seemed to quiver, newly exposed to daylight. Jane had never seen her mother without this prized piece of jewelry; she seemed plain and naked without it.

Her mother touched her bare neck, then removed her hand. "If my daughter is to go to the Pump Room, she shall be fit to be seen."

Jane gasped and shook her head. "Mama—"

"Listen now, Jane. This will smooth the deal, for the father especially. This confirms we are not paupers." She raised her chin.

"Mama, you loved that necklace."

Her mother seemed to wince. "This is my fault, Jane. I let you sit with your father and read, when I should have taken you to balls and parties. I should have shown you how to make tea."

"I know how to make tea."

"You make it very ill, Jane. You forget the leaves until the brew tastes like tin. If we had reprimanded you, helped make the most of your appearance, you'd be married by now. I failed you, Jane. I let you run wild. Let me buy you this dress."

Jane paused to recall the joy that running wild had brought her. She glanced at her mother's bare neck once more, shaking her head. She never understood her. "All right, Mama."

Mrs. Austen smiled for an instant, then returned to her frowns. She gestured for Jane to change, and when she returned, Mrs. Austen placed the banknote in the shop hand's claw. He grinned and snatched the money before taking the dress from Jane and wrapping it. She took possession of the white dress, having never owned anything so beautiful before.

Chapter Four

As they approached Sydney House, they saw a handsome man of thirty-two, who cut a dashing figure as he waited in front of the building. A black ribbon tied back his sunflower hair. Jane gasped in surprise. "Hello, Henry," she called to her brother.

"Hello, Jane," he said with a smile.

Eliza, his wife, held his arm. "Bonjour, Jane," Eliza said.

"I thought you were at the Dawsons' until Thursday?" Jane said. Her brother and his wife, who had been visiting friends in Cornwall, were not due to visit the Austens until a week's time, on their way back to London.

Henry shook his head. "Mama wrote to us express and demanded we change our plans. We shall come with you to the Pump Room tomorrow. We are all so happy for you, Jane. Truly, this is such wonderful news."

"Indeed," Mrs. Austen said, kissing her son and his wife hello. She nodded, proud. "This is more important than silly Robert Dawson."

"Mama, no!" Jane cried, her voice panicked. A catastrophic feeling held her. "We get ahead of ourselves. I have met this man once."

"Jane, do listen," Henry said with a smile. "You have been invited to the Pump Room. Everyone becomes engaged there. No one goes for any other reason, except to drink that horrid water." He laughed, his white teeth shining in the daylight. "On top of this, you are Jane Austen, the loveliest, cleverest woman of my acquaintance. You will make the best mother, and the best wife. Sorry, dear," he added, nodding toward his spouse.

"Don't apologize," Eliza commanded softly, in the French accent of her birth. She never spoke, only purred, and exuded an exotic glamour Jane could never have attempted without looking foolish. "I agree with you." Eliza nodded to her husband. "And now you have the dress," she added with a smile. "No man will resist you."

They all dined together. Mama made jokes and Papa opened a bottle of wine that a rich parishioner had given him back in Hampshire.

"What is Darcy up to lately?" Henry asked Jane in the middle of the meal. He offered her a cheeky grin as he shovelled a piece of lamb into his mouth and chewed. A hush swept through the dining room. Everyone knew of Mama's threats to burn Jane's writing, and Henry, always the rebel, loved to tease her. They all looked to Mrs. Austen and waited for her reaction.

But if anyone hoped for an outburst, Mrs. Austen disappointed them. Instead of shouting, she smiled. "Nothing you say can vex me tonight, my son. Jane may write as much as she likes when she is married."

Henry erupted with laughter and applauded. The others joined in. A strange mood descended on the home for the first time in years: happiness. Henry sent everyone into fits of laughter with stories of the characters he dealt with at his bank. Eliza played the pianoforte, and Revered Austen, normally crippled with shyness, even joined in the singing, to Jane's surprise and joy. Mama's excitement seemed to radiate from her body in little breaths and gasps, her cheeks rosy from the wine.

Jane had never realized how dull and sad the house was before; she had caused this change in them, or her luck in love had. She swallowed, nervous at the weight of the emotion, at how the ease of her parents depended on her marital status. She excused herself.

Henry found her on the stairs. He embraced her again. "I am truly so happy for you, Jane," he told her.

"Henry, this is all so sudden—" she protested.

Henry interrupted her. "Stop this now, Jane. I know Old Man Withers; I have done business with him. He is a sensible man. Sister, the time has come. This man would be a fool to let you go. You are going to be happy, I'm afraid. Time to get used to the concept." He flashed her a giant smile. Henry had a happy nature; he always smiled.

Jane nodded and allowed herself to be silenced.

When Mrs. Austen suggested a walk, which they used to do as a family back in Hampshire, everyone agreed happily. They donned their coats and boots and stepped out into the cool evening air.

Henry and Eliza walked ahead, arm in arm. Mrs. Austen left her husband's arm and joined Jane, who walked alone. As they strolled away from Sydney Place, Mrs. Austen attacked Jane with schemes for romantic scenarios to best engineer a proposal. If Jane fell into the Avon or perhaps a bear pit, suggested Mrs. Austen, Charles Withers would have to rescue and then marry her. Jane said she knew of no bear pits in Somerset, which did not deter Mrs. Austen. She also provided Jane with a script of sweet things to whisper at the man's ear and a selection of unachievable styles in which to wear her hair. Where Jane normally protested, now she smiled and praised every plan, her mind elsewhere, allowing Henry's conclusion of the situation to at last sink in.

"There is Miss Harwood. Let us pay our respects," her mother said as they stepped into Cheap Street. A small woman with gray hair and mended gloves waved to them from her doorway.

"Please, Mama, no more well wishes," Jane said. But her mother had already turned toward the woman's house and bade her good evening.

"I did not witness your approach," said Miss Harwood. "I have been much engaged all night, though I suppose I could brew a pot and rustle up some cake." She made to go inside.

"Thank you, no, Miss Harwood," Jane's mother replied. "We must get home. We have merely stopped to inquire after your supplies of coal."

Miss Harwood smiled. "My level of coal is excellent, madam. I have no need for a fire, in any case." She wrapped her shawl tighter around her shoulders.

"You have no fire?" Mrs. Austen said. "The ground frosted yesterday and will do so again tonight."

Henry and Eliza looked over from their position by the bridge. Miss Harwood lowered her voice and looked down. "I do not waste coal when it is but me inside."

"How much coal do you have, Miss Harwood?"

"Three."

"Three bags of coal? Why, that's plenty."

"No, three," she said.

"What, three . . . lumps?" Jane said.

"I thought your brother came last week?" said Mrs. Austen.

"Samuel is an important man, madam. Many appointments." Miss Harwood raised her chin.

"Come by Sydney House and Margaret will fix you four bags of coal," Mrs. Austen said. "I will require one of your paintings as a payment," she added.

"I already have the idea," Miss Harwood cried in a relieved tone. "A landscape of Pulteney Bridge."

Jane's mother praised the woman on the originality of the concept. "But please do not exhaust your hands," she added.

Miss Harwood looked to Jane and their eyes met. She looked away. "Would you inspect my hearth, Mrs. Austen?" Miss Harwood said. "The chimney may possess a blockage."

"Of course, Miss Harwood," Jane's mother replied. She ducked under the door arch.

Once Mrs. Austen had disappeared inside, Miss Harwood grabbed Jane by the arm. "You are due at the Pump Room tomorrow, I heard. If all does not come to pass, seek me out," she whispered, and pulled Jane closer. Jane drew away. The words so shook her with their strangeness, she thought she had misheard.

"Excuse me. Of what are you talking, Miss Harwood?" Jane said. She peered around the street and hoped no one had seen them.

"This is not the only path," Miss Harwood said. She shook Jane's arm with such force that had she not possessed roughly the dimensions of a sparrow, she might have loosened the bone from its socket.

"You do hurt my arm, Miss Harwood."

"You think me a pathetic soul. Pitiable and ridiculous."

"I do not," Jane lied.

"We must stick together, ladies like you and me." Jane searched the older woman's face. Miss Harwood's eyes darted left and right. A strand of wild gray hair escaped from her bonnet. She blew it from her face with a spit of breath. "Promise you will come to see me," Miss Harwood demanded. Jane agreed, and the strangeness of the promise rang in her ears as she and her family returned home, crossing the River Avon at the bridge Miss Harwood had threatened to paint for her bags of coal.

Chapter Five

The next morning, as Jane came downstairs and the family admired her new dress, the doorbell rang, surprising them all.

"Who could that be?" exclaimed Mrs. Austen. "And at this crucial hour. Our entire acquaintance has been informed we are off to the Pump Room."

Margaret answered the front door and announced the caller. "If you please, ma'am," said the housemaid, "Lady Johnstone."

The Austen family looked and shrugged at each other, all seeming to think the same thing. Why did she visit now?

Lady Johnstone threw her coat at Margaret as she strode inside. Mrs. Austen curtsied to their neighbor. "Lady Johnstone," she said. "To what do we owe the pleasure of your company?"

"Can I not take tea with my closest neighbors without suspicion?" Lady Johnstone replied in an outraged tone. The widow of a solicitor from Putney elevated to the knighthood, Lady Johnstone had never deigned to take tea with the Austens since the day they first arrived at Sydney House. She had selected quite the moment to condescend to them now.

"But of course, madam," said Mrs. Austen. "However, we are expected in town this morning, and don't want your meeting rushed. This is my son Henry and his wife, Eliza. Henry owns a bank in London."

Henry bowed and Eliza curtseyed.

Lady Johnstone nodded toward them with eyes closed. "I've heard of your small operation," she said. "Perhaps you knew my late husband, Sir Johnstone of Putney."

"I knew of him, my lady," Henry replied.

"Perhaps, my lady, you could return this afternoon when we shall all be at your leisure?" Mrs. Austen said.

"Nonsense," Lady Johnstone said. "I am a quick drinker of tea and will consume but a slice of cake. I shan't be ten minutes." Lady Johnstone proceeded up the hallway as she spoke. Jane's father peered at the grandfather clock in the hall and scratched his head. "I delighted in making an acquaintance with Mr. Withers of Kent," Lady Johnstone said, showing herself into the sitting room.

"Indeed. He is a fine young man," Mrs. Austen replied as they all followed her into the room.

"Do sit down," Jane's father said, though Lady Johnstone had already taken his chair. He joined Jane and Mrs. Austen on the settee, while Henry and Eliza squashed themselves onto the couch. Everyone looked quite foolish, sitting inside with their coats and boots on. Jane was barely listening when Lady Johnstone spoke next.

"I shall be delighted in congratulating Mr. Withers on his engagement," said Lady Johnstone.

A moment of silence passed as everyone in the room seemed to digest the words. Finally, Mrs. Austen spoke, jumping from her chair and pointing at Jane with joy, seeming to figure it out.

"Jane," Mrs. Austen exclaimed, half-accusing, "you have said nothing!" The rest of the room all gasped and smiled, as though finally they joined Mrs. Austen's thinking.

Jane shook her head. "Nothing was communicated to me," she insisted. Her heart thumped inside her chest.

"A terrible frost occurred in Bristol yesterday. It detained much post and ruined many travel plans," Lady Johnstone explained. "This would be why you have not heard yet."

"We did not know this, my lady," said Mrs. Austen. "Thank you, madam. You have done us a great service." Reverend Austen grabbed Jane's hand. His fingers felt warm and soft.

"On what score?" said Lady Johnstone.

"You have broken the news to us of our daughter's engagement," said Mrs. Austen with a laugh.

"Beg pardon," said Lady Johnstone, laughing also. "I am excited to congratulate Mr. Withers on his engagement to Miss Clementine Woodger of Taunton. They struck the deal yesterday, in Bristol." The solicitor's widow assembled her face into a sneer of glee.

Jane and her mother and the other Austens all took a moment to react to the news. Jane could not see inside her mother's head, but she imagined that Mama conducted some important discussion with herself, for she smoothed down the folds of her best skirt, folding and refolding each piece of blue muslin. Jane said nothing either, though she did stare at the floor and breathe as her heart fell away.

Her mother thankfully broke the excruciating silence a moment later. "We shall congratulate him also," she replied finally, in a bright tone. Jane rose to stoke the fire with a poker and met eyes with no one. Mrs. Austen offered more conversation quickly. "Miss Woodger is of large fortune?"

"Her father, Sir Woodger, is a solicitor," said Lady Johnstone. "His speciality is conveyancing. He has an office in Putney."

"Putney?"

"Yes. Putney. Clementine, his bride, is not twenty-one years of age."

"So young," Mrs. Austen noted.

"It is not young at all. For marrying, one is past their prime at twenty-two."

Jane stoked the fire more.

"Anyway. Much engaged today," Lady Johnstone continued, rising as Margaret entered with the tea tray. "Do not bother with him now," she added, pointing at the teapot. She smirked and took her leave.

JANE SAT STILL for a time.

At first, hope existed that Lady Johnstone had made a cruel joke. But then Margaret returned from the market with word from the washerwoman of the house at which Mr. Withers was staying. Mr. Withers had become engaged yesterday in Bristol.

Mrs. Austen expressed disbelief and confusion, claiming dark forces were at work. "Someone or something got to him," she declared. Jane nodded, but secretly suspected that far more banal powers had influenced the day. Common sense—and likely, his father—had prevailed upon Mr. Withers. Laughing around the fire on a Tuesday evening for the rest of their lives held less value to him than lying as the wealthiest man in Gravesend Cemetery, and in the end, Mr. Withers had likely performed an act no more evil than taking the path his fortune and breeding demanded.

"I am so sorry, Jane," Henry said. Jane's father did not speak. A feeling of horror and nausea gripped her; her stomach felt curdled with embarrassment. The nerves and joy of last night and the morning evaporated. Mrs. Austen wiped a tear.

"You should return to the Dawsons, Henry," Jane said in a cool voice.

"No, Jane. Of course we will stay here with you."

"Nonsense. I insist you go back to them. A stupid waste of your holiday to stay here." She stood. "I'll check with your driver to see if he can't take you back now." She turned for the door.

Henry stood up. "Stop that, Jane. I will go." He walked past her and into the parlor.

"I'm sorry for ruining your holiday, Eliza," she said.

"Don't be sorry, *ma chérie*," Eliza said gently. Everyone looked at the floor. Jane spotted on her father's desk the letter she had almost sent to Cassandra extolling Mr. Withers's handsomeness and wit and winced.

Jane excused herself from the drawing room and walked upstairs. The clock read eleven o'clock, but she climbed into bed. She did not come down for lunch. She told Margaret to go away when she knocked to tell Jane that Henry and Eliza were leaving. Jane did not come down to say goodbye; she heard Henry and Eliza leave through the front door in the midafternoon. She did not take supper. She lay awake all night until, eventually, she fell asleep at five o'clock the next morning.

JANE WOKE AN hour later and jumped from her bed. She buzzed with agitation: words filled her head. She threw back her bed pillow, looking for something. Yes, she had kept one there once, but no longer. Jane paced the room. An object glimmered on the floor. She ran over. A small pale rod nestled between two floorboards. She fished it out with a smile; her mother had found dozens in her sweep of the room but missed one. Others declared the buttery brown flesh of the oysters the best, but for Jane, this thin white stick represented the beautiful part of a goose. Jane took the spine between her thumb and forefinger, and her tendons moved it into the crook of her hand on instinct.

She flung open a pine chest at the end of her bed and burrowed through its contents. She found a glass pot the size of an apricot and held it up. It contained nothing, so she threw it into the corner of the room and mined through the chest once more. She found a second pot, but it too held only dust. She tossed it over her shoulder to join its twin. She dug down to a bolt of lace meant for a veil. She flipped it from its coffin and flung it to the floor. A third pot lay underneath, and this one held a tiny mound of powder comprised of tannin, vitriol, and acacia gum. Jane held the pot aloft like a trophy. She needed water.

A vase of brown, decaying roses sat on the windowsill. Jane upended the stinking flowers and squinted into the vase. A finger's worth of putrid water lay at the bottom. Jane poured the filthy liquid into the pot, rushing but careful not to spill. The mottled sand crystals dissolved to liquid.

Now she needed paper. But the room contained none! She could fetch some from the drawing room, claiming she wanted to write to Cassandra again, but her mother would surely see her face and suspect her true intention. Panic redoubled its caresses of her mind, as phrases and words began to depart her head.

She stiffened; the room did contain paper. She dug her nails into the crack of one floorboard and pulled until a loose plank rose up. She reached into the floor cavity. Six hundred pages, double-sided, in Jane's own hand lay inside. She had begun its composition on her fifteenth birthday. *First Impressions,* she called it. It had been to London and back, rejected by Cadell the publisher, and then Jane had kept it hidden for nine years, lest her mother find it and put it to the torch.

Jane lifted the pages and ran her fingers over the yellowed paper. It smelled of vanilla and wood. She turned over the last page and found a space, brushed an inch of dust off her desk and dipped her quill.

Chapter Six

Isobel Thornton now understood the feeling of wanting something she could not have.

Melbourne House grew intolerable. Isobel's mother took to her room with the complaint that she had never been so wronged in her existence. When that action provoked insufficient attention from the others, she returned to the parlor to make the same noises. Isobel's father was worse. Instead of joking with his daughter about this latest of romantic mishaps, he took to his study and avoided all conversation. Isobel sensed they all felt as she did: they entertained flattery to believe a man like John Wilson would interest himself in a woman of her station and age.

When the servant expressed a need for mending ribbon, Isobel demanded she undertake the mission herself, if only to exit the house. But when Isobel bade Mrs. Turner good morning in the ribbon shop, the reply came not from the shopkeeper but from a customer. "Good morning, Miss Thornton," said John Wilson, the very man and source of her current pain, the man who had rejected her, a man she hoped never to set eyes on again. He swallowed and turned his head away as he spoke, then inspected a bureau of scarves with violent attention.

Isobel felt determined to remain calm, to show no sign his presence distressed her. She wondered if decorum permitted a minimum time she could remain in the shop before departing without rudeness. She allowed the clock to add three seconds and turned for the exit.

"You are not leaving?" said he.

Isobel sighed, resigned that some conversation was required. She offered polite opinions about the assemblies in town and remarked upon the recent storm. But when her thoughts on plays and rain were exhausted, she felt dismayed to find Mr. Wilson making no reciprocal efforts for conversation. There were several topics into which a gentleman could enter: the wetness of the roads, for example, or the speed of postage. But he said and did nothing, though it seemed words were not far from his lips. She despised him for his lack of gallantry and longed to be gone from the room. Mrs. Turner, who watched from the register, possessed little fame as a discreet woman, and Isobel imagined the report of this humbling interaction reaching Ramsgate by supper.

Isobel grew enraged. She shed her earlier pretensions to demureness and shifted her campaign to the offensive. "I wish you every happiness and joy, Mr. Wilson," said she, and met his eye.

"Thank you, Miss Thornton," said he, though the scrunching of his face indicated confusion.

"Do you make for Kent soon? Or do you plan to travel first?" she asked with a cringe, feeling fresh humiliation to inquire about the honeymoon plans of the man who had spurned her.

"I plan to stay in Somerset for several weeks more," he replied, with another perplexed face.

"Is Mrs. Wilson keen to enjoy the upcoming assemblies?" offered Isobel, growing more exasperated by the second. "There is a revival of a Cowper play next month, if to her standards."

"My mother is fond of Bath but shall remain in Kent for now. But I thank you for the wishes for her theatrical pleasure."

Isobel furrowed her brow and winced at the indignity of being forced to clarify this most sensitive of topics. "I beg pardon," Isobel said. "I refer to Mrs. John Wilson. Your new wife."

The gentleman ceased his scarf inspection and looked up; a glimmer of hope seemed to dance across his face. "Ah. Perhaps you refer to Mrs. Francis Wilson. My new sister." He moved toward Isobel.

"Mrs. Francis Wilson!" repeated Mrs. Turner from behind the counter.

John Wilson continued his path across the shop. Isobel, breathing heavily, turned away from him and grew fascinated with a mound of lace.

"Miss Isobel, I was detained in Bristol to celebrate the engagement of my younger brother, Frank, to Miss Bernadette Martin."

"Then you are not engaged?" Isobel said.

"I am not engaged. There was a frost in Bristol, and I was apprehended for the night. I sent word via express. Considering the roads and the state of the English post, it shall reach you sometime next week. I rode through snow to find you."

Isobel was relieved of the power of speech.

"We arranged to visit the Pump Room, Miss Thornton," he said with a tender smile. "Isobel. If you will do me the honor, we shall go there now."

He held out his arm and Isobel took it, and she and John Wilson proceeded to Stall Street. While her face remained still and she said nothing, she allowed her heart a small leap of what a sentimental person might claim to be joy.

*J*ane put down her quill and cracked her knuckles. She read it back. She would improve the words later, but for the moment, the pain in her chest had departed. The revelation that it was the man's brother who married offered a brilliant solution. This story lay in its infancy—she did not know where it would go and what words and characters would lead up to it—but this climactic scene would make a fine ending to a novel. A miscommunication tore lovers apart. The confusion now cleared up, the man and woman could reunite. The bond repaired, happiness restored.

The effort of willing new words from a blank page had the quality and consistency of torture. Jane knew the horror of painting oneself into a corner on the paper, and the ecstasy of escaping with no smudges made on the floor. She smiled at the speed at which the words had entered her head. She laughed at how they fell to the paper and almost wrote themselves. She wondered how many more words waited. Inspiration like this came rarely. Her mind lapsed into a thought of Charles Withers, of what he might be doing. She surrendered the pages to the desk and climbed back into bed.

JANE AWOKE TO a companion in her bedroom.

"You will ruin that gown if you sleep in it," Mrs. Austen said. Jane looked down at her twenty-pound dress and winced at the sight. Creases devoured the delicate silk overdress, some gold ribbon had come loose, and Jane's blanket had crushed the petals of the embroidered roses.

"What time is it?" Jane asked.

"After three," Mrs. Austen replied. She did not look up but read from a page in her hands.

Jane sat up and rubbed her eyes. "What are you reading, Mama?" she asked, though she already knew the answer. "Give that to me," she said. The words caught in her throat.

"You told me you wrote no stories," Mrs. Austen said.

"Aye. That is old work, Mama," Jane protested.

Mrs. Austen scrutinized the pages. "These are the stories your father sent to London. That was cruel of him to put ideas in your head, to give you false hope. Why have you kept these and tortured yourself, daughter?" She turned the page over. "And this?" Mrs. Austen held up the last page of the manuscript, which contained the fresh scene. Jane did not answer. "You are a grown woman," her mother continued. "Do you disagree?"

"No, Mama," Jane said. "I am a grown woman."

"I came to see if you were all right. Clearly you are." She stabbed the page with her finger as she read. "While the rest of us know how serious this situation is, marriage remains a joke to you. You have little idea how low you will sink when we are gone. But while we run our nerves ragged trying to help, you please yourself."

"That is untrue, Mama. Please give me those pages." But Mrs. Austen gathered the pages into a pile and rose to her feet. "Where do you take them?" Jane begged.

"This is for your own good," Mrs. Austen declared, then dumped the novel into the fireplace.

Jane screamed. The fire, which had died earlier, roared to life with the added kindling. Jane dashed to the hearth. When she was a child, words describing fire had entertained Jane. She preferred *incalescent*: growing hotter or more ardent, set ablaze. Cassandra and their father had little interest in candles and flames, but Jane loved to observe things burning, as did her mother. She stuck her arm into the flames and managed to snatch out a single scrap of paper, as well as the now-charred pink ribbon that had once tied the pages together. The flames devoured the other pages in a gleeful roar. A ball of heat seared the room, the dry pages seemed to explode, and the force blew Jane back onto her haunches. The show dazzled her. The room filled with the aroma of smoked paper, which both comforted and horrified her. Once nothing more remained to burn, Mrs. Austen left the room.

When the fire died, the ashes of *First Impressions* smoldering in the hearth, Jane held the single scrap of paper she'd retrieved from the pyre. She placed the piece in her pocket and exited the house.

Miss Harwood waited on her doorstep. She opened her door and ushered Jane inside.

"You knew how it would go with him," Jane said.

"Yes, badly," Miss Harwood replied. She offered Jane a chair. Jane sat down.

"What is wrong with me?"

"You are different," Miss Harwood said. She stoked the fire, newly ablaze, the hearth now filled with coal.

"I do not want to be," said Jane.

"Do not fret." The woman scribbled something on a piece of paper and handed it to Jane. "You will travel to London."

Jane flinched. The heaving, rat-infested capital? "London is a day's journey away."

"Do you have a better option?" Miss Harwood asked.

Jane shrugged, taking the paper. "At this point, I have nothing."

As JANE TRAVELLED to London the next day in a carriage of ill repute, she worried how to make it there without discovery. She selected the most dilapidated postal carriage she could find, which left from the back of the Black Prince Inn at ten o'clock in the evening and guaranteed passage to London via the quieter roads, in darkness. A man in a torn waistcoat and a stained admiral's hat was Jane's only companion in the public coach. He stank of rum and refused to meet Jane's eye, a level of communication that suited them both. As he made no comments to Jane about the crime of a single woman travelling alone, Jane supposed he lay in worse trouble than she. Whatever fight he'd embroiled himself in or debt he'd racked up in the card houses of Bath, he seemed keen to leave the West Country in as quick and anonymous a manner as possible, which rendered him the perfect travel companion for Jane. He shut his eyes before the carriage moved.

Chapter Seven

Of all the dishonor Jane had brought on her sex over the years, this night's actions far exceeded it. A single woman travelling alone through the countryside, negotiating her fare, paying her own way, and riding with strangers were acts reserved for harlots and witches. No good woman who was the property of a respectable family corrupted her soul in such a fashion.

Guilt had racked Jane as she slipped from the house that evening. Everyone had retired to their bedrooms for the night and she had exited out the back of the building via the kitchen, whose door no one would hear. In her pockets, Jane placed three biscuits from the larder (the hard ones no one missed) and a little over five pounds—all her money in the world. She'd told no one where she was going; she could only imagine the mayhem that would greet the house when they discovered her absence. She felt glad she would likely have arrived in London, one hundred miles away, by then.

The carriage left Bath at a little past ten and made its way east through the outskirts of town. The honeystone Palladian columns out the window gave way to stone cottages, then huts with smoking chimneys, then the endless fields of Somerset.

The rolling fields of the West Country became the oak forests of Berkshire. They stopped at Reading to water the horses. The driver stretched his legs but neither Jane nor her snoring companion left the safety of their wooden cage. She peered gingerly out of the carriage window and looked around the Reading town square, half expecting her mother to come bounding into the carriage and demand she return home.

Another post carriage travelling back toward Bath stopped on the other side of the road. The driver did the same as theirs, watering the horses and himself. Jane looked at the other carriage, in which a family laughed and chatted, their faces illuminated in the torchlight from a nearby alehouse. From their bright clothes and large suitcases, Jane imagined they were on their way to holiday in Bath. She considered jumping inside with them. There was one space spare. She could return to Bath before the alarm was raised, no harm done. She placed her hand on the carriage door, but then the driver took his seat and flicked the reins once more. The carriage rolled forward, and Jane sat back. If she'd had any desire to hold on to what shreds of her dignity and reputation were left, she obliterated it now. There was no turning back.

On the outskirts of Windsor, light from a farmer's bonfire illuminated a spectacular holly oak at least fifty feet high by the side of the London road. Jane momentarily forgot her humiliation and turmoil and turned to admire its glorious branches, which had withstood the weather and the years. Nothing else marked the road from then onward except field after darkened field, and as the bump and roll of the wheels eased into a rhythm, Jane fell asleep.

She awoke as the carriage drove through Kensington. The sun had risen long ago; she estimated the time to be around noon. The smells hit her before the sight of the pretty buildings did: above the green of Hyde Park and the grandeur of Kensington Palace she choked on a perfume of coal smoke, sewage, and a decomposing estuary at low tide. The capital city seethed and tumbled, spewing forth a fragrance of people and buildings, alleys and grime. As the carriage rolled along the Thames, a factory on the south bank disgorged plumes of black smoke into the air and a pipe that led out from its bottom dumped rotting animal matter into the river. Jane recalled her hatred of the capital, with its screeching hawkers, the Machiavellian court, the soot and fog. She chose trees and grass over marble and people. But it was here, in the grime of Bow Street, that Fielding wrote *Tom Jones*; among the pomp of court where Frances Burney wrote *Evelina*; under the vapor of Southwark where Shakespeare wrote *Hamlet*. Jane nodded her head with begrudging respect to the miserable city that produced such genius. *Pressure makes the diamond,* she noted. *Grit makes the pearl.*

Jane disembarked at the last stop, in Piccadilly. Miss Harwood had given her an address for a house in East London, two miles away. Jane looked up; Sir Christopher Wren's dome loomed in the east. She walked toward it along the north bank, stopping once to hold her nose at the perfume of the Thames.

As Jane left the precinct of St. Paul's and travelled east, the characters changed from bishops, curates, and well-heeled parishioners to those they were charged with saving: the seamstresses, flower sellers, and laundresses of Cheapside. The architecture transformed from elegant marble columns and cerebral brass domes to rotting timber and crumbled brick. The lanes were paved with jagged cobblestones and painted with mud, the elegant drainage systems of Mayfair and Piccadilly replaced by homemade remedies of bucket-emptying and gravity. Grease washed the wattle-and-daub buildings in a film of grime. Jane had never visited such a place. A man in a soup-stained cravat poked his tongue out at her, declared that he loved her, and then followed her down a lane. Seeing as though they had never met before, she doubted his love was genuine. She hurried ahead of him and told him her father was a constable. This seemed to satisfy him, for he sat down in a pile of rotting cabbages and began to snore.

Jane walked three blocks more and arrived at the house in question, double-checking the address on the paper. This was it. Jane scratched her head. It was a two-story structure in the Tudor style, sandwiched between two large modern buildings. The black timber frame sagged at the center. Yellow stained the white clay walls and the thatched roof caved in. It was a structure suspended in midcollapse.

Jane tapped the oak door. No one answered. The lattice casement windows were blacked out and sealed shut. She knocked once more, louder this time, and called, "Hello?" She looked up to the roof. The chimney puffed no smoke.

"Who are you?" a voice said. Jane turned around. A woman limped toward her. Her white hair reached her navel; with no pins or ties holding it from her face, it roamed free around her in a great volume of fuzz, like spun sugar. She had patched up her black dress with swatches of mismatched material: a plaid square covered one shoulder; a brown rhombus attempted to repair a giant hole in her skirt. She bundled several cabbages under her bosom; the exact number was hard to tell.

"My name is Miss Austen," Jane replied. "Are you Mrs. Sinclair?"

"That depends," the woman replied. She unlocked the door, went inside, and closed it behind her.

"I come on the advice of Miss Harwood," Jane called through the heavy oak door. The door inched open. Jane stepped inside, gingerly, wondering if she was walking toward her demise. The blacked-out windows encased the dwelling in virtual darkness.

"Are you going to help? These won't light themselves," Mrs. Sinclair said as she lit a candle. Jane fumbled around, found another, and did the same. "How is Emily?" the woman asked.

"She lacks for coal," Jane replied, looking around, "but she investigates her prospects as a painter." The women lit another few candles and the room was illuminated. Jane saw a dirt floor, a hearth, and two chairs. "A homely abode," Jane offered with a nod. She wondered why the woman bothered with the candles; there was nothing to warrant illumination. She squinted at the woman in the candlelight. Her face resembled a raisin.

Mrs. Sinclair lit a fire. "There always has been, and always will be, someone like me in this place."

Jane raised an eyebrow. "I don't doubt it." She looked around the dirty room. A thousand such decrepit buildings littered Cheapside.

"What do you want?" asked Mrs. Sinclair. She motioned for Jane to sit down.

"What is it you do?" asked Jane in reply, seating herself in a rocking chair so old it had ceased rocking.

"I am a matchmaker," said Mrs. Sinclair.

Jane stood back up. "How wonderous!" she said. "I have travelled across half of England, ruining whatever shreds of my reputation remained, all to visit a matchmaker. At home there stand three on every corner." Jane kicked herself for her gullibility and desperation. She had known not what to expect on her way to London and had given little thought to what she would find there, training her focus instead on escaping the house without suspicion. But whatever she had imagined, another stupid matchmaker did not make the list. She moved to the door, beyond annoyed.

"I am not that kind of matchmaker," said Mrs. Sinclair. She shifted a log with a blackened poker and a flame bloomed.

"What kind are you, then? How are you different from the multitude who slither around Bath?"

"I deliver."

Jane scoffed. The fire cracked and spat and devoured the kindling. She thought of her manuscript, nothing but black flakes now, and sat down once more. "You can deliver for me? I need a husband," she said.

"So fetch one, then."

"Therein lies the issue," Jane said. "I appear to have little talent for husband fetching."

"Why do you think that is?"

"Because I am old and poor," Jane replied.

"Bah," Mrs. Sinclair replied. "The young speak of love like they invented it and think it exists when we are at our prettiest. Love is revealed when we are at our ugliest. I have seen older and poorer than you marry. Uglier ones, too. There must be something else. Perhaps you do not want to marry."

"I have no aversion to marrying," Jane protested. "All the men have not wanted me. Are you a matchmaker or not? I have money. I will pay."

"Your one true love is not amongst these men. To find him, you must go on a journey," the woman said in a portentous tone.

Jane paused. "I have been on a journey. I came fourteen hours in a rickety carriage from Bath, my only companion a man who may or may not have been a pirate."

"You make a joke of everything. It does you no favors," Mrs. Sinclair said.

Jane quieted.

"It is not that kind of a journey." Mrs. Sinclair put down a cabbage. "I can help you. But if you want no part in this, you are free to leave."

Jane sighed at the price she had already paid to get there. "I suppose you want payment," she said. "For your magical matchmaking that will defy the efforts of the many women before you."

"I do. I want something of yours that is valuable."

Jane placed four pounds and some shillings on the table, the balance of her assets after purchasing her fare to London. "This is all I have." It was no huge sum, the same as any matchmaker asked. Jane was glad she had no more; she felt sure the woman was swindling her.

"I do not want something that costs. I want something of value," Mrs. Sinclair said.

Jane sighed again and shifted in the rocking chair. Tired with the idea already, she compiled an inventory of the items of potential wealth on her person. The crucifix around her neck, presented to her by her younger brother Frank, which he proudly and lovingly declared to be brass, though with the way the bronze flecks often dusted her collarbones, she felt more comfortable with its classification as painted tin. Her coat and gloves were of a sturdy fabric but old; in her efforts to darn them she demonstrated her happy talent of both closing the tear while destroying the garment. She wore no rings on her fingers or jewels in her hair. She truly possessed nothing of value to tempt this woman.

"As I am sure you can see, madam, I am not a rich woman. The only thing of value I possess sits on the table." She pointed to the banknotes. "Apart from money, I have nothing."

"You do not listen," Mrs. Sinclair said, tucking a strand of white hair behind her ear. "I do not want something that costs. I want something dear to you."

Jane threw up her hands in frustration, then dug them into her pockets. Her hand grasped something flaky and crisp. She turned the item over in her fingers, then pulled it from her pocket and placed it on the table.

Chapter Eight

It was a scrap of burnt paper, not half a page in size. The heat of the fire had baked it to yellow and spattered it with brown spots. Black charred the corners in half and quarter moons, as though some black-lipped monster had taken bites. Every surface that remained was covered in the neat lines of Jane's hand, words written sideways and in the margins. She always wrote small, for paper was a luxury. The words came from a chapter toward the middle of *First Impressions*. The item represented the sole remaining scrap of Jane's life's work.

"This no doubt appears as nothing," Jane said, "but this is the most valuable thing I own."

"That will do perfectly," Mrs. Sinclair said. She picked up the burnt page and stared at it.

A minute passed; Mrs. Sinclair made no sound. Jane grew anxious. "Is there a problem?" she asked.

"Shush," said Mrs. Sinclair. "I am reading."

Jane sat back in the rocking chair.

"This is rather good," Mrs. Sinclair said at last.

"You are too kind," Jane replied in a dead voice. She smiled to herself.

"And you are willing to give this up, in the pursuit of love?" She held the burnt paper toward Jane.

Jane shrugged. "It is but a scrap of paper. Of course." She had memorized the words written on it long ago.

"How much do you want love?" Mrs. Sinclair asked.

Jane shifted again, startled by the question, and considered it. It made no difference now, for he married another, but she and Mr. Withers had shared a moment when they walked under a tree in Sydney Gardens. He had stopped to fix his cuff button, then turned his head to Jane. Their eyes met, and he smiled at her and she returned the smile. It was the smallest of interactions, and they had known each other only minutes, but in that moment, she did not stand alone in the world. She could not recall a warmer feeling.

Jane nodded to Mrs. Sinclair. "I wish for love more than anything," she said.

Mrs. Sinclair stared at Jane, then nodded. "As you are certain," Mrs. Sinclair replied, "you shall have it." She sharpened a quill. "Let us write your wish down." She turned over the scrap of manuscript and wrote something on the underside. "This will work but once. It is reversible. Again, but once. Give me your finger," she said when she was done. Jane presented her left index, which Mrs. Sinclair nicked with the nib.

"Ow!" Jane protested. A bead of red dripped onto the page. "What is this madness?" She was reaching the limit of her patience.

Mrs. Sinclair shut her eyes and a chant passed her lips. Jane scowled and sucked her finger. "Say those words," Mrs. Sinclair said, then turned once more to her cabbages.

Jane laughed. "Beg pardon. That is all?"

"Did you want more?" Mrs. Sinclair asked.

"Where am I to go? To which man shall you introduce me? Which men have I paid for with my blood drops? I don't understand."

"I introduce you to no one. You will meet him on your own."

"Who?" Jane said. "Who will I meet?"

"Him," Mrs. Sinclair replied. She handed Jane back the scrap of blackened manuscript and said nothing more.

Jane took the paper and stood there, impotent. It became apparent that Mrs. Sinclair was finished with her. She began cutting a cabbage. Jane turned in a circle and sighed. "I guess I shall be going, then?" she said. Mrs. Sinclair nodded but again said nothing. Jane let out a grand sigh, frustration boiling within her. Finally, she left. She exited the house, stepping out into the cobblestoned lane. A devil creature strolled down the road toward her, a supernatural beast blackened with soot from head to toe. It smiled at Jane and a set of bright white teeth gleamed from within a pitch-black face. Jane gasped and leapt backward in fright.

"Evening, miss," it said, tipping its grimy cap at her. The figure was no hellish ghost; it was a chimneysweep, his shoulders laden with long-armed brushes, blackened with soot, walking home from the day's trade.

Another man wheeled past with a stinking barrow of eels laid out in a slimy heap. "Move yourself, silly tart!" the man yelled at Jane. The glistening sleeves of scales slipped and slithered as the cart bounced over the cobblestones.

"I have business here, sir," said Jane.

"You do not." The man laughed as he bustled past her. "You are another lovesick girl. They come day and night to that door," he said.

"What for?" said Jane.

"To be taken in," he said. "She's a charlatan. She preys on the softheads and hysterics." He chuckled again and shook his head, then rolled his reeking vehicle down the lane.

Jane shut her eyes. What a fool she was. The hilarity and strangeness of the day evaporated into the soot-laden Cheapside air and reality returned. Her desperation and humiliation had transformed her into a gullible woman, willing to travel by herself to London, and now she stood alone in one of its filthiest, seamiest sections. She commanded her silly heart to stop beating, to stop making a spectacle of itself.

She turned for St. Paul's and trudged back along the north bank, not bothering to cover her nose at the Thames. She boarded her return post at Piccadilly, the only passenger this time, and began the fourteen-hour journey home.

JANE RETURNED TO an assembly gathered in Sydney Place. The entire population of Sydney House, most of Sutton Street, and some of Great Pulteney Street were standing about the front of the building. From the concerned looks and nods, there appeared to be some great event taking place that everyone was happy to delay their lunch to observe. Jane proceeded toward the group to inquire as to what unfortunate incident had befallen some unlucky family, but then froze and hid behind a hedge on the corner when her own mother emerged from the building, her cheeks stained with tears. A constable stood beside her who nodded as she spoke and jotted notes in his notebook. Her mother's hair, usually pulled back in an elegant cultivation of curls, hung limp and wet under her riding bonnet. Jane furrowed her brow. Why was her mama dressed so? She never saw her with wet hair.

Jane shuddered. She realized she had been gone almost two days. She had left no word of where she was going, no plan of visiting friends or travelling with an organized party. She studied her mother. Mrs. Austen's favorite blue gown, always pristine and starched, was muddied and blackened, with the right sleeve torn. A thin line of red ran down her soft cheek, the type of scratch a branch might make. Her mother had gone out looking for her.

Jane peered more closely at the neighbors gathered. Lady Johnstone stood at the front, corralling guests and chatting to everyone. She bounced around the crowd in celebration. They would remember this for years: the great Austen scandal. There was one reason a parson's daughter might exit her home unannounced, and it was not a chaste one. Anticipation seemed to ripple through the crowd at what new crimes of Jane's might soon be confirmed. No one seemed to mind it was raining; they huddled happily under parasols and awnings, training their ears for any updates.

Jane looked back at her mother. Mrs. Austen did not seem to share the crowd's happy emotions. She paid no attention to them but turned to the constable with his notebook. In her hand was a portrait of Jane, one Cassandra had drawn. It was a poor likeness, too beaky, and in truth Cassandra had rushed it, but it was enough like Jane to do the trick. Her mother must have scoured the house for it. She had not realized her mother even knew of the portrait's existence. It was a pitiable little picture, but her mother cradled it in her hands and brushed a drop of water off it that had fallen from the policeman's hat. Jane had never seen her mother hold a picture of her. She contemplated walking to her mother then, perhaps touching her arm and smiling. They could say things they had never said before. But her mother's act of novel incineration still burned in Jane's mind, so she stood back and witnessed her mother's suffering instead. *How we delight in punishing those we love.* Besides, she could muster no energy for the spectacle to follow as she reunited with her family before every matron, fishwife, parishioner, and concerned citizen in town.

She ran instead to the Fairy Wood and took shelter in an abandoned woodsman's cottage. She'd hide until nightfall, when the gathered townsfolk abandoned hope of Jane's return, their hunger for supper overtaking their hunger for scandal. Jane would go home and deal with her parents then. She sat in the stone cottage and waited.

She removed the scrap of *First Impressions* from her pocket and turned it over in her hand. Mrs. Sinclair had written a single line of text on the back. Jane scowled. Not only was Mrs. Sinclair a swindler, her handwriting was impossible. Jane knew shocking penmanship. Her brother Henry's, for example, with his excited, cheerful scribbles that looked more like drunken ants had beached themselves on the page, or her brother Frank, who, when writing to Jane from the sea to thank her for his new shirt, smeared most of the Atlantic Ocean on the page as if wanting to truly show her what sea life was like. But their crimes against handwriting were petty larceny compared to the high treason of Mrs. Sinclair. It took Jane minutes just to conclude which was the page's correct way up. It was not as though the writing was obscured by the elegance of a Germanic script, or calligraphy. It was not ornamented with circumflexes or long tails the way an *s* was once written as an *f,* as one might have found on the bill for

A Midsummer Night's Dream at the Globe. There was no glamour to its illegibility. It was a deranged spray of black globules, interspersed with a random assortment of angry black sticks. She'd achieve a neater display upending the ink pot and sneezing its contents onto the page.

Jane raised the paper in front of her person, the way Mama did when the candle burned low and her eyes were tired. Her eyes moved to the starting point of the demented scrawl. The first letter was *T* for certain. What was the next letter—*a*? Yes.

"*Take*," read Jane aloud. The first word. The next was simpler. It was but two letters, each being different enough in shape to make them decipherable: "*m-e. Me. Take me.*"

Jane read on. The next word was *to*, and the word after, *my*. The following one was a gathering of splotches. Jane could not decipher the number of letters, let alone their meaning. The middle blob was her clue. It curved at the top. Her choices were thus *r, q, o, p, n* . . . It was *n*!

"*One*," Jane read. She smiled. She was a fearsome knight, slaying the dragon of bad penmanship, one letter at a time. The next word began and ended as the first. It was *true*.

She identified the final word with ease. "*Take me to my one true love,*" Jane read aloud. She sat back and smiled, satisfied to have broken the code of blobs. She grimaced at the mawkish choice of words. Then the room grew dark and snow fell. Jane gasped; the flakes fell from the ceiling, from inside the cottage. Then the room whooshed and with a crack like thunder, Jane dissolved into particles and a breeze that entered the cottage blew her away.

Part
Two

Chapter Nine

Sofia Wentworth stood in the wings of the Bath community hall and blew into a brown paper bag.

She looked down at her empire-line Regency costume and cringed. Blue and brown stripes bloomed from her body like a rancid flower. An ostrich feather protruded from her head so far it brushed the ceiling. Altogether, she resembled a vindictive peacock, one of those disheveled kinds who hides in the bushes, then attacks brunch revelers in a park and has to be put down.

She grabbed the brown paper bag once more and inhaled.

A runner jumped into the backstage area and opened a stage door. "Ms. Wentworth, are you in here? Rehearsal is due to start," he called out in a panicked voice.

Sofia hid behind a theater drape. It might have been beneath the dignity of one of the world's biggest movie stars to cower behind a pile of curtains, but it was the appropriate tactic for the moment.

The runner gave up looking and returned to the hall.

Sofia sucked more air from the bag. She blew out again. She cursed her therapist, who had suggested this in a soothing voice as a fix for any panic attacks that might rear their head. Unfortunately, a brown paper bag was not quite enough for the moment she was experiencing. A dram of absinthe and some tranquilizers might have hit closer to the mark.

She fetched her phone from the pocket of her period costume and dialed Max Milson. "Max, I'm afraid I can no longer do the movie," she said when he answered.

"What's wrong?" her agent replied.

"I'm unwell. I'm pregnant," she said. She could only imagine his expression.

"Congratulations!" he said automatically. "When are you due?"

She'd not thought of that. "May seventh?" she said.

"That's . . . eleven months away," Max replied.

Damn. Forgot to carry the one.

"Sofia, what's going on?" His weary, fatherly tone betrayed the effects of the twelve long years they'd worked together.

Sofia looked down and winced. "My outfit. It's hideous."

"In what way?"

"It does my figure no favors."

"It's a period film," Max said. "Those are the costumes. What did you think they'd put you in, a bikini?"

"No. Merely, I didn't expect the past to be so . . . comical."

"You're playing Mrs. Allen, Sofia. She's supposed to be comical."

He was right. The production designer had fulfilled her brief in good faith and designed a costume that made Sofia look ridiculous. Sofia had known the character was a silly woman going in and cursed herself now for thinking this would be okay. Indeed, saying those witty lines of Austen's, dressed in this ludicrous way, she'd likely steal every scene she was in. To the uninitiated, this sounded great. But to Sofia, this posed a problem.

She was used to stealing the scene—she had built a career on doing just that—but she stole the scene by making every straight man in the audience (and, likely, a few of the women) want her. She did this with such ease it had become her calling card, the reason she was cast in films, the reason studios shifted production schedules to suit her. Her way put bottoms on seats, it drew crowds in, it turned turkeys into profit-makers. Now, she would be stealing the scene for all the wrong reasons. She would be the butt of the joke. Audiences had never seen this side of her, and they wouldn't like it. They wanted her to arouse them, they wanted to sit down and live a fantasy for two hours, and she was about to dump a bucket of cold water on their dreams. Everyone else would tell her she was being silly, but Sofia knew that she was good for one thing only in this business—to look hot. Walking out there looking like this would be a mistake.

Fifteen years had passed since she first rocked the acting world as Ophelia at the Old Vic, straight out of the Royal Academy of Dramatic Art. She was "sex on legs," as one critic had declared in frothing tones, and it had transformed her from actress to celebrity. She'd signed with a Hollywood agent, and in less than five years was playing Batgirl, the lusty sidekick to Batman, in the world's most lucrative film franchise. It was the fastest ascendancy from theater tights to leotard for a British actor to date. She married the director, Jack Travers, after they fell in love on set. Ten years of walking red carpets, holidaying on the Riviera, and shooting action films in Slovenia passed like nothing.

Then, the day after her thirty-seventh birthday, the trade papers announced a plan to film a new installment of *Batman*. The news was happy for everyone but Sofia, who learned that the role of Batman's perky dream girl, his partner in crime, the role Sofia had made her own for a generation of fans, had gone to Courtney

Smith, a twenty-three-year-old Los Angeles native who brought "energy" to the role and "always knew" she was the "real Batgirl." Sofia had not landed a starring role since.

"He won't care what you're wearing, Sofia," her agent said carefully.

"He will," she replied.

"Could you not just concentrate on your performance?"

Sofia scowled. "Never say that to me again, Max."

Max sighed. "I thought this was a bad idea from the start," he said. Sofia felt inclined to agree with him but didn't verbalize it. She had been the one to insist on the part. "Why do you do this to yourself, Sofia?"

"Working with Jack Travers is an honor," she said in a robotic voice, repeating the sound bite she had given to seven separate news agencies when she first signed on to do the film. "He is one of the best directors in the world. How could I pass up the opportunity?"

"It's an honor for anyone who is not his ex-wife."

"Not divorced yet, Max." Sofia sat down.

This was the real reason for the panic attacks, the paper-bag blowing, the hiding. She and her husband had signed on to do the Jane Austen picture when they were still together. Jack Travers wanted to do a period film, and he had a family connection to Jane Austen; he was a descendant of one of the author's brothers. Secretly, Sofia knew the real reason was that Jack wanted to add a statue to his mantelpiece. After years of breaking box office records with his violence-heavy CV, now he wanted cred.

Sofia had joyfully joined the ride, because she loved Jane Austen, and because it gave her the chance to spend time with Jack. Hilariously, she had originally signed on thinking she would be playing the lead. When she quietly discovered she was play-ing Mrs. Allen, the *chaperone* of the lead (*chaperone*—was there a frumpier-sounding word in the English language?), she nodded enthusiastically and pretended like she had known this all along. It still allowed her to hang out with her husband, which was the part she wanted.

Then a few months after contracts were signed, as Sofia pre-sented Jack with a three-egg-white-and-spinach omelet she had made herself in their stainless-steel kitchen in the Hollywood Hills, Jack announced he was leaving her. They had grown apart, he said.

Everyone had voiced their kind words and support; the pro-duction company had offered to release Sofia from her contract so she wouldn't have to work with him. But Sofia, quietly heart-broken, vindictive, and secretly hopeful, insisted that if anyone was going to leave the film, it should be Jack. Jack stayed on, and Sofia took this as a sign. She hatched a plan.

Film shoots were long: after spending that much time to-gether, he would fall back in love with her. They had fallen in love during the crazy time of a film shoot, and they could do so again. Unfortunately for Sofia, she remained horribly in love with her husband. Nothing she had ever felt compared to that first falling for him, and you got such things once. Everyone has their one, and Jack was hers. And now she planned to use this film to get him back.

She had spent the last few months dealing admirably with the potential end of her marriage. She'd learned the unique torment of separating from someone in the public eye. Sofia used to be one of those people characterized by headlines about her basic move-ments: "Sofia Wentworth Stuns in Black Leggings While Walking

Dog." Recently, the headlines about her had changed. "Friends Worry for Sofia's Mental Health" was one (she didn't know who these friends were), "Poor Sofia Hides Out After Separation," another. Strangers approached her on the street, offering her marriage advice as though they knew her—owned her—which, in a way, they did.

Despite all of this, she maintained a dignified silence. She'd avoided drowning her sorrows in those jumbo tubs of ice cream that caterers buy for weddings, she'd not sobbed on the kitchen floor. She'd gone to the gym, preserved her waist at its pre-breakup measurements, kept her glorious red mane coiffed to its usual perfection. Her husband was an aesthete: he loved beautiful things, and he appreciated talent and confidence.

But now, as she wore this bejewelled outfit resembling a flightless bird, all her hard work would be ruined. If she presented herself to her husband for the first time since their breakup hidden beneath these comical folds of fabric and making a fool of herself, it might be hard to maintain the irresistible veneer of happiness she carefully fostered, the appearance of being okay. She was not one of those women who could gleefully and gracefully send themselves up; she did not appear on talk shows wearing chicken costumes or dressed up as a man for laughs, allowing herself to be roasted or made fun of. She wore beautiful clothes and people wanted her. Now she was about to destroy all that. Not only would she turn off her fans with this role, she would turn off *him*.

Her confidence, once unshakable, wobbled. Hiding behind the curtain, she uttered, "I don't know if I can do this, Max."

Max sighed. "I will chat to wardrobe. See what I can do."

She exhaled into the phone. "Thanks, Max."

"He's not there tonight, at least."

She brightened. "I know."

"Will you go back to the rehearsal then, please?"

She nodded into the phone. "Okay."

"Make lemonade, kiddo. You never know. This might be good for you." He hung up.

Sofia put down the phone. The giant feather in her headpiece caught on a theater rope and bored further into her cranium. She wished she could agree with Max. But as she took a final breath of paper-bag air and reminded herself that she was about to betray her audience and prevent the love of her life from ever finding her attractive again, she felt quite sure this Jane Austen film would be the worst mistake of her life.

Of this she felt even more certain when she turned and witnessed, from a pile of theater curtains in front of her—the same ones she had cowered behind moments earlier—a person materialize out of thin air.

Chapter Ten

Jane opened her eyes. She no longer sat in the woodsman's cottage in the forest; instead, she rested on the floor of a dark, airy space. An ebony sea of fabric seemed to swim around her on all sides. Ropes and more black fabric hung from the ceiling and dangled down toward her. Curtains. Jane sat up. A woman stood in front of Jane, staring at her.

"Were you a witness to what happened to me?" Jane asked the woman.

"You appeared in that pile of curtains" was the woman's reply. She wore the same style of gown as Jane's, à la grecque, but the fabric sparkled in an unnerving fashion. The material glimmered so brightly Jane squinted to see past it. A giant ostrich feather adorned the woman's head, and she breathed into a reticule made of brown paper.

Jane stood up from the curtain pile. "Where am I?"

The woman in the shiny dress scrunched her nose. "Bath?"

Jane sighed with relief. She must have fallen asleep in the woodsman's cottage and sleepwalked to this place. It was odd, for Jane did not think herself a sleepwalker, but a first time occurred for everything. Her head throbbed with dull thuds. She rubbed her eyes and took a proper look around. She and the shiny-dress woman stood in the stage wings of some sort of theater. She felt unnerved, but also glad to have emerged from her escapade alive. She could have sleepwalked into the Avon. "I would appreciate assistance. My name is Miss Jane Austen."

The woman glared at Jane. "Is this *Candid Camera*?" she asked. She turned her head to the ceiling, then breathed into the bag again. "You think you can trick me?" she announced toward the ceiling. "I'm not signing a release for this!" She stalked off down the darkened corridor.

"Please come back," Jane called. But the woman did not stop. Jane followed her and arrived at the entrance to a large hall, the lights of which momentarily blinded her. Inside, a country ball was taking place. Men and women danced in two lines. There was music, but no orchestra performed. An older woman dressed in men's trousers stood at one end of the space and shouted instructions to the dancers as though they were children.

"One, two, forward, back two, forward," she barked. "You in the white, you've missed your cue," she said. She was looking at Jane.

Jane pointed to her chest as if to say, *Who, me?* She jumped when the woman nodded. "I do not care to dance, thank you," Jane called across the room. She normally delighted in dancing but felt too gripped by confusion at this juncture to seriously entertain the notion.

The trousered woman glared at her. "You're not paid to watch," she said.

The other woman, the one from the curtains, joined the line of dancers. She stared at Jane again and raised an eyebrow.

"Well, then?" the fierce woman in the trousers asked.

Jane shrugged. She felt unsure why the woman demanded she dance. She recognized no one at this assembly and knew of no halls in Bath that looked this way. She searched for an excuse. "Madam, I do not know the steps," Jane offered, hoping that would suffice as a way to avoid joining in.

"Don't you 'madam' me. It's Grimstock," the trouser woman said. "We've practiced this dance for weeks."

"My dear lady," Jane said with a laugh, "I may not be the world's finest dancer, but I can safely say that was no Grimstock."

The music stopped midnote. A dancer gasped. Both rows of dancers turned their heads in unison. Everyone in the hall stared at Jane. The woman stormed toward her with deliberate strides and halted in front of Jane's face. "This is the exact Grimstock they dance in *P and P* ninety-five!" she declared. "Where is your partner?"

"I have none," Jane said.

The trousered woman turned around. "Fred," she said, pointing at a man who stood by himself in the corner of the hall. "Want to dance in a movie?"

The man jumped at the mention of his first name, then hid behind a pillar. "No, thank you," he said from behind the column.

"You could be famous, like your sister!" the trouser woman added in a bright voice.

"I'd rather not, cheers!" the man said with a laugh.

"But you are so handsome and statuesque! What bone structure! You should be up at the front here."

"Steady on, Cheryl, you're making me blush," he replied.

She chased after him around the pillar. "Look. You're in costume and you're standing there. Please, Fred. For me?" The pleading seemed to have little effect on the man; he quickened his gallop around the pillar.

Jane watched the odd exchange and shook her head. She could not make head or tail of what was occurring.

"I'm a terrible dancer." He waltzed another ring around the column. "Trust me, Cheryl, this will hurt you more than me."

"You will be fantastic," said Cheryl in a bright, aggressive voice. She caught him by the arm and dragged him toward Jane. "This is Fred," she said quickly.

Jane blanched at the informality of the introduction. "I beg your pardon, madam. May I know his family name?"

"You may not," she replied. "Fred, meet . . ." She studied Jane and scratched her head. "Right, I've misplaced your name." She nodded at Jane.

"I have not told you it," said Jane. "Miss Jane Austen."

The woman glowered at Jane. "If I wanted sarcasm, missy, I'd spend time with my daughter." She scowled and turned to the man. "Fred, dance with . . . this person," she said dismissively. She pushed Jane toward the man she branded only "Fred."

Jane stumbled into his chest and blushed. "My apologies, sir," she said. He helped her to regain her balance. His hands felt strong as he gripped her elbows to lift her up.

"No worries," he said, a strangely confident phrase that Jane comprehended but had never heard before. Cheryl walked away. The man smiled at her awkwardly, and Jane smiled back.

She scratched her head at the strangeness of finding herself about to dance with a man she'd never met, in a hall she'd never been in before. Still, queer as it was, it would be inconceivably rude to refuse to dance with this Fred, so she turned toward him and prepared to Grimstock. "I suppose we should dance, then," she said with a nervous laugh. She put her shoulders back, ready to start.

The man called Fred leaned in toward Jane, then shook his head. "I'm sorry, I really don't know how to dance. I'm not even supposed to be here. But if you go see the third AD—that's the one over there who looks unnervingly like Danny DeVito—he will find someone else for you to dance with, okay? Cheers." He nodded and walked away from Jane.

A moment passed before she realized for sure that he was indeed leaving her. She gasped. "Have you no decency, sir?" she called after him on instinct. She did not even want to dance, and the whole event confused her, but still, she would not take such discourtesy so easily. "You are despicable!" she declared, for effect.

He stopped walking and turned. "I'm sorry?" She expected him to react with anger, but instead he smiled at her. "Did you just call me despicable? I don't think I've ever been called that before, and I've been called a great many things." He smiled at her again, which infuriated her. She suddenly found herself indecently angry at his rebuttal. She did not understand what she was even doing here but since she was, she would not let a rogue whose trousers were too short for his legs refuse to dance with her.

"You heard me perfectly well. How dare you agree to dance with a woman and then renege on the deal." He walked slowly back toward her as she spoke. She tried not to let this distract her. "Don't flatter yourself that I even wanted to dance with you. My feelings extend merely from the fact that an agreement was struck, and now you have backed out. The terms of the contract were ideal to *neither* party, I assure you, but nevertheless, here we are. You have ridiculed not me, but everyone, by refusing." He kept walking toward her and had almost reached her. Jane ignored him, cleared her throat, and kept talking, in a faster and higher-pitched voice. "Indeed, will the first thing to crumble be not *society itself,* when people no longer dance with each other!" She raised a fist to indicate her outrage, then, realizing she may have ruined the effect with overstatement, put it down again. She coughed and gazed at the floor.

"I don't care if you find me the most hideous woman in Christendom. You said you would dance with me," she added, in a softer voice. She swallowed. She said none of this for herself, of course—she did not even want to dance—but for spurned women in general. It was the height of rudeness to withdraw an invitation to dance, and this man deserved to be educated.

"I don't find you hideous," he said. He looked at her and their eyes met.

Jane exhaled and hoped he did not see. "So, what is the problem, then?" Jane said, coughing and looking away.

He shrugged. "I don't like dancing."

Jane scoffed. "Too bad."

"I don't dance well. I don't do anything well, really, and you'll be thankful in the end this didn't happen."

"You do not dance well? So, here is an opportunity to practice."

He smiled at her. "You're scarier than Cheryl," he said. "Do you dress down all your dance partners?"

"Only the ones who annoy me," Jane replied.

"So, all of them, then?"

Jane felt the corner of her mouth twitch, like she might smile, but she forced it back down to an even line. She bristled at the exchange, at how quickly she had entwined herself in an argument with a stranger.

He opened his mouth and laughed, and she stifled a gasp at the sight of the whitest teeth she had ever beheld. A perfectly straight row of ivory pegs shone back at her from his mouth, with no stain of tobacco or food, nor any incisors or canines missing.

"Your britches are too short," she said in an accusatory voice. She pointed to his knees and looked away.

"'Britches'? Is that what they are called? It's all they had. I'm just an extra, sort of. I'm tagging along with my delinquent sister—she's the famous one up in the front somewhere," he said. "I'm not supposed to dance. I was told to stand and mouth 'rhubarb' multiple times. Apparently, the shape that your mouth makes when you say it looks good in the shot."

"Shot? Who was shot?" Jane demanded, looking around the room with concern.

"No one," he told her, shaking his head with a confused look. "The film shot."

This was the strangest conversation she'd ever had with a dance partner.

"Well?" he said then.

"Well what?" Jane replied.

"Are we going to dance or not?" he said.

"I thought you did not want to," Jane replied.

He smiled and crossed his arms. "I don't, but I'm afraid you'll beat me up if I refuse now. Besides, if we don't dance together, society will crumble," he said dryly.

She did not approve—only she was allowed to speak dryly. He smirked at her.

"Are you smirking at me?" she said, incensed.

"Smirking? I don't know how to smirk," he replied.

"You do indeed. You're doing it now. You appear quite good at it, like you do it often. You'd best stop before you get yourself into trouble."

Jane found two emotions competing for supremacy inside her: one, utter confusion, and two, utter annoyance at the person standing next to her, who seemed bent on infuriating her at every juncture.

"Music!" barked Cheryl. The music began once more, a slow march with a delicate tune. The two lines of dancers snapped to attention and arranged themselves in order. Fred turned to Jane and shrugged. He held out his hands.

Jane looked up at him. She felt too enraged by the situation to decline, so she placed her own hands in his. His hands felt large and warm. "That's the cue," Fred said. The music swelled. He grabbed Jane and towed her down the line. Jane skipped and stumbled and almost tripped over. She missed every step and stood on his toes once or twice. Fred laughed. "You're terrible!" he said. "After all that."

Cheryl rushed over to them with an angry look on her face. "One, two, forward, back, round, and behind your partner," she commanded to Jane in a staccato voice, like she beat a drum. "For a professed expert on the Grimstock, you leave much to be desired. This is your final warning!" She stormed off.

Jane turned to Fred with an anguished look. "I am lost, sir. I do not know my purpose here." She felt tears well in her eyes.

"Well, it's not dancing, that's for sure," he said with a laugh. "You're even worse than me."

Jane ceased her tears and grew irrationally mad. "How dare

you laugh at me in my moment of distress!" she said. "I do not know the steps!" she added.

"I can tell," he said.

She stared at him in utter shock. She had never come across a more odious dance partner in her life. True, she had danced with some shocking people, men who stepped on her toes, who had breath stinking of rum or gravy, or who conducted terrible conversation, but this man reigned as the champion over them all. Her toes remained un-stepped-on and his breath was fresh—perhaps the freshest she'd ever smelled, curiously—but this man committed a more-annoying crime than any of the others: he was arrogant. He wore a dry, self-satisfied grin at all times, like the whole world was a joke to him. "I assure you I know how to dance," she said. "Stop laughing. What will happen if I do not manage these steps? I do not understand this."

"You will get the sack for sure," he said. "Cheryl's a terrifying woman. She made a stuntman cry."

Jane scowled at him. She barely understood what he was saying, but she could tell from his tone that he was teasing her. She felt furious. The woman in the trousers barking orders had mentioned Fred's handsomeness but Jane noticed little accuracy in the appraisal. He was not handsome at all, certainly not. His age exceeded thirty. A short brown beard covered his face, golden whiskers lined his lips, his hair was unkempt, and he was obnoxious.

"Your hair is pointing every which way," she said, motioning to his head. "I wonder if it has ever seen a comb."

"First you hate my britches, now my hair. Anything else about me you have a problem with, while we're here?"

Jane stared at him. "I cannot think of anything right now, but rest assured, I will let you know. Now, teach me the steps."

"I'm not sure that will help," he said, laughing.

"Congratulations, sir," Jane said. "You are the most disagreeable person I've ever met. And that includes my mother."

"Your mother is disagreeable?" he replied. "Then I see the resemblance."

Jane glowered at him. "If you give me even the slightest hint of instruction, if that is at all possible within your small brain, I guarantee I will catch on," she said. "You do know the steps to this dance?"

"I suppose so," he said with a shrug.

"Then please show me," Jane said. She waited.

He rolled his eyes, but then he did a surprising thing. He took her arms and moved them into place. "I think it goes like this. One, two, forward, back . . . ," he said in a soft voice. He placed his hand on her hip. The placing of it rendered Jane silent. She let him move her forward and back, down the line of dancers, across the room. She felt infuriated about him guiding her but said nothing. Instead she trained her concentration on him, following his every direction, trying not to feel distracted by his hand on her hip.

He spoke the steps to her in a whisper as they went. "One, two, good, good," he said. For all his obnoxious posturing, he actually made for a patient instructor. He guided her gently, sensing as she progressed, approving when she got things right, helping when she faltered. They reached the end of the line and Jane exhaled.

"Well, then?" Jane asked him.

"Not bad, I suppose," he said. "Better than the first time, at least, though that's not difficult," he added, jettisoning his patient tone and resuming the earlier, obnoxious one.

They turned to dance again. Fred curled his fingers at Jane's side. She stiffened and hoped he did not notice. The way he held her disarmed her. A familiarity seemed to grace the embrace, though lasciviousness did not define it. He merely held her closer than she was accustomed to.

"Sorry. You're a small person," Fred said. "I hope I don't snap you in two."

"As do I," Jane said.

Fred laughed, and she smiled, admittedly pleased it was her doing. "Ready for round two?" he asked. "If you can manage it? Once more and then it's all over."

"An ending to which I heartily look forward," Jane replied.

The music reached its cue. The strings swelled, the melody quickened, and the sad tune rose to a crescendo. They danced through the corridor of people for the second time.

Fred pulled her gently down the line and their bodies moved in unison. Jane knew the steps now and danced well. But something else occurred that would stay with her for a long time. Every time she moved her arm, his was there to catch it. Every time she turned, he was waiting to hold her again. One body began the sentence; the other finished it. She could feel his breath on her neck, the arch of his collarbone through his shirt. Jane had never danced like this with anyone. It was infuriating and confusing.

How had this obnoxious person moved her about so, commanded her body? He held her tenderly; it maddened her. Despite his claims to the contrary, he was, in fact, a fine dancer, moving smoothly and in time. Jane would breathe this detail to no one, especially him. They reached the end of the line once more and the rest of the dancers cheered and applauded. She smiled in spite of herself. She had not noticed before, but she was panting with the exertion. Fred took a bow as a joke and Jane joined him. He did not look at her, but his warm hand rested on the small of her back.

Cheryl nodded to them. "I've seen worse, I suppose," she said in a begrudging tone.

Jane loved to dance. When she was nineteen, she had never wanted for a partner. She had flung her bashful companions around the room in boisterous joy, pointing at silly hats and ugly sashes and flirting outrageously. People attributed her outspoken manner to the charm of youth. But as she arrived in her twenties and other girls were marrying around her, the offers to dance thinned. By twenty-five, she felt lucky to be asked once in ten dances. She stood by the wall and inhaled as men approached, then felt crushed when they asked her younger neighbor. Sometimes men asked her to dance two dances, then moved off after the first when, she supposed, they realized her age. She let them go with a smile, keen not to show they had hurt her, watching the couples spin around the assembly room, and resolving to temper her conduct. She observed the women who were asked to dance every dance, with their bosoms exposed and their mouths shut, and tried to replicate their behavior.

Cassandra, who had a sweeter temperament, gently counseled her to smile more, to encourage an approach. But it was no good. The more she tried to be quiet, the more of a scowl she wore. By twenty-eight, she sat in the corner and joked of being an old maid. She'd leave in a grim state, muttering about the disappointing society, while her heart ached.

Jane glanced at Fred. He seemed to stare at her with an expression Jane did not recognize. Jane was used to men looking at her in a number of ways. Confusion, for certain, when she spoke of a philosopher she enjoyed. Pity, of course, when she spoke of her love of walking alone in the woods. Her favorite was probably derision, when they moved close enough to see the lines formed around her eyes, realized her age, added it to her poverty, and found themselves offended to be in her company, wasting their time. But this man looked at her in none of those ways. Jane could not place it at all. It was almost as though . . . yes, like he was trying *not* to look at her. Like he gave too much of himself away.

Jane felt her own face doing a peculiar thing also. It was trying to move itself closer to his, as though trying to hear what the infuriating man said or scrutinize his facial expression, though he spoke clearly and his visage sat in full view. Perhaps she was eager to hear what he said, to be close to him so she could offer a quick rebuttal to any inane thoughts he produced. Yes, that was it. She commanded her face to stop, but the order rang hollow in the muscles of her neck, which elected to continue the mission of their own volition.

Chapter Eleven

*T*hank you, darlings. That's a wrap on rehearsal," Cheryl called to the group. The dancers clapped and cheered and embraced each other.

Fred shrugged at Jane. "Look at that, you survived," he said.

"I suppose I should thank you for your help," she said, but then paused and said no more.

Fred placed his hands in the pockets of his coat. "A bunch of these guys go to that café up on May Street after rehearsal. I'm not an actor, but I guess I could slap on a beret and sit in a smoky corner. We could sip lattes and talk about 'craft'?" He coughed and looked away.

It was Jane's turn to laugh. Jane did not understand *beret* or *latte,* but she understood she was being invited somewhere. "I'm sorry, do you request my company in this café?" she asked.

He stared at her, then shook his head violently. "Of course not," he replied. "I'm just saying that's where I'll be. If you're going there as well, I'll probably run into you."

"I thought I was disagreeable, and a terrible dancer," she said.

"You are," he replied.

"Well, then?" Jane said, maddened. "I think you are indeed inviting me somewhere, sir," she challenged him.

"Forget I said anything," he said.

"I'll go," Jane said quickly without thinking. "I have nowhere better to be," she added. She crossed her arms.

He looked at her. "Fine. We should probably go together, unless you know the way?" he said in a tone of such unenthusiasm, Jane regretted the whole idea once more.

"As I'm unfamiliar with the teahouse you mention, you will have to escort me," Jane replied, frustrated. She looked at his face again. He breathed a little heavily, though he was standing still. This Fred person was nothing like Mr. Withers—nothing at all. Mr. Withers laughed and conversed with ease and smoothness. This man's manner resembled more her own: awkward. Jane shook her head. She did not want to go somewhere with this individual; she wanted to go somewhere with Mr. Withers. She was stepping out with the wrong person! But she had already agreed now, and after her grand speech earlier about the importance of keeping one's engagements, she had no choice but to go through with the infernal plan.

He shrugged. "I'll go change out of my costume, then," he said. "Do you want to change out of yours?"

Jane looked down at her attire. "Change, sir? I have no other clothes."

He scoffed. "You're going to walk around dressed like that?"

Jane shrugged. "Yes? Do my clothes offend you?"

"No," he said with a resigned sigh.

Jane scowled at him. He was such a strange person.

"Back in a sec," he said, walking away quickly. By the time Jane had deciphered the meaning of the hyperbolic and inaccurate sentence, he had moved halfway across the hall—in the direction of his other clothes, she supposed—cutting a lean silhouette across the floor. The tails of his coat moved back and forth as he walked. He wore his brown hair short; a few light tufts rested on the back of his collar, messy and rebellious. She tutted at the sight. He resembled a naval man in his coat. She wondered if he sailed the seas, like her brothers did. It would be the only thing to recommend him among a multitude of flaws.

He moved behind the curtains. Jane shook her head. She had never seen him at any of the Bath assemblies, though Mama had dragged her to many. She did not recognize anyone here from the usual Bath crowd, in fact, though she supposed these comprised another group on holiday.

She glanced around the room again. The confusion of waking up in the curtains had departed, but still, certain objects did not sit right with her senses. This ball's guests were such an odd assortment of people, her dance partner included. Their speech differed—not in accents, which remained as she knew, hailing from the south of England, Kent, Somerset, London—but more in the words they chose. These people employed an assortment of contractions and idioms that she could grasp if she thought about them but had never heard before. One dancer beside her said Cheryl "was on the warpath tonight," which she liked, though did not fully understand.

The decor of the assembly hall alarmed her, too. One of the paintings on the wall, for instance. A man smiled in front of what appeared to be Bath Abbey. The painter had rendered the expression of the man, the light, and the landscape in so lifelike a fashion she thought the subject might sit up and talk to her. She still could not figure where the music had come from; she viewed not a single violin, or cello or piano, though the sounds of each still rung in her ears, the music having been so loud it could have originated only from inside the room. The room also smelled of paraffin or some lethal disinfecting agent; it was the cleanest air she'd ever smelled. No fireplace or smoke blemished the air, yet the room was warm. She raised an eyebrow in confusion.

A man dressed in undershorts walked up to Jane and offered her some paper. "Well done, love," he said to her. "Call sheet for tomorrow. Another dress rehearsal."

Jane accepted the page and scoured it. It was a list made by a very good printing press of names and places and numbers. The date printed at the top of the page contained an absurd, make-believe number. "I do not know what this is, sir," she said. She handed it back to him. "For what am I rehearsing?"

He turned back to her and frowned. "What is your name?" He consulted some list that rested in his hand.

"As I told the others. It's Jane Austen."

"Your real name, thanks."

Jane shrugged and said nothing.

"What agency are you with?" he asked, squinting at her with suspicious eyes.

"I do not know what that means," Jane said in a friendly voice.

The man checked his piece of paper. He shook his head. "Are you supposed to be here? How did you get in?"

"I came from the wings," Jane said. "I am unsure how I got inside the building."

That seemed to enrage him, for he grabbed her arm. "You're another one of those Austen loons, aren't you? Here to tell us we've sewed the costumes wrong. You're wasting the time of busy people. This is the most ambitious production in years. You need to leave."

"But I must wait for my dance partner," she said reluctantly.

While she certainly did not care about leaving Fred so rudely, she was not a barbarian, and even an obnoxious person such as he deserved an explanation before she disappeared on him.

"I don't care about that," the man replied. "You're lucky it's just minor cast and extras here tonight. If Jack Travers were here, I'd call the police. You'd best bugger off before I ring security." He pushed her toward the door.

Jane shuddered. No one had ever addressed her so, let alone put their hands on her! "Please. I must tell my . . . companion," she tried. But the man tipped her out the door and into the darkness. The door shut behind her and the click of a lock echoed in the dark. Jane turned back and knocked on the door but received no reply. She turned out to face the night air and looked around. She walked a loop around the building and found another door at the front; she tried but could not open it. She waited for Fred to come out, but thirty minutes must have passed and he did not appear. No sounds or lights came from inside the building. Everyone seemed to have left.

She wished to wait longer, but the case seemed quite hopeless. Fred had clearly departed already to the next destination without her. On top of this, the hour by then must have reached a hideous number, and Mama likely tore hairs from her head. Eventually, she sighed and realized she must give up the cause. It was time to return home to face the scandalous fate that awaited her. If she saw Fred again at another assembly, she would force out an apology and attempt to sound sincere.

Jane walked down the lane toward town and sought her bearings. The black iron spire of St. Swithin's rose up into the sky in the distance. Jane walked toward the landmark. She arrived at the brick steps to the church and looked around. A cobblestoned road led to Pulteney Bridge. She followed it, then turned left and crossed the bridge. The Avon rushed below her in a soft current. She scurried down Great Pulteney Street. The grand houses of the row loomed above her in shadows of blue and black. She reached Sydney Place and turned left again and walked toward her house. She sighed with relief. The crowd of concerned townsfolk had dispersed from Sydney House, at least. No one walked in the street.

Jane knocked on the main door. No one answered. "Margaret," she called up to the first-floor window. The housemaid did not come, but a man opened a window.

"What do you want?" he called down to her, startling Jane. He wore nothing but underclothes, and from the window he stood at, he seemed to be standing in her bedroom.

She scratched her head. "I am Jane Austen, sir," she called up to him. "I live in this house. Please let me in."

"Please leave," he called down to her. "I've told you groupies before, if you come around here at night, I'll call the police."

"I don't understand," Jane said to him. "I'm cold. Won't you please let me in? Or fetch Margaret, at least—she will open the door for me." She felt her face make a forlorn look.

The man sighed. "Look. While I applaud your passion for her— and I think your costume is spot-on, by the way—I'm trying to run a hotel here, and if you keep shouting, you'll wake up my guests." He shut the window and pulled down the blind. Jane knocked on the door again. "I'm calling them now!" the man shouted.

Jane stepped backward onto the street and shook her head. Her mind raced with confusion. She waited outside Sydney House. An hour passed, but no one came or went. The temperature dropped. Jane shivered in the darkness; she needed to find shelter lest she transform into an ice sculpture. She gave up on Sydney House for now and walked back over Pulteney Bridge, returning to St. Swithin's, a church her father occasionally performed services at even though he'd formally retired. She climbed through the loose iron-glass window toward the rear and jumped down inside. She located a stash of red velvet prayer pillows and lay them on the floor. The cold marble made her shiver but as soon as she rested her head, the nervous energy of the day drained away and exhaustion gripped her. She closed her eyes and soon fell asleep.

Chapter Twelve

Jane woke to a blunt object prodding her shoulder. She opened her eyes. An old man wearing a clergyman's collar was poking her with a walking stick.

"Do you need some crack, dear?" he whispered.

Jane rubbed her eyes. Next to the parson stood an old woman.

"Enough with the crack chat. You're obsessed," the old woman said to him. From the way she squinted at him, with decades' worth of resignation, Jane figured the woman was his wife. "You think everyone is on crack."

The parson shrugged. "She looks like she could do with some." He turned back to Jane. "There's a funny-looking fellow by the stop for the thirty-nine bus. Name's Scab. He's reasonable, I hear. He'll do you a deal," he said.

"Do you know George Austen?" asked Jane. "He sometimes performs services here, when other curates fall ill. He's my father."

The parson shook his head. "Never heard of him. I don't mean to be un-Christlike, but I called the police."

Jane sat up, horrified. "For me? Why did you do such a thing?"

"I'm sorry," said the parson. "I saw you sleeping here, and I panicked! That's why I'm telling you about Scab and the crack.

I feel bad about the whole calling-the-police thing. I thought maybe a nice bit of crack would make up for it. Do you like crack?"

Jane squinted. "I am unsure."

"See, Bill," exclaimed the old woman, "she's not a drug addict!" She shook his arm. She wore a dress painted with sunflowers. The fabric rippled in the morning breeze that blew through the window Jane had left open.

"Yes, Pert. Thank you," said the parson, pulling the window shut with a grimace. "I see that now. But what was I supposed to think with her sleeping on the floor?" He placed a hand on Jane's shoulder. "To recap. I've called the police. That may have been rash. But let's look on the bright side. Now you know, you've got a head start. I wouldn't dawdle."

The oak front doors crashed open. Two men dressed in black entered the church and paused, looking around. "That was quick," said the parson.

Jane sprang to her feet. "Are those the constables?"

"I think one is a sergeant, to be fair," the parson said. He squinted at the two men as they walked down the aisle. "But yes."

"What should I do?" Jane pleaded.

"Make a run for it!" said the parson. "You can escape out the back."

Jane ran for the altar. She darted into the transept to exit through the back door. The wall of the transept held a brass plate. Jane ran past it but was forced to stop at the sight of her name.

Here worshipped Jane Austen 1801–1805.

Jane gazed at the plate in stunned silence. She read it again. It was her name. Her heart raced. She shook her head; the two men dressed in black bounded into the transept and Jane had no choice but to leave the plate that bore her name and escape out the back of the church.

JANE TRIPPED INTO the daylight and gasped at the sight before her.

It looked like Bath for the most part. The honeystone town houses lined the row of Northgate Street, as they always did. The Pump Room remained, rooted obstinately at the bottom of the hill ahead of her. But dizzying structures of glass and metal dotted around each building in the dozens, making her eyes water. A carriage made of green steel galloped past her on the road. It moved on its own, with no horse pulling it. Jane yelped and jumped out of its path, hugging an iron railing for protection. A man in black leather drawers, his hair colored purple, moved toward Jane and offered her a handbill. The paper was painted a vicious shade of pink and shone like a diamond. "March for trans rights, tomorrow at four," he said. "Wear the costume. It's a scream!" He pointed to her muslin dress.

"Heavens preserve us," Jane cried. She ignored the man in his underclothes and pointed at something far obscener. "I see your ankle, madam!" she exclaimed to a woman walking past. The lady wore a skirt that ended at the knee, allowing the ball of bone to be seen protruding lasciviously through her pale skin. How did the poor soul move this far down the street without being heckled or kidnapped? Jane shielded her eyes with her fingers. The woman wrinkled her nose at Jane and walked on. Jane felt dizzy at the confusing sights around her. What on earth was going on?

"You there. Stop," called a voice behind Jane. The policemen from the church appeared at the top of the street and ran toward her. Jane yelped and darted away. She ran south using the faint sun to navigate. The street sign said *Northgate,* like it always did, but now the sign hung on an impossibly tall building made of steel. She turned left into the lane, which was the shortcut to Pulteney Bridge, but the lane was gone. She slammed instead into a brick wall. She rubbed her skull and turned in a daze, then continued straight ahead instead, toward the Pump Room, the thing she recognized. Jane had known by heart the layout of Bath almost as soon as she first moved there. Since she was a child, she had possessed a mastery of maps and spaces; her brain had always devoured shapes, names, and numbers. She knew every brick in every miserable lane, the columns of every inane assembly room, the paintwork of every stuffy teahouse. But now she felt flummoxed as her memory was insulted over and again. Nothing was where it promised to be.

But while she tried to locate lanes that weren't there and stumbled around buildings she'd never seen before, the two men who chased her navigated the streets like it was second nature. They rounded every corner at speed and cleared every pothole with ease, and though she had a decent head start, the two men now bore down on her from less than twenty feet away. Jane ran on and attempted to bottle her panic. Being caught by the constabulary in this confusing Bath-but-not-Bath place would be less than ideal.

She glanced toward the plaza and gasped as she saw someone she recognized. "You!" Jane cried. It was the woman from the night before, the one Jane had spoken to in the wings of the theater. She had changed from her shiny dress and now wore a man's shirt and trousers. Giant black eyeglasses enveloped the top half of her face. The woman scowled and moved off down the road. Jane chased after her. "Wait! You have to help me," Jane pleaded.

"No, I don't!" the woman called over her shoulder. She walked into a crowd of women assembled out in front of the Pump Room, and Jane followed her into the throng. Jane shielded her eyes from the exposed knees and bosoms and weaved through the strange multitude. The sea of people parted to reveal the woman walking between two men dressed in waistcoats and little else. Jane grabbed the woman's hand and pulled her into a side passage near the Pump Room's main entrance.

"All right, fine, what do you want?" the woman said with a sigh. They were shielded from view of the policemen and everyone else. "A selfie? An autograph? A happy birthday video for your grandmother? Whatever you want, it's yours if you promise to leave me alone afterward."

Jane peered around nervously, but to her relief could not see the constables. She shrugged and shook her head. "I don't know what those things are. But I don't want any of them."

The woman exhaled. "Boy, I've wrangled some superfans in my time, but you take the cake. What do you want, then?"

Jane stepped backward and studied the woman. "Why do you keep walking away from me?" Jane asked her. "You did the same thing last night."

The woman placed her hands on her hips. "Let's see. First, you appeared in a pile of curtains from thin air," she said. "Then you follow me through the village, like a stalker. Can you blame me, or any sane person, for wanting to avoid you?" She raised an eyebrow.

Jane nodded. "Will you give me the chance to explain myself? Then you may leave as you please." The woman looked Jane up and down, then shrugged. Jane proceeded. "I fell asleep and woke to find Bath altered," she said. "The people wear less clothing and the buildings are made of glass and steel. Nothing is where it is supposed to be, and now I am being chased by the constabulary. I remain in a state of utter confusion. Please get me out of here. I will do anything. I could help you with something in return."

The woman stared at Jane and appeared to ponder the offer. She crossed her arms and nodded. "Yes. Deal."

Jane straightened at the unexpected about-face. What had she said to change the woman's mind? "You will help me?"

"I will help you," she replied. "If you will help me, that is."

"Of course," Jane said. She felt certain she could offer little in the way of help, but it was her best chance of escaping capture, so she would worry about that later. "What is your name?"

The woman squinted. "Seriously? You don't know who I am?" She removed her black eyeglasses and struck a pose like Venus in, well, *The Birth of Venus*. "How about now?"

"I do not recognize you," Jane said.

"For goodness' sake," snapped the woman, seeming annoyed. "I'm Sofia Wentworth." She held out her hand and Jane shook it.

"I'm Jane Austen," Jane said.

Chapter Thirteen

For Sofia Wentworth, the situation now came into focus, just like it did when you mounted a prime lens on a 35 mm film camera. When the woman had materialized in the theater curtains the night before, Sofia justified the sight as being a simple hallucination from her own brain, which was deprived of oxygen at that point from inhaling too many times from the paper bag. On closer reflection, however, it was clear that the woman appearing in the mountain of black velvet had been conjured not from the hypoxia of her brain but from the mischief of a film producer, keen to secure their big break with that most clichéd of tropes, the hidden-camera practical joke. It was all so obvious now.

She cringed at the tearful call she'd made to her agent. He must have been in on the joke. She had suggested a Jane Austen behind-the-scenes tie-in once, something for the DVD extras. The production had said no, apparently, but she saw now even that constituted part of the ruse, to keep her in the dark so she gave a more natural performance. Of course they had gone for it. Now they were hoping to maximize the extra footage by catching Sofia screaming on camera, and to achieve this aim, they had hired a Jane Austen impersonator to jump out of a pile of curtains and scare her. As she had made no screams when this ghost of Jane

Austen appeared, they had come for her again this morning to get the footage they needed.

Sofia had been minding her own business, reacquainting herself with the town of her birth, when the actress ran toward her down Stall Street. Sofia reflected that the actress chosen to play the author overplayed certain things. This annoyed Sofia. If they could not get even a half-decent actress to play the foil in this farce, they were insulting Sofia once more and confirming a general lack of respect in the business for her own talents. She wasn't asking for much—someone who had completed a summer course at the Actors Centre would suffice—but this woman had likely nothing but failed auditions for shampoo commercials on her résumé, so little was her grasp of nuance. How dare they.

Sofia decided to have some fun. If the producers showed her such little respect, she'd pay it back in kind. Aware of the production costs and crew required to film this extended practical joke, she'd string it along so she could get them to waste as much of their money as possible on hidden-camera operators, costumes, extras, and storyliners. She wouldn't flinch first. She'd call their bluff and play along, treating the woman in front of her as though she were the long-dead darling of English prose. The producers would scratch their heads, all the while filming endless scenes of useless footage. Even better, if the footage was any good, her husband might like it.

"So, you're Jane Austen then," Sofia said.

"That is correct," replied the Jane Austen impersonator. Her eyes darted about to the surrounding buildings, roads, and people who walked past on the street.

"And you agreed to help me, right?" Sofia asked. She refused to let the woman wriggle from the earlier deal.

"Of course," the woman replied in a shaky tone. "How may I be of assistance?"

"Make me look good," Sofia whispered, out of ear- and eyeshot of whatever hidden cameras might be lurking. "Follow my lead. If I walk into bad lighting, steer me toward a more attractive mise-en-scène. It's okay, I've worked with semiamateurs before. I can salvage this disaster of a production. But you need to throw yourself into this part. You need to play this like you believe you are Jane Austen."

"I am Jane Austen," the woman said.

"Perfect! Play it with conviction. The main point is, I need to look attractive, beautiful, sensual. Come now, we can do this." Sofia gave the woman playing Jane an encouraging pat.

"I hope so," the woman said.

"Good. Okay," Sofia resumed in a louder voice. "What now, Jane Austen?" she asked.

"My clothes," Jane said. She pointed to her empire-line dress. "For some reason, they are a beacon for attention."

"Good idea," Sofia said. "Wait here. Sofia to the rescue." She left the passage and walked back up the hill.

Jane stood in the street and called after her, "Do you intend to return?"

SOFIA DID RETURN, with a bag of clothes. "Put these on," she said. She had hoped to dress her new protégée in a chic ensemble from Harvey Nichols, something Hepburnesque, but the only establishment open was the Samaritans thrift store on Stall Street. The boxy sales associate had sold Sofia a brown paisley suit in a safari cut.

"I trust these are the fashions of this place, that I will blend in if I wear them?" Jane said of the clothes. A look of concern danced across her face.

"You'll look fabulous," Sofia declared. Jane would look ridiculous, but it was all Sofia could find at short notice. "Change over there," she added. She pointed to a pile of wooden crates that lay in the alley.

Jane ducked behind them and wiggled out of her dress. "These are men's clothes."

"Women can wear trousers now," Sofia explained, playing along. She turned her head to the sky. A CCTV camera mounted on the building above pointed down at them. Sofia pretended not to see it but turned her shoulders and moved her chin to be filmed from the best angle.

"I've worn trousers before, Miss Wentworth," Jane said. "I played King George in *The Horrible History of England*, a play I wrote and performed with my siblings."

"Please call me Sofia." She didn't want the general public and Jack hearing her called by her last name. It made her sound aloof. And old.

"How peculiar," Jane remarked. "The people last night addressed each other by their Christian names also. Do I leave my underclothes on?"

"You call everyone by their first names here," Sofia said. "Yes, leave them on." Sofia considered how best to play this. She needed to appear like she was unaware the whole thing was a stunt, while secretly saying philosophical, informative things to reendear her to her husband.

Jane pulled up the trousers and tucked her chemise inside. She covered the lumps with the shirt. "Will this do?" Her face bore a look of complete confusion.

Sofia looked her up and down. Jane's tiny frame swam underneath layers of flowery beige polyester. Her Regency hairdo remained, with the tiny ringlets surrounding her face. Altogether, she resembled a shrunken clown. "You look smashing," Sofia said with confidence. She rolled the waistband up on the trousers until they could be rolled no more. Sofia crept forward to the edge of the side passage. She turned her head left and right. The coast was clear for the moment. The so-called police were gone. She motioned for Jane to follow her and they walked out onto the main street.

"So," Sofia began as they walked down Stall Street, "have you been resurrected, then?" She looked around for the next camera. She couldn't see any; they must be hidden. She hoped none were in the bushes. Being shot from below was a most unflattering angle.

"I beg your pardon?" said Jane.

"Or perhaps they cloned your DNA from a bonnet?" Sofia snorted. She was trying to help the young actress along, as she may have been rusty with improvisation. But her new companion feigned misunderstanding at this, so Sofia elaborated. "You're in a different time now. I was just wondering how you got here."

The woman responded better to this invitation and now stared at Sofia with alarm. "What time *is* this?" she asked.

Sofia paused and smiled. The time had arrived for the revelation, it seemed. This formed a key moment in the narrative, and Sofia needed to play it well. "What time do you think it is?" she said in a casual voice.

"It is the year eighteen hundred and three," Jane replied, as if on cue. She delivered the line quite well, with caution and confusion.

Sofia nodded and gave her reply. "Afraid not. It is the year twenty hundred and twenty."

"Heavens preserve us," Jane said. She opened her eyes wide and paced around in a circle. Then she closed her eyes and sat on the ground and seemed to faint.

Sofia shook Jane's shoulder and blew on her face. The woman roused. "The date on the paper. Last night," she said to Sofia.

"What paper?" said Sofia. She wondered if she should tell the woman to get up. But she was acting rather shaken by the news—understandably—and Sofia was loath to interrupt her process.

Jane explained to Sofia about some piece of paper she was handed the night before.

"The call sheet for rehearsal? That had the date, yes. It is 2020," Sofia replied.

The Jane Austen impersonator shuddered. Sofia was enjoying the performance now. She had underestimated this actress. Sofia had delivered the reveal with gravitas, and now the actress responded with a convincing display of disbelief and terror. Though it was behind-the-scenes footage, and likely shot on a grainy video camera, Sofia did not mind. An audience suspended their disbelief at any plot point when they saw genuine human feeling, and this tale of a person from two hundred years ago, trapped in the modern day, would move the hardest of hearts.

Chapter Fourteen

*J*ane leaned over her knees and inhaled. While the only food she'd consumed over the past three days were the biscuits she'd packed for her journey to London, she suddenly felt inclined to deposit that paltry meal across the footpath. She attempted to curtail such a reaction until she was confirmed of the facts. "That's impossible," she said to the woman who asked to be called Sofia. The evidence grew harder to ignore that something had happened to the Bath she knew. But still, she clung to hope that the absurd reality the woman had suggested was a mistake. "I don't believe you," she tried.

Sofia hailed a passerby, another man in his drawers. "Excuse me, sir. What year is it?" she said to him.

"Do I know you?" said the man. He lifted his eyeglasses. "Are you from *Wheel of Fortune*?"

Sofia covered her face with her hand. "No. The year, sir?" she insisted.

"It's twenty twenty," he replied with a huff and a scowl, as though Jane's companion had asked a foolish question. He replaced his glasses and walked off.

Sofia turned to Jane. "See?" she said. Jane winced. This offered a less than ideal situation. Sofia retrieved a newspaper from a bin and showed it to Jane. "And see again." The front page bore a painting of a man making a speech. The painting shared the same lifelike quality of the one that had terrified Jane in the hall the night before. Sofia pointed to the date printed at the top of the page: 2020.

Jane shivered and considered bringing up her meal again. She stared at Sofia. Perhaps Lady Johnstone and her cavalry of gossips were playing some grand joke, hoping to milk the Austen misfortune for more scandal and fun. It proved an unusual tactic to go to such lengths as these for conversation fodder, to fabricate newspapers and pay actors, but the alternative—that this woman told the truth—was even more ludicrous.

Another steel carriage raced past them with terrific sound, again with no horses to drag it. Even if Jane was to entertain the idea that she had moved through time, how had she managed it? What mechanism had she employed to achieve this mind-and-flesh-bending feat? Was it Mrs. Sinclair's doing? But that required a reality more ridiculous than the others combined. That a bedraggled person from Cheapside who smelled of cabbages was in fact a mighty sorceress? That the demented scribbles she'd left on Jane's page were a . . . spell? That she had conjured from her cabbage hearth an opening into time itself and sent Jane through it?

As they walked down the road, Jane studied the sights around her and searched for logical explanations. A third steel carriage sped past her. She could source a reason for this. She mistook a horseless carriage for what was simply a train, powered by steam. Jane and her father had ridden a Murdoch locomotive over fifty yards of track in London when she was twenty. The steam that billowed from the train's chimney in meaty gray puffs astounded her and she had demanded the driver explain how it worked. The bemused man told Papa his daughter was impertinent and that was no question for a woman, so her father had borrowed a book about locomotion from the circulating library for Jane and she taught herself the concepts. The mysterious animation of the carriage she was now looking at could be put down to simple steam combustion. Indeed, no steam billowed from this carriage, but she supposed this was a French version or some alternative design.

She could explain Bath's altered appearance, too. Perhaps some renovations with steel and glass had occurred, which she missed while she walked the woods and groves. They must have overhauled everything quickly since she was in Stall Street yesterday, but as Bath always strained to have everything first, she did not put it past the local gentry to throw up fashionable new edifices in a day.

As she looked around for another item to logically explain her situation, a roaring rumble of wind screamed overhead. She looked to the sky. The sound came from a bird whose coat comprised not feathers, but gleaming white steel. Its length stretched as long as the twenty-four-apartment block of Sydney House. The bird shot through the sky, thousands of feet in the air. It was the second of the species she had observed that morning. Yes, this was where the endeavor came a tad unstuck. No logical explanation existed for a gargantuan steel bird, one thousand times the height of an ostrich, to be hurtling through the sky.

And then Jane slapped her head as she realized a logical explanation did exist for everything. Of course! She herself was insane. Jane, in her humiliation and final condemnation to spinsterhood, had become senile. Like the woman who stood on Stall Street and composed love poems for a shilling, who wore a gravy-stained shawl and a saucepan for a bonnet, Jane too had retreated from the bleakness of her spinsterhood into the warm blanket of madness. She did not doubt that heartbreak was a force powerful enough to fling one into lunacy. She saw now that she had imagined the whole thing—the trip to London, Mrs. Sinclair, dancing with the obnoxious man. It was all a ruse of her own mind to counter against loneliness.

Now that she had identified her psychosis, what was she to do? How was she to behave? The fashionable treatment for hysterical ladies was to offer them a trip to the seaside, and then, after bundling them into a carriage that locked on the outside, to deposit them not at Brighton or Lyme, but Bedlam instead. Jane felt happy to forgo such a glamorous fate for herself. She resolved instead to act as normal as possible and draw as little attention to her madness as she could. She would pretend all was well and go along with whatever her new friend Sofia said. Hopefully Sofia was not part of the hallucination, but just to be safe, Jane would politely decline any offers to visit Brighton.

"I suppose you'll be wanting to get back, then," Sofia said. "To your own time?"

"Indeed," Jane said with a careful nod. "I did not consider that."

"You need to go back so you can write your books."

Jane was still so preoccupied with navigating her recent descent into madness that she almost missed what Sofia said. She stopped walking. "My books?" she said.

"Yes, your books. The ones by Jane Austen?"

Jane opened her mouth but said nothing.

"Come with me." Sofia continued along the path and Jane followed her. "Did you know I'm starring in an adaptation of one of them?"

"One of what, I beg pardon?" Jane asked.

"One of your books. *Northanger Abbey.*"

Jane shook her head. "I do apologize. Again, I do not follow your meaning."

They arrived at a white-stone cottage with a thatched roof. Sofia unlocked the door and showed Jane inside. It was a cozy, comfortable home that made Jane smile. It reminded her of the rectory in Hampshire where she grew up. She did not recognize some of the furniture pieces, made of glass and steel, but the parlor contained a fireplace and a wonderful bookshelf, which took up an entire wall.

"I'm not here by choice," Sofia said, flinging her giant reticule onto the windowsill. "This is my brother's house. But it will do for now." She disappeared into another room, then returned carrying a stack of books under her arm. She laid the books out on the table one by one. "The producer gave them to me as a gift when I signed on to do the film. I'd prefer jewelry, but never mind. These are nice. First editions, I believe."

A momentary silence filled the house as Jane stopped breathing. She stared at the six books that now lay on the table. She read each title in turn. They shared a common author.

"Good God" was all Jane could say. The room spun around her.

"I know," Sofia said. "Cool, right?"

"Might I sit down?"

"Knock yourself out," Sofia said.

Jane did not understand the expression but pulled out a chair all the same. Her hand shook. Of all the tricks her mind played in its current insane reverie, this took pride of place as the cruelest. Jane felt happy to entertain the notion that she had descended into madness, but not if her hallucination included her achieving the status of published novelist, the dearest dream of her heart. It seemed too cruel. For her to see her name in print this way answered a question her soul had been asking for twenty years.

She struggled to overstate the bliss she felt in every fiber of her being. Even if wicked fantasy now engulfed her mind, she allowed herself one indulgent moment to enjoy it. She sat and immersed herself in the idea that she was not insane; she had indeed cast a spell and travelled through time. She found herself in a future moment of human existence, in which her manuscripts were not rejected, but accepted and published, to the point where they now sat on a bookshelf in someone's home. Jane felt glad she had sat down, for all the liquid drained from her head, and fainting felt likely. She blinked and picked up one of the books. The cover read:

EMMA
A Novel
JANE AUSTEN

Jane opened the book. A portrait rested on the inside cover, a watercolor of a woman around age thirty. The woman wore a bone-white gown and her curls poked out from under a lace bonnet. "My goodness," Jane said. "It's me." The nose stretched too beaklike, and the eyes were too round, but the similarity of the portrait to her own face remained remarkable.

"They've cast you well," Sofia muttered.

Once more Jane did not understand Sofia's meaning but she had larger things to distract her. "I've never posed for a portrait in a lace cap," she said, pointing at the picture. The detail seemed odd; the rules of society reserved lace caps for married women. Jane studied the painting of herself more closely and identified the unmistakable broad strokes of a familiar artist. "Cassandra painted this," declared Jane. She felt confused and intrigued; she never recalled sitting and posing for this portrait for Cassandra, yet it was for certain a painting done by her. How?

"Who is Cassandra?"

"My sister," Jane replied.

"Of course, I knew that!" Sofia said. She puffed out her chest. Her ample bosom bloomed into the room. She shrugged. "Shall we go?"

"Go where?" Jane asked. She closed the cover of the novel again.

"Somewhere we might find clues."

"Clues?" repeated Jane. She stared at the novel, still distracted by its strangeness.

"Yes," replied Sofia with a nod. "To send you back to your own time."

Chapter Fifteen

"I believed I had arrived at my capacity for shock earlier," Jane said, "but it has now been exceeded."

They arrived at a modern town house, in the style of King George. From the grayish hue of the sun, Jane guessed the hour reached about three in the afternoon. She also noted that the fantasy sun appeared as gray and disappointing as the English sun of reality. Jane stared at the building's facade. A sign across the top read *The Jane Austen Experience*. Jane inhaled. "This building has my name on it," she declared. Her head still spun from seeing the novels she had supposedly written; now this.

"Isn't it great?" Sofia said. "I thought we could gather some facts about your life. It will look great on camera."

Jane shook her head, her mind whirring. How and why was there a building with her name on it? What could possibly be inside?

They entered through a blue front door. "That is my sitting room!" Jane said with a gasp. The foyer contained the Austens' battered old settee, their French armchairs, and Mrs. Austen's armoire. Why was their furniture in this place? How did it get here? It felt entirely odd to see her family's possessions transplanted whole into this foreign building, their sitting room re-created, as if on display. Jane felt the blood drain from her head once more and sat down on the settee to compose herself.

"You there, in the pajamas!" a voice shrieked at Jane from the corner of the room. "Don't sit on that." A woman bounded over with a furious look. She wore an ill-fitting purple gown and a white bonnet.

"I beg your pardon," Sofia said. "They're not pajamas. That's a safari suit! It's vintage."

"So is that furniture," the bonneted woman cried. "Did you not see the sign? That is an artifact. It is priceless!" She scowled. "Jane Austen sat on that very sofa!"

Jane looked at the sofa. The woman told no lies; in fairness, Jane always sat on that settee in the sitting room and had indeed sat on it the last time she was there. It bore the same crescent-shaped burn on the arm where Jane once spilled a candle while reading in the small hours. A mixture of fascination and unease gripped her. The more real the details became, the more unsettling this dream grew. "Indeed. My apologies, madam," Jane said, still not enough gone into her nightmare to forget her manners. She stood up.

"Two tickets, please," Sofia said to the woman with a smile.

"The next tour leaves in ten minutes," she replied. She studied Jane as she took Sofia's money. "Have we met?" she asked Jane. She seemed to stare past Jane at the wall behind her.

"I believe not, madam," Jane replied.

"Jesus," Sofia said, also staring past Jane toward the wall. Jane winced at the blasphemy but found it warranted when she turned to look as well. On the wall behind Jane, looming over the back of her head, hung the same portrait of Jane that lay on the inside cover of her novel, reproduced now to life-size proportions. Besides the beaky nose and the different clothes, Jane's own flesh matched that of the image with precision. The human Jane wore the identical expression of bemusement as her portrait. "Golly, they *have* cast you well," Sofia muttered once more.

"I still do not know what that means," Jane said, "but I agree with the sentiment."

While the portrait in the book was cropped at the shoulders, this larger reproduction showed more of Jane's figure. Jane saw now she wore the bone-white muslin dress from Maison Du Bois: the one that made her eyes shine, the one Mr. Withers never saw her in. A new detail drew Jane's eye downward. In the portrait, she wore a ring. A band made of gold wrapped around her ring finger, and a turquoise stone sat upon it. The oval stone shone in a creamy blue. She inhaled. She felt the ring draw her closer, as though it had a soul. It confused her, too. She did not own, nor had she ever owned, such a piece of jewelry. It stood out on her finger in the painting, not out of place, but a new addition. She put it down to yet another bizarre detail of her hallucination, but she heard herself asking the woman in the white bonnet, against her better judgment, about the stone's origin. "Do you know whose ring that is?" Jane asked her.

"It is Austen's ring. She always wore it," the woman said with a huff, as though the answer were obvious.

Jane scratched her head. "Where did she get it?" she pressed. "Who gave it to her?"

The woman shrugged. "No one knows where that ring came from, actually. No one knows how it came into her possession. Its origins remain a mystery."

Jane shook her head and added it to the list of unsettling items she had encountered in her reverie of the insane. She stared at the ring and found herself unable to pry her gaze from it, even when Sofia tugged her arm and gently pulled her away. More urgent issues existed to worry about, but the appearance of this ring, on her finger, in this watercolor portrait in the building with her name on the outside, was the one strange item in a cacophony of strange items her mind could not put away.

"The Jane Austen Experience is about to begin," the bonneted woman announced. "Please form a queue at the double doors." Jane and Sofia walked over. They were the only people on the tour. "Welcome to the Jane Austen Experience," the woman said. She was apparently also the tour guide. "And welcome to Bath," she continued, "the home of Jane Austen."

Jane snorted. "My favorite thing about Bath is the road out." The woman glared at Jane again.

"Please be quiet," Sofia whispered to Jane, "or we'll get kicked off the tour."

The woman continued. "My name is Marjorie Martin and I shall be your guide as we travel on a journey back to the time of Regency England and the greatest writer that ever lived."

"I give you leave to like this woman," Jane said to Sofia. Marjorie turned to face the double doors. She threw them open with ceremony. A dark room greeted them. "I don't see anything," Jane said.

"Sit. Both of you," said Marjorie. She gestured toward a small train of open carriages. Jane and Sofia fumbled around in the dark and eventually found seats together in the third carriage. Marjorie sat in the front. She pressed a button and the train moved forward.

"Heavens!" Jane said at the sudden motion.

"Indeed," said Marjorie. She pushed back her shoulders. "We

are the only Jane Austen attraction in Bath with a built-in roller coaster."

"Is the train going to jerk around the whole time?" Sofia asked. "I feel bilious."

"If you vomit, there is a fifty-pound cleaning fee," Marjorie said.

"Fifty pounds!" Jane said. "That's a year's wages."

"Yeah, that's unfair," Sofia said. "I can't be held responsible for the security of my stomach contents! I only had a mimosa for breakfast."

The train entered the next room, which was lined on both sides with glass cases. Marjorie pointed to the first case as the train moved past. "Behold," she said. "We begin at the beginning. Jane Austen's christening bonnet." A tiny muslin cap smocked with grub roses sat on a wooden plinth.

"That is not my christening bonnet," Jane declared. Marjorie turned around and scowled at Jane. Sofia elbowed Jane in the ribs.

"Control yourself," Sofia said. "This woman is not an actor. She's a real person. She could boot us out of here." Jane scratched her head and agreed to stay quiet.

"One of Jane's favorite pastimes was tea-making," Marjorie pressed on. The train moved on to the next glass case. It displayed a china tea set.

"Untrue again," Jane said, more quietly this time. "And that is not my tea set, either." She knew this was all some grand fantasy her mind had concocted, but still, she objected to so many details of her life being arranged so inaccurately and haphazardly.

The remaining glass cases contained an assortment of hats and gloves, James's writing desk, a pair of Cassandra's stockings, a prayer book of her father's, and more spoons and teacups.

"Do you recognize anything?" Sofia said.

"Yes. Not a single thing is mine. Wait," Jane said. "Excuse me please, Marjorie. What is that ribbon?"

A two-foot length of inch-thick silk ribbon, once pink but now yellowed with time, hung from a wooden bar in the final glass cabinet.

"A hair ribbon." Marjorie shrugged. "It is of no great significance. Women wore hair ribbons."

How wrong she was. Jane recognized the ribbon in an instant. Black soot charred the ends of the ribbon that had once tied the manuscript for *First Impressions*. The ribbon had caught the edge of the flames before Jane hauled it out from the inferno. In this charlatan shrine of Jane's fantasy, this one length of silk was more visceral to Jane than the other objects combined. She struggled to believe she had conjured such a detail in a fantasy. The train jerked to a halt.

"We have reached the end of the tour," Marjorie said. "Your complimentary sweet." She presented them each with a small brown disc furnished with a crooked silhouette, which, when Jane squinted, resembled her own head.

"Cheers," Sofia said. She popped the brown disc in her mouth.

Jane observed Sofia and did the same. The solid disc dissolved to cream on her tongue. Jane closed her eyes and rocked backward.

"Are you well?" Sofia asked.

"What do I consume?"

"Chocolate." Jane had heard of chocolate but never had the funds to procure it. "Do you like it?"

"It is the highlight of the tour," Jane said.

They exited the building. Jane reflected on the events of the morning and found that her self-diagnosis of insanity perhaps deserved deeper scrutiny. Was this all truly a hallucination? She began to falter in her certainty. Her own current experience differed from the examples of madness she had observed in the known lunatics of her acquaintance. While the gravy-stained poet of Stall Street, for example, spoke only to herself in her own world, Jane conversed with others of flesh and blood. While the same woman possessed no awareness of the stench of the fish that rotted two feet from her in the gutter, Jane had tasted that chocolate as it melted in her mouth. She had touched the books and felt the fabric of their covers. She had smelled the vanilla in their pages. All five senses remained alert and intact. No one she talked to indulged her as one did a child or patted her head; no one offered her a carriage ride to Brighton. Each person interacted with her in a manner befitting someone who retained control of her senses; they treated her as though she were lucid and sane.

She allowed herself to consider that there might be some minuscule chance lunacy had not taken her, but rather, with a sound mind, she had indeed cast a spell that had moved her through time to the year 2020, where her reputation as an author was such that museums were now built in her honor. It was pure fiction, surely.

Chapter Sixteen

They left the museum. Sofia listened to the Jane Austen impersonator detail her alleged journey from 1803 to the present, about
travelling to London to visit a witch in a falling-down house, of
her mother burning her manuscript, of the witch's fondness for
cabbages. The saga enthralled her, and while Sofia didn't understand why the actress went into such detail, at least she felt
entertained. The actress remembered great chunks of dialogue,
names, facts, and dates. She had done her research. Sofia had
read every Jane Austen novel as a teenager. She loved them and
confessed to being something of a secret bonnet-drama fiend, so
despite the whole thing being contrived for an elaborate candid-
camera prank, she thoroughly enjoyed listening to it all and
threw herself into her own part.

"This was all houses before," Jane said. She pointed to a row of
convenience stores and dress shops that lined the street. Brutalist
boxes of concrete had replaced the famous Bath-stone buildings.

"Bath was bombed in the war," Sofia said, taking her cue.

"Which war? Did the Little Corporal finally invade? The
French are never to be trusted."

"The Second World War. Bombed by the Nazis. We like the
French now. Sort of."

"The whole world was at war?" Jane exclaimed.

"Ask my brother to fill you in when he gets home. He's a history teacher, among other things; he'll have some dusty doorstop of a book to put you to sleep with."

A rusty black sedan drove past. "Where are the horses?" Jane asked. "To pull it along?"

"Inside," Sofia said, waving to the car. "There's a machine that does . . . something." She squinted, trying to appear wise without having to explain how a car worked.

Jane looked confused but nodded. "I like walking," she said. "I walk every day, even in the rain."

"There's no chance of that here," Sofia said. "It hasn't rained in six months. England is in a drought."

"Is this the apocalypse?" Jane asked.

"Maybe," replied Sofia with gravitas. They walked onward. Sofia strained for something else sophisticated to say to keep the conversation going. The Jane actress had remained subdued since the "I am now a famous novelist" scene. "What else have you observed about the present?" Sofia asked her.

"The world smells of paraffin."

"Paraffin? You mean gasoline? That's concerning." Sofia snorted. "Sounds about right, though." She was keen to move on from science and history; they would bore her husband to tears. "Tell me more about the witch," she said, changing the improv to something juicier.

"Her name is Mrs. Sinclair. I visited her at her house in London. Is there still a London?" Jane asked.

"There's still a London," Sofia said. "And this 'spell'?"

"I still have it," Jane said. She reached into her pocket and retrieved a piece of paper.

Sofia examined it. Someone—the props department, likely—had scrawled blobs of black ink across a charred, yellowish piece of paper. "I can't make this out."

"She had terrible handwriting," Jane said.

Sofia held the page at all angles, looking for any type of clue or inspiration. She could not decipher the words. "Did props make this for you?"

Jane slumped. "I was hoping that this occurred often. That you would know what to do."

Sofia shook her head. "I don't know what this is. Sorry." She handed the paper back.

"Am I stuck here?" Jane asked.

"I don't know," Sofia said. "Maybe. Are you fainting again?"

The Jane actress possessed a knack for physical stunts, it seemed. Her knees buckled and she fell to the ground. Sofia rushed over and grabbed her under the arms. It all seemed a bit over the top for this scene, but the actress fainted convincingly, so Sofia let her have her moment. She glanced at another CCTV camera above them and shifted the woman's shoulders toward it so they were both featured in the shot. "Are you okay?" she asked in a tender voice.

"I'll never see my brothers or Papa again. Even Mama," she replied, looking forlorn.

Sofia dabbed the woman's brow with her sleeve and played along. "There, there. I will help you. Hush now, Sofia is here," she cooed.

Jane looked up at her. "The woman who gave me the . . . well, spell—shall I call it a 'spell'?"

"Sure, why not?" Sofia replied.

"It seems a silly word. I still struggle to believe she had any power at all, let alone magic. She was barely a matchmaker."

"'Spell' sounds great," Sofia said, nodding. "The audience will love it." Talk of mystical things always added darkness and romance to a storyline.

"Who?" Jane asked. "The audience?"

"Never mind." Sofia rolled her eyes. Amateurs. "So . . . the spell?"

"Yes. Well, Mrs. Sinclair—the woman who gave it to me—told me it was reversible."

"Excellent."

"Except she did not mention *how* to reverse it. I found the encounter rather ludicrous, you see. I now wish I had listened more."

"Okay." Sofia shrugged. She had neglected this part of the improvisation. "Remind me, who is Sinclair?"

"The matchmaker. In London. When I met her, she said to me, 'There always has been, and always will be, someone like me in this place.' I found it ridiculous at the time, so did not pay it much heed. Now I begin to think it possessed some significance."

Sofia remembered now. The collapsing house, the cabbages. This was difficult terrain to keep interesting for an audience. People were bored by hearing of action that took place off-screen. Still, she did her best to keep the flow going and suggested some forward movement. "So, maybe go check it out? Go back there."

"Back where?" Jane asked.

"Go back to London."

SOFIA SHOWED JANE to a guest bedroom in her brother's house. Night had fallen, and no one had come to tell her what to do next.

No person had jumped out of the shrubbery and yelled "Gotcha!" No production runner had called her offering to reimburse her for the Jane Austen Experience tickets (she kept the receipt anyway). The producers seemed determined to keep the farce going and Sofia felt happy to oblige. Sofia had tried suggesting to the Jane Austen actress that they call it a day once it began to get dark and gently tried to get her to leave, but the woman looked about, forlorn, like she might cry.

"I have nowhere to go," she said. "What if the constabulary arrest me?"

Sofia was unsure about the exact nature of the crime the Jane actress had committed that seemed to make her fear arrest now, but Sofia couldn't risk the whole thing falling through if the actress left town—they had come this far. She decided the safest option was to let her stay in the house. After providing her with a bowl of canned soup she found in the cupboard—which Sofia felt quite pleased with herself for heating up without destroying the microwave—she showed Jane to the guest room. "You can sleep in here," she said to Jane. Sofia walked into the room and switched on the light on the bedside table.

"What is that?" Jane asked, transfixed. She pointed at the light.

"That's a desk lamp," Sofia said.

"Desk lamp," Jane said. She clicked the switch at the base of the lamp, mimicking Sofia's action. The lamp switched off and threw the room into darkness. She clicked the switch once more and the lamp flicked back on. She repeated the motion again. The room was light, then dark, then light, then dark.

Sofia grabbed her hand. "Best just leave it on, methinks."

Jane shook her head. "Extraordinary," she whispered, in a tone of wonder.

"You can wear this to bed," Sofia said. She offered Jane a pink silk nightgown.

Jane studied the dress. "You sew far better than I do," she said. "Though that is no difficult feat."

"Save your compliments for Donatella Versace," Sofia said, and sat down on the bed. "I have a six A.M. call time. Do they want you on set tomorrow?"

"Who is 'they' and what is 'set'?" Jane asked.

Sofia exhaled, feeling exhausted by the continuous state of confusion the actress seemed determined to maintain. "You can break character, you know." She leaned in. "This is private property. The production wouldn't dare put cameras inside here."

"Madam, once more, I have little idea of your meaning," Jane replied.

Sofia sighed. "A method actor, hey? I dig. Okay, I'll respect your process." She would have to continue the farce for a little longer, it seemed.

"I should go to London as soon as possible," Jane said. "To search for information regarding Mrs. Sinclair. If I can locate her house, perhaps I will find clues to reverse the spell."

"Sure. Do whatever you like," Sofia said. She was unsure of the point of this discussion. The hidden camera crew was not going to follow this sweet little extra all the way to London. They were interested in Sofia Wentworth, movie star. Still, she indulged the actress, keen not to ruin another thespian's improvisations. "My brother sometimes goes to London," she said. "Ask him in the morning. Perhaps he'll take you."

"Splendid. Though, is that not improper? Travelling with a man who is no relative, to whom I am not engaged?"

"You could travel to London in a bikini and no one would care."

The actress appeared confused by this. "The address is for 8 Russia Row, Cheapside. Do you know of it?" she asked.

"Cheapside? That's EC2," Sofia replied. "Give me your paper. I'll write it down."

Jane handed Sofia another paper prop she had been cradling, which contained an address for London written in old-fashioned, fountain-pen handwriting. Sofia took it and wrote down the postcode for Cheapside.

"What is that?" Jane whispered. She pointed at Sofia's hand.

"This? It's a pen."

"May I?" she said reverently. Sofia nodded and handed Jane the pen. Jane put the pen to the corner of the paper and scribbled. She gasped. "Where is the ink?" She drew the pen to her face and studied it.

"Inside the barrel," Sofia said. "It's more convenient than a quill, I suppose?"

"It's the finest thing I have ever seen," Jane said. She held up the pen as though she examined a gold nugget.

"Keep it," Sofia said.

"I could not possibly," Jane said. "A self-inking quill must cost a fortune."

"It's yours."

Jane gasped and nestled the pen in her hands.

"Now, I must get my beauty sleep," Sofia said. "You have everything you need?"

"I am well, thank you," Jane replied, still staring at the pen.

The interaction struck Sofia as odd, though not unpleasant. The Jane impersonator seemed determined to uphold the farce, despite Sofia's insistence that no cameras existed inside her brother's private property. Still, Sofia didn't mind. She could not put her finger on it, but something otherworldly surrounded this actress. What Sofia had earlier written off as bad acting now struck her as something different altogether. Jane appeared to be genuinely taken with the pen and the desk lamp. She showed an interest in everything Sofia said, whereas most people zoned out the minute Sofia opened her mouth. She seemed to be one of those annoying types who liked people. Sofia commanded herself to remain frosty and professional with the woman, however, to not like her too much, for Sofia was the movie star, and this Jane was a nobody, employed by a film studio to make fun of her. With any luck, she would just stay the night and be gone by the morning, and Sofia would never see her again.

"Good night, then, Jane Austen," Sofia said.

"Good night, Sofia," Jane replied.

Sofia left the room and shut the door.

Chapter Seventeen

*F*red sat in the Black Prince Inn and drained his third lager for the evening.

Four weeks ago, his sister, Sofia, had showed up on his doorstep and turned his life upside down. It was the first he'd heard from her in three years in any meaningful way; she flew around the globe from red carpet to film set and they exchanged brief, humorous text messages around birthdays and holidays with a distinct lack of any real emotion. That's how they did it in their family, with jokes and booze. When he had learned about her separation from her husband (on the internet), he'd made an awkward, half-hearted offer to call, but she hadn't replied, which he had been grateful for, for he had no idea what he would have said if she'd taken him up on his offer.

In the last few weeks of living with him, she'd already managed to destroy his stereo, scratch his car, drink all of his wine, and somehow spill rice into every drawer in the kitchen and corner of the floor. Grains of rice still stabbed his feet when he got up in the night.

She'd returned to Bath to shoot some period film—a Jane Austen movie, like they all were in Bath—and she'd asked to stay with him, declaring that no hotels in Bath met her standards. The request had startled him. Sofia wasn't just some actress. She was a movie star, and the last time he had seen her face, it had been on a thirty-foot-high billboard in Piccadilly Circus. She didn't stay with relatives, she stayed in presidential suites and on yachts, and bunking down in the little cottage they had both grown up in seemed several levels beneath both her taste and price range. He'd tried to assuage her concerns and reassure her of the quality of hotels in Bath; after all, the city had hosted Roman emperors and kings for two thousand years; there were more than a few decent rooms in town with appropriately eye-watering price tags. "None good enough for me," his sister had insisted. "I'll have to stay here." She'd scratched her face then and gazed at the floor. He had never seen his magnificent big sister look so tired and small. They still hadn't discussed her marital split, and he didn't plan on bringing it up anytime soon.

"You'd better stay here, then," he'd said, realizing she wasn't going to budge.

She'd done an odd thing then. She'd hugged him. He recalled her leather jacket crackling like crushed cellophane as she held him tight. She reeked of French perfume and money. She embraced him for almost a minute, saying nothing. She hadn't hugged him—or perhaps anyone, from what he could gather—in a long time. It was all very strange.

"Don't tell anyone I did that, or I'll crush your bollocks," she muttered afterward.

Next thing he knew, he was acting as an extra on the set of her new movie. "It will be fun," she had said when making the ludicrous request. "Sister-brother bonding!"

Fred had laughed; normally Sofia couldn't get far enough away from her family, and now she wanted a member of it lurking around her workplace. Something was up. "Please?" she added, when he scoffed at the idea. The *please* signified more than the request itself. Sofia never said *please*. "It would be nice to see a friendly face on set," she'd mumbled then, and looked at the floor again. He'd never known his big sister to be anything but brimming with obscene confidence, pouty and haughty. He'd finally agreed to go to set with her, and relief had danced across her face like he'd never seen.

Almost as soon as he agreed, he regretted his decision. For two weeks already, he'd been initiated into the ludicrous world of film sets. Moviemaking seemed mostly to involve standing around and occasionally being shouted at by people with headsets. The production people dressed him in a Regency-era costume that included a frock coat and jodhpurs. He complained of feeling silly but this was the one part of the whole thing he secretly enjoyed. He often instructed his A-level students on the Napoleonic Wars, and he also suspected he looked quite dashing in the clothes, maybe like someone who fought pirates. They told him his character was an officer in the navy and gave him a plastic sword to complete the look. When no one was watching, he swished it back and forth.

The set teemed with attractive women—fantasy women, really, from magazines and commercials, who looked unreal at close range, with ludicrously svelte figures and angular, alien faces. But any grand plans for one of those on-set romances the magazines rejoiced in were thrown from his mind as soon as he spoke to these people. They were only interested in one thing: Sofia. Either they wanted to know the gossip on her breakup, or they wanted to be introduced. Fred refused to indulge in the first, but he did naively introduce a couple of them to his sister early on. He regretted it almost instantly. The first woman gave Sofia her show reel. The second woman ignored him afterward, defeating the purpose.

He sipped his beer. That's why when he'd met Jane, she had confused and infuriated him. She spoke nothing of acting, dancing, show reels, agents, platforms, publicity, high-protein low-carb, or influencing. She bore none of the falseness of the other women, who were nice to him solely to get to Sofia. In fact, her behavior was quite the opposite. She made no attempt to conceal her dislike for him. She was downright hostile. He still found himself reeling from the exchange, and he felt agitation. She infuriated him. She was bewildering.

Fred put down his beer again, a little too hard. Paul looked at him and sighed.

"Okay," Paul said. "You asked her out. She turned you down." He sipped his drink.

"She didn't turn me down. I asked her out and she said yes," Fred argued.

"Then what happened?" Paul asked.

Fred shrugged. "Then she ran away," he mumbled.

Paul folded at the middle like a hinge, silently chortling. He taught PE and Health at the school where Fred worked. His preferred teaching method for safe-sex education was to show his students close-up photos of gonorrhea.

"Are you finished?" Fred asked. He rolled his eyes.

"Sorry," Paul said. He composed himself and sat up. He raised his glass. "A toast. To the woman who ran away. Good luck to her, I say!" He offered his glass toward Fred's. Fred made no move toward it. Paul scoffed warmly and chinked the glasses together anyway. "I'm so happy right now," Paul said. "It annoys me how much luck you have with women. I really like this Jane character. Too bad she ran away from you. I would have liked to shake her hand. First woman to turn 'Mr. Sexy Eyes' down. You normally don't even try. Women just flock to you."

"They don't," Fred said.

"They do," Paul said with a nod. "You've got that dark, brooding, self-destructive look about you that women go gaga for. And you've got great hair, like your sister. You never have to romance women. They just sit next to you and flick their hair and then it's on for young and old. No one ever flicks their hair at me."

"You're married," Fred said.

"That's even worse," Paul said. "Not even Nadine flicks her hair at me, and she's legally obliged to. It's ironic." He sighed. "The first woman you're actually interested in, she runs away from you."

"I wasn't interested in her," Fred insisted.

"Sure," Paul replied. "I'd happily believe that, but you've had a great many admirers over the years, and this is the first one you've ever spoken to me about." He took another sip of his beer and looked over for Fred's reaction. "Another one?" Paul asked.

Fred looked down; he'd emptied his glass.

"Thanks." He shrugged. Why not? He'd checked with Sofia three times that there was no rehearsal tonight until, eventually, she told him to stop asking and declared he was weird. Fred and Sofia had both inherited the same creative streak from their father, a deadbeat poet and drunk. Sofia embraced it, while Fred buried it deep down, so it only revealed itself in odd, strangled places. Teaching was safer.

"Fred. We've been mates since teachers' college," Paul said then. He put his glass down and cleared his throat.

Fred watched him, uncomfortable. It felt distinctly as though a declaration of manly affection was looming. "Because I feel sorry for you," Fred said, hoping to bat the conversation in a less serious direction. "No one else will talk to you."

"I'm not good at the mushy stuff, so don't expect a grand speech."

"I'm fine, seriously, Paul. I will be fine," he insisted, a little too loudly.

"I know you will, mate, this is about something else. Yikes." He looked at him with mock concern.

Fred swallowed and nodded for him to continue. "What's it about then?"

"If it's not too much trouble, will you be Maggie's godfather?" Paul looked proud, hopeful.

"Oh," Fred said. He inhaled. He had expected an invitation to an ill-planned hunting trip in the woods above Bath, where one of them ended up shot in the buttocks, or a hastily booked drinking weekend to Prague, where they each lost a shoe and their dignity. Those were the invitations he normally received from Paul. But this? To be the guardian of the most precious and beautiful little bundle, whose hobbies included drinking milk and smelling like heaven? He smiled. "I'm flattered, Paul, thank you. Maggie's an awesome little girl."

"She's pretty cool, isn't she?" Paul said with a smile.

Fred nodded and held up his glass. "To Maggie," he said.

"To her godfather," Paul replied, raising his own.

"Fred?" a female voice called. Paul and Fred both looked up.

"Hi," Fred said. Two women, vaguely familiar, were walking

toward them. He searched his memory frantically for their names.

"It's Laura, from St. Margaret's?" the first woman said mercifully. "We played against you guys at Teachers' Games."

Of course. "Laura, hi," Fred said. "You guys creamed us, as I recall."

"I didn't want to say, but yes," she replied, with a laugh. Fred remembered now: Laura, the bubbly lady who had turned into a swearing dominatrix on the netball court. She'd almost made Paul cry at one point. "Netball is a tough game. You guys did okay, considering."

"I think the ref could have thrown a few penalties our way," Paul said. "That game was unfair."

"How was it unfair?" Laura asked. A fire danced in her eyes, terrifying Fred. He harked back to a moment when she had torn the netball from him and growled like a wildebeest.

"You guys were really good, and we were crap," Paul said. "Not fair. We should have received a head start."

The woman behind him smiled. Fred remembered her—Simone, was it?

"I'm Simone," she said.

"Goal attack, right?" Fred asked. She was a graceful player and had scored many points.

She nodded.

"What are you guys up to tonight?" Laura asked.

"Just drowning our sorrows," Paul said. He glanced over; Fred elbowed him. "Ouch," he added.

"We're heading to Infernos," Laura said, mentioning a notorious establishment around the corner. Upon exiting this nightclub, most people resembled a public service announcement on the dangers of binge-drinking. "They're doing two-for-one buckets tonight."

"What's in the buckets?" Fred asked.

"Alcohol," Laura replied in a satisfied tone. She pumped her fist like she'd scored a goal.

"Amazing," Paul said. "Keeping up the grand tradition of teachers getting sloshed."

Simone smiled again, at Fred this time. Paul seemed to notice, and he raised an eyebrow at Fred.

"You guys are free to join us," Laura said. "I can show you some netball moves, point out where you were going wrong with your passing, stepping, shooting."

"We'd love to," Paul said.

"We'll think about it," Fred said.

"No pressure. We're heading there now—maybe we'll see you guys a little later."

"Maybe," Paul said. The women waved and walked off.

Paul turned to Fred. "Okay, enough of this moping," he said. "Did you see her smile at you? Not Laura the netball monster, the other one."

"Simone," Fred said.

"Exactly. We're hitting Infernos."

Fred laughed and shook his head. "No way. You have a wife and a child."

Paul shook his head. "Nadine put me up to this," he said. "My wife, after hearing your tale of hilarious woe, insisted I be your wingman tonight."

Fred sighed. "A tempting offer but I think I'll hang here. Thanks, Paul. Another time."

"Are you sure?" Paul stared at him for a moment.

"Positive," Fred replied.

Paul exhaled. "Oh, thank God. For a minute I thought I was going to Infernos. I was getting a hangover just thinking about it."

Fred laughed. "I knew it."

"Okay, mate," Paul said. He smiled and patted his pockets for his keys. "See you tomorrow?"

Fred shook his head. "Off to London tomorrow. Meeting those French exchange students we've got coming."

"Yikes. Enjoy, mate. See you Thursday, then." They shared an awkward fist bump where each fist missed the other, and then Paul left.

Fred looked around the dilapidated, half-empty pub and walked to the bar. Perhaps he should kick on at the nightclub? Maybe he could go on his own? It could even turn into an amazing night. He could dance and drink from a bucket!

As he mulled over the idea, one pint on his own turned into three, and when he tripped over the poker machine at twelve thirty A.M., the publican had no choice but to ask him to leave.

Fred agreed. Fair call.

STUMBLING HOME, FRED, the full-time brooder and part-time underachiever with great hair, who had always had luck with the ladies until last night, tripped through his front door. Earlier he'd seen a commercial promoting an *Alien* marathon that would be playing on the television at midnight. Splendid. What did he need her for, when he could watch five films' worth of galactic carnage? He nodded at the certain genius of his plan. By morning all would be well, and he'd be done thinking about that infuriating woman.

The television in the spare room wouldn't wake Sofia. He made a detour to the kitchen and found a half-drunk bottle of pink Moscato in the fridge. He stumbled through the house with the bottle, putting it down briefly to unbutton his shirt and fling it into the air, where it landed on the blade of the ceiling fan. He unbuckled his trousers and let them bundle to the floor, mid-stride. If he was to give five *Alien* films his full attention, he needed to be unencumbered by clothing.

He pretended his belt was a whip and lashed an imaginary snake on the floor. Then he picked up the bottle again, danced up the stairs, and entered the spare room in his boxer shorts.

He switched on the television. The first film had started, but no aliens yet.

Splendid.

He took a swig from the wine bottle and remembered why it had been left half-drunk, then backed onto the bed and sat down on someone's head.

Chapter Eighteen

*J*ane woke. She tried to scream but a tremendous weight on her head muffled any sound. It also blocked her sight, and she couldn't breathe. She battered the unidentified object with her fist. The weight shifted off her and she pulled back the bedsheet and jumped out of bed, gasping for air. A figure loomed above her in the darkness. Jane felt around for a defensive weapon; she located her leather boot on the floor and bashed the intruder's head with it.

"What is the meaning of this?" Jane demanded into the darkness, striking the intruder once more.

"Youch!" shouted the figure. "My head!"

"Who are you and what business have you here?" Jane asked.

"It's my houshe!" they slurred in a drunken voice. "What business have *you* here?"

Sofia rushed in. She lit the magic candle in the ceiling and light flooded the room. Jane stood by the bed in her pink nightgown and surveyed the scene. An inebriated man of at least thirty swayed in his underclothes and rubbed his head. The picture frame mounted to the wall portrayed a theatrical scene, but unlike a painting, where the actors froze as eternal statues, the characters in this frame *moved*.

"This pervert attempted to have his way with me," Jane said, pointing to the man in his underdrawers.

The man glared at her and raised his arms in surrender. "Steady on. I came in to watch the telly," he said.

Jane scoffed and regarded the man in front of her. He presented a preposterous anatomical display of muscle and skin; her cheeks flushed all manner of pink and crimson, offended by the sight. Their eyes met, and Jane looked away.

"You're her," he said. "From the rehearsal the other night."

Jane appraised his face. He was right; they had danced together. Her heart thumped.

"What a shurprise," he said. He stumbled. "This must be awkward for you."

"I do not follow your meaning, sir," Jane said. She reminded herself of how much she disliked him.

"You know, if you didn't want to go out with me, you could have said up front. No skin off my nose. You didn't need to stand me up!" He grabbed the doorknob for balance and almost toppled over.

"Jane, this is my brother, Fred," Sofia said. "Fred, this is my . . . colleague, Jane."

Jane and Fred stared at each other. Jane felt her cheeks heating once more. She grabbed the bedsheets and wrapped them around herself.

"Okay. Show's over," Sofia said. She grabbed Fred's arm. "Fred, you can continue this party alone in your room." She shovelled him out the door, then turned back to Jane. "Are you okay?"

Jane nodded.

"He didn't really interfere with you, did he? He doesn't seem the type."

"Goodness, no. He merely surprised me. I am well, thank you."

"Good. Sorry about that. Fred's a civilian, not an actor. He won't play along."

Jane gave Sofia a confused look.

"Don't do the whole 'I'm Jane Austen' thing with him," Sofia said. "Just trust me on this one. He didn't vomit on you, I hope?"

Jane shook her head and Sofia wished her good night. Jane lay back down in the bed and stared at the ceiling. The obnoxious man—the one who had refused to dance with her, the one who had annoyed and teased her—was Sofia's brother. He lived in this house! She forced her mind to stop focusing on how much this aggravated her and tried to sleep.

Jane stood in the bathroom the next morning in astonishment. Kensington Palace apparently had an indoor privy, but to see running water with her own two eyes was enough to make her admire the water closet for forty minutes. Sofia had departed for her profession earlier that morning and left her with some clean clothes and instructions for using the waterfall that spilled over the bathtub. She called it a "shower."

"This is hot, and this is cold," Sofia had said, pointing to the taps. She turned them on to demonstrate. Steaming water poured from above. Jane had stared at the marvel before her.

Now she attempted the feat herself. She turned the cold tap to the left and admired the icy stream that spouted down. She had seen taps before, in water pumps, but the water came out of them in blobs and drips of yellow, nothing compared to the elegant crystal stream that now poured forth from the silver head. Next, she turned the hot tap to the left, in increments, as Sofia had showed her. She placed her fingers in the stream and felt the water grow warm. She turned the tap more to the left and the room filled with steam.

In her house in Sydney Place, her family possessed a bathtub that Margaret filled every Sunday with water she boiled in a pot. Jane's father, as head of the house, used it first, then her mother, then Cassandra. Jane, as the youngest, used the water last. By the time she stepped in, the water ran beige. Now Jane looked up at the steaming, pristine waterfall that she had all to herself. She tested the water once more. It felt warmer than anything she knew. She inhaled, then removed her pink nightgown and laid it over the chair. She stood in the room naked and imagined herself luxuriating like Cleopatra about to bathe under a goat-milk waterfall. She climbed into the bathtub and stood under the water. The hot water bubbled and rolled over her back. Her shoulder blades prickled. She placed her arm on the wall as the water tumbled over her. "Oh," she gasped. "That is obscene." She stepped back from the water and stood in the freezing air. She shivered but did not return to the water. If she went back, she might decide to stay there forever.

The doorknob shook. The bathroom door cracked open. "This room is occupied!" Jane shrieked in a blind panic. She covered herself in horror and turned to the back wall. She tried to reach for the towel Sofia had showed her, but it sat on the rail out of reach. She considered turning and lunging for it but that risked exposure of her front.

"Oh, yikes. Sorry," said a man's voice. Fred! Sofia's brother backed out of the doorway almost as soon as he opened it, shutting the door. Jane leapt from the shower and inspected the doorknob.

A brass dial sat underneath the handle, which she turned, and the lock clicked shut. She tested the door three times. It remained locked. She sat on the floor, mortified. No man had ever seen her shoulder, let alone anything else. Jane caught her breath and began to dress.

She allowed herself a momentary departure from the horrors of her embarrassment to ogle with confusion at the clothes Sofia had given her to wear: they were a man's shirt and trousers. She pulled them on; they felt odd on her skin. Women wore trousers now, not for mumming in a play but as everyday garb. Did women act as men now? How would people treat her, dressed this way? She might own three estates by now, earning twenty thousand a year. The thought bewitched her until she heard a chair shift across the floor in the room outside, and the reality of her present, crushing embarrassment returned. Fred. The horrid man had managed to upend her comfort once again. She had hoped he would have absented himself from the house, if not the country, in preemptive chivalry, but instead he sat right there.

She opened the door and located him. He sat with his head slumped on the dining table. Jane crept through the doorway and took her chance, hoping to move past without him seeing. But just as she reached him, he lifted his head from the table and their eyes met. Jane wondered how much those eyes had seen in the bathroom. She could feel her cheeks blooming to a shade of crimson again.

"Sorry, again," he said in a garbled voice.

"I am simply mortified, sir," she said. "Horrified."

He shook his head. "Why didn't you lock the door?"

"Did you not hear the water and deduce the room was occupied?" she protested.

He stood. "Fine, why don't you see me naked? Then we'll be even." He began to unbuckle his belt.

"Certainly not!" Jane cried. "Stop that."

He fastened his belt. "No? Something else embarrassing? I could make myself fall over. Or you could beat me with a vegetable? I could eat some rubbish?"

Jane tried not to smile; the ill feeling of the other night had returned, but she overcame her embarrassment to recall how much he annoyed her.

"You look different," he said, studying her.

Jane grabbed her man's shirt, suddenly self-conscious once more. "These are Sofia's clothes. Are they inappropriate?"

Fred shook his head. "It's not the clothes. It's your hair. You changed it."

Jane patted her head. The steam of the bathroom waterfall had relaxed it to its natural state. The Grecian curls, which she dutifully set with rags every night, had vanished. Her hair, now loose, reached halfway down her back except for the hair around her face, which she kept short for easier curling. She tucked the pieces behind her ear.

"Your hair was done in period style for the rehearsal," he stated. "You looked like a character from the nineteenth century."

Jane nodded. "And what do I look like now?" she asked in a soft voice.

He shrugged. "Like a woman," he said. He coughed. "You missed one." He pointed at Jane's arm.

She looked down to where he was pointing; the button at her cuff lay undone. "Yes. I was unable," she explained.

"Don't you know how to dress yourself?" he asked dryly.

"I dress myself every morning!" she protested. He must have

thought she was some princess, with a lady's maid to dress her; she was quick to correct him of that falsehood. "There are a great many buttons on this shirt," she explained in a huff.

Fred moved toward her.

"What are you doing?" she asked quickly.

He moved close enough that she could feel his breath on her shoulder. She froze; their eyes met, then he looked down. He said nothing but took the pearl-white disc between his thumb and forefinger. Jane watched him. He slipped it through the buttonhole. Jane did not know where to look. She was struck by the tenderness of the gesture, but also that a man she found so annoying could act so gently with her. She commanded her breathing to still, to not appear so riled up. She begged herself to speak calmly, to show no sign of the effect his closeness had on her, but she could think of nothing to say in that moment.

"For what it's worth, I hardly saw anything. In the shower," he said softly. He finished with the button and placed Jane's wrist back by her side. "I saw nothing to be embarrassed about. Quite the opposite, actually."

Jane nodded without looking at him, too mortified to meet his eye. "Do you have business in London today?" she said, keen to break the mood which scared her.

"I'm going to Paddington," he replied.

"May I accompany you?"

He gave her a confused look. "You want to come with me?"

"Yes. Is there a problem?" He stared at her. "I assure you I will be no burden."

"Suit yourself. Fine by me," Fred said quickly. He shrugged.

The idea of going to London with a man was suspect at best; now to impose upon this obnoxious member of the opposite sex, this horrid specimen, filled her with dread. The day would be awkward, and she did not want to go with him. But she could see no other way to get there. She would have to endure this uncomfortable experience to maximize her chances of returning home.

"How shall we get there?" Jane asked him.

"We'll take the train," he said. He excused himself and left the room. Jane waited by the door. He returned a minute later. Something about him looked different. "Ready?" he asked.

Jane studied him. "Did you comb your hair, just now?"

His hair stood neat and tidy off his face, swept to the side, behind his ears. "Some woman harped that it was messy. I wanted to stop her nagging," he said.

She refused to admit how nice it looked. With the hair off his face, his visage was not as disagreeable as she'd first thought. She mentioned naught of this to him. "Good for you," she said instead. "You own a comb indeed."

Fred rolled his eyes and said nothing, then showed her out the front door.

Chapter Nineteen

Sofia sat in the makeup chair and gave a nervous smile. The past two weeks had consisted of wardrobe fittings and dancing. Today, proper rehearsals began. Lights flooded the space. Technicians checked their light meters, gates, gauges. Most importantly, Jack was somewhere on set. He had flown in the previous night from LA, someone said. She had last seen him five months ago; now it might be minutes before he stood next to her again. Sofia commanded herself to remain calm.

For the first time in a decade, production, insultingly, had assigned Sofia the general cast makeup artist, another indignity she swallowed so she could spend time with her husband. The friendly looking man named Derek met her in the makeup truck and introduced himself. "Ms. Wentworth. I've worshipped you since I was twelve," he said.

Sofia scowled; this was a rocky start. "Oh dear, that's horrible. How old are you, son? How old does that make me?" she said. She touched her throat.

"That's not what I meant!" Derek replied, quivering and looking panicked.

"It's all right," she said, trying to soothe him. She needed him to remain calm. After all, she could not have him shaking while he applied her makeup. "No harm done. So, for my makeup I was thinking an English rose look. Something simple, but classic—pink cheeks, big beautiful eyes." she asked. "Very British, very Austen."

"That sounds stunning, Ms. Wentworth," Derek said. "Unfortunately, the brief is for powder only. No actual makeup."

Sofia paused, stiffening. "I don't understand," she said. "I thought I heard you say no makeup."

Derek nodded.

"Do you mean to tell me this production is requesting that I, Sofia Wentworth, who once played Batgirl, who was once brand ambassador for a very prestigious soda corporation, walk onto set and appear in a film with no makeup on?"

Derek nodded again and took a cautious step backward, away from her.

She surveyed her face in the mirror. "No foundation, no primer, no mascara—everything's banned?"

"Of course not! Not everything's banned," Derek said quickly with a relieved laugh.

"Thank heavens," she said with a sigh. "What products are allowed, then, Derek?"

"I'm supposed to put on moisturizer and lash gel," he replied confidently.

Sofia scowled. "Lash gel? What is that?"

"I'm not sure exactly." He held up the bottle and studied it, tipping the bottle sideways; a clear substance moved from one end of the tube to the other.

"Derek, that looks like water to me."

"I agree with you," he said, his voice growing less confident by the second.

"And the moisturizer?"

He showed her a pot of cream with a shaky hand. "Is that supermarket moisturizer?" she asked, horrified. He checked the pot's label and nodded cautiously. "I'm already wearing moisturizer that costs two hundred pounds a pot. It has crushed-up sea creatures in it, I kid you not." She paused. "So you're saying my face will be stripped bare, my eye bags visible, my blemishes and blotches on display. I'm already walking out there in a dress with leg-of-mutton sleeves. What else would they like? My firstborn?"

This wouldn't be good for anyone. Parade her bare, wrinkle-mortified face to the whole world? She would be a laughingstock.

"Jack will hate this," she said.

"It was his idea," Derek replied.

"What?" She shuddered, struggling to decide which horror to concern herself with most—that her public would be seeing her for the first time since her breakup with no makeup on, or that her husband would.

Jack. Oh God. He was going to see every blotch and crow's-foot, every eye bag and burst capillary, every sag and crack. If her chances of getting her husband back were slim before, they were nonexistent now.

"Derek, I don't know if you understand the power of makeup to transform."

"Believe me, Ms. Wentworth, I know," he said. He held up a brush, as if to remind her of his profession.

"Right, so you understand what a tragedy this will be for everyone if I walk out there as myself."

"It won't be a tragedy," he said in a kind voice.

"Don't sugarcoat this, Derek. You make us both feel cheap. This is catastrophic and you know it. The last time I walked outside without makeup, I was twelve years old. I don't plan to start up again now at thirty-eight! You don't understand, Derek. They're going to laugh at me."

Derek bowed his head. "I'm so sorry, Ms. Wentworth."

She looked at the floor. "Derek, I'm not sure if you know, but my husband is the director of this film. I have not seen this man in five months, since he walked out the door after a decade of marriage."

"I know, Ms. Wentworth." Derek sighed and touched her arm.

"I had this grand fantasy that I'd stroll onto set today with pro hair and makeup. Jack would see me and feel like he'd made the worst mistake of his life." She laughed. "I thought my husband might want me again. No chance now."

Derek's lip quivered; he looked like he might cry, too. She cringed; she did not want pity. But then he brightened. "I think eye drops are allowed, too?"

Sofia smiled, defeated. "Thank you, Derek. That will be lovely." She leaned back and he dropped some liquid into her eyes as she heard the door of the makeup truck open and a pair of feet climb the stairs.

"You don't mind, do you?" a woman's voice said. With her eyes full of saline, Sofia could not see who sat down next to her—just blurry shapes—but her ears pricked up at the California accent. She recognized the voice, she thought.

"How long do these drops take to clear, Derek?" she asked anxiously.

"A few seconds," he said. Sofia opened her eyes and turned to the chair next to her. Her eyes were still blurred and now also stung as the drops ran down her face, but as she squinted, Sofia could make out a svelte, twentysomething natural blonde.

"We've never met, but I am a huge fan," said the chair's oc-
cupant with a giant smile. Her teeth were so white they seemed
blue.

"I appreciate that," Sofia said. She squinted again, feeling like
a mad scientist looking into a microscope.

"Courtney Smith," said the girl and held out her hand. "I came
to welcome you to the picture."

Sofia's eyes suddenly cleared into sharp focus. She gripped
the hand of the zygote who had replaced her as the female lead
in the planet's most lucrative film franchise. "Sofia Wentworth,"
she said. They shook hands. Sofia felt a soft wetness grip her
palm in a slimy hold.

"Just washed my hands, sorry," Courtney said. "It's so cool
to be working together." The moment marked itself with auspi-
ciousness: Batgirl and the girl who took her job, meeting for the
first time. If the paparazzi knew, they would have camped themselves outside.

"Have you come to have your makeup done, too?" Sofia asked.
"Considering the brief, I won't be long."

"No, this is the reserve truck, for supporting. I have my own
truck," Courtney said. "I came to welcome you to my movie."

"Oh, cheers." Sofia laughed at the comment. She did not care
what role she played, so long as Jack was directing, but she had
swallowed a few bags of pride when they announced that Courtney
Smith, the woman who had replaced her in the *Batman* movies,
was playing Catherine Morland, the lead.

"What are you putting on her face?" Courtney asked Derek
with another giant smile.

"It's moisturizer," Derek replied.

"Cool. I think that's allowed. Don't worry, I'm not checking up on you. You've been briefed on the 'no makeup' idea, right? It's so exciting." She threw her hands in the air.

"Yes! I'm keeping my excitement on the inside," Sofia replied.

"It's awesome Jack wants to go down this road. It will lift the production value," Courtney said.

"Maybe call him Mr. Travers—he likes that," Sofia said. "An affectation, I know"—she rolled her eyes and smiled— "but trust me, he prefers it. It will put you in his good books."

Courtney nodded with a smirk. "Jack is pumped for us to wear no makeup. He wants everyone to look their age."

Sofia paused, shocked, and nodded. "Message received, loud and clear," she finally replied.

"Gotta run. See you on set," Courtney said in a bright voice. She exited the truck, jumping onto each step as she went down.

Derek shut the door and sat down next to Sofia. "Ms. Wentworth, I need to tell you something." He leaned in close. "Courtney Smith is wearing makeup."

Sofia laughed and sat up. "She said she wasn't."

"She's put primer on there, concealer, foundation, lashes, bronzer, highlighter, the works. All very subtle—perhaps she used a spray gun—but it's there."

Sofia chewed her lip. "I'm going to walk out there with no makeup on, while a woman fifteen years my junior will wear a full face?"

"Afraid so," he said.

Sofia's earlier concern hardened to aggravation. Derek stared at the door for a moment and shook his head, then touched Sofia's arm and spoke in a casual tone. "Ms. Wentworth, what Courtney did . . . I could do something similar for you? Nothing outrageous—a little touch-up?"

"That's against the rules, Derek." She shook her head.

Derek shrugged. "I wouldn't suggest it if Courtney wasn't doing the same."

Sofia scratched her head. "What did you have in mind?" she asked him innocently.

"A little 'no-makeup' makeup," he replied in an equally innocent voice. "I'm the master at it," he added. He raised an eyebrow.

Sofia winced. "But what if Courtney notices? She will say something for sure."

He shook his head and smiled. "She will say nothing, Ms. Wentworth, because she has done the same thing. If she says something, you will say something. Mutually assured destruction."

"I don't know," she said, looking at him cautiously.

"Let me do this for you. When I'm done, Jack won't be able to look away."

It was the one thing she couldn't say no to. She nodded.

He smiled. "Lie back, Ms. Wentworth." Sofia did so.

ABOUT A MONTH after Jack had left her, Sofia had fled from LA back to London to escape the scrutiny. She needed to feel the green of England. Stupid idea, it had turned out, as every tabloid journalist seemed to have set up camp on the front porch of her London town house. One day the doorbell rang, and Sofia yelled at the journalists to go away, but it wasn't a reporter. It was a messenger, with a package from her husband's lawyers. He had served her with divorce papers.

He'd mentioned nothing of divorce earlier. Sofia had expected a trial separation, but he moved fast. She'd holed up inside her house and read the legal papers in shock. Finally, after three days in hiding with no food in the house, she realized she might actually starve, which would be an even more embarrassing headline— "Beleaguered Hollywood Darling Dies of Starvation, Alone." She snuck out to buy dinner, but after what happened next, she wished she'd stayed inside.

Someone must have tipped off the press that Sofia Wentworth, newly served with divorce papers, was attempting to purchase a microwave dinner from the local Marks & Spencer, like a sad person. All she'd wanted was their lovely shepherd's pie, which she'd planned to eat in peace with a bottle of red and a slasher movie box set, preferably one where everyone died, when the camera vultures swooped. By the time she left the store, an honor guard of paparazzi was waiting for her, lining the exit.

One of the photographers said something to her as she walked out, something she would never forget as long as she lived. And Sofia did something she normally never did. She reacted.

"Just let me eat my shepherd's pie in peace!" she screamed at the man with his camera.

For days afterward, every gossip rag and entertainment news show replayed those immortal words. Sofia had regretted it instantly, but the retort had flown from her mouth involuntarily; an act of self-defense. "What did that man say?" her agent asked her later. Sofia refused to repeat it. She knew the photographer had said it to get a rise out of her, to get a picture he could sell. But the words stuck with her: "What a pity," the paparazzo had said, shaking his head and tutting with disappointment. "You were a poster on my bedroom wall. Now you're no use to me."

"DONE, MS. WENTWORTH," Derek announced.

Sofia opened her eyes.

"What do you think?"

She checked her reflection in the mirror.

Derek had worked magic. The crow's-feet had faded; the eye bags lifted. She still looked like herself, but she felt a little beautiful. He had erased all the evidence, too, like an evil genius at a crime scene.

"Derek, you have a gift."

Derek smiled. "I just brought out your natural beauty," he said.

Sofia grimaced and looked at the floor, fragility returning. "What if Jack still doesn't . . . ," she said, not finishing the sentence. *What if he still doesn't want me?*

Derek bent down and smiled at her. "Impossible," he said. She smiled back and inhaled. He touched her arm. "Ready?"

Chapter Twenty

Jane stood next to Fred on a raised platform forged from stone. The structure apparently housed some sort of station that received not post carriages, but a train. Two steel tracks sat below her on the ground and stretched to the horizon in either direction. The sight overwhelmed her. Jane looked westward, then east.

"Is this where the train comes?" Jane asked.

Fred nodded, before rolling his shirtsleeves to the elbows, a custom in which Jane had only ever witnessed farmers partake. She glanced at his exposed forearms and blushed. The awkwardness remained from earlier; she still could not look him in the eye. He seemed to look over at her himself, then looked away. He bent down to tie his bootlace.

"That's the third time you've tied your bootlace this morning. Is there a problem with your shoe?" she asked him.

"No," he said, laughing incredulously. "I did not tie my laces three times."

"You did," Jane replied. "Once in the kitchen, once on the road here, and now." He coughed. "Are your laces broken?"

"My shoes are one hundred percent fine, thank you," he said. Jane eyed him curiously. He truly performed many acts that confused her. She could not tell if his oddness was due to him being a person from the twenty-first century, or whether it was simply his natural state. He took a small orange card from his pocket.

"What is that?" Jane asked him.

"My ticket?" he answered.

"Does one need such a thing to ride the train?"

"You don't have a ticket?"

Jane shook her head, and Fred led her inside a stone building by the middle of the platform.

"Return to London, please," Fred said to a man who seemed to sit inside a glass box.

"Sixty-one, please," the man replied. "Cash or card?"

Jane smiled. "Sixty-one shillings? A little more expensive than the post carriage, which is only twenty, but never mind. I have the amount." She rummaged through her trouser pocket. She had retrieved seventy shillings from her white muslin dress earlier that morning in case she needed it in London. It would not go far at these prices, but she would have to make do.

The ticket man scowled. "Sixty-one pounds."

Jane gripped the steel bars that lay across his window. "Sixty-one pounds," she repeated. "What madness is this?"

"What's the problem?" Fred asked.

"This man wants sixty-one pounds for his train ride. I could pay the King of England to drag me to London in a golden carriage for sixty-one pounds. With him as the horse. I don't have such money."

"No money, no ticket, love," the man in the glass box said to her.

Jane looked at the floor, mortified.

Fred shook his head. "You seriously don't have any money?"

"Not that kind of money," Jane said. She turned to the exit. "I guess I shall walk back to the house."

Fred grimaced. "Don't be stupid. Here." He reached into his pocket and pulled out two red banknotes, each marked £50.

"Good God. Are you a sultan, sir? I cannot accept," she said, eyes wide. One hundred pounds exceeded the allowance given to her over an entire year.

He shook his head. "Pay me back if you like."

"I don't know how I could ever repay such a sum." She felt doubly mortified.

"We'll worry about it later," he said. "Train's almost here." He passed the notes under the glass window. The man produced an orange card like Fred's. Fred collected the ticket and the money and handed them both to Jane. "Keep the change."

"I couldn't possibly," she said in a horrified voice.

"Keep it," he insisted. "You might need it." He reached into his pocket again. "Here's an Oyster card, too, in case you want to take the tube. You'll have to top it up, though." Jane took the small blue card, which resembled in no way an oyster, nor any sea creature for that matter, and studied it from all angles. She knew not its use but did not want to sound like an imbecile, so she placed the object in her pocket with the banknotes, the coins, and her ticket.

"Thank you, Fred," said Jane, truly grateful. She felt flummoxed by his generosity. All their past interactions had been filled with aggravation, teasing, and mocking; where had this kindness come from? Why had he given her a hundred pounds of his own money? He must still feel bad about the morning, she figured, and everything else.

They returned to the platform. A great horn boomed, followed by a clacking rhythm of steel hitting steel. Jane turned to face the source of the sound. A giant green oblong moved down the track. Words on its side read *Great Western Railway*. Jane jumped backward in fright on its approach, convinced no force in the world existed to bring such a thing to a halt. But halt it did, and the doors opened by magic. People streamed from the carriage, thirty or more, all dressed in the odd clothes of the day.

Fred stepped onto the train. Jane followed him inside the carriage. It smelled of cut metal. Rows of seats lined the carriage, as though they stood inside a narrow theater. Jane spotted a free seat and sat down next to a man in a gray coat. Fred shrugged and sat in the row behind her. The enchanted doors closed on their own.

Somewhere below her, metal again screeched on metal and the green leviathan lurched from the station. Jane looked across the man in the gray coat and watched through the window as the landscape moved. The train picked up speed as it reached the edges of the city. Houses and roads and shops transitioned to trees and paddocks; the crumbling stone walls of the Norman invasion still divided the fields as they did in the year 1803, and the seven centuries before that.

As they approached Windsor, they passed a magnificent oak tree. Jane gasped. It was the same tree she had encountered the last time she travelled to London, now likely two hundred feet tall. She wondered of the things it had seen.

Jane knew things worked differently in her own time than in the years that came before it. Serfs, stake burnings, and blackbirds in pies littered the Middle Ages, for example, and a woman had sat on the English throne in earlier times. It bore consideration that the year 2020 also produced a similar degree of advancement upon 1803. But how exactly did human progress manifest? One thing stood for certain: twenty-first-century humans had eradicated manual labor and replaced it with magic. A steel box washed the clothes. Another washed the crockery. Magic lit the candles and moved the steel carriages.

Jane looked around the carriage. A woman in the seat opposite, dressed in underclothes, gazed at a steel box she held in the palm of her hand. She pressed at it and smiled, fondled it and laughed warmly at it, as though it both entertained and comforted her. She seemed to treat the box like it were as dear to her as a child.

The box rang like a bell then; the woman scowled at it and lifted it to her ear. "I can't talk now. I'm on the train," she said, speaking into the box. Jane shook her head at the sight, bewildered. Who did the woman talk to? After a moment, the woman removed the box from her ear and resumed poking and fondling it.

At first Jane believed that the twenty-first-century humans ruled over these steel boxes. Now she was unsure. The man who had sold Jane the train ticket obeyed the box in his ticket booth. When Fred gave him the money, he spoke to the box with his hands and then the box presented him with money and a ticket, which he passed on to Fred. The more of these boxes Jane witnessed, the more she decided the humans did not enslave the boxes, but the reverse.

Jane felt so fascinated, she did not know which held more delights for her eyes, inside the carriage or out the window.

"You seem so delighted," Fred said to Jane, leaning forward from the row of seats behind to speak to her. "It's a train."

"I am!" Jane replied. "We have invented such wonders. Do you not agree?"

He chuckled. "I agree. But I've never seen anyone so enamored with a battered old train."

"What is the purpose of your appointment in London?" she asked.

"Professional engagement day. And yes, it's as boring as it sounds."

"Not at all. You have a profession? That does not sound boring to me."

Fred laughed. "I have a profession. I'm a schoolteacher. I teach history and English."

"How marvelous," Jane replied. "You must have the patience of a saint," she added. "I could never instruct children."

He shrugged. "Some days are better than others."

"Does your profession bring you joy, sir?"

"Joy?" he asked with a laugh. Then he seemed to think on it a little more. "Actually, it does."

"How wonderful," Jane replied, smiling. The awkwardness with Fred remained, and was now added to, with the mortification of receiving money from him and now being in his debt. But she had so many things at which to look and marvel that she found her first train journey to London only half as terrible as she expected. She looked out the window once more.

THE TRAIN ENDED its journey at Paddington, arriving at a gargantuan terminus hall. "Shall we?" Fred said, interrupting her reverie. Jane looked around. The other passengers had left; the carriage lay empty. The man sitting next to her must have shuffled past her to get out; she hadn't even noticed. Jane's brain still whirred at the sheer mathematics of the journey. The steel beast had raced over a hundred miles of country in little over an hour. Jane stepped from the green monster and joined Fred on the platform. A sign read *Platform 8*. Eight platforms! That meant at least eight of these gigantic serpents roamed the countryside. Jane looked skyward and her mouth dropped open. A vaulted steel-and-glass ceiling loomed above her. On either side, people rushed back and forth along the multiple stone platforms, and trains arrived and departed, lurching forward and grinding to a halt. Everything moved at a tremendous speed. Jane's mouth grew dry from falling open for so long.

Fred guided her to the exit. They walked out of the station and onto Praed Street. She looked around, amazed at the changes, the new buildings of glass and steel, the people. "Right, I'm going that way," Fred said. He pointed west. "You'll be right from here?"

"Oh," Jane said, caught off guard.

"Do you know where to go?" he said to her, seeing her look. "I can stay with you."

Jane could think of no excuse to keep him there. It was unlikely he suspected she was secretly a time traveler from the year 1803 who might need assistance navigating a witch hunt through twenty-first-century London. "I know where to go," she lied. She pushed her shoulders back, hoping the move would imbue her with confidence. "Do not trouble yourself," she added. "You have your appointment. Please attend it. I will be well."

"I'll see you back here at one," he said.

"One o'clock? In the afternoon?" Fred nodded. She hesitated then, feeling guilty. She hoped to arrive at Mrs. Sinclair's house, find the way to reverse the spell and return to 1803. She had no intention of returning to Paddington. "Yes, fine. Good. One o'clock," she lied again. She looked away. "Goodbye, Fred," she said solemnly. This was likely the last time she'd see him.

"Bye," Fred replied. He went. She put him from her mind. She had made it to London; now it was time to return home. She looked at the gray sky, attempting to find her bearings.

She had walked Praed Street once before, with Henry while visiting him in 1801. A few things had changed since then. Three red steel boxes the size of pantries stood to her left, serving what function she knew not. Two buildings taller than she could fathom emerged from the earth to her right. People rushed past her in waves, more humans than she had seen in one place in her life. More colors and brightness bombarded her eyes than they could take in. A cacophony of sounds she did not comprehend assaulted her ears: beeps and buzzes and whistles. She prided herself on her education and mind, but every object and person moved faster and louder than she could predict. A wooden bench lay on the other side of the road. As she walked to it, a horn bellowed. Jane turned around. An immense steel carriage bore down on her. She jumped from its path just in time.

The driver stuck his head out the carriage window. "Stupid cow!" he shouted to her. Jane shrieked and sat down on the bench. Her fingers tingled with shock.

Jane took a moment to assess the situation and evaluate her chances of succeeding in this mission. She sat alone in the middle of London, intending to navigate her way through a city that had moved two hundred years beyond her. She composed a list of ways she might be killed and arrived at a dozen methods. Forgetting the geographical challenges of her predicted journey east for a moment, she decided the bigger risk lay in her dying somewhere along the way. Attempting to leave the bench on which she sat posed a risky enough proposition, let alone forging a path to Cheapside.

Chapter Twenty-One

Further up the street, a man in rumpled trousers struggled to open the front door of some sort of shop with one hand while balancing a pile of books in the other. He wore a red woolen coat and his gray hair protruded from his head in a bushy mop. Grasping the bundle under one arm, he turned the key. The books came loose and tumbled to the ground.

Jane walked over. "Allow me to help," she said. She collected the books that had fallen and handed them to the shopkeeper. Paint peeled from an elegant old sign above him that read *Clarke's Books & Periodicals*.

"Thank you," he replied, reaching out to take the books from Jane. Another book came free from his arm and fell. Jane caught it in midair, preventing it from landing in a puddle on the sidewalk. "Good catch! Please, come inside." He ushered her into the shop. Inside was an astonishing sight. It was a tiny space, no larger than a bedroom, but the man had made the most of it. Shelves lined the walls from floor to ceiling. Books burst from every shelf and spilled to the floor in glorious streams of red, blue, and yellow. Greek columns of novels rose up from the floor and almost reached the ceiling. It resembled a cave, or a little underground chapel, consisting entirely of books. A warm mustiness filled the room, and it smelled of ink and wood.

"A bookshop!" Jane said. She had never beheld a store dedicated to the purpose.

The old man laughed. "Indeed," he said, watching Jane look around the room in happy amazement. "Will you take one?" he said.

"No, thank you," Jane said. She ran her eyes over the shelves, envious. She had read no books in three days, when often she read one a day. She could devour some literature. But books were expensive, and she needed to conserve the money Fred had given her.

"I meant for free," he said then, as if sensing her hesitation. "As a thank-you for helping me. I'm George." He held out his hand for her to shake. Jane was still adjusting to strangers calling themselves by their first names, but she smiled. The name belonged to her father.

"Jane," she replied. She shook his hand. His skin bore an old man's softness, like her papa's. "Thank you for the kind gesture, but I cannot accept," Jane said.

"You can accept, and you must, for you rescued a treasure from death by puddle." He held up one of the books Jane had collected. The title read *Tess of the d'Urbervilles*. "A second edition," said George. "Do you like to read?"

"Yes," Jane said. She scanned the nearest shelf's contents and recognized fewer than one title in ten. The sight delighted her; usually she walked into a library and slumped at having already read its contents. She would need years to make her way through these books.

"What do you like? Fiction? Thrillers, science fiction, romance?"

Jane stiffened with curiosity. "Science fiction?"

He showed her to a shelf by the window. The books bore thin, colored covers in shades Jane did not recognize. "Have you read this one?" He handed Jane a book titled *Dune*.

Jane shook her head. "I have read little in this area."

"This is a classic," he said with a smile. A well-stuffed armchair squatted at the back of the shop; love-worn green leather covered the seat and arms. "You're welcome to sit and read for as long as you like," said George. "You will be keeping me company."

Jane grew excited. Instead of sitting on a bench and wallowing in her failure, she could sit in this shop in the twenty-first century and read a book.

"Do you . . . have anything by Jane Austen?" she asked on a whim.

"Of course. She's not science fiction, though." He led Jane across to the opposite side of the shop where a hand-painted sign read *Classics*. Nervous anticipation suddenly filled her. George handed Jane a small book. Its red cloth cover had faded to orange and small gold letters embossed the cover. *Pride and Prejudice, by Jane Austen*. Jane ran her hand across the title. "This is a seventh edition, I think. Printed in 1912." Jane nodded and said nothing, bewitched by the contents of her hand. She opened the book; the spine made a crackling sound and a glorious smell of almonds rose up. The pages felt crisp, like someone might have left them in the sun to dry.

"I picked that up from a high school in Walthamstow," George said. "They were renovating their library. From the looks of it, this poor little one took a beating."

Jane turned to the title page. Someone had written *Property of Hilary Dawe, 12F* across the corner. Jane stared at the detail. "Who is this person?" she asked him. She pointed to the inscription.

"That's a student, I suppose. It's in the syllabus."

"The syllabus?"

"*Pride and Prejudice* is taught in schools. You did not read it yourself, in secondary college?"

Jane inhaled and gripped the book tighter. She scoured her brain for a suitable reply. "Perhaps I read it. I must have forgotten."

"Every child in England who completes A-level English reads some Austen, I believe."

Every child in England. Jane stared at him.

"I daresay a great many children in the States, too."

"The States?"

"America," he replied.

Jane stared at him again until her eyes grew dry from the lack of blinking. Her position in this new world, in the bookshop even, took on a new dimension. Just how many people were aware of her? How many people read her novels?

Jane closed the book and read the cover once more. What was this "pride and prejudice" of the title? She was dying to know what she had written. Had she changed her style? Perhaps now instead of country farces, she wrote about pirates—proud ones. Was this the reason for her new, widespread fame? She turned to a page and read. She worked her way through a paragraph, then a second. She exhaled.

No new story of pirates greeted her. No new style graced those pages, not even new prose. These were not new words written in some future life, should she ever succeed in returning to her own time; she had read these words many times before. The book she held in her hand told the story of a young woman, spirited and clever, but poor, who rejects a marriage offer from one of the richest men in England because of the low opinion she forms of him when they first meet. It was *First Impressions,* the novel rejected by Thomas Cadell and incinerated by Mama on the hearth. Somehow the words had made their way to a more sympathetic publisher, or one with better taste. They resonated enough that they were now taught in schools. A rush of what she could only describe as fire coursed through her veins.

Lord knew what George made of all this. He was unlikely to deduce the person holding the battered little tome was the time-slipping author of the words inside it. Instead, he likely saw a woman breathing and sighing and stepping backward and forward on the carpet. "Do you like it? It's yours," he said.

"I could not possibly," Jane replied.

"I think you must," he said. "Anyone who has a reaction like that to a book must keep it forever. I insist."

Jane scanned the other titles on the shelf. A *Collected Works of Shakespeare* sat next to *The Theban Plays* by Sophocles; *The Canterbury Tales* by Chaucer took the position to the other side of her own novel. Jane shook her head. Her books sat beside giants. The time had arrived for more sighing and carpet-pacing.

"I have others by Austen," George said. He selected another title from the shelf: *Mansfield Park.*

Jane again selected a page and devoured it in a breath. If

possible, this novel presented more excitement than the last. She observed at once her own style as she read: her phrasing and quips bounced off the page, so different from the earnest adventures and romances of her contemporaries, whom she tried to emulate, but always found her own stubborn words fighting through. But while she recognized her style, she did not know this story. The tale told of a young woman, Fanny, who was clever but again poor and lived as some sort of ward with rich relations. Jane read three pages in quick succession. She sat down to see what she would write, settling in to consume the book.

"Cup of tea?" George said. "I'm so delighted to have such a great reader in the shop."

Jane smiled in acceptance. What a thrill to read something she had not yet written. She turned back to the first page and began:

> About thirty years ago Miss Maria Ward, of Huntingdon, with only seven thousand pounds, had the good luck to captivate Sir Thomas Bertram, of Mansfield Park . . .

As the words entered her mind, she closed the book as quickly as she had opened it. She put the book back on the shelf and stood.

"Are you all right, Jane?" George said. Jane stared at the floor. This was a thrill she could do without. How could she be reading something she had not yet written? This was no good. To sit there and congratulate herself on a book she had not yet slaved over was not only hubris, it was dangerous. There was but one way out of this: she needed to find the way back to her own time, so she could write this book. Jane handed George the novel.

"You don't want the Austen?" he said.

She shook her head politely, then sifted a piece of paper from her pocket. "Do you know this place, sir?"

George read the address. "EC2? I know it."

"Is there another way I could arrive there, rather than walking?"

"Yes. If you're game."

Jane beamed. "How?"

"You can take the tube."

Chapter Twenty-Two

Sofia walked onto set. A grip smiled as she walked past, to her delight, and a production assistant nodded hello and showed her to the sound stage. She had to break herself away from their approving smiles, however, when she spotted the man she had loved from almost the first moment she saw him, sitting on the other side of the room.

Seated in his director's chair, Jack wore a look of concentration on his face as he read the day's rehearsal sides. She studied him. Five months apart had not tarnished his leading-man bone structure, and his full head of hair remained, even though he was approaching his midforties. He looked more like a film star than a director. He should be reclining in a private jet dressed in a tuxedo rather than sitting on set, wearing a beige utility shirt. Sofia breathed in. This would be the best part of her day, before he saw her. She could watch his beautiful face and pretend for a second they were still together, about to meet up and go for coffee. She was too old to act so childishly, gripped by juvenile longing, but then love never aged. She'd feel the same at eighty.

She became aware of the whispers around her; the gaffer and the electricians were staring and pointing. The moment made for a great story—the artist and his muse reunited, for the third act in the fairy tale.

Jack looked up from his pages, then down again. Then he looked back up at her and their eyes met. Sofia told her heart to be still. She smiled, casually, and tried not to inhale too sharply. Jack rose from his chair and walked toward her. Sofia picked up her skirt and did the same. They met in the middle of the sound stage.

"Hey," said Jack. He did not smile.

Sofia paused, momentarily thrown. "Hey yourself," she replied quickly, hoping she appeared composed.

"Someone should have told you. We don't need you yet. I'm not happy with the light on Courtney." He paused, and then continued. "I didn't see the 2K come out of the truck this morning. I told you I want lens flare on all shots."

Sofia winced. These were the words to leave his mouth when they had not spoken in five months—generic greetings and camera stipulations? She told herself to remain calm. This wasn't about her; this was about work. She focused on the issue at hand. Jack's usual anxieties had evidently returned. Lens flare flooded a frame with a glowing light, which created beautiful pictures. *Northanger Abbey* should have a Gothic feel, plenty of shadows, which Jack's cinematographer knew how to create. Lens flare would render each frame like a hipster soda commercial. Sofia cringed for Jack, but this also made her happy. Had the prospect of seeing her conjured this agitation in him? Should she say something? No. She chose to indulge him, to help. "Okay, lens flare it is," Sofia said. "I'll go ask someone."

"What? No, I was talking to him," said Jack with a grim chuckle.

He pointed to a camera assistant behind Sofia, who fixed a lens to a large black camera.

"Right, of course," Sofia said, feeling stupid. The cameraman smirked and walked away. "How are you?" she said to Jack in a bright voice, trying to remain upbeat.

"Busy," Jack said. "They've cut two locations. It's John, the EP in the States, I know it. He's got it in for me. If this picture ends up looking like a movie of the week, it won't be my fault."

Sofia nodded, her mind racing, and waited for him to ask about her. She tried not to let this bother her; this was how he was on all shoots—always abrupt, always businesslike.

THE FIRST TIME Sofia had met Jack Travers, she'd been twenty-five years old. She had been cast as Batgirl in the *Batman* movie, which made her famous, and Jack had signed on as the film's director. At the first rehearsal on set, Jack ignored her the entire day. He warmly addressed Peter, the actor playing Batman, chatting with him about baseball and throwing jokey uppercuts and jabs toward his giant frame.

But not a word to Sofia.

When she asked a question about her character, Jack excused himself to go to the bathroom. Rage filled Sofia; she refused to stand for it. After a week of being ignored, she asked around, found his address, and took a cab to his house, perched high in the Hollywood Hills.

She thumped on his front door. "What is your problem?" she spat out when he opened it.

He looked her up and down, genuinely shocked to see her. "What's my problem?" he asked, laughing grimly. "How long have you got?"

He showed her inside. His home looked like some sort of giant Escher painting, a fantasy house with different levels, different wings. He offered her a drink from a bottle that resembled an ice sculpture, pouring the spirit into a carved crystal glass with a solid gold bottom. Sofia scoffed at the outrageousness of it all. She had grown up in a three-bedroom cottage in Somerset.

"My problem is that I have exactly zero clue what I'm doing," he said as he poured.

Sofia almost spat her whisky onto the geometric marble countertop. "What do you mean?" she asked with a laugh.

"I mean I have absolutely no idea how to direct a feature film." She studied his face and saw only anguish. "I've only been on a film set twice," he added. "Once, visiting my dad. The other was directing *Short Stack*."

"What's *Short Stack*?"

"My short film," he said. He puffed out his chest.

"Never heard of it."

"It won a bunch of awards," he protested. He finished pouring his own drink and clinked her glass. She clinked his back politely and studied him again. The smooth, creamy spirit sank into her throat and made her insides feel like they were glowing. WASPs always had the best booze.

"I'm sorry, how is it possible you've only been on two film sets?" she said, laughing again. "I've been on"—she counted in her head—"seven this year. It's only June."

"Show-off," he replied. "My dad got me the job." His father was Donald Travers, Hollywood royalty from the seventies, winner of the Academy Award for Best Director and, from what Sofia had heard, one of the most unpleasant and arrogant people in the business.

Sofia raised an eyebrow. "This film has an eighty-five-million-dollar budget. How did they . . ." She shook her head. "Never mind."

Sofia watched Jack take another sip of his drink. His hand shook. She could not wipe the amused smile off her face, and yet she needed to help. She refused to have her Hollywood debut ruined by a director having a nervous breakdown. "I'm going to let you in on a little secret, Mr. Travers," she told him. "Directing is the easiest job on set."

He scoffed at her. "What do you mean?"

"I worked on a TV show back in England, a children's show. The director was a bit of an alcoholic—a lovely guy, but he fell asleep on set once, and we couldn't wake him. We were hours behind in the schedule, and the producer told us to keep going. So we did. The assistant director ticked off the shots we needed, the cameraman filmed, the actors acted. We shot everything for the day without a director. We even went home early. That episode won a children's BAFTA. The screenwriter has done well with this script—it's much better than the usual dross I'm given. And the casting is good, obviously. So you don't need to do much at all. A killer cinematographer and a great AD are all you need to shoot a film. If you have those, the only words you'll have to speak on set all day will be your coffee order."

He stared at her for a long time.

"Are you well?" she said to him when he still said nothing.

"Who are you?" he finally asked, searching her face with a look of wonder. "How do you know all of this? You're too beautiful to know all this."

Because I live and breathe this, she replied, but not out loud.

In truth, she loved it all, the battles on the film set, the sweat and the tears. One prepared for it like one went to war. When she was young, she would walk to the video store and rent an armful of films at a time. She'd watch them from Friday night to Monday morning, blinds drawn, devouring all the old classics, films from the French New Wave, works by the Russian masters, titles from the Italian giants. She laughed at how her shell did not mirror the inside, how that exterior of hers did not match her brain. But then, thinking back over people she knew, when did it ever?

She looked up at his face then to find him still staring at her, with an expression she knew to be desire. She met his eye and swallowed. He was damn handsome. For a second, Sofia felt a little intimidated, but then she reminded herself she was damn handsome, too. She looked into his soft blue eyes and smiling face. She bit her lip.

The next day on set, Jack fired his cinematographer, a sarcastic older man who had been undermining him, and replaced him with a young German cameraman who had just won an award in Europe, recommended by Sofia's agent. For good measure, he also replaced his first AD with an all-business woman recommended by Sofia. Both crew members were still shooting his films for him today, and Sofia became his sounding board, and his friend.

That first night at Jack's house, they did not kiss—they barely touched the whole night—but they talked about movies for hours, and when she finally called a cab and wished her director good night, she knew something much larger than a film was beginning. Over the next few months, Sofia fell in mortifying, terrifying love. She possessed no memories of that time except the ones spent in his company. She must have brushed her hair, washed her clothes—breathed—during that time, but it was as if the hard drive of her brain had decided these moments were insignificant, inconsequential to the operating system, and deleted them all. All that remained of that time for her was him smiling at her, laughing with her, finally kissing her.

HER RECALL OF this first meeting was interrupted by the sound of crunching, as Jack deposited the last bite of a protein bar into his mouth. It was an American brand he liked—perhaps the production had shipped a crate in for him. Jack chewed, then exhaled a little burp that he covered with his fist. The little emission both disgusted and comforted her; she had never seen him burp in front of a stranger. In this repulsive but intimate action, he at least treated her like they remained together.

She tried to think of something to make him feel better, to distract him from his work woes. "How's the Aston Martin? Does he miss me?" she asked. His eyes lit up and he put down his phone.

"I got it detailed at this auto shop in Los Feliz. You should see the rims." He spoke at length about the new exhaust, how the car purred now. Sofia sighed, gratified she still knew his passions. She nodded and smiled as he talked, buzzing inside with little leaps of ecstasy at having Jack all to herself for a few minutes.

Then Courtney walked over. "Hey, guys," she said, before performing a double take. She squinted and seemed to study Sofia's face from several angles. Sofia swallowed, recalling the extensive secret restoration work Derek had performed on her face. Courtney opened her mouth, and Sofia prepared herself to be called out—her no-makeup makeup exposed to everyone—but then Courtney closed her mouth and said no more, possibly, thankfully, thinking better of it. Sofia breathed a sigh of relief and made a note to thank Derek later, not only for his makeup wizardry but also his cunning grasp of interactress politics.

Courtney smiled at her instead and seemed to take a different tack. "Sofia, sorry, you don't mind, do you?" She pointed to the floor. "You're on my mark. We're behind?"

"Oh goodness, sorry. Yes, of course," Sofia replied.

"You understand, Sofe? We're busy," Jack said. "We've got work to do."

"Sure! We'll talk later," Sofia replied quickly. She suddenly felt stupid, like a thirty-eight-year-old child. She felt like reminding everyone she had been working on film sets for fifteen years. A runner showed her off the sound stage.

She sat down on a chair and watched the rehearsal. After a minute, Courtney seemed to look over.

The runner returned. "Sorry, that's Ms. Smith's chair," he said to Sofia.

"Oh, no problem," Sofia replied. She stood up. "Show me where my chair is—I'll sit on that."

He stared at her, then looked around. "There isn't one." He seemed terrified.

She saw he told the truth. Four directors chairs sat near the monitors, each with a name printed on the back in white letters. One read *Courtney Smith,* another *Jack Travers,* and another two had the names of the producers. None of them read *Sofia Wentworth.*

"Here, let me get you a chair!" The runner ran off and returned with another chair, a very nice one, better than the others, fashioned from leather and with wheels. Sofia smiled at him. "Thanks." She did not sit down but walked toward the makeup truck instead.

Hot, nauseating embarrassment bubbled up through her torso. She could feel the back of her neck prickle and sweat. Maybe the brown paper bag was still somewhere around; she could blow into it. She felt so stupid, playing the lovesick girl, trying to restore her marriage on a film set. It would be all right if it worked, but Jack had paid her efforts no attention. He appeared ensconced in his job, as he should be. She reached the edge of the sound stage and ran straight into Jack, reading his pages alone beside another, smaller monitor. She cursed herself for choosing this route off the stage and tried to avoid him, but he'd already looked up. "Where are you going?" he asked.

Sofia swallowed, attempted breeziness, though she felt like crying. "Back to the truck," she said lightly. "I prefer it there. My crib," she joked.

Jack nodded and looked back down at his script. She swallowed and walked on.

"Sofia," he called to her as she walked away.

She turned to him.

"You look great, by the way," he said. He looked up from his papers; their eyes met. He gave her a smile and she recognized the look: it was the smile he used to give her when they first met, a crooked smile from the corner of his mouth, brazen and cute. He suddenly looked ten years younger, full of energy.

"Oh, thanks," she said, as casually as she could muster. She turned away from him and walked on. She waited until she was well clear of him, then allowed herself to smile. She didn't know if Derek usually received obscene tips from his clients, but he would do so today.

Chapter Twenty-Three

Jane attempted to conquer London. She approached a giant undercroft of metal and bricks. A sign above read *Underground*. She held the card with *Oyster* printed across it in bold blue letters that Fred had given her earlier. A man in a ticket booth had taken four pounds of her remaining money and somehow added their value to the card, or so he alleged. He squinted at her when she asked him, "How long is this tube?" But then he exhaled and explained in a bureaucratic register how to use the card.

"Put the card on the circle. The gate will open," he told her, in a slow, deliberate tone, as though talking to an invalid, which she felt horrendously grateful for. "Take the brown line and change at Oxford Circus onto the red line. Down there," he said and pointed to a tunnel. "First time in London?" he asked with a smile.

"First time in a while," Jane answered.

Jane walked down the tunnel and searched for the elusive circle of which he proclaimed. She felt unsure as to what size sphere she should be looking for. The size of a saucepan? The size of a pond?

She reached a row of steel fences. On one sat a yellow circle, the size of a gentleman's palm. Jane placed the card on the circle. A gate retracted with magic between two of the fences, inviting

Jane inside. Jane hurried through. The gate shut behind her with a crash and she grabbed her bottom on instinct. The gate behaved the way of a farm gate on springs, with a mind of its own, opening and closing whenever it deigned to. She exhaled with relief at not having been taken into its jaws.

More people entered through the maniacal farm gates behind her. One man fared not so lucky; the gate snapped shut before he could enter. He smashed his loins into the gate, barred, and rolled his eyes. He cursed and complained to a man wearing some sort of uniform. Jane's fear redoubled. Even people from the twenty-first century were no match for these capricious gates. She looked up. A maze of signage hung above her. One sign announced *Baker-loo Line* with a brown line painted underneath. Jane recalled the ticket seller's directive and followed the sign. As she shuddered at what might lie in store next, a river of bodies engulfed Jane in their current, and she was rushed down the tunnel, her feet barely touching the ground.

Up ahead, people walked forward then disappeared downward into thin air, though they moved too slowly to be falling. Jane approached the area with trepidation and gasped at the sight of people riding a moving staircase down to a lower level. Jane stood back and observed. People stepped onto the beastly contrivance with a concerning nonchalance. Huge steel teeth lined the edge of each step. The silver jaws glinted in the lurid yellow light of the tunnel, like the neatly aligned fangs of a metallic animal. How did people avoid the staircase eating them? She paused, held her breath, and leapt onto it. She had a stair in mind, but she misjudged the landing and ended up on the same stair as an old man in a checked suit.

"Do you mind!" he said.

"My apologies, sir," Jane said. "I am not from these parts." She jumped up to the next step. "These things are a danger." The moving staircase descended for no short time. Soon, she must have stood at least thirty feet below the earth. She looked down. The staircase ended up ahead; the stairs flattened and disappeared into the ground. She feared being eaten once again. The people ahead of her stepped off without looking up. "Here we go," Jane said to the old man. She inhaled, and the stairs levelled. She closed her eyes and stepped off and landed on solid ground. "Well done, everyone!" she said to the people in front. The old man in the suit shook his head. The others ignored her and continued moving forward.

She followed the signs to the brown line and arrived on an underground platform. A red-and-white train, smaller than the Bath train, pulled up to the platform. The doors opened like sentient beings, the same as the others. Jane stepped inside the train and gripped a pole running from floor to ceiling. The doors closed themselves and the train pulled away from the platform. It then entered a tunnel, plunging the view out the windows into darkness.

Jane studied the people. Once again, almost every person in the carriage seemed to possess a small thin rectangular box, which they cradled in their hands and gazed at. They smiled at these boxes, laughed at them, worshipped them. Jane shook her head, filled with curiosity at what wonders these little rectangles possessed. She glanced at one and found a theater production playing inside the box. She felt flabbergasted and terrified. Actors reduced to tiny proportions moved inside the screen and waved and spoke to each other. She shook her head and stepped away, gripped with shock. More magic. She understood now why people paid these enchanted boxes such attention.

Next, she studied the faces. Either flower sellers filled the carriage, or people no longer considered face painting obscene. A woman in a spotted coat was painting her mouth red. Another who read a novel had lined her eyes with black, like Cleopatra. One woman exposed the top of her bosoms. A man in a striped evening suit glanced at them, then returned to watching his little rectangular box. How did women and men interact in the twenty-first century? Had things changed? Did marriage still represent the goal? Before she could delve deeper into her anthropological study, the tube train arrived at the station for Oxford Circus. Jane alighted the carriage.

As soon as she did so, Jane wished she could jump back into the safety of the warm train. A scene of mayhem greeted her, with more people rumbling and streaming through the confined space than Jane thought humanly possible. Bodies pushed in and out of the carriages, through and across the stone platform in every direction, like rats escaping a sinking ship. As Jane again looked upward for signs, a sea of people swept her along and moved her forward, whether she wanted to go or not. A sign with a red line loomed overhead. Jane fought her way out of the seething wave of bodies and followed it.

She boarded another two moving staircases at great peril and walked down another tunnel, then arrived at the red line. A train pulled up. Jane boarded the train and found a seat. Before she had time to catch her breath, the tube arrived at St. Paul's station and Jane alighted again. She exhaled, bewildered at the pace and the noises, the heat and the people. She mounted yet another lo-

comotive staircase, this one travelling upward. She touched her
card on the circle once more, exited the gates, and was spat out
into the daylight.

Once her eyes adjusted, she fixated on the facade of St. Paul's
Cathedral, which seemed to bloom before her from the ground
into the sky. For a moment, she thought she had returned to 1803.
The baroque structure stood as it had the last time she was there,
but then she turned around in a circle and found monsters of glass
and steel now surrounded it on all sides. Giant red carriages with
two floors carried dozens of people through the street. Horseless
monsters moved everywhere, up and down the street, sounding
horns of alarm and anguish.

But if she momentarily thought she had returned to her own
world at the sight of St. Paul's, she banished the mistake when the
next building lured her inside. The smell of fresh bread wafted
from its doors, and she walked toward it, her stomach sucking
with hunger.

Above the doorway, brilliant white letters before a bright orange background read *Sainsbury's*. Magic glass doors slid apart
as she approached. Her nose followed the wafting smell of hot
sweet bread, but her eyes concerned themselves with the most
abundant and grotesque display of food she had ever seen. Some
sort of indoor marketplace happened there, like the one in her
own world on Stall Street, but at least ten times the size. In one
direction, a field of exotic fruits and vegetables bloomed across
a giant floor. A mountain of oranges spilled forth from a giant wooden crate. Jane had seen an orange once, sitting next to
Queen Elizabeth in a painting. Apples liberated from a thousand
trees bloomed from another leviathan mound. Giant domes of
lettuce squatted across the landscape. Tremendous glass boxes

that felt cold to the touch were filled from floor to ceiling with paper cartons, with each carton bearing an Italian title. *Bellissima Gourmet Pizza,* one read. Huge cases strewn with chipped ice encased rows of haddock, salmon, and sea creatures she knew only from storybooks: octopus, crab, and lobster.

Corridors of shelves were stacked row upon row with boxes and packages of dried foods, biscuits, bottles, sauces, and grains spewing from each ledge. She walked down one corridor at random and the sight of at least a hundred pound bags of sugar wrapped in brightly colored paper assaulted her eyes. A wall of sweetness. If any lingering doubt remained that this was all a dream, she now firmly knew she had travelled through time. Not even in her wildest fantasies could she conjure such a biblical plethora of food. Jane needed to sit down.

"Can I help you with something, love?" a woman in an orange shirt asked her.

"What is that?" Jane replied. She pointed to the woman's chest, where a name hung on a little sign.

"That's my name tag. My name is Pam." Jane felt astounded at the brevity and forwardness of the introduction. People now wore their names on their clothing and introduced themselves before you met them.

"Why does no one guard the sugar?" she asked Pam with wonder. Pam looked at her curiously. Jane walked further down the corridor and reached the end, where more cold glass cases stood at the back of the store.

"And where did all of this milk come from? Where are the cows?"

Pam studied the mysteriously cold shelves stuffed with bottles of creamy white liquid. "I honestly don't know," said Pam. "No one's ever asked me that." They walked back to the corridor with the sugar. Jane had reached El Dorado, the city of gold, the land of milk and honey, and it was named Sainsbury's.

"Pam, you are a genius," Jane said. "You must have abolished starvation with your indoor market." At least four children had starved to death in Bath the month prior; Jane knew this because her papa had christened each of them before they died. "Enough food now exists to feed everyone," she declared.

"People still starve," Pam said.

Jane turned to her with surprise. "How is that possible?"

"Not around here," Pam said, shaking her head. "I've heard children starve to death in Yemen, though, poor darlings."

"How is that possible?" Jane repeated. She picked up a sugar bag.

Pam shrugged. "People are still people."

Jane sighed. "You are wise, Pam. How much is this sugar?"

"Fifty p for the bag," Pam replied.

"Do I have enough?" Jane asked. She offered her handful of remaining banknotes and coins. Pam nodded. Jane had felt happy to forgo buying a book, but it equaled the utmost of follies to walk past sugar in such abundance and not buy some. "I shall take one bag, Pam." She offered Pam her money. Pam offered her another curious look.

"Pay at the front, miss. At the checkout." Pam showed Jane how to purchase the sugar. There were more silver boxes and ringing sounds and mayhem and confusion, but finally, together, they completed the transaction. Pam packed the sugar in a shiny reticule that also read *Sainsbury's* and Jane exited the building.

She returned to the road that stretched beside St. Paul's Cathedral and took one last detour to walk inside the grand church and look around; she could not help herself. The monstrous dome loomed over her head, and glorious dusty light streamed downward into the church in shards of yellow. The giant naves of the structure stretched out like the lungs of a whale. Twenty-first-century people wandered about in pairs and trios, whispering and pointing at statues and paintings, dwarfed by the monumental stone walls. Each of them in turn stopped and looked upward, turning their head to stare at the giant dome and the circular opening it offered overhead, a window to the heavens. Jane had done the same once, on the date of her twelfth birthday, when she travelled with her father to London. She had felt compelled to peer aloft, on instinct, as they did, and she repeated the act now, looking upward, smiling at the warm sun on her face, and sending a prayer of thanks up there for having made it across London alive.

$\mathcal{J}$ane exited the church and walked the three blocks east down Cheapside as she had before. Her thoughts turned to what Mrs. Sinclair had told her: she would be gone now, but there would always be someone like her in that house. Questions filled Jane's mind. Why was she sent here? Had Mrs. Sinclair simply made a mistake? Sorceresses likely erred as much as the next profession, especially the ones who lived in Cheapside. But above these, one question stood for which she required an answer: How could she reverse what she had done and return home?

As Jane arrived at Milk Street, her heart raced. The ale house on the corner was still called the Duck and Waffle. A smooth black lane replaced the cobblestones, but the public house was the same brownstone building as in 1803. She continued down the street. The same military church and warehouses sat there, cleaner than before, but they remained. Apart from the refurbished road, the frame portrayed a scene almost identical to the one she had left.

She quickened her pace, her heart skipping with excitement. She turned the corner and stepped onto Russia Row.

The sagging Tudor building was gone.

Jane shook her head in disbelief. She confirmed the address on the paper, with its strange numbers and letters that Sofia had added. She stood in the correct place, but the house had departed. In its place stood a block building of glass and mortar, five stories tall. The ground floor of the building appeared to be a restaurant; a blue sign out front read *Pizza Express*. Jane stepped back in shock. She felt sure the house would remain; all the other houses in the street did. Some mistake must have occurred.

Jane walked inside the restaurant.

"For one?" a woman said to Jane.

"I beg your pardon," said Jane. "Is this the address of 8 Russia Row?"

"Yes," said the woman. "Just you for lunch?"

"What happened to the house that was here?"

"I've only worked here two months. I know nothing," the woman replied. "What do you want to order?"

Jane looked at the woman and tried not to cry. She had salivated with hunger before in the indoor market but had now lost her appetite.

"I'll give you a minute." The woman walked away.

Jane sat down at a table. She could not understand it. She had crossed twenty-first-century London and not been killed once. She had earned the right to arrive at this house and find it intact after navigating her way through underground trains, maniacal farm gates, and crazed drivers of horseless steel beasts. Jane felt nauseated with worry as the waitress returned. What could she do now?

"I am sorry. I still do not know my order," Jane said.

"I've just come to tell you this is a new building. My manager told me."

Jane sat up. "Thank you. And what happened to the house that stood on this plot before?"

"It fell down. Last year."

"That cannot be," said Jane. "That house was always supposed to be here."

"It was in the newspaper," the woman said.

"But I came all this way," Jane said. Tears formed in her eyes. "I am stuck."

The woman touched her arm. "I came to this country, too. I don't know anybody. I am so lonely." She spoke in a sad, deep accent Jane did not recognize. The woman scratched her brow. With her long face and high cheekbones, she resembled Catherine the Great. "But then I made friends. Okay?"

Jane smiled at the kind, futile words and thanked the woman. She told the woman she had lost her appetite and walked back outside. She stood on the corner and exhaled, all hope faded.

"Can you take our picture?" a voice asked.

Jane turned her head to the voice's source. A man of about twenty-five addressed her; he was pointing to himself and a woman standing beside him. "Yes," Jane answered, unsure of what he meant but relieved to be distracted from her despair by a smiling face. The man held out a shiny, thin rectangle of steel. "Everyone has these things," Jane remarked. "I am unversed in their operation, with regret."

"Here," he said, standing next to her and holding the object in front of his body. It contained a frame like a painting. The man's companion stood by the wall of 8 Russia Row. She appeared in the frame. The man pressed a white button and a painting appeared by magic in the frame. It was a picture of the woman who stood by the wall in front of them.

"It captures the moment," Jane exclaimed. The man laughed at her, kind and unmalicious. "It's a memory," she added. "You capture it and stow it in your pocket."

"Hold it up like this," the man said, handing the object to Jane and moving her arms into position so the box pointed at his female companion once more. Jane stiffened at the feeling of the man's hands on her and hoped he did not notice. He positioned Jane's shoulders so the woman now appeared in the center of the frame. The man rushed over to join his friend and, once he was comfortable in his portrait pose, he nodded for Jane. "This building fell down last year," he said.

"I heard," Jane replied. She pressed the white button on the box, as he had, and the box made a clicking sound.

The man rushed back over to Jane. "Beautiful!" he said, as he examined the painting from all angles.

"A good attempt, perhaps," Jane said. "That was my first try." She puffed out her chest.

He laughed another generous laugh. "Well done," he said, and smiled at Jane. "Have a great day."

"And to the both of you," Jane said as they turned to leave. "Pardon me, sir, but could you tell me the time?"

The man consulted the steel box. "Twelve thirty," he answered.

"Thank you," Jane said. It required fifteen minutes on the tube train to return to Paddington; she had earlier observed the time on the clock that hung in the train station. It was the best and only option now; with nothing left for her in Cheapside, she should return to Fred. She winced at the idea of seeing him again; she had never expected to do so. But it could not be helped. She proceeded toward St. Paul's and steeled herself for another harrowing ride on the moving staircase of doom. She crossed the plaza of St. Paul's Cathedral and descended once more into the earth. She reached the solid steel fence and fished in her pocket for the card she would place on the circle to open the magical gates, but the card did not appear in her hand. Jane spread her fingers wide in her pocket and sifted through the folds in the fabric. But the pouch of fabric stood empty. Jane scowled. She must have allowed it to fly open.

She proceeded to the glass booth to purchase another ticket, then stopped. Her pockets contained no money, either. She dug into both folds of fabric and turned them inside out. All their contents had departed: the card, the money. What a fool she was! She'd let everything fall from her person. She held only the bag with the sugar. Jane scowled at herself for her carelessness. She reached to her neck to run her fingers along her necklace, which she often did when thinking, but touched nothing.

Jane grabbed at her neck. She fell to her knees and swept the ground. Frank's crucifix necklace had disappeared. How had she managed to misplace her jewelry? Perhaps it had fallen off somewhere along the way. Maybe if she dashed back there now, it would lie on the road to Russia Row. How long had it been missing? She recalled playing with it as she walked down Milk Road. Jane's stomach fell. The man with the metal box who'd asked Jane to make the picture, his hands on her shoulders. She felt sick. He had robbed her!

Jane moved back up the stairs and onto St. Paul's piazza in a horrified daze. The day in London, which had begun so well, now fell to pieces. She shook her head in a panic, unsure of what to do, then finally arrived at her only remaining option. She shrugged and slumped and began walking in a northwesterly direction.

SHE DID NOT allow the changes to distract her. Piccadilly Circus still stood, as did the Thames, though now it smelled a far sight better, and three new bridges straddled its waters. She reached Oxford Circus. Giant brick and glass structures now surrounded the chaotic square on all four sides. People streamed from every doorway and corner. A shop window contained her books. She gasped and ran over to it. The shop had put her books in a special display, with her portrait in the window. The busiest shopfront in London displayed her novels!

She glanced at a clock in the shop window. The hands read two fifteen. She sighed. Two fifteen! She was already late, more than one hour past the agreed time, yet she had reached only halfway across London. She ran, trying not to consider the futility of her task. Even if she guessed the correct path from here, by the time she arrived at Paddington, it would be, at the very least, more than two hours after she and Fred had agreed to reunite. Her devastation at the day transformed into panic. It was terrible enough to be denied returning home, but now a worse fate confronted her. If she did not reunite with Fred, she'd be left in New London, with no money, no food, and no convincing story to tell anyone. She had winced with anticipation of how awkward their reunion would be and dreaded spending any more time in his company, but now that seemed like paradise compared with the option of never meeting at all.

What chance existed that he had waited for her? She had already let Fred down once by not meeting him after agreeing to do so. A grown man with appointments did not wait to be made a fool of a second time.

AFTER WHAT SEEMED like days, Jane turned down Praed Street in Paddington, red-faced and puffing. A flap of skin came loose from her ankle where Sofia's leather shoe rubbed it raw. She ignored it and ran forward.

As she moved down the street, she glimpsed the bench she had sat on earlier that day. A man sat upon it with his arms crossed over his chest, shivering. Jane inhaled.

It was Fred. For some reason she could not grasp, he had waited for her.

Chapter Twenty-Five

"You're two hours late," he said when she reached him.

"Thank you" was all she could reply. She bent over to catch her breath.

"We've missed the train," he said.

"I am sorry. Thank you for waiting. I am glad you did not leave," she said. She meant it.

"Did you get lost?" he asked. His voice was curt.

"No."

"It's fifteen minutes on the tube to St. Paul's from here. What happened?" A mixture of emotions seemed to dance across his face: frustration, of course, but also something else. Was it relief? "I thought you'd stood me up again," he said finally.

"No," Jane replied quickly. But she had more bad news. Her face burned a shade of crimson. "I walked."

He turned to her. "Why on earth?"

"I misplaced my Oyster card. Your card, really."

"You didn't buy another one? I gave you extra money."

Jane bowed her head. "I lost your money. The ticket to Bath, too. I lost everything."

Fred stared at her, incredulous.

Jane felt her voice breaking. "I was robbed, do you see? They took the money, your Oyster card, and my necklace. The house was not there. Now I'm stuck here!" Her eyes blurred. Mortification gripped her as tears threatened to emerge. She cared little for Fred's opinion of the event; she hoped only that others had not seen. She turned and began to run away from him back down the street.

"Don't run away," he called after her.

"Go. I shall make my own way," she said.

"No, you won't." He caught up to her and took her arm.

Jane blinked, willing her eyes not to cry. But it was no good. Hot, embarrassed tears tumbled down her face. She waited for Fred's reproach and contempt. Instead, his face seemed fixed in a look of pain.

"It's okay. It's only money," he said.

She nodded. "You don't understand," she said.

He put out his arms—what for, to hold her?—but Jane flinched, and he took them back. He offered her a handkerchief instead.

"Thank you," she blubbered, and accepted the cloth. Jane dabbed the handkerchief to her eyes. She could not believe she was crying in front of this obnoxious man, to whom she was now indebted for money, for Oyster cards, for basically saving her life. She mopped up as many of the offending drops as she could.

He sat down on a bench and motioned for her to sit next to him. "Any good?" he asked, pointing to the handkerchief.

It was white and made of a strange substance, a cross between cloth and paper. "It does the trick," Jane said. "Commendable liquid absorption." She handed him back the handkerchief.

"Keep it," he said.

"You don't want your handkerchief back?" she asked.

"It's just a tissue," he said. "I have more." He showed her a small package with five or six of the tissues inside. She shook her head. He must be very rich to own so many.

"Very well," she replied. "Thank you."

"What did you buy at Sainsbury's?" he asked. He pointed to the bright orange bag, which Jane had forgotten she was holding.

"Oh, a bag of sugar," Jane said. She lifted the package from the bag and showed it to him. "I paid the most extraordinary price for it; I've never found sugar so cheap."

"Do you keep a keen eye on sugar prices?" he asked with a gentle smirk.

"Do you not?" Jane asked him.

"I don't, but maybe I should," he said. "Clearly I am missing some bargains."

"I apologize. I used your money to purchase this. Here, take it, it's yours." She held up the package of sweet crystals to him.

He shook his head. "I wouldn't dare take your sugar." He seemed always to stare at her with a bemused face, though not unsmiling. She had always interpreted this as some sort of contempt; now she wondered if she was mistaken, if it was something else. She could not put her finger on it exactly, but either his face had softened, or she was looking at him differently.

She blushed. "I'm sorry I made you miss your train," she said.

He shrugged. "There's another one in an hour."

"I'm sorry for wasting your hundred pounds and for destroying your handkerchief," she added.

"Please stop apologizing," he replied. He smiled at her again in a way that made her swallow.

"How was your appointment?" she asked him.

"It was a disaster. I was supposed to be doing something clever and failed miserably."

"What happened?" Jane said. She turned her knees toward him and listened.

He glanced at her knees, then spoke. "We've organized some student exchanges with our sister school in Normandy."

"Student exchange?" Jane asked.

"A student of ours stays with a French family and attends school there for a couple of months. They tour battlefields, visit Paris, learn a bit of French. A French student, in exchange, comes here and learns British customs—they make tea, visit the Tower, learn how to queue properly. It's all great fun, and the students love it. Some of the French students and teachers arrived in London this morning and I went to meet them."

"Goodness, we are such friends with the French now. We exchange students with them and everything," Jane remarked.

Fred smiled. "That's where all the good cheese is. Anyway, Madame Cluse, our French teacher, normally accompanies me on these outings, but today she was unwell, and I went alone. I was there representing the history department. I don't speak a lick of French, except 'bonjour' and 'croissant.' Only once I arrived did I realize they don't speak a lick of English."

"Oh dear," Jane said. She did not understand many of his words, but she felt the warmth and wit of them. He spoke in a relaxed way, smiling and animated. Jane wondered at the change. Their interactions up to this point had felt so strained, but it seemed when he spoke of something other than her—when they weren't speaking of the dislike and agitation between them—he became a different person. As if she brought out some tension in him that melted when he switched to easier topics. She did not feel dismayed by this, only intrigued.

"Madame Cluse will be very cross with me because I think I

ruined everything. 'Sacré bleu, Fred,' she will say. 'You are an imbecile.'" He smiled. "All I needed to give them was some information about visiting Bath, but I think instead I provoked some sort of international incident between the British and the French. I tried to communicate with my own made-up sign language. I also kept talking in English with a bad French accent, thinking they understood me." He put his head in his hands in a gesture of mock agony.

Jane laughed kindly. "A diplomatic disaster," she said.

"I offended them," Fred continued. "Now there are three French people roaming around London doing who knows what. I hope I've not provoked a war. We'll have to start calling chips Freedom Fries again and boycotting cheese imports." He raised an eyebrow.

"Do the French students and teachers still wait at the place you came from?" Jane asked him.

"I guess so," Fred said with a shrug. "They're probably still eating lunch, and besides, they don't know where to go otherwise."

"I should like to meet these Norman folk of yours," Jane said.

Fred checked his wrist clock and shrugged. "This way." He showed her down a lane. They proceeded north toward the old village of Westbourne Green until they arrived at a row of town houses with pointed roofs below Westbourne Park Road. A shop selling teas and cakes sat on the corner. Fred showed Jane inside.

"Allo," said a male voice in a thick Norman lilt as they entered the shop. A large man stood from one of the tables. He spoke in a soft, nervous tone and glanced at Fred with a sheepish look. Two adolescent children sat beside him, dressed in school uniforms.

"Bonjour, monsieur," Jane said. She walked to the man, who

raised his eyes in hope to Jane. "Are you the teacher, sir?" she continued in French. Fred snapped his head toward her.

The man smiled his delight. "I am, miss. Claude Poulan, at your service," he replied, also in French.

"Welcome to England, Mr. Poulan. The French are most welcome here."

Claude beamed and chuckled a deep, barrel-chested laugh. "Thank you. But please, call me Claude."

Jane turned to Fred and returned her speech to English. "What shall I tell him?"

Fred smiled at her and shook his head. "You don't own a watch or a phone, but you speak perfect French."

"*His* French is perfect." Jane shrugged. "Mine could be better." Jane turned back to Claude. "Where are you from in France, Claude?" she asked him.

"Brittany," said Claude.

"Beautiful. Do they still call Brittany 'Little Britain'?"

"They do. Are you a teacher, miss?" he asked her.

"Goodness, no. I have not the patience, nor the skill," Jane replied. "Monsieur Fred is an excellent teacher, though, from what I have heard." She smiled at Fred and he shook his head again, searching her face.

"I have no idea what you're saying, but it sounds brilliant," Fred said. He cleared his throat.

"Please tell Mr. Fred I apologize," Claude said. "I want to explain. Another teacher was supposed to be here, Miss Rampon. She speaks English, but she is ill and remains in the hotel. Now I have wasted everyone's day."

Jane explained the situation to Fred. "Is your day wasted, Fred?"

Fred shook his head. Jane did not need to translate this to Claude. The giant man smiled with relief and shook Fred's hand, then kissed him twice on each cheek.

"Whoa, easy there, big fella." Fred laughed.

They missed the next two trains back to Bath.

WHEN JANE AND Fred finally boarded the 6:17 P.M. service, the sun had set. They sat next to each other. The steel monstrosity pulled out from Paddington station and made its way to the West Country once more. Fred looked out the window.

"I was sent from the hall, the other night," Jane told him. He ceased his looking out the window and turned to her. "A gentleman made me leave. I searched for you, but I could not get back inside." He nodded. "I waited by the front of the building for at least an hour."

"I looked for you, too," he said. He smiled. Silence fell between them; the only sounds were the train's wheels clacking below them and the wind whooshing against the glass outside. "That place you were looking for today—why was it so important?" he asked her after a time.

"It was there last time I went to London. But it is no longer," she said. "I hoped it held information I need."

He nodded. "What kind of information?"

Jane hesitated and wondered how best to answer without ignoring Sofia's instructions. "Information to help me return to my home," she said. "Once I have it, I shall leave you in peace."

Fred looked out the window again. "Do you want to leave?"

"Yes," Jane said. "Well, no. But I must."

He nodded and made no remark.

The machine trundled through a tunnel of blue hills and

stars. Jane stared out the window up at the sky and smiled. The stars looked the same as they did in her time. The constellation of Orion still blazed across the blackness, Rigel still sparkled in blue white. Time passed more slowly up there, it seemed, changing little. She lost track of time staring upward; when she finally turned back to the carriage and looked over at Fred she found he had fallen asleep. She watched his face; it was relaxed, at peace. A piece of his hair had fallen into his eyes, the hair he had combed for her that morning. She shook her head at this strange twenty-first-century man, whom she had found so infuriating at first—and still did, in many ways—and wondered if, ever so slightly, she may have misjudged him.

He shifted his position and she thought he might wake, but he relaxed into the seat once more. She felt a weight on her leg and looked down. His hand had dropped to his side and come to rest on her knee.

Several events presented themselves as worthy candidates for reflection as Jane rode the train with Fred asleep next to her. She had walked through the London of two hundred years in the future. She had beheld her own novels for sale in a bookshop. Both were ideal things to captivate her brain and occupy her thoughts, so she was surprised when the item lingering in her mind from Maidenhead to Bath was instead the time she had spent in the company of the man who now slept beside her, and the feeling of his hand now resting on her leg.

Chapter Twenty-Six

*W*hen Sofia saw Jane the next day, she seemed surprised. "You're still here?"

"Yes," Jane replied. "I was unable to return home."

Sofia looked confused. "I wonder how much longer this prank can go on, is all. Surely their budget has run out by now," she whispered.

Jane scowled. "Yes, well. I found no sign of the house."

"What house?"

"Mrs. Sinclair's house. In London."

"You went to London?" Sofia said. Her face bore a look of surprise.

Jane nodded. "With your brother." She commanded her cheeks not to blush; they disobeyed her. She told Sofia of the house's removal from the London landscape, the robbery, the people-eating staircase.

Sofia poured herself a goblet of wine and nodded. "You're sticking with the witch backstory, huh?"

Jane nodded. "I saw my novels in a bookshop," she said.

"Okay, sure." Sofia sat down at the kitchen table and drank the wine in one swallow. She exhaled a long sigh, then shook her shoulders and nodded. "I'm a professional. I can keep this charade up for another day. Which ones?" Jane's six novels still lay on the table. Sofia picked up *Persuasion* and held it in front of Jane. "Did you see this one today?"

The novel then performed two acts that were to dominate their discussions and occupy their actions for some time after.

First, the book shook and turned to dust in Sofia's hand. Jane gasped. Sofia shrieked.

Second, the dust gathered together, and then disappeared into thin air. The women, in almost perfect mimicry, repeated their previous reactions.

JANE STARED AT Sofia's right hand, which remained outstretched and empty, with naught but air where the little book had earlier sat. Sofia stared at the hand, too, and poured another goblet of wine with the other. She drained the goblet, all the while keeping her eyes on the hand where the novel had formerly stood. "Did you see that happen?" Sofia asked Jane in a strangely calm voice.

"The book disappeared from your fingers," Jane replied, equally calmly.

"There was a solid object in my hand. Now there is not."

"I concur with that observation," Jane said, her voice shaking.

"That's a relief," Sofia said. "I thought I might have been hallucinating. Can you explain what is going on?" She peered under the table.

"I do not know," Jane said. It was the truth. Her head spun. "What are you doing?"

"Looking under the table for your book," Sofia replied, doing as much. "Perhaps I dropped it."

"You did not drop it," Jane said.

"Perhaps if I do this"—Sofia shook her hand and wiggled her fingers—"I can bring it back." She flapped her hands. The book did not return. She paced the room. Jane followed her movements back and forth and grew dizzy. "Let's start from the beginning," Sofia began in her strangely calm tone. "Did CGI make the book disappear?"

"I do not know what that means," Jane replied.

"Fair enough. They do fancy things with iPads these days, but even a computer cannot make molecules disappear," Sofia said. "And we've ruled out drunken hallucination, for you saw it too. Are you drunk?" Jane shook her head. Sofia stopped pacing and slammed her hands on the table. "I'm going to ask you a question now and I want you to answer truthfully," she said.

"Proceed," Jane replied.

"Are you or are you not an actress pretending to be Jane Austen in a candid-camera scheme concocted by the producers of the film I am starring in?" She looked Jane in the eye.

"I am not," Jane replied. "What are you doing now?"

Sofia had sat down and was lowering her head between her legs. "I am stopping my head from exploding. I suggest you join me."

Jane secured her head at her knees. Her skull burned. She had never witnessed anything like what had just happened. Except for the occasion where she had travelled through time in a similar fashion.

"Explain to me, then, who you think you are," Sofia said after a moment.

"I am Jane Austen," Jane replied.

"I see. Well, putting my head between my legs didn't work." Sofia sat back up again. "I shall return to my first tactic." She poured herself a third goblet of wine, then pointed at Jane. "You are try-ing to tell me that was not CGI? You materialized in a pile of cur-tains?"

"I do not know what see-gee-eye means."

"You expect me to accept you are Jane Austen. The writer who lived two hundred years ago."

"Yes?" Jane replied. "As I have said."

"The novelist who wrote *Northanger Abbey*. The ambitious and doomed film adaptation of which I am now acting in."

"While I've comprehended little of what you have said, I am nevertheless compelled to answer yes."

"And you arrived here how?"

"I said a spell, and—"

"The witch, the cabbages, et cetera," Sofia said, waving a hand. "That is all *true*?"

"Yes."

"When you appeared in the curtain. What happened to you?"

"Difficult to say," Jane replied. "It was similar to the thing that occurred with my book."

"The dust particles and the disappearing?"

"Yes," Jane said.

Sofia nodded. "You are not an actress? Not an avatar?"

"I do not believe so."

"You are not a cartoon?"

"Not that I am aware." It dawned on Jane then that during the entirety of their short acquaintance, Sofia Wentworth had com-prehended a different version of events from the real one. "You did not believe me before?" Jane asked her. "When I said my name is Jane Austen?"

"I thought you were an actress!" Sofia said. "A poorly trained one," she added.

"Do you believe me now?"

Sofia drained the goblet. Jane waited for an answer.

"What I want to believe is that you are a performer, sent to trip me up, whom I instead planned to maneuver into making me look good on camera and somehow wrangle my husband back. I hoped your appearance out of thin air, and your book's disappearing act, were tricks of the theater." Sofia sighed.

"Here's the thing. It was so strange when it happened. Dust became a person. Excuse me for a moment." Sofia got up and located a second bottle of wine. She opened it and filled her goblet again. Then she opened the front door. Jane peered after her. Sofia squinted at the sky and tipped the glass to her lips. She swallowed and gulped. Jane thought she might pass out about halfway through, when she seemed to choke and stop breathing, but then she resumed her gulping once more and drained the goblet. She returned inside.

"To summarize. You are Jane Austen. You cast a spell you got from a witch and disappeared from your own time, then reappeared here in a pile of curtains. Stop me if I have left anything out."

Jane made no remark.

"Are there any disadvantages to me if I cease disbelieving you, and accept this story as truth?"

"I see only advantages to you believing me," Jane said.

Sofia nodded. She stood and cleared her throat. "On behalf of everyone, welcome to the twentieth century, Jane Austen."

"I believe this is the twenty-first century?"

"Right. What are your plans while you are here?" Sofia asked.

"To find a way to return home," Jane answered.

"Makes sense." Sofia shrugged. "Now we have that answered, we arrive at the next question."

"What is that?" Jane said.

"Why did a novel, written by you, disappear into thin air?"

Chapter Twenty-Seven

Sofia led Jane out of the house and began walking toward the center of Bath.

"Where are we going?" Jane asked as Sofia strode down the road ahead of her.

"To gather more clues," Sofia replied. "Hurry up." She walked even faster.

"You move remarkably well for a woman who recently consumed a bottle of wine," Jane called after her, shaking her head.

"Thank you," Sofia said with a nod. "A talent of mine." Jane caught up to her. "My husband, Jack, is your great-great-great-great-great-great-great-great . . . something, by the way," Sofia said as they turned down Railway Street. "How many 'greats' was that?"

"Eight," Jane replied.

"That's not right," Sofia said.

"How many 'greats' should there be?" Jane asked.

"I don't know. Not eight. Anyway, he is your relative."

Jane stiffened. "Am I to understand a relative of mine, a descendant, my flesh and blood, walks this earth?"

"Yep. He's handsome, too," Sofia replied.

"He is a descendant of my immediate family? The Austens of Hampshire?"

"The very same. He's related to you, Jane. That's the whole point. He has thirty of your letters in a shoebox in our attic in London."

"I do not understand. Your husband has my letters in his possession? Why?"

"His mother left them to him. They're collector's items."

Jane reveled in the thought. "Whose child is he? Rather, from whom is he descended?" Was this her great-grandson? Was she destined to return to her own time to marry and bear a child, who through generations of careful marriage and breeding would produce a handsome descendant named Jack? Who was she destined to marry, then?

"James, I think?" Sofia replied.

"Yes," Jane said with a disappointed nod. "I have a brother named James. I see."

"Jack is your great-great-great—et cetera—nephew, I believe," Sofia said.

Jane felt deflated. Still, it did not mean there weren't others. "Is there any resemblance between us? May I meet him?"

"Who?"

"Your husband," Jane said. "Does he live here in Bath?"

"No. We are separated," Sofia said. She swallowed and gazed at the ground.

"Oh," Jane said with horror. "I am sorry."

"Don't be sorry," Sofia said. Jane caught a look of turmoil on Sofia's face before she turned away. It was a complex expression, one of both hope and pain. Jane could not respond. She had never met anyone whose marriage had ceased to be. She knew plenty of

persons who remained roped to another human in misery, infi-
delity, and hatred, yes, but no one who had abandoned the marital
bed, or whose spouse had deserted them. "Perhaps you can come
to set, where they're filming the movie?" Sofia said. She seemed
to force her face into a smile. "It's your novel. Jack will be there."

"Mov-ie?"

"Like a theater production, but fancier."

Jane felt so overcome with delight, confusion, and intrigue that
she needed to sit down again. "I might like to see that," she said.

THE TWO WOMEN entered a honeystone building in the center of
Bath and rode a travelling staircase to the second floor. "I have
been on several of these!" Jane remarked with joy. "Observe my
technique." She jumped on a stair with a wobble.

"Not bad," Sofia said. She led Jane inside a large room filled
with shelves of books.

"A library." Jane smiled. "Whose is it?"

"The plebs," Sofia said. "Anyone's."

This concept greeted Jane as entirely new. In her own time, a
man brought a cart filled with books into the village; one could
borrow them for a week. Indoor libraries were private and the
domain of the rich. Jane's brother Edward had inherited a spectacular example from the Knights when he became their heir, and
whenever Jane visited, she spent days lost among its shelves, devouring mountains of books. Her brother did not use the library
himself. "I am astounded by the number of books in the twenty-
first century," Jane remarked.

A man in rags walked up to them and elbowed Sofia with a
withered arm. "I loved you in *Doctor Zhivago*!" he said. He wore a
perfume of old potatoes.

Sofia rolled her eyes at the man. "Though I'm not one to turn down a compliment, that was Julie Christie."

"She was beautiful in that film. Can I get a selfie?" He put one arm around Sofia to pose and held out his other arm in front of them.

"You don't have a camera," Sofia said.

"No," he replied. He put his arm down. "How about an autograph?"

"You don't have any paper. Or a pen."

"That's true," he said. He stared into the distance.

Sofia sighed. "We're off to the information desk. If you find paper in that time, I'll sign it when we get back. Always nice to meet a fan." She led Jane away.

"You are a woman of fame," Jane remarked to her. "I recall other times when people have stared and pointed at you in the street."

Sofia nodded. "I am an actress, Jane."

"How wonderful. A poor player that struts and frets her hour upon the stage. Do you play Ophelia? Do you play Electra?"

"I used to," she said with a smile. "Then I grew famous, and I played ingenues, sexy action sidekicks, and hookers with hearts of gold. Now that I'm the wrong side of thirty-five, I play fish-wives and grandmothers."

"Oh. But you have a profession? You earn an income for this acting?"

"An income? Jane, I have six swimming pools across my various houses. I've never even swum in most of them."

Jane shook her head in disbelief. "I have never met a woman who earned her own income before. Do other women have professions? Or only actresses?"

Sofia shrugged. "Sure. Women are doctors, lawyers, garbage

collectors. You can do what you want. You'll get paid less than a man"—she snorted— "but you'll get paid."

Jane's brother Edward, who picked things from his ear and ate them, had been adopted at age twelve by a childless couple, the Knights, who were cousins of Jane's father. Jane far exceeded Edward in mathematics, languages, wit, and talent, but Edward had the talent of maleness, the most important talent of all. By the time Edward reached twenty-five, he had inherited three estates, from which he earned a rental income of ten thousand pounds a year. When Jane had reached the same age, she inherited nothing. When one day she'd expressed aloud a desire to earn her own income, Edward pronounced her a prostitute. The last time she had spoken to her brother involved a letter asking him of his recent holiday to Ramsgate. Edward had replied that it was a wonderful tour and she might have joined them, if there had been room in the carriage.

Jane stared at Sofia, her income-earning female friend, feeling gripped with admiration and agitation. How did she feel earning her own way, existing as a burden to no one? What was it like to be beholden to none?

Sofia showed Jane to the back of the room, where a woman sat behind a desk. Sofia greeted her. "Where can we find *Persuasion*, please?"

The woman squinted at the large steel frame on the desk. "Who is the author?"

Sofia froze. "The author is Jane Austen."

The woman laughed. "No. Jane Austen never wrote anything by that title."

Jane balked. She had memorized those six titles in an instant when Sofia showed the novels to her. They had become as precious to her as children's names.

"Could you check on your computer, please?" Sofia asked the woman.

"Don't need to. Jane Austen never wrote a novel called that. But to humor you . . ." She operated the frame and turned it to face Sofia. "See?"

Sofia examined it and scowled. "Out of interest, how many novels did Jane Austen write?"

The woman behind the desk shrugged liked it was obvious. "Five."

Jane shuddered.

Sofia thanked the woman. "Let's go," she said to Jane.

Next to the library was a shop selling coffee. Jane's sister-in-law Eliza had written from Paris of such things, and Henry had tried some once in London. Sofia pointed to a table and chairs. "Sit down, I'll order us coffee. I need to sober up," Sofia said. "This is a disaster," she added. She ordered at the shop's counter, then returned and sat down next to Jane.

"I understand something is wrong," Jane said, "but I am unsure exactly what."

"Jane. Your book has disappeared. You don't write *Persuasion* anymore! You once wrote six novels, now you only write five. I was in a time-travel movie once. I played the girl who lived next door to a man called Rob. Rob had the power to move back and forth through different periods in time, from the sixties to today and back again. Every time Rob moved from one era to the next, he inadvertently changed events and outcomes in the other time, to the detriment of everyone. A person he spoke to in the past ended up killing a whole bunch of people in the future, for example, and someone who never met their hairdresser because they were talking to Rob instead received horrid haircuts from that day on." She paused and shrugged. "The film was not a masterpiece, to be fair. *Variety* called it 'a poor take on the genre.' But that's beside the point."

"What is the point?" Jane said.

"The point is, the actions Rob made in one time affected what happened in the other time. He went back and forth, changing things and erasing events until eventually, he erased himself and, if I recall correctly, the *universe*." Sofia stared at Jane.

"That does not sound ideal," Jane said.

Sofia nodded. "If you stay here, that is what will happen."

The drinks arrived. Jane sipped hers and scowled. The hot, brown liquid sank to the back of her throat, strangling her from the inside. "The bitterness of this substance astounds me," she said. "But I feel strangely compelled to drink more."

"It's coffee, Jane. Suck it down," Sofia replied. She took a large gulp from her own cup. Jane did the same and found herself buzzing like a bumblebee. She felt disgusted by the drink, but also glad; in some way it made everything seem clearer. She focused her mind back on the issue. The moment when the book had vanished from Sofia's hand disturbed her—not the magic of it, which unnerved her, of course, though no more so than the other strange acts she witnessed—but the true feeling of horror came from the thought that something she had written, which had been published and sent out into the world, now ceased to exist. "What can we do?" she asked Sofia.

"I don't know. The damage might already be too great." Sofia cleared the table and held up a saucer. "This plate represents you in your own time line." She placed the saucer with great ceremony at one end of the table. "You are a woman from the year 1803. At some point in your life, you write a series of novels. These books are published and remain in print two hundred years later. That is your story, your time line." She ran her finger along the table in a line. "But this teacup is you now." She picked it up. "Instead of following your destiny to write those books, you have come here." She moved the teacup away from the saucer. "You have created an alternative version of events, a new time line."

Jane looked at the cup, then the saucer, then back again. She blinked.

"The longer you stay and immerse yourself in this world, the less likely it becomes that you will return to your own time. If you are not in your own time, you cannot write the books for which you become famous." She threw her hands up. "I don't know what I was thinking, showing you that museum. Jane, don't you see? Going out into the world, interacting with people—you changed history. I shouldn't have let you go to London. One of your books has already disappeared. More will follow. And if you keep doing it, eventually all of your novels will disappear. *You* will disappear."

She touched Jane's arm and lowered her voice. "It's quite the confusing thing to get one's head around," she said. "It might take you a while to understand."

"If I never return to 1803, I never write those books," Jane said.

"Or it might be quite easy for you to understand."

Jane raised her china cup and blinked down another large gulp. The bitter substance coated her tongue and lingered in her throat. It seemed to prickle her insides and ring her mind like a bell. She found herself jumping in her seat a little. "What can be done?" she asked with a flinch.

Sofia picked up her own cup. "We need to get you back to your original time line."

"But Mrs. Sinclair is gone! How do we do that?"

"I don't know. But you should take a good look around. This is the last time you will be leaving the house."

Jane looked around the shop and surveyed the contents. The steel box that produced the coffee gleamed from the serving counter, wooden tables and chairs littered the room in ramshackle pairings of twos and threes, and the transient gentleman from the public library dozed in one corner. "I feel unsure as to what I am taking a good look at," Jane replied.

"It's an expression, Jane," Sofia replied with a sigh. "I was trying to be dramatic. You're not supposed to be looking at anything." She grabbed Jane's head, turning it away from the room and back to her face. "I meant I want you to stop falling in love with the twenty-first century. Don't you understand? You went out into the world, you talked to people, you saw your books, you rode the tube! You took a photograph—with a phone! The more you grow to love this time and place, the less likely it becomes that you will leave! We're going straight back to Fred's and you won't be going outside again. You cannot risk further reducing your chances of returning home."

Jane nodded. "But if I remain inside your brother's house, how will I discover the means to return home?"

"You cannot go outside," Sofia said. She drained her cup and stood with determination.

"What is it?" Jane asked.

"It's up to me, Jane. This is my hero's journey. I am going to get you home."

Jane nodded, confused. "Oh. I am honored. Thank you."

"No problem. Now close your eyes and I'll escort you home."

Jane and her savior walked home.

Chapter Twenty-Eight

*T*he next morning, Sofia dragged Jane out of bed and filled her ears with a list of rules and demands, designed to protect her from erasing herself and, if correctly recalled, the universe. "Rule one: You must not go outside," Sofia declared, as she passed Jane a plate of toast, butter, and a boiled egg.

"May I go in the garden?" Jane asked, pointing out the window. She placed a piece of toast in her mouth and chewed with delight. The bread was far softer than the loaves from the Austen house, baked by Margaret the housemaid, which possessed roughly the density of stone.

"Yes. But try not to observe too much. Don't make a study of the telegraph poles. Don't peek over next door's fence. Who knows what might set you off, what stimuli will send you further down the novel-destroying path?" Sofia marched around the kitchen, placing steel boxes in cupboards. "You might witness electricity, become enamored of it, and decide you want to stay," she explained, hiding another contrivance. "Then, whoops, you don't go back, and all your novels—gone!"

"What is electricity?" Jane asked.

"See? You're showing an interest already. Luckily for you, I don't know what electricity is so I won't be tempted to explain it to you. Just accept like the rest of us that it's there, it's useful and move on."

"What shall I do all day then, if I may take an interest in nothing? Stare at the wall?"

"If you like," Sofia said. She gasped. "That reminds me. Do not switch on the television." She stabbed her finger in the air as she said it, speaking in a horrified whisper. Jane gave her a confused look. "The paintings that move," Sofia explained.

"That's called television? How interesting. *Tele* is Greek, meaning 'far away.' *Vision* or *visio* is Latin, meaning 'to see.' I'm warmed that the tradition for clumsy hybrids continues in the English language."

"Yes, well, enough of that," Sofia said. "Rule two: No more finding things interesting. Just promise me you will not watch television."

"I promise," Jane said. It was an easy promise to make; even if she located one of the modern inventions, she doubted she would be able to operate it.

Sofia ceased hiding kitchen objects and sat down next to Jane at the table.

"Perhaps I could read?" Jane asked. "To occupy my time."

"I suppose there's no harm." Sofia walked over to the bookcase. "Let's see." She scanned the titles. "You are restricted to things you could read in your own time. Here we are." She took two large heavy books from the shelves and handed them to Jane.

"'*Sermons to Young Women*, by James Fordyce,'" read Jane, "and '*The Complete Works of William Shakespeare*.' That's it? These two?"

"They will keep you going. Above all, you must not read these." Sofia gathered up the remaining five Austen novels: *Emma, Sense* and *Sensibility, Pride and Prejudice, Northanger Abbey,* and *Mansfield Park*. "What's the matter?" she asked then, when Jane scowled.

"I read some of *Mansfield Park*," Jane said. She swallowed. "In a bookshop in London. Only a little, a page or two. Three pages at most."

"Austen!" Sofia cried. "What were you thinking? That's probably the culprit! I cannot spell out enough the dangers of this. Rule three: No reading your own work." She placed the books in a pile in the glass cabinet, next to a dusty sherry bottle. She locked the door and pocketed the key. "Fingers crossed that does the trick."

Jane stared at the small tower of novels behind the glass. "When shall you be home?"

"As soon as I can," Sofia said.

Fred emerged from the bathroom, bleary-eyed. He wore only a towel, wrapped at the waist. He saw Jane and Sofia at the table and jumped. "What are you doing up?" he said to Sofia. He shot a nervous smile at Jane. "Good morning."

"Good morning, Fred," Jane replied. It was all she could muster in light of the sight before her. Previous to this, she had never seen a man's chest before in her life. Now she had seen the same one twice in three days.

"I have a six A.M. call time," Sofia explained. "Look, Fred. Jane is going to be staying here a few days, okay? She won't be in your way."

"Fine," said Fred, a little too quickly. "Makes no difference to me," he added, coughing. He shrugged and his towel came loose. He caught it awkwardly before it fell. He looked at Jane, and she looked away. She felt certain her cheeks now shone a shade of beetroot. "Where's the kettle?" he asked. He stared at the place on the worktop where the shiny steel pitcher used to sit, the one Sofia had stashed in the cupboard.

"It's broken," Sofia replied. "Get coffee at school. By the way, what's a book about time travel?"

Fred scowled at her. "*The Time Machine,* H. G. Wells. Why?"

"When was it written?"

"I don't know, 1850?"

"Sorry, won't work," Sofia replied. Fred frowned at her, confused. "Never mind," she said.

Fred raised an eyebrow at Sofia and turned to Jane. "Can I get you anything to make your stay more comfortable? Any food you like to eat?"

Jane shook her head. "The food is wonderful, thank you."

"Look at you," Sofia cried to Fred. "Now you're Mr. Hospitable? You never offered me special food!"

He ignored Sofia. "You don't have any clothes, or bags?" he asked Jane.

"I've given her some clothes," Sofia said.

"And my dress is being washed by the white box," Jane added, pointing to the box by the kitchen sink that rattled and spun. Her white muslin dress swished behind the glass window in a sea of suds and froth. "I don't know what women do with the seven hours spare every week," she rejoiced, "liberated by the drudgery of clothes washing!"

Fred laughed kindly and excused himself.

Sofia waited until he was gone, then turned to Jane. "You can't say things like that, Jane," she hissed. "You have to pretend like you're from this day and age." Jane furrowed her brow, not following. "I saw you appear out of those curtains," Sofia explained. "It's my quest now to help you get back to your own time. But if you tell another person you're from the nineteenth century, that you're Jane Austen, MI6 will take you away for experiments."

Jane looked at her curiously, still not following, and now even more confused than before.

"Bad example," Sofia said, shaking her head. "Just don't tell Fred you're Jane Austen—remember, like I said before? Time travel is not a normal occurrence. It's actually quite weird. Fred has no idea who you really are. He thinks you're an actress from my film. If you tell him you travelled here from 1803, he will think you're crazy."

Jane went green as the mortifying realization dawned. Sofia had indeed told her earlier to keep her true identity a secret, but she had never fully understood why. "I've been speaking to him all this time as though he is aware that I have travelled here from a long time past." She recalled all the conversations she had had with him and cringed. "What must he think of me?"

Sofia raised an eyebrow. "Why, what did you say to him?"

"I commented at length about the price of sugar, among other things." She placed her head in her hands.

"Don't worry," Sofia said.

"But how should I behave around him?" she asked in a frantic voice.

"Don't panic. That was probably the last time you will see him. But if you are forced to engage with him, just remember your cover story. You are an actress. You are from the twenty-first century."

Jane nodded. "I am an actress. I am from the twenty-first century," she repeated.

"Do you know the expression 'when in Rome'?" Sofia asked.

"Indeed. Augustine, 390 AD."

Sofia smirked. "For now, how about you 'do as the Romans do'?"

"I shall observe and replicate the modern custom," Jane said.

"It won't be a problem anyway, as you won't be leaving the house." Sofia bade Jane farewell and shut the front door behind her.

FRED EMERGED A few minutes later. He wore a blue shirt. "I'm off to work," he said, in the casual way everyone now seemed to speak. Many times, Jane's brain chased down the meanings of the phrases that littered the new vernacular. "Faster than a speeding bullet" she liked, though it had required a full twenty seconds of cognition, staring into confused space, before she gathered its meaning. "Did Sofia go already?" he asked her.

Jane nodded. She searched his face for any signs of residual awkwardness. Where did things between them now stand? She wasn't sure. There had been some softening between them after their trip to London, but it did not undo the hostility that had existed during the events before it. Were they friends now? Certainly not. But did he still dislike her? It was hard to tell.

"She's left you here alone all day?" Fred asked. "They don't need you on set?"

Jane hesitated at the unexpected question and scrambled for an explanation. "I am unwell," she lied. She coughed and hoped the accompanying noise approximated the severity of a head cold. "I am to stay inside. I shall be fine. I have a book to read."

The excuse seemed to work, for the next thing she knew he was offering to make her a fire. "You should keep warm," he said. Despite Jane's protests, he walked outside to the back garden. "Stay inside," he commanded. Jane watched from the back window as he selected a two-foot-long log from a pyramid of wood stacked against the house's back wall. He rolled his sleeves to the elbows and placed the wood on a stump. He raised an axe over his head, then brought it down with ease, splitting the log in half. The muscles in his jaw tensed and relaxed as he raised the axe and carved three more logs.

A memory struck Jane, from when she was twelve years old. The lid had stuck on a jar of pickled carrots in the kitchen of the Austens' rectory in Hampshire, and Jane and her mother had quarreled over how to liberate the vegetables from their briny sarcophagus. Jane favored a scientific approach, warming the lid while cooling the glass beneath, whereas her mother preferred to bash it across the bench. They each tried with their own system, yet the lid remained tight on the jar, as though cemented in place. Martin, the rectory steward, had entered then—summoned no doubt by the dulcet tones of the discussion between Jane and Mama—and gently took the jar from them. A young man in his twenties, Martin held the jar, and with no warming or bashing, turned the lid with his fingers and popped it open like it was nothing. Jane witnessed the muscles flex in his forearms and realized for the first time that men existed, separate from women.

Fred brought the wood inside and knelt at the hearth. He laid the logs well; he placed the kindling at the base, and then built the larger logs around it. He drew a spark from a box he took from his pocket. He lowered the flame to the wood and held it there, watching. It did not catch at first, so he left his hand there and waited. Jane watched him, astonished at the sight. The wood caught fire, but he held his hand there, watching the orange flame lick his fingers. This startled her. She could not be sure he did this deliberately; perhaps he simply wanted to make sure the fire caught fully. But he left his hand there well longer than required, and the sight evoked a piece of his character that disarmed her. She sensed a small darkness in him, some recklessness or desire for ruin she had not seen before. Finally, he retracted his hand.

The fire grew with assured speed and soon a prickly warmth glowed through the room. Jane thanked him, unsure of how to profusely to do so. "Thank you. Producing a fire is not easy," she said to him.

"You're welcome," he said.

"And the night we danced, I recall you telling me you did nothing well," she said. "But you did that well," she added.

He nodded. "I do some things well," he said. He smiled but did not look at her.

Jane swallowed, unsure of how to take the comment. She tried not to inhale too deeply.

"Feel better, Jane," he said, and touched her elbow. He took his leave.

Jane felt startled by the uncommon mix of teasing and tenderness that seemed to pervade her interactions with him. One moment, he appeared annoyed and distant with her, mocking and making fun, or away somewhere else; the next moment he was patient and attentive, anticipating her needs. She could not make head or tail of it. She ordered herself to stop dwelling on the mystery of his regard for her, for it played no material part in her present predicament. Mulling over the intentions of a person so wholly unconnected with her was a pointless endeavor when her focus should be on returning home.

The fire crackled in the hearth and Jane stared at the clock. The hands read seven o'clock. Jane sighed and, in the absence of a better plan, hoped Sofia would succeed today in finding the means to send her back to 1803. She needed a way to pass the time until then, so she sat in an armchair and opened Fordyce's *Sermons*.

Chapter Twenty-Nine

*J*ane finished Fordyce's *Sermons* for the third time. She had attended to this book previously as an aid to sleep, but now that she had the opportunity to read it in full, she saw it also presented great potential for comedy. The two-volume compendium of lectures on the morality and chastity of young women abounded with sound advice. But after the third reading, she'd exhausted even her capacity for laughter and felt dismayed to discover the hour only reached eleven.

Disobeying Sofia was not her intention. She possessed every desire to do as directed, to make no interaction with the advancements of the twenty-first century, lest she erase herself, her novels, and then the universe, as Sofia had prophesied. She took special care to ignore the candles that turned on from the wall switch and burned brighter than any candle she had seen. She made sure not to marvel at the steel box in the kitchen that froze water and kept the foodstuffs cold. She spent the morning closing her mind off from any sort of admiration, fascination, and calculation about the wonders and advancements of the future time in which she found herself, lest she grow so enamored with the place she might elect to remain, thus ruining everything.

This required no small feat of discipline. The world fascinated Jane. She had taken the grandfather clock apart when she
was eight to see how it worked; her mother declared her insolent
and destructive. Asking a person who spoke her first word at eight
months and taught herself to read at two to not show curiosity at
the world around her rivalled the futility of asking a lioness to
save the antelope for later.

Besides, what harm could it do? Sofia had declared that any
sort of investigation on Jane's part into the twenty-first century
would make her fall in love with it and then change the course
of history, but this notion bore further scrutiny. Not every object
in their future world posed a danger to Jane's existence, surely;
a simple tour of the house to prevent her from descending into
boredom-induced madness could not hurt. Jane promised herself
not to observe too much. Once Sofia discovered the key to Jane
returning home, she would be back in the year 1803 anyway. Jane
nodded to herself, satisfied she committed only a justifiable in-
fraction, and put the sermons down.

She began in the kitchen, which appeared similar to a kitchen
in her own time, a place for storing and preparing food, though
with many of the objects different and without any house staff.
She opened the white box, the one that chilled the foodstuffs
without any ice she could see. Cooked meats and vegetables in
an assortment of boxes and bottles sat inside. She peered at one
bottle. The bottle was made of a clear substance, though not
glass. What was this mysterious substance of which every box
and bottle seemed comprised, which possessed the transparency
of glass but felt much thinner and lighter and smelled faintly of
peat moss? She shook her head yet again at these people and their
inventions. They had conjured so many devices to save time and

to make life easier, yet everyone walked around faster and looking more anguished.

Moving on from the bottle, Jane sighed once more at the abundance of food. She tasted each meat. Spices filled her mouth. One
wore garlic around one's neck to ward off the plague; one did not
put it in food. She tested each bottle of sauce—tasting even more
spices—and then replaced them. She attempted to heave the white
box from its place so she might inspect its posterior to ascertain
how it chilled the items, but it gripped the floor with its weight,
planted heavy as a tree stump, and she abandoned the endeavor
when her back began to ache.

She studied her muslin dress, which lay limp inside the box
of soapy water, which had now ceased washing of its own volition. She attempted to retrieve her dress but could not pry open
the door. She left it alone for fear of enraging the steel box. Upon
opening the drawers and cupboards, she saw they contained
knives and saucepans, some different shapes and sizes than she
had seen before, others exactly as in her own world. Scissors were
the same. She produced water from the fountains in the wash-
room and depressed the flushing mechanism of the indoor privy.
She gasped at the pristine water that filled the white bowl.

She moved on, proceeding down the corridor. She opened the
next door with a gasp; she had assumed it led to the dining room,
but it escorted her to Fred's sleeping quarters. She closed the
door again and stood in the corridor. She refused to violate his
privacy. What lay inside, though? No interest in Fred's personal
belongings gripped her; she desired no discovery of hidden se-
crets, but she did want to see the general layout of a man's bedroom. She had never entered a man's private quarters, not even
her brothers', and saw a literary duty to preserve the accuracy of

any descriptions, should she ever write one. No one was expected back until nightfall; it hurt none to snatch the briefest of glances inside. She pushed the door with her foot. It creaked open.

Inside was an airy space with a bay window that looked out into the garden. A fluffed duvet of duck-egg blue sat upon an obscenely large bed, and a brown leather chair in the corner hosted a man's shirt and trousers. By the window was a set of drawers. Jane opened the top drawer and found a thick pile of paper. Printed words of black, as from a press, covered the pages. A letter sat on top of the pile. Jane picked it up.

Dear sir,

Please find enclosed the first 10,000 words of my young adult novel, Land's End. *I include a self-addressed envelope for the return of the manuscript. Please be in touch if you're interested in reading further.*

Jane scowled at the page, fiercely curious. She remembered back to when her father sent her own novel, *First Impressions,* to Cadell, and the heartache when the publisher sent his reply.

Jane put the letter to one side. The printed title of a manuscript lay underneath. Jane inhaled a slow breath. A floorboard creaked; she looked at the door, guiltily, but the doorway lay bare. The house remained empty, except for herself and this manuscript. She turned to the first page.

Chapter One
It was four P.M. on a Tuesday when George Drummond first decided that firecrackers make terrible pets.

Jane stiffened. Fred had written a novel! She sat on the window ledge and read quickly and with excitement. Phrases she had never heard before littered the pages, as well as enough curse words to make her blush. But once she adjusted to the modern phrases and vernacular, the story engrossed her. A tumor afflicted a woman. In his desperation to save her life, her twelve-year-old son ran some sort of footrace—meant for adults, over an extreme distance—to raise funds to pay for her treatment. Jane found herself turning page after page, hurrying to see if the boy accomplished his task, if he finished the race, if he saved his mother. Before long, she had read halfway through the stack of pages.

"Hello, Jane," a voice said.

She spun around in horror. The manuscript's owner stood in the doorway. Jane froze.

The smile on his face faded as he looked down at her hands. "What are you doing?" he said.

Jane scrambled for an excuse. "I am sorry. I lost track of the hour," she said. She commanded herself to breathe; she felt filled with horror and shame. "What are you doing home? I did not expect you back so soon."

"I came home for lunch. And to see how you were." He shook his head and peered at her with a sheepish look, then held out his hand for the manuscript.

She flinched as he took it. "Why did you never send it?" she asked. Despite her embarrassment at being caught, she could not help herself.

"What?"

"Your manuscript. Why did you never send it to the gentleman in the letter?"

He made no reply. Jane shifted her feet. They stood there in silence until he finally said, "I need to change clothes."

Jane bristled at his tone—not angry, quieter. She wanted to cry. "Goodness, yes. I'm so sorry. Forgive me." Fred said nothing as she scuttled past him and he closed the door behind her.

Jane sat in the kitchen like a scolded child, mortified. Fred emerged from his room wearing the shirt and trousers that had been laid out on his chair.

"Fred, allow me to apologize," Jane said.

He walked past her and did not meet her eye. "Don't go into people's rooms without asking," he said in a soft voice.

"Yes," she said. "I am sorry." He walked out the front door without a farewell. Jane returned to the armchair in the sitting room and opened the sermons once more. She turned to the one entitled "On Female Reserve" and read it in full.

Chapter Thirty

Try as she might, Jane could not chase from her mind the image of Fred's face when he'd discovered her. She reminded herself she did not care one way or the other what he thought of her, but still, she wished for their awkwardness to be reduced as much as possible. She was staying in his house and her journey home relied on his and Sofia's help, and thus to be asked to leave at this juncture would be most inconvenient.

Fred was due home in the late afternoon. Jane planted herself in the armchair and stared at the door, awaiting his return. He walked in, finally, later than expected. Jane sat up from the armchair and waited for his salutation. He removed his brown coat. He nodded Jane a hello but said nothing, then walked to his room. The politeness and indifference of the greeting annoyed her. Silence posed a more worrying challenge than anger; she would have preferred for him to shout at her.

She found herself caught between two worlds of feeling. The first was a desire to make amends with Fred quickly, to restore her good standing in the house. This required that she speak no further of his novel or its characters, but to move quickly to lighter, prettier topics such as the weather or his favorite color. The second was an overwhelming, flame-licked burning to speak

to this man about novels, about writing, about the light and fire
of her life. She waded in with the second, treading softly, and followed him down the corridor.

"Fred, please allow me to apologize again," she said. Fred
closed his door, and Jane stood alone in the hallway. "I know what
I did was unforgivable." Jane spoke to him through the door. "I am
a terrible, horrid person." She hoped this would suffice to placate
him. She waited at the door. He did not open it.

She sighed. "It's of little consolation, but I found your novel
to be beautiful," she mumbled. There continued to be no answer
from behind the door. Jane slumped and wondered how long it
would be before she was asked to leave the house. She nodded and
returned to James Fordyce to await her fate.

After a moment, Fred appeared in the doorway to the sitting
room. He shuffled a foot back and forth and gazed at the floor.
"You liked it?" he asked after a pause.

Jane put down her book. "The story broke my heart," she stated
plainly. "In the best way. I had reader's pain from it."

He furrowed his brow. "'Reader's pain'? What's that?"

"The pain one feels when they must keep reading. My eyes and
brain were exhausted, for I had read so much already, but I kept
turning the pages for I simply had to know what happened next."

He smiled. Jane's heart leapt a little. "There was one thing I did
not understand in your novel, however," Jane said excitedly.

Fred's face fell. "It doesn't make sense. My novel doesn't make
sense."

Jane's heart fell, too, as she recognized how quickly she had
undone all her good work with one imprudent remark. "No, I
apologize!" she said quickly. "What I meant . . . oh goodness," she
cursed herself. She of all people should know better than to criti-

cize someone's work, to offer an opinion, informed or not, with its power to crush. "It shined with brilliance and sweetness. Forget I said anything," she pleaded. She would soon be shown the door if she continued this way.

"No, please tell me. I'd like to know," he said. "Something's not working with it. I feel stuck. I can't seem to write more." He searched her face with pleading eyes.

Jane cringed. She chose her words as carefully as she could. She knew their power; she knew she had a nastiness in her, a judgmental nature. "I could not understand why the little boy danced with his mother," she said. Part of her hoped he asked no further.

"How do you mean?" he asked her.

"It doesn't matter how I mean. I don't know anything, I am a stupid woman, I should never have said anything."

"But you have said something, so please explain what you mean." He placed his hands on his hips and exhaled.

"In the novel, as it is now, the mother asks the little boy to dance, and he does so."

Fred nodded. "What's wrong with that?" he asked.

"It bears false witness to the boy's character." Goodness. Jane could not believe the words leaving her mouth. She insulted his story; now she assassinated his characters. She felt like a pernicious word beast, a horrible witch, monstering his little story, which in all honesty, she found beautiful. "Shall we speak more on this another time?" she offered in a weak voice.

Fred laughed and crossed his arms. "No. What do you know about writing?" he said.

"Nothing, for certain," Jane said. "This is my opinion. I likely misread it."

Fred nodded. "Even still, go on."

Jane inhaled and launched her case about the novel's protago-
nist as quickly as she could. "The scene with the dance did not
ring true. The little boy is angry at his mother, is he not?"

"No, he loves his mother. She's a great woman."

Jane nodded quickly. "I agree. The little boy loves his mother,"
she said. "She hugs him always and remembers his favorite sup-
pers, she kisses his scabs and mends his clothes even though he
never thanks her, she listens to his stories even when the day has
exhausted her. But that does not mean he cannot be vexed with
her. He blames her for the father's abandonment."

Fred sat down in an armchair and was silent.

"I am wrong," Jane said. "I apologize. I should have said
naught."

"I don't know," Fred said. He stared at her and seemed to search
her face. "Please go on," he said, and waited for her to continue.

Jane spoke in her gentlest tone, aware now that this was more
than making amends simply to prevent her being forced out into
the street. She held another writer's soul in her hands, and she
reminded herself not to crush it. "Even though she listens to
him, cares for him, feeds him, the little boy cannot help himself.
He rages against his father's leaving and turns this toward the
only person he can, the parent who stayed. On the day in question, it is the mother's birthday, correct?"

"Yes." Fred scratched his head.

Jane nodded. "The mother tells her son what she wants for her
birthday. 'I don't want any presents. I don't want a cake,' she says.
'My wish is for you to dance with me. I shall put my dress and my
red shoes on and when you come home from school we will dance

to "My Girl." All I want is for you to dance with me.' What is it?" Jane said, noticing Fred's expression.

Fred stared at her. "That's what she said, verbatim."

Jane swallowed. She always remembered words this way, as though reading them from a painting in her mind; others had commented on it before, and it embarrassed her. "Beautiful words are easy to remember," she said quickly, shrugging. "In any case, the boy doesn't want to dance with his mother. He is emerging from childhood, interested more in skylarking with school friends than in his home life. He feels embarrassed by her sentimental request. He makes excuses that he will be busy at the agreed time, but the mother secretly believes he will come. The clock ticks by and the boy does not appear. He has not honored their appointment. The mother curses herself for weeping at the small thing but cannot stop. She takes off her shoes and prepares for bed. Then, at the last minute, when all seems lost, the boy comes. He runs home and as the mother is trudging to bed, he bursts through the front door. He takes his mother's arms and dances with her. The mother cries tears of joy and they are a family once again."

Fred's face bore a look of pain. "What's wrong with that?" he said again in a feeble voice.

Jane watched him and inhaled. "I think the boy does not go home. He refuses the request—out of momentary embarrassment, perhaps a little spite, too—and never dances with his mother."

Fred stared at her then like she had accused him of murder. He shook his head. "No way. It can't happen like that. That's terrible."

"It is terrible. It is sad and horrid and something one might instantly regret, perhaps for the rest of one's life. That's the point. That is life, full of regret."

"But if he doesn't dance with her, we will hate him." Fred stared at the floor now, his face red and sad.

Jane spoke softly. "I liked the little boy a great deal. He was a delicate soul, with a great sadness in his heart. He cared for his sister and loved his mother dearly."

Fred looked up at Jane and their eyes met. His gaze fell once more, like that of a scolded child, and Jane saw the novel's subject in front of her. She likely sat in the room where the scene she spoke of had played out.

She spoke again, softly. "Did you run a footrace for your mother? One meant for adults, though you were still a child?"

"It was a walk from John o' Groats to Land's End. A fourteen-day endurance event."

Jane gasped. "How old were you?"

"Twelve. I entered without telling anyone. When I turned up at the starting line, they tried to stop me. But I ran past them. People cheered for me along the road—a little boy trying to run a man's race. It was great for a while. But on the fourth day, I grew sick. I didn't know how much water you were supposed to drink. I kept walking until I collapsed. I woke up in hospital, with dehydration. A doctor told me I almost died. I wanted to keep going, I even tried to escape the hospital bed, but a nurse caught me." He laughed and bowed his head.

"How far did you go before you collapsed?"

"Two hundred and thirty-two miles."

"You *walked* two hundred and thirty-two miles?"

He nodded.

"What funds did you need to raise?"

"My goal was to raise eight hundred pounds. It was to fly my mum to America. They had invented a new cancer treatment there. Eight hundred pounds was the cost of the plane ticket."

The words flew at her and she received them with curiosity and wonder. How on earth did one *fly* to America? Like a bird? And what magic treated cancer? She reminded herself to remain with the issue at hand. "Did you raise the sum?" she asked him.

"My story made the news. I raised twenty-three thousand pounds."

A fantastical sum. Jane gazed at him with wonder. "Goodness! And your mother, how did she react?"

He smiled, then shook his head and said nothing. He shifted his feet and scratched his head in a way Jane imagined he must have done since he was small. Finally, he spoke.

"I was horrible to my mother," Fred whispered. "I was a spoilt little boy. She did everything for me, and I teased her and was cold to her. I never danced with her, and then she died. I never told her I loved her, not once. Though she said it to me every day."

"You were a little boy. Boys never tell anyone they love them."

"I could have said it once. She died thinking I didn't love her."

"You walked across England to save her. Your mother knew you loved her," she said. Fred shook his head. "It means more if the little boy does not dance with his mother in the novel," she whispered. "We will love him more, the more human he is."

Fred's eyes darted back and forth across Jane's face.

"Are there more pages? I could only find half a novel when I— with an ungallantry which haunts me—entered your quarters."

"I never finished writing it," Fred replied.

"You must!" Jane cried. "Why did you stop?"

Fred shrugged. "I didn't know what to write next. Maybe some of the scenes rang false." He leaned across and tapped her arm with his fist in a playful way. She shivered and blushed at the affectionate touch. "Besides, do you know how hard it is to get a novel published?"

"I have some idea," Jane replied.

"Do you know how many people write novels every year, and they go nowhere? There are enough books in the world. We don't need any more."

"What a dreadful thought."

Fred shrugged. "It got too hard. I didn't know if it was any good. I showed some of the early pages to a friend at work. They offered a few benign, constructive comments, and I shriveled into a ball of embarrassment and vowed never to try anything creative again."

"That is the point at which you must persevere," Jane declared. "The blackest time is before a breakthrough. That moment when all seems lost? That is the moment to keep writing. You must trust your heart, though no end lies in sight. No one can write this story but you. Writing is a lonely profession."

"And what about when the words don't come?" he asked.

Jane nodded. "You grit your teeth and grip the pen and keep going."

"Sounds like agony."

"It is," she replied. "And you fill the page with words, and you read them back and despair."

"Great," he said with a laugh.

"Then the next day, you read it once more, and find two words in the page that were not terrible," she said. "And your heart will sing in a register to shatter a stone." She cleared her throat, aware her voice had risen. "Or so I have heard."

He raised his head and stared at her. When she could no longer meet his eyes, she looked away. "I'll think about it," he said.

"Good. Do," Jane said. She coughed again.

He met her eyes once more and fixed his face in a different look. "Thank you, by the way," he said. "Not for the invading-my-bedroom part, but thank you for the rest. For reading my novel and telling me you enjoyed it. That's not nothing."

"You are welcome," Jane said.

He excused himself to attend to a work appointment and she watched him go. She barely understood how this had unfolded. Earlier she had been in a pit of despair, shunned by him as a room-invading criminal, and she had prepared herself to be imminently jettisoned from the house. Now they were friends again. Not only friends, but comrades. The man before her knew the torment and ecstasy of toiling over a page, as she did, of gambling one's soul to tell a story.

She began to feel a turmoil inside her, a strange instability that had not been there before. The awkwardness between them remained, but it was softer now, and alongside it there was something deeper and more disarming. The way he had begun to look at her, to regard himself around her, was something altogether new, and her behavior toward him had altered, too. There was a familiarity to their actions now, as though they had been through something together, which in a way they had. But there was also a new foreignness to the way they interacted, as though each was wary of the other, equipped with new information, or new feeling. Everything had become tenser.

A part of her wished to never see him again, to no longer be confronted with him. There were more important aims to satisfy, other tasks to complete, like returning home so she could write her books. She needed to stop thinking of him.

Jane tried to remind herself of the things she disliked about him and spent several minutes attempting to compose a list of his faults in her head. When that did not work, she looked for another distraction. She fetched Fordyce and pleaded with herself to begin the next sermon. She ran her eyes over the lines of text and read nothing but reassured herself that eventually, distraction would come.

WHEN SHE GREETED Sofia in the kitchen that evening, her eye caught the glimmer of the glass cabinet that held the liquor and her books. She turned toward it to discover only four books now sat in the pile on the little glass shelf.

A second book had disappeared. *Sense and Sensibility.*

"Did you move it?" Jane asked Sofia, pointing to the empty space where her novel once rested.

Sofia shook her head with a look of horror and picked up a bottle of wine. "I don't understand," she said. "We've done everything right. You've stayed in the house, have you not?"

"I have," Jane replied.

"You have not committed any interactions with the twenty-first century that might jeopardize your chances of returning to 1803?"

"I cannot think of anything," Jane said. "I've spoken to Fred and spent the entire day inside."

"Well, those two acts hardly warrant the calamity we see before us!"

Jane nodded. She made no mention of invading Fred's room,

discovering his manuscript, and everything else. She doubted they posed any relevance to the present predicament.

"I'm sorry, Jane," Sofia said. "I have been lax on my quest. I've preoccupied myself with getting my husband back and rescuing my career. But I will do something now."

"No, Sofia, you have been wonderful. It is I who have erred." Jane swallowed and felt racked with guilt.

Sofia shook her head and placed her hands on her hips. "It's time for drastic measures."

"What will you do?" Jane asked, concerned.

"I will go back to the library. A bigger one this time."

Chapter Thirty-One

Sofia entered the atrium of the University of Bristol library. To say she felt out of place was an understatement. The cavernous redbrick building stretched over four stories. Stacks, computers, and men in cardigans filled the floor. This cathedral of literature, for serious book people, did not exactly welcome her inside. The last literature she'd read was by a journalist who was ruminating on the size of her bottom. Sofia worried that someone might ask her to leave.

It had not always been so. She'd loved reading as a child: she devoured Judy Blume, solved crimes with the Famous Five, and went on a trip with Lewis Carroll. She blamed Noel Streatfeild entirely for her consumptive obsession with shoes. She was once rendered so desperate on a dreary holiday in Blackpool that she had picked up the phone book and read half. Above all, she loved Jane Austen. But Sofia hadn't read a book in so long, she thought she might've forgotten how.

She reached a line of ancient stacks, picked a row at random and trudged down it with a scowl. She felt lost already. She scanned the titles.

"Can I help you?" whispered a voice from the next shelf over.

Sofia peered through the row of books at eye level. The voice came from a librarian, who pushed a cart of plastic-covered books down the opposite stack. "No, thank you," Sofia lied. She pretended to peruse the shelves some more.

"*The Almanac of Ukrainian Poetry,*" he said. He pointed to the book Sofia was pretending to look at. "A cracking read. Many verses on potatoes. Can never have too many poems about them, I say. I have the pocket version on my bedside table." Sofia glared at him. He wore a black collared shirt and creased black trousers, unfashionable and scruffy. "Ah, there. A little smile," he said. "I knew my Ukrainian jokes weren't that bad."

"I'm fine on my own, thank you," Sofia said. The librarian held up his arms in a mock surrender and returned to reshelving books. Sofia moved to the next shelf over.

"Bulgarian poetry is also good," said the librarian. He peeked through a gap in the books again. "They're more laissez-faire with their potato imagery, but you can't have everything."

Sofia sighed.

"Tell me what you're looking for," he said. "I'll let you in on a secret. I've been here before. I might even know where it is."

"No," Sofia answered.

"Is it naughty? It's a naughty book you're looking for, isn't it?"

"No," Sofia said.

"I know. It's *The Da Vinci Code!*" he shouted.

"Lower your voice! We're in a library."

"I'll keep shouting until you tell me."

"Fine," Sofia said. "I'm looking for a book on witchcraft." She coughed.

"That wasn't so hard. Not a problem." He parked his book cart. "I'm Dave Croft, by the way."

"Sofia Wentworth."

"I'm a big fan," said Dave. He held out his hand. Sofia rolled her eyes and shook it.

Dave showed Sofia to the fourth floor. He ushered her into a small room with stacks of dusty shelves. "We have a whole witch section," he said cheerfully. "We burned them like mad in the West Country." He offered Sofia a book. It was bound in heavy black leather. "The *Malleus Maleficarum*, 1487. The seminal work on witches from the height of the craze. Written by a priest who was quite angry, it seems. This is your A1 guide to witches. How to spot 'em, how to arrest 'em, how to burn 'em." He smiled brightly.

Sofia picked up the book. "Do you have anything more vocational?" she asked.

He raised an eyebrow. "Vocational?"

She shrugged and spoke casually. "You know, from the witch's perspective. Like how one might make a spell, for example."

Dave smiled. "You mean a spell book? You want to cast a spell?"

"Don't be silly," she said with a laugh. She paused. "Actually, I want to reverse one. A real spell. Made by a real witch."

"Does this witch have a name?" Dave said.

"She did, in fact. Her name was Mrs. Sinclair," Sofia said. "What?"

"Oh gosh, sorry," Dave replied with a laugh. "I thought you were joking."

"I know you think me a fool. That I'm just some beautiful actress, chased into insanity by tragedy and scandal." She adjusted her sunglasses.

"I don't think you're a fool. What's the spell for?"

"If you must know, Jane Austen is living in my house." She cleared her throat.

He stared at her and seemed to stifle a smile. "Jane Austen."

Sofia nodded. "Witty writer lady. She's living here, in my house—my brother's house, actually; I don't buy ones that small. She cast a spell and was magicked through time and ended up here. Now she needs to reverse said spell to travel back to her own time. Yes, I understand how loopy I sound. No, I don't expect you to believe me. See, I told you, bookman. It's better if you leave me in peace. Thank you for your help, but now I have work to do." She gathered up her enormous tote bag and shawl.

"Hey. Don't go," said Dave. "I'm sorry." She ignored him and made her way out of the stacks. "At least leave a number where I can reach you," he called after her.

She paused and turned. "What for?"

He shrugged. "In case I find anything."

She scoffed. "You won't." But she walked back to him and wrote a number on a slip of paper. "Here. Happy? Can I go now?" She handed him the paper, cursed herself for coming there, and walked to the elevator. It opened and she stepped inside.

"Wait, stay," Dave followed and called after her. But she pressed the button and the doors had already closed.

THAT AFTERNOON, SOFIA rejoiced in her first dress rehearsal with Courtney Smith. Derek once again fashioned her face to flawless perfection with his no-makeup makeup, but his finest efforts were rendered pointless when Courtney again stepped into the truck.

"All right, missus?" she said in a reasonably decent Yorkshire accent. Sofia ran her mind back over the inflection and was disappointed to find it accurate. She bristled with jealousy.

"Sorry about that. I've been chatting with Mick the grip? He's from a town up north. Thought I'd try some British, to get me into the mood. Show me your costume, then," Courtney said.

Sofia turned around and smiled. This at least she could be proud of. Her agent had spoken to the producers. Sofia now wore a very pretty, slim, cream silk gown, demure and elegant. She resembled a lovely, sparkly Greek column. Her fans—and Jack—would love her in this gown.

"I'm not sure," Courtney said, pointing to the dress.

"I beg your pardon?" Sofia said with a laugh. "What is the matter?"

Courtney shrugged. "I could be wrong, but maybe that dress isn't right for this picture?"

"How? It's exactly the style of the period."

"I know, but it's wrong for your character. Mrs. Allen is a humorous person, not a sex symbol. She's supposed to make people laugh."

Sofia grimaced. Even if Courtney was right, who was she, an actress, to be commenting on another actress's costume?

"I'll be back," Courtney said. Sofia and Derek looked at each other and shrugged. Courtney soon returned with a wardrobe person who looked worried. The woman carried another dress on a hanger. "Try this on," Courtney said, and offered the dress to Sofia.

She studied the dress and gasped. "I will not."

"It's just a rehearsal. Try it on. If it doesn't work, you can take it off again."

Sofia rolled her eyes and ducked behind the curtain to change. She reemerged and stood in front of them. Derek snickered.

"What is it, Derek?"

"It's hysterical," he said, his face falling as he saw Sofia's expression. "Oh. Is it not meant to be?" Sofia ran to the mirror and surveyed her reflection. Lime-green velvet composed the dress's main features. A giant purple bow, also in velvet, festooned the bosoms. The accompanying headpiece had actual fruit in it. If she had looked like a peacock before, she resembled a frog now.

"It's perfect," Courtney declared.

"What? No, you must be joking," Sofia said.

"You look hilarious," Courtney said with a nod. "It's a brilliant costume. The audience will howl with laughter."

"Too bad," Sofia said with an outraged laugh. "I already had a dress. I'm going to change back into it."

"What's wrong? Leave it on," Courtney said. "It's what Jack wants."

Jack. Oh God. "It most certainly is not."

"Let's ask him. Go get Jack," Courtney said to the wardrobe person, who scurried away with a look of fear.

"Don't bring Jack into this! Oh, hi," Sofia said as Jack appeared.

"Whoa," he said as he stepped into the truck. He stared at Sofia.

"Exactly," Sofia said. "Thank you." She felt a mixture of two things: relief that he did not like the dress, and embarrassment that he was seeing her in it. "I'll take it off. I have a lovely cream dress which I'll slip into. Excuse me," she said and moved to change.

Courtney touched his arm. "No, Jack, you're missing the point." Sofia blinked at the way Courtney spoke to him. He wouldn't stand for it.

"What is the point, young lady?" he said to Courtney with a smile. Sofia's heart sank a little. He seemed to be standing for it.

"The point is, Sofia's character is meant to be humorous. Jane Austen wrote comedies, remember? This will honor that."

Sofia bristled. She found herself in a battle of two warring parts. On the one hand, she wanted to look devastatingly glamorous on-screen in a beautiful gown, break hearts, and show Courtney up. On the other hand, she worshipped Jane Austen, and doing right by the little woman now living in her brother's house would involve honoring this infernal child's suggestion. She cursed Jane for the dilemma.

Jack looked at them both. "It's a good idea," Jack said. "You don't mind, do you, Sofe?"

"I suppose not," Sofia said. She didn't mind most things when he called her "Sofe." He used to call her that all the time.

"Cool," he said.

"Cool," Courtney repeated. She winked at him and followed him out of the makeup truck.

Sofia stood there and watched them go.

ONCE UPON A time, Sofia's beauty had disarmed. When she was fourteen years old, a man had walked up to her on a darkened train platform, drunk. "You're the hottest piece of arse I've ever seen," he declared. He was at least thirty-five. She was terrified. Then she learned to use it. She studied herself in the mirror each day until she had shaped a set of looks, walks, and laughs. By the time she was fifteen, tales of her beauty swept the length of her village.

The body matched the face in perfection. Sofia was not just thin, she was curved, like the hood of a race car. If you wanted to get all scientific about it, as some of the movie nutritionists did in awed voices, she maintained a fat percentage homeostasis known as bikini, hovering around 18 percent, never wavering, and most of that was bosom and bottom. She never counted calories, anguished, or starved. If she indulged over Christmas, she would eat carefully for three days and be back to her best. Nothing else was required; she was born that way.

She had made her way to London as soon as she could, one of the youngest students ever accepted into RADA's hallowed halls. The other students pointed and whispered; they said she didn't get in on talent, she wouldn't graduate. Eight months out from finishing, when the Royal Shakespeare called looking for an Ophelia, Sofia auditioned, was offered, and accepted the role. So the students were right.

She did TV and theater for a few years, good British stuff, always playing the same role whether she was a policewoman, a lawyer, or a medical intern. She was the harlot with the heart of gold, the damaged love interest. Too beautiful to play anyone serious. She eked out a good living, but she wanted more. As soon as she had enough money saved, she bought a one-way ticket to Los Angeles. Three months later, she was Batgirl.

When Sofia first slipped into that batsuit, the black oily skin hugging her hips and breasts like a glove, no straight man in the audience (and quite a few of the women) was the same again. It was only a comic book movie, but desire transcended even the silliest of settings. Bronwyn, the hair and makeup designer, dyed Sofia's hair red to go with the slinky black leotard, old-Hollywood style, like Rita Hayworth's. It turned out to be a masterstroke: Sofia already looked like no one else, but with the crimson hair, she was truly in a league of her own. Sofia was only playing a supporting character, but she romped and whipped her way through the film. Under the lights, her hair bouncing on her shoulders in voluptuous flaming curls, Sofia stole the show. History was made, records were broken, and a star was born.

Sofia liked the red hair so much, she kept it. The color became her calling card, a tidal wave of rich ruby velvet that crowned her head, like no other.

Then one day, at age thirty-four, Sofia caught her reflection in a mirror in daylight. A crow's-foot stared back at her. Minuscule and imperceptible to anyone but her, a trench ran from the corner of her left eye and dragged gently down her cheekbone. Sofia knew she was still a fine-looking woman, by world standards. But she did not live in the world. She lived in magazines and on billboards, where pores were magnified and wrinkles were to scale. She'd gasped at the small crack in her face and pleaded with herself to remain calm. But by the end of that year, a second crow's-foot had joined the first. Her skin grew coarser and sagged in places. But under certain lights and with makeup, she still looked damn good, she told herself.

A few months later, a director did not return her call, something that had never happened before. She thought she would be good for a part in his next movie, the love interest of a naval officer trying to find himself. The part went to someone ten years her junior and she felt incredibly foolish. The next month, a fashion brand quietly severed its contract. She reassured herself that things would be okay. She had traded in only one currency for over a decade; now its value had dropped. But surely people didn't love her just for her looks. That power she'd first wielded at fourteen was gone, but she had other things of value to offer, no?

Sofia stood in the makeup room, on the wrong side of thirty-five, and tried to convince herself she was right.

"You know why Courtney's doing this, right?" Derek said. "The green dress, the no makeup? She's trying to make you quit."

"What?" Sofia replied, tearing herself away from her reflection and turning to him. "I would never quit," she said in a stern voice. But then she considered it. If she quit, she would never have to appear in that horrid dress again. She would never have to make a fool of herself on camera, alienating her fans and destroying her career. Quitting seemed quite the attractive option in certain respects. But then, what about Jack? What would happen between them if she quit? She would likely never see him again. It was not an option. No quitting.

She turned to Derek. "I'm not quitting, mister," she told him.

Derek nodded. "Good for you, Ms. Wentworth."

Then she caught her reflection again and laughed ruefully, regretting the statement as quickly as she'd said it. "But what should I do? I don't even want to step onto the set again. Acting beside her is horrible. It's one embarrassment after another. She hates me. I feel like I'm at school, being bullied by the ugly, smelly girl. Only she's not ugly and smelly, she's beautiful, younger, and smells rather good."

Derek grabbed her shoulders. "You want to take down a bully?"

Sofia felt startled by his enthusiasm. "I suppose," she answered carefully.

"Speaking as a person who encountered some bullies in their time," he said, "bullies only understand one thing—weakness. They go after the weakling. Are you a weakling?"

"I don't believe so."

"No, you are not," he said forcefully.

"So what do I do, then?"

"Stand up for yourself," Derek replied.

"How? I can't compete with her," she said wearily.

"Yes, you can."

"But, how—"

He interrupted her. "You're a smart woman. You already know what to do."

She glanced at herself in the mirror once more, thinking. She turned to him and nodded and tried to form a plan.

Chapter Thirty-Two

*J*ack requested a lens flare on all of Courtney's shots, so while a polite gaffer from Shropshire ran around looking for a teeny tiny mirror, Sofia stood to the side of the sound stage watching Courtney rehearse on her own. "Could you move, Sofia? You're in my eyeline," Courtney called out. Everyone turned to look at Sofia.

Sofia realized she was staring into space. "Goodness, sorry. Of course." She stepped aside, embarrassed.

Courtney finished her rehearsal and walked over. "Sorry for shouting just now," Courtney said, smiling with bright, insincere eyes. "My eyeline is important to me."

"It's all right. I know," Sofia said apologetically. "I was daydreaming, I made an error."

"It's understandable," Courtney said. "It makes sense—you're from a theater background. Eyelines don't matter to you."

Sofia stiffened. "I understand the importance of maintaining an eyeline."

"But you do come from the theater originally?"

"Well, yes."

Courtney tossed her hair. "All I was trying to say. Makes sense now. Why you lost *Batgirl*."

Sofia turned to her and glared. "I beg your pardon?"

Courtney laughed. "I just mean, you come from the theater—you didn't train in film, so your acting is theatrical, old-fashioned. Maybe you do better in the theater."

Sofia burst out with laughter. "You think I lost *Batgirl* because I'm a theater-trained actress?" She searched the girl's face. What was she playing at?

Courtney smiled back at her. "Of course," she replied in a deliberate tone. "Why else?"

"It will be another five on that mirror, ladies," an assistant director said to them, scratching his head. "Take a seat."

A runner brought over some chairs and they sat down. "Where did you go to school, then?" Sofia said to her.

"Beverly Hills High," Courtney replied with a yawn.

"Sorry. I meant where did you train? USC? The Actors Studio?"

"I didn't go to drama school."

"Oh." Sofia raised her eyebrows.

"It's never been a problem."

"You never studied acting?" Sofia said it with genuine interest and surprise, but it seemed to touch a nerve.

"I'm proud I didn't go to drama school," Courtney said. "This stuff can't be taught. It's all about instinct."

"You don't think there are benefits to studying acting, learning dramatic process?" Sofia said.

"Nope," said Courtney with a grin. "You either have it or you don't."

"I studied for five years," Sofia said.

"You can tell," said Courtney pointedly. "Yours is better for specific roles, mine is better for others."

Sofia smiled. "Yours is better for, say, Batgirl?"

"Obviously." A small crowd of camera assistants began to lean toward them, craning their ears as they fixed a teeny tiny mirror to the camera.

"I was super concerned coming into this," Courtney said. "I can reveal that now. I mentioned to a few people that our acting styles don't match."

"In what way?" Sofia asked through gritted teeth.

"Mine is natural. Yours is theatrical. You were so lucky to get *Batman* again the last time."

Sofia scoffed. "And what do you consider 'natural' acting, dear?"

"Natural acting is feeling it," Courtney said. "You know, getting into character. I don't know!" She threw up her arms, like she was making an offering.

"And you believe you are the better actor?" Sofia asked.

Courtney shook her head violently. "Of course not!" Then she shrugged. "Well, if we look at what part I'm playing, and look at what part you're playing . . ." She shrugged again, then sighed. "All I'm saying is, acting is easy. You take it so seriously, whereas I am so much more relaxed. I just let things flow. And it shows in my work." Courtney began talking faster, growing more out of breath. "It's not the end of the world, we can't all be the best." More crew people, lighting and grips, moved toward the camera to check if they needed help affixing the mirror. They aimed their ears at the conversation as they helped.

Sofia inhaled. "Care to have a little wager?" she asked. "Why don't we both act out the same scene and decide who is the better actor?"

Courtney spluttered with laughter. "What? No way."

"You don't think you will win?" Sofia said.

Courtney looked around. An entire crew of people were watching. "Of course I will," she spat. "Fine. You're on," she said.

"Splendid," Sofia replied.

The crew now abandoned their mirror-affixing pretense and turned to watch, clearing a space on the rehearsal set without comment. Courtney saw the gathered crowd and exhaled with a bored look. "Fine. What's the scene? Something from *Batman*, I bet," she said. The crowd chuckled.

"The scene is 'Fill me a bucket with water,'" Sofia replied.

"That's it?" Courtney laughed to some of the crowd. The crowd sniggered back. Sofia could not tell how many of the crew were on her side, and how many would be for Courtney. She had heard that Courtney had been rude with many of them, issuing demands for coconut water and imported gummy bears like a sugar-addicted tinpot dictator, but perhaps they still loved her out of fear, or because she was the young, pretty one.

Sofia swallowed and hoped she was doing the right thing. She didn't know if she had the requisite nerve left to pull this off. "There is a tap over there," Sofia said. She pointed to the opposite side of the sound stage.

"I don't see it," said Courtney. She squinted. The crowd all looked over as well. "There's no tap there," she said.

"It's called acting," Sofia said.

"Oh, ha. I get it. The tap is imaginary. I'll bet the bucket is too, right?" said Courtney.

"You are a smart one," Sofia said. "Here is your challenge. Walk to the tap, fill your bucket with water, then carry the bucket back here and place it at my feet."

"That's it? No dialogue?"

"No dialogue. Just fill and carry a bucket."

Courtney rolled her eyes. "Fine with me." She shook her arms and lunged, then stretched her neck, touching her head to each shoulder. "Just warming up," she said, to giggles from the crew. She exhaled a long, exaggerated breath, then she skipped over to the "tap" and turned it on, waited for her "bucket" to fill, then skipped with it back to Sofia. She swung the imaginary bucket back and forth and whistled the theme tune to *Batman* as she went. She swished her shoulders and sashayed across the floor. She popped her hips and winked to a camera assistant, who blushed and fondled a light meter. The performance oozed with cuteness; the crew chuckled and wolf-whistled. Finally, she flung the imaginary bucket at Sofia's feet and saluted like a gymnast who had finished a difficult routine. The crew laughed and applauded. "Your turn," said Courtney. "I bet you can't do it whistling."

"You have me there," Sofia said. "I don't know how to whistle. One of the great tragedies of my life. Nevertheless, I shall endeavor to match the rest. First, may I inquire about your bucket?"

"My bucket?" Courtney repeated.

"Yes. The bucket you carried the water in, just now. What kind was it?"

Courtney scoffed. "It was just a bucket, I don't know."

"Was it a plastic bucket? Or steel?"

Courtney shrugged, looking bored. "What the hell? Plastic."

"Wonderful. How much water does it hold?"

"How should I know? It's a make-believe bucket! Who cares?"

"Make-believe is your livelihood, dear. I care." The crowd shifted and went quiet.

Courtney glared at her. "I don't know, six gallons," she said.

"Six gallons. My goodness! I'm afraid I cannot confess as much expertise with imperial measurements as you. Another paradox of British units of measure, you see—while we're all inches and feet for distance, we're mils and liters for volume. No matter. I guess six gallons is about twenty liters."

"Twenty-two," Derek called from the crowd, smartphone in hand.

Sofia beamed. "Twenty-two! Thank you, Derek. Now, here's one equation I do know: that wonderful metric system which says one liter of water equals one kilogram of weight. Love the neatness, don't you?" Courtney nodded and made no remark. "How rude of me. I know what a kilogram is, but you don't, of course. Let's see if I can find an equivalent for you. Derek, you have a nephew, do you not? The lovely young man who visited set yesterday."

"I do," said Derek, with a delighted look on his face. "John."

"How much does John weigh?"

"Three and a half stone, I'd guess. About twenty kilograms."

"And how old is your nephew?"

"Ten."

A gasp rippled through the crowd. Courtney turned to the sound and swallowed. She focused again on Sofia, a worried look now gracing her face. "Ten years old," Sofia repeated. "I'm thinking the bucket you carried to hold that much water, Courtney, big enough to fit a ten-year-old inside, might be one of those white buckets with the thin steel handle, the ones fishermen put the fish guts in?"

Courtney blinked. "Fine."

"Good, then." Sofia stood. "May I borrow your bucket?" She pointed to the ground by Courtney's feet where there was nothing but air.

The younger actress rolled her eyes. "Be my guest."

Sofia picked up the imaginary bucket and walked over to the imaginary tap. She turned the tap to the left. "Righty tighty, lefty loosey," she sang. Courtney, who had turned her hand to the right, swallowed. Sofia waited at the tap for a full minute while the imaginary bucket filled. Courtney sneered and tapped her foot. "Right to the top, you filled it?" she checked with Courtney. The girl glared.

Sofia turned off the imaginary tap and bent her knees with great ceremony. She picked up the imaginary bucket with two hands, wincing at the imaginary weight. She passed the bucket over to her right hand then waddled to the other side of the room, dipping her hips with each step to catch the bounce of the imaginary bucket onto her thigh. She reached halfway across the room and swapped to her left hand, stretching out her right hand in relief. She dropped the imaginary bucket at Courtney's feet with a thud and wiped her brow.

Mutters and chortles rose from the assembled crowd. "Clever," said Courtney. "Too theatrical for most people's taste, though."

"I see I have not won you over yet," Sofia said with a nod. "I wonder. I think I saw one of those white buckets by catering. You, sir, could you investigate?" She pointed to the runner, who scurried off. Courtney sneered at Sofia, but Sofia just smiled back.

The runner returned. "Splendid!" Sofia patted him on the back and turned to Courtney. "You as the star of this film, please do us the honor. Show us how it's done." She offered Courtney the bucket.

"No, thanks," Courtney said. She tried to walk away but the gathered crew had crowded by the exit, smiling and waiting, and she could not easily pass through. She turned back.

"Come now, we are but students of your easy acting style," Sofia said. "There's a tap over there. Unless you don't want to? Unless you're worried?"

Courtney took the bucket and walked over to a real tap by the back wall of the sound stage. She turned it to the left and water poured into the real-life bucket. Courtney had filled her imaginary bucket for all of two seconds. It took exactly a minute for the real bucket to fill.

"Takes forever, doesn't it?" Sofia said.

Courtney grabbed the handle and lifted. Her arm wrenched, and the bucket stayed on the floor. She winced. She bent her knees and tried to lift it again, this time with both hands. She grimaced, and the bucket came off the ground. She waddled across the room with gritted teeth. The bucket bounced on her thigh and she almost tripped over. She reached the halfway point and it seemed she could stand the bucket no longer in her right hand, bogged down with the weight of a ten-year-old child inside, and switched it to her left. Despite every impulse to resist, she stretched her right hand out, red and aching from the task. She could not have managed a closer match of Sofia's own bucket-carrying if she did so on purpose.

She dumped the bucket at Sofia's feet and stormed off. The crowd stomped and whistled and cheered Sofia's name. Sofia stifled a grin and nodded, keen not to appear a sore winner.

Derek held up his hand for a high five and Sofia slapped it with her own.

"Wow, Ms. Wentworth," he said.

"Okay, moving on, everyone," the assistant director called out to the gathered crowd. "We've got the mirror sorted. We're back in five." The crew dispersed, revealing Jack standing over by the camera. He looked at Sofia, a hint of amusement on his face. Her heart leapt.

"I've never seen that before. You showed her," Derek said.

Sofia nodded and kept her eyes on Jack across the way, enjoying his smile. Then she squinted. "What did I show her, exactly?" she asked Derek.

He shrugged. "Youth is more important than talent."

Sofia smiled but said no more. Jack walked back to his trailer and Sofia watched him go.

"Ms. Wentworth. I want to tell you something, and I mean this in the nicest possible way," Derek said.

Sofia turned to him. "What is it, Derek?"

"Ms. Wentworth. You can act."

"Thanks, Derek," Sofia said with a laugh.

She knew this somewhere deep down, but the words had a greater effect on her than he likely intended.

Chapter Thirty-Three

You like good stories, then?" Fred asked Jane that morning. "Are you a movie buff, too?"

"Mov-ie? I don't know what that is." They were in the sitting room; Jane was reading her sermons again.

Fred laughed. "You don't know what a movie is? You're acting in one."

Jane inhaled sharply, aware she had again hinted at her unorthodoxy. She scoured her brain as quickly as she could. *Mov-ie.* Sofia had mentioned it, she remembered now. The theater production, but fancier. "Yes, I know this thing!" she declared eagerly, hoping it was enough to remedy the situation.

He laughed and shook his head. "You are a strange one," he said. He did not say it derisively or cruelly, but still, it bothered her. In fact, it made her irrationally angry.

"I am not strange, thank you. I am entirely normal," she insisted, breathing heavily. She of course detested this line of conversation, well aware of how strange she truly was. An author who had travelled through time: on a scale of strangeness, that likely sat toward the high end. More than that, however, she disliked being called strange by *him*.

He laughed again. "Sure, whatever you say." He crossed his arms and leaned on the doorframe.

She eyed him suspiciously and felt relieved. He seemed not to have discovered her secret just yet. But she also felt outrageously annoyed at his teasing. What had happened to the rapprochement of yesterday, the deliverance and intimacy of sharing in his writing? It had gone back to him making fun of her, and her reacting with indignant anger.

"Want to go to one?" he said. He cleared his throat and looked at the floor. "A movie, that is."

Jane scowled. He clearly disliked her, yet once again he seemed to be inviting her to some sort of event. She shrugged; he must be a glutton for punishment. "Oh. I don't know," she replied.

"We can go this afternoon, when I get home from school."

She stared at him. "Are you sure? You've made it quite clear I infuriate you each time I open my mouth."

He smiled at her and scratched his head. "You do infuriate me each time you open your mouth. That's why we're going. You have to be quiet at the movies."

She narrowed her eyes. "Actually, no. I cannot go outside," she replied in a haughty tone. She spoke the truth. Sofia had been firm on this. She felt glad for the excuse to refuse him: she did not want to go now he was obnoxious once more.

"That's the beauty of the movies—they're inside." He coughed again.

"I see." She found herself unable to think of another reason to say no. She could not tell him the truth, obviously, so she decided the safer option was just to accept his invitation. "All right, then," she said. "I will go with you."

"Looking forward to it already," he said.

"And I," she shot back. She shook her head again, confused as to why this man, who clearly found her disagreeable, kept inviting her on outings. She had never understood men before and seemed on no path to reaching further comprehension anytime soon.

Later that day, they walked to some sort of theater house at the corner of one of the lanes behind the main square of New Bath. They entered the foyer.

"Who are they?" Jane exclaimed, gasping at a curious sight that stood inside. A group of ten women, laughing and chatting, walked toward her in muslin gowns, à la grecque, as she donned herself in her own time. They wore bonnets, gloves, and pelisses, and giggled and gossiped as though they made their way to a ball or an assembly. Jane thought she had stepped into 1803 once more.

Fred looked to where she pointed and smiled. "Hey, man. What are the costumes for?" he asked a young person who swept the floor with a wooden broom.

"We're hosting a Jane Austen film festival," the sweeper replied. "To celebrate the new movie being shot in town, we're showing all the films made from her books."

"Cool," Fred replied. "This is one of the actors from the shoot." He pointed to Jane.

The young man put down his broom and held his hand out. "Nice. What part do you play?"

"Oh, I, um . . ." Jane stared at him, wide-eyed, and scrambled for a suitable answer. The only line she could recall was one Sofia had taught her; she spat it out in a strangled voice. "I am an actress. I am from the twenty-first century," she said.

The man stared at her with a smile and seemed to wait for her to elaborate. She did not. "I get it. Top secret, huh?" he said. "You could tell me but then you'd have to kill me?" Jane stared back at him and sighed, understanding nothing, then nodded dumbly and hoped it was sufficient.

"Okay, then," he said mercifully, and returned to his sweeping.

"Shall we see a Jane Austen movie?" Fred said to her.

"Yes," Jane said, burning with curiosity, and then, "No!" almost as quickly. "Sorry, no, I don't want to," she added. She was aware she acted rather strangely, yet again, but this time it could not be helped. She felt well-versed by now in the risks of exposing herself to her own creative output, and as she was already breaking one of Sofia's rules by venturing outside, she did not feel the need to violate another for the sake of something as silly as a movie.

"That's okay, we'll see something else. Not a fan of Jane Austen, huh?" Fred said with a smile. "You don't like her stuff?"

"No," Jane said, keen to maintain the ploy. "Dreadful stuff."

Fred nodded. "Probably feels a bit like work, I guess." He purchased tickets and ushered Jane inside a darkened theater.

"What is this place?" she asked him.

"The movie theater?" he replied with a resigned laugh, pointing to the stage area. "As I said, you are a strange one."

Jane glowered at him again and went to provide him with a rebuttal, but she found herself too astounded by the sights around her to argue further.

A huge screen of fabric, twenty feet high, stood across the stage, from which a sort of theater production beamed out to them with lights and sound. Jane gasped. They sat down and the theater grew dark. The crowd hushed; the main show began. Jane watched the actors move and perform in the frame. "It's like tele-vision, only bigger," Jane whispered to Fred.

He turned to her and chuckled. "That's right."

The story unfolded over various scenes. A ship moved through the universe, past planets and the sun. The ship's crew rivalled Odysseus and his men for their prolific touring and adventures. Jane hung on every word. During a quiet moment in the story, she looked around the theater. The audience all stared up at the screen, as she did, bound by its spell.

A realization came to her. In the theater next door, those women, dressed in their muslin gowns, watched a production in the same vein as this, with the terrific sounds, actors, and theater sets. Only there, the theater played a story from Jane's own head. Jane inhaled. Her mind leapt in circles.

"I see now!" she cried out in the darkened theater.

"Do you mind?" a young man in the row of seats behind them said.

"A thousand apologies," she said. She turned to Fred. "They watch a Jane Austen story next door!" Multiple audience members turned in their seats this time and hissed angry shushes at her. She apologized again.

Fred nodded to her with a laugh and whispered, "Yes, a Jane Austen film plays in the other theater."

Jane inhaled. She looked once more at the audience who watched the screen, and then thought of the women in the muslin dresses and bonnets. They were there for *her*. The idea required such leaps of her mind and stirrings of her soul that she could barely grasp it fully. Seeing her books in print, the museum built in her honor, now this . . . it all contributed to a growing suspicion that she might not know the half of what she was to become—what she meant now. Jane closed her eyes for a moment, before watching the rest of the story in awed silence.

When it ended, the audience stood to leave. "Did you like it?" Fred asked her.

"Can we see another?" she asked him.

Fred chuckled. "Sure. Whenever you like."

"Thank you," Jane said to him. "That was extraordinary." She felt too filled with wonder to argue with him now, so she settled for genuine feeling. She looked over, expecting him to be laughing at her, but he was not. His face bore a look of joy.

"Good to get out of the house," he said. They walked home and spoke at length of the story, the ship on its journey through space, the characters. They did not argue; there were other things of which to speak.

LATER, FRED CAME to Jane, and asked, "Now that you're well enough to go outside"—he still believed this lie, bless him—"do you not want to explore Bath?"

"I have been to Bath before," she answered.

"Bath is beautiful, even if you have already been here."

"I do not care for it," she replied. She spoke the truth.

"Yes," Fred said. "You've said so, a few times."

Jane bristled. "I have not."

He nodded. "Once yesterday, you said how much you disliked Bath. The day before, I think you may have sneered when I mentioned Stall Street."

"Utter nonsense," Jane scoffed. She was dismayed, both that her dislike of Bath was so obvious, and also that he recalled things she had said, as though he was interested in what she had to say and had made note of them.

Fred laughed. "What do you not care for? The buildings? Not the people, I hope." He raised an eyebrow.

"While I am loath to criticize the town of your birth, it is the most incurious place in England," she said. "Some of its people have charm, I grant you," she added quickly.

Fred leaned on the door. "It's not all bad."

"Name one place in Bath that is at all clever or interesting."

"How about the Pump Room?"

"The worst place of all!" Jane cried. "Tea drinking and schemes. A forum for gossips and blockheads." She heard her voice rising. She stared at the floor.

"Oh. I found it quite nice. The bath itself is incredible," he said.

"Perhaps," Jane said. "I could not say. I have not been inside."

"Unfair, then; you cannot critique it. That's as bad as burning a book you haven't read."

"You make a good point," Jane said begrudgingly. "It was not that I did not want to go," she said in a soft voice. She stared out the window and hoped he did not detect the pain in her voice and pity her. "I never had reason to go there. I am not the type they like in their establishment."

"I find that hard to believe," Fred said.

She swallowed. "I was invited once," she said.

He looked at her. "What happened? Why didn't you go?"

"The gentleman . . . it never eventuated," she said. "I am not welcome there," she added quickly. She stopped talking then, commanding herself to stop feeling pain over such an idle memory.

Fred looked surprised. "Trust me," he said. "You'd never say you hate Bath again, once you've laid eyes on the Roman baths. The original foundation is almost two thousand years old. The emperor built it for his sweetheart. It's romantic."

Jane was well aware of the story; she had been told the same thing herself many times. She may have even read one or two books on the subject, on the baths and their history, on how romantic, magical, and beautiful the place was. This was all well and good, and not for her.

"I do not care for the concept of romance," Jane stated flatly. "Romance is fakery. Flowers from the hothouse and sweets do not equal regard."

"I agree," said Fred. "Those things aren't romance."

Jane frowned. "What is romance, then?"

"Romance is being thoughtful. It is rubbing someone's feet after their long day. Even if their feet stink."

"Sounds dreadful," Jane declared, though secretly she found the image lovely.

"Romance is knowing someone's secret desires and fulfilling them," Fred said.

Jane swallowed.

"Will you go somewhere with me?" he asked then.

"Where?" Jane asked. Her heart still thumped from his last remark.

"It is a surprise. Something I want to show you."

Jane shook her head in frustration and found herself unable to contain herself any longer. He infuriated her. "I am sorry, sir, but I must say, your behavior confuses me."

He raised an eyebrow and laughed. "How do I confuse you?" he asked.

"I struggle to see why you persist in inviting me on outings," Jane said to him. "You have made clear your dislike for me," she began.

"Have I?" he asked.

"Yes," she insisted, flinching. "You tease me and laugh at me and you have mistaken my character. You don't know who I am. You do not see me at all."

"I see you perfectly well."

"What do you see?" she said, squinting.

"I see a person of intelligence, so much that it scares me," he said.

Jane swallowed. "Really," she said incredulously.

"I see a cold person with a warm heart. A judgmental person, but with good reason. Someone who has been hurt so is watchful now." Jane stared at him. "Someone who doesn't suffer fools, and why should she? I see someone who loves people, despite what they may have done to her. I see an optimist—"

"An optimist?" Jane interrupted. She scoffed. "Hardly."

"An optimist, yes," he said. "Someone who pretends they hate the world, when really they see such beauty in it that they want to live as long as they can, try everything, see everything." He scratched his shoulder. "I see a person so beautiful it takes my breath away." He paused and looked right at her. "Which part of what I have said is wrong?"

Jane found herself gripped with such astonishment that she felt unable to speak. She could not meet his eye. No one had ever said such things. She glanced at the ceiling, then the floor.

A minute might have passed, or maybe an hour. Finally, he spoke again.

"So, will you go with me?" he said.

She remained stunned to silence. She could still move her head, though, so she nodded.

"Meet me downstairs, tomorrow," he said. "At a quarter to midnight."

"A quarter to midnight?" she asked. "What purpose requires such a late hour?"

"You'll see." He looked at her with a conspiratorial eye that made her swallow again. "Until then, Jane."

"Until then," she replied.

Jane returned to the book of sermons and forced herself to read once more. She heard herself inhale and exhale loudly and told herself to be calm. She coasted dangerously close to something—she was not quite sure what—and although she wanted to stop, she felt like there was not a force on earth that could do so.

WHEN SOFIA ARRIVED home that night, she said, "I'm so sorry, Jane. My voyage to the library was a disaster. I found no information on how to return you home. You've been waiting patiently inside all day with nothing to do and you entrusted your future life and happiness to me. I tried to find help and failed miserably."

"You did not fail, Sofia," Jane replied. Sofia's face looked pained.

"I had a rough day. But I promise I will keep trying."

"Thank you, Sofia. I appreciate everything."

"Unfortunately, you won't be returning to your own time today. I hoped to have better news. You'll have to stay here another night. I'll try again tomorrow. Don't hate me."

"Of course not," Jane replied. "I could never hate you." She looked across the way as Fred walked into the kitchen. She turned back to Sofia quickly, hoping she hadn't seen. Jane swallowed. She felt gripped between anxiety that her chances of returning home were slipping away, and relief that she was allowed to stay one more day.

A chime of oddly metallic bells sounded from Sofia's clothes and broke her reverie. "Is there a bell in your pocket?" Jane asked.

Sofia scowled. "Oh. It's my phone." She turned to Jane and squinted. "Don't ask me how it works." She pulled a thin steel box from her pocket, the same as those everyone seemed to possess in this time, and studied it. "I don't know this number," she said with a grimace, then stiffened. "It must be Jack! He must have a new phone. I feel sick. Why is he calling me?" She paused. "He is calling to apologize!" She turned to Jane. "Quick, what do I say to him? How about this voice? Hellooo," she said in a deep, husky voice.

"You sound like you have consumption," Jane said.

"Okay, a little brighter," Sofia said. She practiced again. "Hell-oh!"

"Better, I suppose," Jane said, confused.

The box rang on. Sofia shook her head. "I used to be good at this stuff. Okay, here I go." She put the box to her ear. "Hello, sexy man," she purred.

"Is this Ms. Wentworth?" asked a shaky male voice. The voice came from the steel box. Jane leaned in closer to listen.

"Yes. Who is this?" Sofia removed the attempted huskiness and resumed her normal voice.

"It's Dave Croft. From the library."

Sofia sank into her seat. "How did you get this number?"

"You gave it to me," the voice in the box said.

"Oh. What do you want?"

"I wanted to apologize for before."

Jane stared at the box. Sofia spoke into it the same way the woman had on the train. How did it produce sound? Did the voice inside it belong to a person? Jane moved even closer to the magical thin rectangle, her eyes bulging.

Sofia shrugged and waved her arm in the air. "No need. I wasn't bothered," she said.

"I hope not. Because I did a little digging of my own. About your witch problem," the voice replied.

Jane sat up in her chair.

"Funny," Sofia scoffed. She rolled her eyes. "You found the crazy lady's witch, well done."

"As a matter of fact," said the voice, "I did."

Chapter Thirty-Four

Sofia entered the University of Bristol, again, the law library this time. Dave the librarian was waiting for her in the foyer. "Why are we meeting here?" she asked him.

"Good morning," he said. "Mrs. Sinclair is inside." He held the door open for her, then pointed to her clothes. "New threads?"

"Just something I'm trying out." She wore a pair of leather trousers and a T-shirt that may or may not have said *Bazooka* across the chest. She could not be sure, as she was not wearing her reading glasses. Her eyeballs were instead ensconced behind a large pair of rainbow-framed sunglasses that she was sure afforded little UV protection. Courtney Smith had worn the same ensemble on the cover of last month's *Teen Vogue*. She swallowed. "I look horrendous, don't I?" She bowed her head.

"No. You look great," Dave replied. "Fashion-forward. You looked great before, too. This way."

He ushered her toward the central reading room. The ceiling of a recital hall loomed overhead. Rows of brown study carrels lined the great room, each cubicle occupied by a student, many of them sleeping. Dave led Sofia up a steel spiral staircase and onto the open mezzanine. Rows of stacks lined the floor. He took a blue legal volume from a shelf and searched. Sofia observed his eyes as they ran down the pages; his gaze seemed gentle and nervous. He blinked with a twitch.

"Why are you helping me?" she asked then, eyes narrowed.

Dave closed the book and looked up at her. "I'm sorry?"

"You can't be more than twenty. I'm . . . in my thirties. Do you have a fetish for older women?"

"No?" said Dave. He laughed and read on. "And I'm twenty-nine."

"I can't help you get your screenplay made, if that's what you're thinking."

"I don't have a screenplay," he replied.

"I'm not going to sleep with you."

"I don't want to sleep with you."

"Yes, you do!" insisted Sofia. "Everyone does."

Dave said nothing.

"Don't tell me you're a nice person. I hate those."

Dave put the book down. "Do you remember *The Warmest Hearth*?"

Sofia rolled her eyes. "The long-running soap opera in which I played the buxom parson's daughter, Nanette? I have tried these many years to forget it."

"It was my mother's favorite show."

"I pity your mother," Sofia said.

"No need. She's dead." Dave turned back to the book.

Sofia slapped his arm but spoke in a soft voice. "Why did you have to ruin it by telling me that? My mother up and died, too. It was very rude of her, dying right when she was beginning to grow on me. Quite messed up my year," she said.

"Mine too," said Dave. "I can't go one June twelfth without thinking of her, silly woman. Or any other day for that matter."

"Our mothers are both thoughtless."

"My mum's favorite storyline on *The Warmest Hearth* was when Father Matthews fell in love with Nanette," Dave said.

"Ah yes, Father Matt, the sexy priest. It was quite the scandal. The Beeb got so many letters. I wonder what Ryan-o is doing these days. That's the actor who played Father Matt," she added. "Probably dead in a ditch somewhere. I should give him a call. Anyway, please continue."

"Every day I arrived home from school, and me and Mum watched *The Warmest Hearth*. When Nanette and Father Matthew finally . . . you know . . ."

"Had a holy union?" Sofia said.

Dave nodded. "Mum was so excited. We watched it and taped it, then watched it again straightaway."

"Videotape? Stop reminding me how old I am; you're not doing yourself any favors."

He shrugged. "Anyway, that's why I'm helping you."

"You're helping me because I was in a soap opera so old you pirated it on VHS?"

"Because you brought my mother, who was so riddled with cancer that in the X-ray her body looked like a treasure chest of pearls, a bit of joy before she died."

Sofia stared at him. "Fine," she sniffed. "I give you permission to help me. Wait. Just so we're clear: I claim Jane Austen lives in my brother's spare room. You don't think I'm crazy?"

Dave shrugged. "If you say you saw Jane Austen, then you saw Jane Austen. If you're for real, then, wow. You've got one of the greatest writers in the English language in your house. If you're crazy, then I've got a great story to tell down the pub. It's a win-win for me." He picked up the book and flipped through the pages. Sofia stared at him again. "Here we are." He paused on a page.

"Besides, if you've made this all up, it's a sophisticated lie." He pointed to a line halfway down, then handed the volume to her.

Sofia turned to the book and read the passage aloud. "Summary notice. February second, 1810. Emmaline J. Sinclair of 8 Russia Row, Cheapside, v. Rex." Sofia gasped. "That's Mrs. Sinclair? Jane is telling the truth?"

Dave pointed to the entry. "Is that her address?"

"It's absolutely the address Jane gave me. My God. I don't know what to say." She laughed, astounded. "Okay, explain. What are we looking at?"

Dave held up the book. "We're looking at a court listing. Your Mrs. Sinclair was charged with a crime."

Sofia straightened. "A witch trial?"

Dave read the lines below. "No. She was charged with grand larceny."

Sofia scowled and shook her head. "Which is?"

"Stealing clothes," Dave replied. "It was a thing back then."

"Was she found guilty?" Sofia said.

Dave read the passage. "It doesn't say. We need to check the archive. Ground floor."

Sofia and Dave descended. Her mind whirred. Jane was telling the truth: Mrs. Sinclair was a real person. She found herself at the beginning of a mystery. Dave showed her to a shelf containing the dusty tomes of the Old Bailey. "This is rather exciting," Sofia said. "I feel like a treasure hunter. But with books."

Dave riffled through the pages of one volume, then tossed it to one side and grabbed another.

"You're enjoying this," Sofia said with a crooked smile.

"Thoroughly," said Dave. "Here." He settled on a page. His face fell.

"What is it?" Sofia asked.

Dave shook his head. "Mrs. Sinclair was found guilty as charged. They sentenced her to transportation."

"Transportation? To where?"

Dave read on. "Australia. But she died. On the *Earl Spencer,* the ship that took her to New South Wales."

"How inconsiderate of her." Sofia scratched her head. "Well, I'm utterly confused now."

Dave sat on the floor between the two stacks. "So am I."

"You're disappointed," Sofia said. "I must admit, that was rather an anticlimax."

"I thought I was onto something there," said Dave. "I'll keep looking."

Sofia checked her watch. "I have to go."

He looked up. "What if I find something?"

"If you find anything, bring it to set."

Dave straightened. "You mean the film set?"

Sofia shrugged. "Why not? I'll put your name on the visitors' list."

Dave looked starry-eyed. "Wow. A real-life film set! Where the magic happens."

"It's not as glamorous as you might think," she said, and waved her hand glamorously.

"To you, maybe. But to me . . . so exciting! There will be film stars there."

Sofia rolled her eyes. "Yes, Courtney Smith will be there."

"I meant you," Dave said.

"Oh," she replied. "Whatever." She walked off, concealing her smile.

Chapter Thirty-Five

*C*ourtney took Sofia's arm and leaned in. "I heard a rumor," she whispered with a smile. They stood on the sound stage once more for afternoon rehearsal. Courtney wore her Grecian goddess gown. Sofia had redonned her lime-green sack. The tension and passive aggression between them fizzed and buzzed in a symphony; they seemed to loom on the verge of an all-out war, but their tones and gestures remained tightly controlled for the moment. They were like a couple of expensively dressed, impossibly glamorous gunslingers from the Old West, waiting in the street for the shoot-out to begin, each daring the other to flinch or fumble their jewel-encrusted gun. "You have a secret admirer."

"I do?" Sofia said. She kicked the ground and feigned uninterest. "Who?" All she could think of was Jack. Had he said something? Was it obvious? Her heart leapt.

"Pete likes you," Courtney replied. She raised her eyebrows and nudged Sofia in the ribs.

Sofia scowled. "Who is Pete?" she asked.

"Pete, the unit manager?"

Sofia scanned through names and faces in her head and came up with no one. Finally, Courtney pointed across the set. A tattooed man of seventy exited a portable toilet in a high-visibility vest. An eczema-mortified bottom crack poked out from his trousers.

"That's him. He won't kick you out of bed. I think you should go for it."

Sofia rolled her eyes. "No, thank you."

"Why not? You're single. Take a chance, you might find love." Courtney beamed at her with sinister glee. Sofia looked over at Pete the unit manager as he stacked some chairs. He was probably a lovely person and had no idea Courtney mocked him. Sofia felt sad and embarrassed for the both of them. She hoped Courtney had said nothing to him as some cruel joke; he probably just wanted to do his job in peace. She suddenly felt incredibly mad.

"Can't, sorry," Sofia said in a confident voice. "I'm already seeing someone." She winced at the lie as soon as the words left her mouth.

Courtney blinked and straightened. "Oh! I'm happy for you. What's his name?"

Sofia inhaled. Oh dear. She had started the falsehood and would now need to continue it. Quick, what were sexy men's names? Bertie? Reginald? Horatio? No, those were all unsexy. She tried to conjure a person from her imagination, but was saved from having to answer by Jack, who walked over.

"We're almost ready," he said, pointing to the camera. "We'll go from the top."

"Jack, did you know Sofia is seeing someone?" Courtney asked.

Sofia cringed at the repeated lie. But Jack did a double take and met Sofia's eyes. It was the smallest of flinches on his part, but it was enough to gratify Sofia for the rest of the day.

"I am," she said, defiant.

"I'm happy for you," said Jack, in a hollow voice.

"Tell Jack his name," said Courtney.

Sofia gritted her teeth, keen to follow through with the adolescent lie because it was making Jack sweat. But now that he was looking at her with what might have been sadness, she found she couldn't think of a name.

"Did you make him up?" asked Courtney, grinning.

"No . . . I . . ." She couldn't think of a name. She didn't want to think of a name. She was exhausted by the whole thing. She could not compete with a twentysomething Californian.

"Even imaginary boyfriends have names," said Courtney. Her cornflower-blue eyes gleamed with joy. A camera operator chuckled nearby.

Then a figure moved toward them through the crowd. The crew parted. Dave Croft emerged from where he must have been standing for some time. He strode up to Sofia and placed his arm around her shoulder.

"Hi," he said.

Courtney and Jack and the rest of the crew seemed to take in the scene with a general sense of bewilderment. Sofia was as shocked as anyone but had the good sense, and the acting talent, to say nothing.

"Sorry I'm late. Got held up at the gym," said Dave. "Lifting loads of weights." He wore his librarian clothes and leather shoes. Dave turned to Jack, whose mouth was still wide open. He held out his hand. "Dave Croft," he said. "The boyfriend." Sofia stifled a laugh. The whole performance was so ludicrous, but also so endearing, that she found it difficult to imagine anyone would possibly believe it. To her surprise and delight, everyone seemed to.

"Jack Travers." They shook hands. Courtney stared at them with wide eyes. A vein throbbed in her temple.

"Of course," Dave said to him. "*Forrest Gump* is one of my favorite films."

"I didn't direct that," Jack said.

"I know," said Dave. He grinned and turned to Courtney. "And you are?"

Courtney's mouth dropped open. "Courtney Smith?" she said.

Dave smiled and shook her hand. "Nice to meet you."

Courtney stomped off. Dave turned to Sofia. "Are you free, babes?" He croaked when saying *babes*, as though he had never said the word before. "I want to show you something."

"You can't have her," blurted Jack. "We're rehearsing a scene, pal."

"I'll be five minutes, Jack," Sofia said. "You don't need me quite yet, anyway." She walked away and motioned for Dave to follow her outside. She knew from experience that Jack would be watching her go.

"So sorry about that," Dave said, once they were outside. "Putting my arm around you and saying I was your boyfriend. I said that because I overheard them talking. I didn't mean it. I know I'm not your boyfriend."

"Good, I should hope not," Sofia said, though she still smiled. "Thank you, though. Kind of a rock-star move."

Dave smiled. "Oh." He shuffled his feet.

"What did you want to show me?" she asked him quickly.

He cleared his throat. "Right. Check it out," he said, and opened his bag. "I dug deeper on Mrs. Sinclair." He pulled out a book and began flipping through its pages. "I thought about the records we have of Jane Austen. Biographies of her are patchy. Dickens, Hardy, Tolstoy—we have reams of information on them. But for Jane Austen, we know basically nothing. She is an enigma."

"Why? She is a huge writer."

Dave shrugged. "No one thought to keep them. I don't know."

Sofia scowled. "Can we not ask her about the facts of her life herself? She does live with me."

"I know she does," he replied.

Sofia smiled. Any normal person was within their rights to call her crazy when she claimed she lived with a nineteenth-century author. But he did not. Which perhaps made him not normal, but it was still nice.

"But here's the thing," he added. "The Jane Austen in your house is still a young woman. She's had no books published, no achievements. In the time she's come from, she's not famous yet. The information we need she doesn't yet know herself." Sofia nodded. "But there was one source of information I hadn't considered. In her lifetime, Jane Austen wrote three thousand letters. One hundred and sixty of those survive today."

Sofia raised an eyebrow. "Did Jane write Mrs. Sinclair a letter?"

"No," he replied. Sofia scowled. "But Mrs. Sinclair wrote one to Jane."

"What?" Sofia said. She inhaled. "Show me."

He handed Sofia the large blue book. The cover read *Sotheby's Annual*. The opened page contained auction-house listings.

"This is like the sports pages for antiques geeks," Dave said. Each line contained names and dates. "These are the details of known letters written to or from Jane Austen."

Sofia scanned the page and gasped. "Here!" She pointed to an entry on the page and read it aloud. "*Mrs. Emmaline Sinclair to Jane Austen*. She wrote Jane a letter in 1810!"

Dave nodded. "Before she went to Australia."

"What do we do, then?" Sofia asked.

"We find that letter."

"How exciting! We are intrepid book hunters!" Sofia said. She smiled at him.

He blinked and smiled back. He gazed down and flipped through the book again.

SOFIA ESCORTED DAVE over to catering. "Grab yourself a coffee before you return to the library." She walked back to Jack and Courtney to rehearse. Neither of them said anything unrelated to camera angles and script coverage for the rest of the scene.

At one point during the rehearsal, Sofia looked over to the catering table where Dave was attempting to make himself a coffee at the espresso machine. He loaded the beans into the machine, but when he pressed the button only scalding water emerged. He swore and jumped on the spot. He glanced around to see if anyone noticed. Eventually he shrugged and seemed to give up. He threw a tea bag into the cup of hot water and sipped it instead. Sofia watched him and smiled. In her beauteous youth on the stage, Sofia had been romanced by Lancelot, rescued by Robin and his bow, proposed to by Romeo, and seduced by Tristan. But as far as acts of chivalry went, Dave Croft, with his soft stomach and scuffed shoes, standing beside her before and doing what he did, maybe trumped them all.

A FEW HOURS passed in happy uneventfulness. Rehearsal wrapped for the day and Sofia returned to the truck to change and go home. When she stepped inside, she gasped. "When did these arrive?" she asked Derek, who was washing makeup brushes in the sink.

"About twenty minutes ago, Ms. Wentworth. They're so beautiful."

Derek told the truth. Three dozen long-stemmed roses were arranged in a crystal vase. Dew covered the cherry-red blooms and glistened in the afternoon light.

"Who are they from?" he asked. "There's no card."

Sofia did not need a card to know who'd sent them. "They're from Jack," she said.

"Such a beautiful color," Derek said. "Such a glorious shade of red. I can't put my finger on where I've seen it before. It's the same shade—"

"As my hair," Sofia whispered. She tucked a strand of her red tresses behind her ear and stared at the flowers on the table. Her heart raced. Jack always used to give her red roses like this, the same color as her hair, when they first started seeing each other. She could not catch her breath.

Sofia's phone rang. Dave Croft's name appeared on screen. Dave! She thought of answering—it might be something important, something to do with Jane, but she let it go to voicemail. Dave would understand. If he had news, he'd leave a message. She watched the screen and waited. No voicemail popped up. She shrugged; he'd call back. She glanced at the roses again. This was going to be a great shoot.

Chapter Thirty-Six

*I*f Sofia had been asked to locate the turning point in her marriage, the moment when things changed, an event from four years prior would have come to mind.

At first, she and Jack had dedicated themselves to making their Hollywood relationship an exception to the rule. "We'll do things differently," they said, noting in sanctimonious tones the long list of Hollywood unions that ended in divorce, and vowing to do better than those couples.

Jack's role as director required him to remain in Los Angeles for months at a time, to oversee postproduction, screenings, meetings. Meanwhile people put Sofia on jets and sent her wherever crew labor ran cheap and the US dollar went far, to Eastern Europe mostly, and even Australia in those days.

Sofia returned to LA every chance she got. One time, she found Jack on the floor of an edit suite, in the midst of a panic attack—his worst one yet—over the edit of the *Batman* sequel. The movie had come in at almost five hours long, and Jack was crippled by indecision over which shots to lose. Sofia sat with him in that windowless room, soothed him, and gently suggested to him to let this or that shot go, applauding him whenever he made a decision.

In truth, Jack overthought things. A good director made decisions, even if they were the wrong ones: the act of deciding was the important part. Sofia was not like him; she knew innately what to do. She knew how to tell a story with a look, a shot, a word. She watched him on the floor of the edit room, trembling and close to tears, and shook her head at why he did it to himself, why he had convinced himself that this career was what he wanted. Sofia loved him, so she always helped him. They completed the edit together.

The film succeeded. Sofia and Peter had built on the chemistry they'd had in the first movie, and the scriptwriter added real heart this time, above the usual convoluted comic-book plotting. The trade papers reviewed the film in celebratory tones, declaring it an action masterpiece. The film broke records, earning the highest box office ever for a sequel, and Jack was feted everywhere he went.

It was at about this time that things seemed to change.

They went straight into preproduction on *Batman 3*. They shot it and wrapped, and the edit loomed once more. Jack struggled, and Sofia sat with him again, night after night in the edit suite. Jack asked her to be at the studio screening, and she gladly attended, but sat in the back of the room so as not to be in the way. She glanced at the back of his head as he watched the cut on the big screen above. He relaxed his shoulders. The movie looked good. She smiled, happy for him. He'd be in a great mood later.

As she turned to leave the theater, an executive leaned over to Jack in his seat and spoke to him. Sofia overheard the words. "Does the carpet match the drapes?" The executive pointed to the screen, where Sofia, as Batgirl, jumped into frame, her flame-red hair dancing across the screen. Sofia stiffened. She turned to Jack and inhaled, waiting for his rebuttal. She wanted to hear how Jack Travers dressed down pissants who insulted his wife.

Jack seemed to pause and look around. Some other executives snickered. He looked to them. "No," he replied. He chuckled. That was all he said. The darkened room erupted with laughter.

Sofia left the theater. She spent the morning in the edit suite, tweaking the cut, helping Jack with everything. Then she went home and cried. When Jack arrived home a few hours later, she confronted him. "Does the carpet match the drapes?" she asked.

He looked like a guilty child who had been caught stealing a cookie. Then he grew defiant and angry and waved her away. "What could I do? They're the money."

"I'm your wife," she said.

He doubled down then. The pressure rested on him to do the job, he explained. She just stood around looking good in that leotard and her task was complete. He made decisions—hundreds of them—and they had to be the right ones.

She swallowed this with horror and vowed never to help him again. *See how he does without me,* she thought. The *Batman* installment succeeded and records were broken once more, the highest trilogy takings of all time. More parties were thrown; people inside their LA bubble behaved toward Jack as though he had cured cancer. Sofia went off to shoot another film in Prague, while Jack stayed in LA. Their relationship remained suspended in a frosty holding pattern.

The studio ordered a fourth *Batman* in the wake of the trilogy's success. The trade papers alleged that paychecks for director and stars would run to eight figures. But Peter was looking quite old by then, maybe too old to play Batman once more. He had reached his late forties; he'd lost weight and his neck skin hung loose. Rumors abounded: the studio would be replacing him; they were already searching for a new Batman.

Sofia called Peter every day in support. He had a fierce team of agents and handlers who put up a fight, and everything came to a head between the studio and Peter's camp. Words were thrown, endorsements were threatened, and Peter looked set to depart.

Turned out, they did not replace Batman. They replaced Batgirl.

To make Peter look younger, they put him next to a younger woman. As soon as Sofia heard their decision, she nodded with wisdom. Of course they'd replaced her, not him.

As for Jack, he privately raged to Sofia about unfairness and disloyalty, but he said nothing publicly. When a few journalists asked him his opinion about no longer directing his wife in the film series that had made them both famous, he said it wasn't appropriate to comment when the new film was still in preproduction, like it was a court case and he didn't want to influence the jury. Sofia took the sting and added it to the list of tiny treacheries they had enacted upon each other. When Sofia returned to LA, they separated.

She had always thought this was the moment when Jack changed. She thought she could change him back, if they could just spend time together again, but it was Sofia who had changed, and actually Jack had been the same all along. Even on that first night, he'd thought of her a certain way.

"You're too beautiful to know all this," he had said to her when she'd arrived fuming on his doorstep and told him how to direct a movie. She had taken it as a compliment at the time, which it may have been, but now she saw another side to those words. It was as though Jack had accused her of treachery, of misrepresentation, of some cunning trick, that she'd gone to his house pretending to be one thing, then turned out to be something else. She knew Jack thought she was beautiful, but if that were to change, would he value her at all? In the beginning, he had seemed to adore her, to need her so much. Sofia was sure Jack had loved her, at least for a while, but now she suspected there was also a bit of hate mixed up in that love.

Chapter Thirty-Seven

As the time drew near for Jane and Fred's midnight departure to the secret location, Jane marked the whole endeavor as folly. She sat by the sitting room window and chewed her lip. Sofia had again promised to get Jane back to 1803, assuring Jane she'd made progress on the mission, before leaving the house with a cheerful wave. Jane had thanked her, racked with guilt. She possessed a singular ally in Sofia, and to sneak from the house and defy her in this way not only invited censure, it abounded in stupidity and took Jane one step further down the path of not returning to 1803. Leaving the house invited only ruin.

Yet she could not bring herself to decline him. She put on the nicest of the shirts and men's trousers Sofia had given her and brushed her hair many times, cursing herself as she did so. She clicked a magic candle on and off and worked herself into such a state that she did not notice when Fred entered the room.

"What are you doing?" Fred asked her with an amused look. He wore a green shirt with the sleeves rolled to the elbows and black trousers, and his eyes shone an agitating shade of emerald.

Jane ceased her abuse of the candle switch. "Nothing at all," she said with a shrug. "I merely admire this desk lamp." She ran her finger along the lamp's arm and pretended to study it.

Fred smirked. "You are a fan of desk lamps in general? Or this one in particular?"

"I am an ardent fan of all lighting contrivances," she replied. She looked up from the apparatus. She did not know how to feel at that point: annoyed at his continued teasing or terrified at what was about to happen. She settled for a combination of both.

"Shall we go?"

They walked through dark streets to the center of Bath. "Where are we going?" Jane said. Fred did not answer.

They arrived at a cast-iron gate. Fred opened a heavy lock and slid back a chain. He swung the gate open and held out his hand. Jane took it and he led her inside a stone building. Jane strained her eyes to see where they were, but darkness enshrouded them. His hand felt warm on hers; she commanded her breath to slow. Her mind darted this way and that; she could focus on no single thought for longer than a moment.

They stepped under an arch and entered a cavernous tunnel, carved from stone. A rocky path of smashed flagstone lay under their feet. Fred pulled her along. Jane tripped on a jagged paver and Fred caught her before she tumbled to the floor. He lifted her up and they continued forward.

"Are you leading me to my demise?" she managed to ask him.

"Almost there," he replied. They reached the end of the tunnel and entered a larger space.

"We are outside again," Jane declared. She could see nothing, but the air had changed. Fred let go of Jane's hand and walked away. "Do not leave me here, sir!" she demanded.

"Back in a tick," he said cheerfully.

Jane stood on the spot and hoped a ghost did not seize her. She could see less than a foot in front of her, making out stone blocks and perhaps a column. The air felt warm and wet on her shoulders and face. "If you do not return in an instant, I shall scream," she announced into the space.

"Ten seconds! Almost there," Fred called from somewhere.

Jane counted to ten in her head. Nothing happened. She opened her mouth to scream, then a yellow light beamed above her. Jane looked up into it and it blinded her. "Goodness," Jane said. "I see spots."

"Don't look straight into the light. Maybe I should have mentioned that. Sorry!"

Jane's eyes recovered. Light bathed the area. She stepped back and gasped. "Oh my," she said.

A double-story cloistered courtyard stood before her. Greek columns carved from warm golden stone held up the walkway, and gargoyles looked down on them from above. The middle of the courtyard did not consist of grass or stone, but rather a giant pool of pastel green water.

"It's a bath," Jane said with astonishment.

Fred laughed. "It's *the* bath. The greatest of them all." Fred angled his giant lamp and the beam hit the surface of the water. Steam whorled across the surface in loops and wisps.

"This is the Roman Bath?" Jane asked. "Of the Pump Room?"

Fred nodded. "This is the bath that Bath was named for. Does it live up to its name?"

Jane looked down at the sacred spring. It stood lovelier than it did in her dreams. "I believe it might. How are we permitted to enter at night?" she asked.

"We're not," he replied. "Shhh, don't tell anyone." She waited for him to explain. "See those Roman statues?" he said.

Jane looked up. She stood corrected: the statues above her

formed not gargoyles, but Nero, Claudius, and Julius Caesar, rendered in stone. They loomed over the pool, observing the scene. "They are marvelous," she said.

"They get covered in acid rain," he said. Jane squinted. "The restorers come in every so often and clean it off. We're bringing the students here tomorrow for an excursion, to check out the restoration. One of the caretakers is a friend of mine and he gave me a key," Fred said. "Do you like it?" He gestured to the baths.

"I had no idea it looked this way," she said. She could scarcely believe she was standing in a place she had never been permitted to enter before.

Fred beamed. "The Romans were master builders," he said.

"They could not have been that masterful," Jane said. "They built no roof. All the heat escapes." She pointed. Steam rose from the water's surface, then evaporated into thin air.

"There is a roof," Fred said with a nod.

Jane frowned. "I do not see one."

"You can't see it from this angle. You have to get in to see it." He nodded toward the pool.

Jane scoffed. "In the water? Impossible."

Fred laughed. "This is a once-in-a-lifetime chance! The pool is not open to the public to swim in."

The frigid night air already made her shiver. "I will freeze to death," she said.

"You won't. I promise."

"Is it safe?"

"Sure. The restorers drained and refilled it yesterday," he said.

"It looks rather green."

"Don't drink it then," he replied with a laugh. "Are you scared?"

"Not at all," Jane said, petrified. She scrambled for an excuse. "I have no sea-bathing clothes."

"I thought you might say that. Here." He handed her a ball of fabric.

She unraveled it. "What is this?"

"A swimsuit," said Fred.

Jane held up the fabric and gasped. It was a tiny scrap of material in the shape of underclothes. "I am to wear this?" Jane's eyes bulged. "That's obscene."

"Oh," he said. He looked concerned. "I'm sorry. The woman in the shop said her grandmother has the same one." He showed Jane a small card attached to the underclothes. It was a picture of a gray-haired woman holding a large orange ball; she wore the bathing clothes. "She's having fun."

"She looks drunk," Jane said. Perhaps that was the only possible mind-state in which to contemplate the scenario: inebriation. "You promise me this is no trick, that this is what women wear? For bathing. In public."

Fred laughed. "I promise."

Since arriving in this time, Jane had seen enough women in their drawers with exposed ankles and bosoms to know this bore truth, but the idea of wearing such a miniature outfit herself mortified every creed and protocol of her existence. "I am sorry. I cannot."

"I promise I won't look," he said. "Is that what you're worried about?"

"No," she lied. She turned toward the pool. The water sparkled. The surface seemed opaque.

Jane's brother Frank had written to her once of swimming in the Praia da Luz in Portugal with his fleet. He described the water as warm and golden, and the experience as heavenly. He even claimed to have seen a mermaid. It was a rare line of poetry from Frank. The Austens had a soft spot for a body of water; they were all seduced by its mystery and immersion. Jane shared the attraction, but her experiences were theoretical up to this point.

"Go on, take a chance," Fred said.

Jane held the bathing suit and winced. The vicar preached the message from every pulpit: exposing one's flesh to a man was to place one's soul in mortal danger. A woman's body was meant for singular consumption. Once a man's eyes looked upon the flesh, his gaze spoiled her for all others.

She was aware that her thoughts on this score were outdated compared to the social mores of this time. She imagined standing before him, wearing this item. Fred placed his eyes on her, smiled politely, then averted them once more.

Jane fidgeted and scratched her head. Fred spoke to her then in a soft voice. "This is not meant to be torture, Jane. I thought you might enjoy it. You don't have to do anything you don't want. We can leave."

Jane had longed to go bathing all her life. "I am not upset," she said. She recalled his accurate pronouncement of her character the night before, of her wanting to see and try everything. She looked at the pool once more. The green water held only opaqueness; she could see nothing of under the surface. She had an idea.

"If you agree not to look until I am in the pool?"

"I shall stand over there behind the column," Fred said with a nod. "I won't look at all."

Jane inhaled. She took the sea-bathing suit from him and moved into a cave behind the cloisters.

Chapter Thirty-Eight

Jane removed her clothes, then stepped into the leg holes of the suit and pulled it upward. She shuddered. It felt even smaller than she had first thought, and barely covered anything. She cursed herself for agreeing to this mad scheme.

"I am coming out," Jane called.

"I will be here," Fred called back. "I'm behind a column. I can't see anything."

Jane inhaled and walked out of the cave, looking around. She could not see him. She hurried over to the edge of the pool and placed a toe in the water. "It's warm," she whispered, and jettisoned her fear of freezing. As her foot touched the water, it rippled and radiated small waves to the middle of the pool. She pulled it back and stepped her other foot into the water; it fizzed on her skin. She had never felt anything like it. She inhaled and plunged into the pool. The hot green liquid reached her waist.

In her dreams she had imagined this place, but the reality fared a thousand times better. The dreams did not include how the limey water felt on her skin. It never mentioned the smell in her nostrils, salty and sweet. It omitted the cracks in the Roman statues, the moss on the stones, the sand and mud under her toes.

The fantasy never spoke of the flesh-and-blood man, somewhere behind her.

"Are you in?" Fred's voice called to her from somewhere at the far end of the cloisters.

"I am in," Jane called back. She looked around but saw only shadows and columns.

"Lie on your back," Fred's voice shouted.

Jane scowled and wondered how to manage it. "That does not sound feasible," she announced to the shadows.

"Swing your shoulders behind you," he called out. "Use your hands and feet to paddle."

She tipped her head back. The water bubbled on the back of her hair. She lifted her hips and sighed with delight. "I float!" she exclaimed.

"Look up," he called to her.

Jane looked up and gasped. "Good God," she whispered. The night sky hung above her. A thousand—no, a million—white stars reigned overhead, puncturing the blanket of black with twinkling diamonds.

"There's your roof," Fred said. Jane smiled and felt her eyes water.

All her life she had been a burden, a nuisance: someone who earned nothing and stood only to drain the household. Jane held reticules while others danced and watched over naughty children while their parents attended assemblies. She served where she could to pay her way, to justify her room and board. No one had ever brought her to such a place; she never deserved it. Jane stretched her arms out. She floated out to the middle of the pool. The sky swirled above her, and a thousand sparkles blurred and danced. No one had provided her an activity of idle pleasure such as this; she drank it in greedily.

She inhaled—too deeply, it turned out—and breathed in water instead of air. She coughed and lost the ability she had earlier possessed in floating. She lowered her legs to stand up but found no ground beneath her. She wiggled one leg around and grasped for the bottom of the pool. But the water reached too deep; she could not stand. She'd floated to the deeper end. She coughed again. "Help me. I cannot swim!" She breathed in a goblet's worth of green water and spluttered. Her head went under.

She sank down into the depths of the pool. Murky water clouded her eyes. She flailed her arms but could not return to the surface. She sank down further and swallowed more water. She hoped Fred had heard her call out. Finally, her toes touched the pool's bottom. The water surface now appeared to her as a ceiling, a person-length above her. She inhaled, stupidly, and swallowed another mouthful of water. She closed her eyes and struggled to think. She felt herself falling to sleep, peacefully.

Then a hand surrounded her waist and moved her upward.

Fred pulled Jane to the surface. She gasped and coughed and inhaled a wondrous, painful breath of air, the water leaving a limey and bitter taste in her mouth. He helped her to the side of the pool; he had dived into the water with his clothes on.

She grasped the edge and held on. "I swallowed water," she said. "It looks prettier than it tastes." She wiped her eyes. Her nose stung to breathe. Her fingers prickled.

He held his hand on her, somewhere under the water. "Why didn't you say you couldn't swim?" he asked.

"I don't know. Thank you," Jane said.

He waited until her breathing slowed and returned to normal. "Are you all right?" he said. "I'm so sorry. I didn't know you couldn't swim."

Jane nodded. "I am quite well," she said. "Perfectly healthy. I swallowed some water, that is all." She smiled at him to assure him she felt well. He smiled back. It took several minutes of reassuring words and nods before his face relaxed from a look of horrified guilt to a happier one.

"I feel terrible. I almost killed you."

"You did nothing of the sort. If anything, you've brought me to life." The words slipped out before she could stop them. "Thank you, for showing me this," she explained.

He stared at her. Jane grew aware he still held his hand on her under the water. The other held the edge of the pool. He seemed to grow aware of it, too. He sighed but did not move. He swallowed. "You're sure you're all right?"

"Please stop asking that," she said, silencing him.

The air seemed to shift around them; the mood changed. She felt his breath on her collarbone. He moved his eyes downward and looked at her mouth.

In terms of experience in such matters, Jane could lay claim to the title of "limited." In her twenty-eight years on the earth, pitifully, no man had ever put his hand there, or moved his eyes so, or shown any intentions toward her of doing what Fred now seemed to want to do. She stole a glance at his face and beheld a look in his eyes both noble and brazen. Her heart beat wildly; her mind moved. She wondered if he was aware of her inexperience, if he detected a childishness in the way she held herself or breathed, if it disappointed him, if she should move differently. He continued to look and smile at her; nothing he did seemed to indicate he was anything other than pleased, and perhaps a little scared, of the current situation, and of what might come next. She inhaled and waited and ordered herself to keep breathing.

Unfortunately, possessed with a brain like a chess player's, always contemplating several steps ahead, she found her mind moving forward over the pleasant parts and on to the things to worry about.

It was not so much the act itself that concerned her, though she was curious and petrified of that, too; it was the afterward that put her mind in a spin. What happened next, beyond him doing the thing he intended? Could she happily return to her own time, once she had known what a kiss from him felt like? She glanced at his face. Once he had kissed her, she knew with her heart, as feeble and inexperienced as it was, she would find it difficult ever to leave him. How glorious it might feel to become swept up in a thing like this. But the hard times afterward could never atone for a few moments of magic. Surely not. Indeed, the act comprised nothing but folly.

"How can you have reached adulthood without learning to swim?" he asked in a kind voice. He leaned his head toward hers, so close now that she inhaled sharply. She prayed for strength.

She searched for a tactic to halt the operation. She arrived at a compelling one. She closed her eyes at how compelling it would be.

"Because I am Jane Austen," she declared.

The words had the desired effect. Fred drew his head back and blinked. He gave the reaction of any sane person offered such a declaration. He studied her face. "I'm sorry?" he said. His eyes were filled with hope, as though perhaps he had misheard her.

"I am Jane Austen," she repeated.

"The writer," he said with a disbelieving nod. His eyes went blank.

Jane nodded.

"I see," he said. He dropped his hand from where it had been and frowned.

What did he think now? That she was insane, appropriating the writer in some hysterical hallucination? Or did he think she mocked him? Either way, her words had done their job.

"You don't need to make up stories," he said.

"It is no story, sir," she said.

The damage was complete. He moved more parts of him away from her. He assisted her from the water, gently, deliberately, as one did a child. He shrouded her in a towel.

"I speak the truth," Jane tried again. She did not know why she felt the need to insist, now that the moment had passed, but she kept doing so.

Fred nodded. "Have you been telling this to Sofia?" he asked in a soft voice.

"I am from the year eighteen hundred and three," Jane continued, though it was futile. "I journeyed to this time. You do not believe me." She preached the ludicrous gospel for effect, to drive him away. But she nevertheless felt a sting that he had not accepted it.

"You've taken advantage of her. I'll take you home." He looked at her with sad eyes.

"I shall be gone from the house as soon as it can be arranged," she said.

Fred nodded.

Jane put her clothes back on over her sea-bathing suit. Water dripped from Fred's clothes. His shirt fabric clung to his body. She offered him the towel. He shook his head.

"Please, I insist. You shall catch cold."

He relented and accepted the towel. He dried himself perfunctorily and handed the towel back.

They returned to the house in silence. Fred walked ahead of her, close enough for her not to lose her way in the dark streets, but far enough that all communication was impossible.

Upon arriving at the house, Fred bade her good night and closed his door. Jane lay in the guest room in her wet clothes. She stared at the clock on the wall. How lovely it would be to turn back its hands.

Instead she closed her eyes and offered a grim nod of recognition to herself. Her behavior toward Fred was not purely an act of self-preservation, it was something else, too. She had treated other men the same way. While no man had tried to kiss her before, others had wanted her. Mr. Withers had likely spurned her because she was poor and old, but what she kept to herself was that she too had let men go: nicer, poorer suitors who made better matches for her station. She had rejected these men in earlier times, before her age became a problem.

Jane sat on the bed, her hair still dripping, and reflected upon a list of three to four decent men who, given enough time and quiet, she may have grown to love in a resigned, wise way. They came to her hopeful, and she found them dull, and rebuffed them with jokes and scorn and made them feel as though they had short chance of making her happy. A little voice inside had always instructed her to flee. These men were happy with other women now, as Jane discovered in letters and passing conversations; each of them had married someone else in time, most likely a woman who made them laugh less, but cared for them more.

She always enjoyed some reassurance of the safety that lay in loneliness, some desire to run when others drew near. She let a feeling of oblivion sink in, sensing she must possess some death wish inside her to think this way. Or perhaps she just liked to be left alone, really, to walk and to think and to be, to live without concerning herself with another. She wondered if this made her a horrible beast of a person; it probably did.

Jane gritted her teeth. She had told Fred the truth of her identity, but he did not believe her. She felt glad, for it made her decision to depart easier. She had achieved a suitable outcome. Nothing good could come of the other thing, an idle fancy she felt glad to have shushed. She directed her mind to a more useful topic instead: helping Sofia secure the means to return her home.

Chapter Thirty-Nine

Fred enjoyed his job as a schoolteacher. Some days were diamonds, full of academic joy and scholarly insights, where delight danced across a child's face when they finally mastered a concept. Other times, the greatest achievement possible was arriving at the end of the day with everyone still alive. He suspected today belonged to the latter category. He and Paul had twenty-five twelve-year-olds under their care, taking them on an excursion to the baths to study the new restorations.

As they corralled the children into the honeystone building, he felt in awe of those mother ducks you saw crossing the road, with a line of ducklings following with cute but military precision. How did the mother duck do it? He and Paul had no such endearing, fluffy followers in these children; instead a brutish gaggle of perspiring, gossiping adolescent bodies dragged their feet after them down the street, with no one looking left or right when crossing the road, and random children shooting off in multiple directions at once. It was only nine thirty in the morning and Fred already had a hoarse voice from shouting things like, "Walk quickly but sensibly!," "Don't eat that!," and "Has everyone been to the toilet?"

They arrived at the Pump Room, miraculously with the same

number of children as when they'd set off. Fred cautioned the students again on politeness and motioned them inside. A small pocket of disobedience erupted at the front of the line, some shouting and laughing and pushing. Fred rushed ahead to quiet them. Tess Jones stood at the front.

"Tess swore at that old lady, sir," another student complained to him. The student pointed to the old lady in question, just in case Fred could not see for himself. An unimpressed-looking woman with gray hair and a volunteer's badge bearing the Pump Room's insignia glared at them all.

"I did not," Tess said. "All I said was 'bollocks.'"

The lady in question, still within earshot, huffed and glared some more. Fred pulled Tess aside.

"What's going on, Tess?" he asked her.

She sniffed and stared at the floor. He never used to have to worry about Tess, but her parents had recently separated, and her behavior was slipping. She'd been caught drinking, skipping school. She was super bright, one of his best students. Just last week she had given an excellent speech in elective history about Nero, where she'd quoted texts and hadn't even plagiarized. Some teachers wanted to expel her, but Fred felt that was too hasty. *Separated*. He knew from his own heart the things that tied themselves to that word.

"Tess, explain yourself," he said.

She shrugged. "Sorry, Mr. Dub" was all she said.

The kids at school all called him "Mr. Dub." He was well-liked, especially by the difficult children. Paul joked it was because he read Russian literature, had good hair, and liked a drink, but Fred knew it was something else. Some things he'd experienced when he was young still bothered him and those kids were drawn to that. He sat in the shadows sometimes, and misery loves company.

"Just stay away from that lady, Tess," he said.

She nodded. "Sorry, Mr. Dub," she said again.

He sent her to the back of the line. He needed to keep an eye on her today.

Fred felt exhausted, but also glad for the distraction. He stood twenty feet from the Roman Bath but could not have felt further from the night before.

Jane Austen. How ridiculous.

"What happened with Jane?" Paul asked Fred for the second time. "Did she run away again?"

"What? No," Fred replied. "Well, sort of."

"Why?" Paul asked.

Fred stiffened. He couldn't explain; there were not words for such a strange situation. Actually, there were. A woman he liked— who did not like him back—had made a joke to reject him. Pretty simple really.

"She hurt you, mate," Paul said to him. He spoke softly.

"Just my pride," Fred replied in a joking tone, not wanting to get into it. He smiled.

Paul shook his head. "I don't like her anymore," he said. "That's not cool, her stringing you along like that. Even a handsome devil like you has feelings."

Fred wasn't hurt at the rejection. It was far worse and more embarrassing than that. He felt sad. Sad that the things he felt were deluded. Now he had to make peace with the fact that none of it was real. She didn't feel the same. He'd only known her for a few days, but that made it worse.

They gathered the students and walked into the courtyard,

where the pastel green pool loomed before them. The kids stopped their chatter to point and gasp. The deep lake of green water looked different in the day. Fred stared at the water and shook his head. Jane was odd, sure. But in an endearing way—not in a time-travelling, science-fiction way. There was the absentminded addressing him as "sir." There was the insistence on referring to her person as "oneself." The harshest swearword she seemed to know was *blockhead*. Fred had put these down to an actor's affectations, getting into the part for the period film.

If she was an actor, she was a good one. She appeared genuinely fascinated with any and every machine. She spent an inordinate amount of time staring at the fridge and had broken several light switches. He remembered when she'd told the dance instructor at the first rehearsal her name was Jane Austen. She had appeared flummoxed when the instructor accused her of joking.

An odd sound made its way into the courtyard then. A pitter-patter. It came from the roof above. "What is that sound?" Fred said.

Paul shook his head. "No idea."

"It sounds like—"

"It's raining, sir!" one of the kids exclaimed. The other students gasped.

They looked at each other, then at the roof.

"How long has it been?" Paul asked him. He pointed to the water falling from the sky.

"Eight months," Fred replied.

The rain spluttered and dripped in through the cracks of the buildings. It dripped down on old windows and into the foundations. It splattered drops into the pool, radiating waves outward.

The kids jumped and laughed, and screams of excitement rippled through the group.

"All right, people, we've all seen rain before," Paul cried to the kids. His words had no effect. Children reacted the same way to rain the world over, with madness. Water fights erupted between pockets of kids. Students leapt and skidded over the wet floor. The elderly volunteer from before, the one whom Tess Jones had said bollocks to, howled at the scene in horror. Fred and Paul herded the kids under the cloisters.

"I think that's recess," Fred said. Paul nodded.

They gathered up the students, found a cafeteria across the road, and corralled everyone to tables and chairs. Fred performed a head count. Twenty-four kids. He counted again and got the same number. Someone was missing.

"Where's Tess?" Fred called to Paul. Paul looked around and shrugged. Fred moved to her friends and asked them, "Where's Tess?" No one knew. Paul stayed with the students while Fred headed outside into the rain.

There a level of mayhem even greater than what usually accompanied a school excursion greeted him. The rain had apparently put everyone in a jam. The townsfolk rushed back and forth across the roads and pathways, ducking under roofs and under crofts for shelter from the deluge. No one had an umbrella. He turned his head and spotted Tess standing in the middle of the road, staring up at the rain. She had picked the wrong point at which to stop walking.

"Get off the road, Tess," he called. She turned around. She had been crying. Fred slumped, but smiled at her. "It will be okay," he said. "Come with me."

The rain poured down on his head, reminding him of the

previous night. Could the woman staying in his house truly be Jane Austen? As ludicrous as it seemed, at least it offered a better alternative than the present one—that she'd pushed him away.

Tess nodded and walked toward him. She picked a somewhat foolish path, straight across the road, into oncoming traffic. Real danger. A car swerved to avoid her.

Fred remembered laughing at a public service announcement that cautioned people to be careful driving if the drought broke. In the strangely calm tones that characterized English bureaucracy, signs and radio broadcasts had announced that driving in newly wet weather could pose a danger, as the car oil that had pooled on the roads could make them slippery, causing serious accidents. Fred had smirked at the time but now had the unique opportunity to watch the prophesied conditions in action.

As the car swerved to avoid Tess, it lost traction and collided with a telegraph pole. It was quite a tame accident by world standards; the car could only have been travelling five miles per hour and gave the pole no more than a bump. The driver was, thankfully, unhurt; he had left his vehicle and was already walking over to reassure Tess.

Tess began walking to the side of the road herself, when Fred observed that the end of a wire from the felled telegraph pole had come to rest in a newly formed puddle on the side of the road.

"Tess, wait!" Fred shouted. She kept walking, so he darted toward her, quickly pulling her back from the innocuous-looking, but rather dangerous, electrified puddle. Distracted by the rain, the chaos of the day, and one or two thoughts of Jane, however, he stepped in the puddle himself.

As he ruminated on the thought that this might have been a bad move, a spark seemed to agree with him. It moved from the puddle and entered Fred's left foot through his toe, where it shot up through his leg into his torso. It volleyed through the liquid of his chest, tickled the corner of his left ventricle, leapt through his shoulder, danced down his arm, and shot out from his body through his right thumb, then escaped into the earth through the telegraph pole he was now holding. He flew across the street like a bird and came to rest against the iron-latticed window of the building opposite.

Chapter Forty

$\mathcal{J}$ane felt unfortunate to have upset Fred, but it made sense in the scheme of events. She would not see him again. She stared out the window at the back garden, where a glorious sight greeted her. Rain poured down and splashed onto the grass. The yellow foliage seemed restored to green.

A knock rang out at the front door. Jane went to answer it; perhaps Sofia had forgotten her key. She hoped it was not Fred. She opened the door. A man in a red shirt stood on the porch. "May I be of assistance?" she asked him.

"My name is Rob. I am to take you to the hospital."

"I do not understand," Jane said.

"Ms. Wentworth sent me. I'm a runner from set. Her brother had an accident."

Jane held the doorframe. "What type of accident?"

JANE'S FIRST RIDE in a horseless steel carriage went without ceremony. She rode in the passenger side while Rob, the runner from set (whatever that meant), steered the carriage to Bath Hospital. She commanded herself to marvel at the speed of it, the size, the air rushing in through the opened window. She ordered her mind to ponder how the engine was powered without steam. For some silly reason, it grew obsessed instead with the definition of the word *accident* in the twenty-first century. Accidents where she came from were whispered about rather than spoken of. They meant someone had lost a limb, an eyeball, or a head. But with all the advancements of two hundred years, with the steel buildings and train tubes, surely the big accidents had been wiped out, gone the way of the dodo bird. *Accident* probably denoted something minor now, like a cut from paper or a stubbed toe. Definitely nothing to vex oneself over. She cursed herself for wasting her debut voyage in a horseless steel carriage occupied by such thoughts.

THE BOY IN the red shirt deposited Jane at Bath Hospital and a member of staff showed her down a corridor. Jane had visited a hospital once before, at age nine, for someone to inspect her inflamed tooth. She and her father had travelled in a post carriage to Winchester, and her father had held her hand while the village barber, who also claimed the title of its doctor, relieved Jane of her left molar with a pair of pliers. She had not been fond of hospitals since. She hoped the physicians who treated Fred were gentler than hers, if only for his comfort.

Jane arrived at the room where Sofia waited. Sofia embraced her. Tears bathed her face. "I don't know anything," she said to Jane. "I haven't seen him."

"It was only an accident," Jane said. "I am certain all is well." Her voice sounded confident.

Jane and Sofia waited in silence. Steel boxes sat everywhere, beeping and ringing. Another member of staff, a nurse perhaps, escorted them after a time to the room where Fred lay. Jane felt annoyed. No stubbed toe or paper cut greeted them. Aside from a little bandage above his eye and one on his arm, Fred lay before them with naught a scratch on him.

Sofia embraced him. "What happened?"

Jane remained in the doorway and came no closer.

"Is my hair spiky?" Fred asked. He wore a short-sleeved white gown. Jane's gaze fell to the floor.

Sofia pounded him with a fist. "We thought you were dead. No one told us anything!"

"I'm fine. Never felt better. Might go to the gym after this," he said. Fred moved his eyes to Jane as Sofia spoke. He moved them back to Sofia again and made no other acknowledgment of her presence.

Jane felt foolish and out of place; she invaded a family scene. She wished she had not come.

A man entered the room. He had a bald head and soft brown eyes. "Which one is the sister?" he asked them. Sofia raised her hand. "My name is Dr. Marks."

Jane observed the man. Doctors dressed differently now, it seemed. Where Jane's own physician wore riding boots and a frock coat, this one wore green pajamas. Sofia seemed unconcerned by the nightclothes and shook hands with the doctor. He turned to Jane and held out his hand. "And you are?" he asked.

"Jane," she replied. "I am no relation." She shook his hand. Fred looked at her again.

"What happened, Doc?" Sofia said.

"Mr. Wentworth got a bit too close to some electricity," Dr. Marks replied.

"He's always been a bit daft," Sofia said affectionately. "May we take him home?"

The doctor studied one of the boxes beside Fred's hospital

bed. It shone with lights of green and blue lines and beeped in a rhythm. He wrote something down with a self-inking quill and turned to the box again, then repeated this several times, watching and writing, as though the box dictated to him a song that he transcribed in his notes. "We'd like to keep him here for a few hours," he said.

"Is that necessary? He's acting his normal, annoying self and he looks healthy enough," Sofia said. Her face pulled into a rubbery smile to show she was joking, but her eyes looked worried.

"We'd like him to stay," he said with a smile. He finished his conversation with the box and left the room.

"Is it cold in here?" Fred shivered. "I feel like they turned the aircon up too high."

"It's always cold in these places," Sofia said.

"Could someone get me a blanket?" he asked.

"I am not your maid," Sofia said.

"I will go," said Jane. Anything to leave the room.

"No, that's okay, Jane," Fred said. She searched his face for feeling. He stared into the distance.

"I insist," Jane said, and started walking away.

Sofia stayed by the bed. "What are you looking at, Fred?" she asked. "Fred?"

Jane turned back. Fred stared at the floor for some reason. Jane followed his gaze. No point of interest presented itself in the spot where he peered, except a shiny white floor. His eyes lay unfocused. His body remained in the bed, but his mind seemed to have left the room.

"Fred?" Sofia called again. Fred lay his head on his shoulder and slowly closed his eyes. He did not move; he appeared asleep. Sofia pushed his shoulder, hard enough to wake him. He did not stir but continued sleeping. Sofia ran to the door. "Someone?" she called down the hall. "Help!"

A woman with strawberry hair entered the room. She addressed the steel box first. Then she moved to the patient. "Mr. Wentworth?" she asked. She shook Fred's shoulder. "Mr. Wentworth, can you hear me? Do you know where you are? Mr. Wentworth?"

Mr. Wentworth gave no answer.

Chapter Forty-One

*T*he strawberry-haired woman consulted the steel box once more. Numbers flashed across its frame, changing constantly, each figure moving up and down in a rapid blink.

Two more people entered the room. They all looked at the box. A line ran across the box's frame, patterned like the stitches on a blanket. The woman pressed a red circle on the wall. An alarm sounded in the room and rang out in the hall. Not an echo, but the same alarm repeated, from another source.

The line that was a procession of blanket stitches now shaped into a chaos of troughs and peaks, moving across the frame at random heights and spaces. "Ventricular fibrillation," the strawberry-haired woman called out, using pieces of Latin that Jane understood but rearranging them into words she had never heard. "Lower the bed," she commanded. One of the other people turned a crank on the bed. Fred, who had been sitting upright, now lay flat. A man gently moved Jane and Sofia to the edge of the room. "Please wait outside," he said to them. They moved outside the room but lingered and watched from the doorway.

The strawberry-haired woman jumped on top of Fred, as one jumped on a horse. Small and round and at least in her sixth decade, she leapt onto the bed with the grace of a gazelle and thumped his chest with her fist. Again, she checked the steel box. Of all the boxes Jane had seen, this one reigned supreme. All in the room obeyed its commands; it told them to smile or frown. The woman frowned. She placed her hands, one on top of the other, over the middle of Fred's breastbone and pushed down and released. She repeated the motion in a rhythm. After several cycles, another person tapped her shoulder and indicated that he could take over. He stood beside the bed in readiness to do so. Jane watched the strawberry-haired woman, tiring but determined, and saw that this required intense work, to move a person's chest up and down for them.

Words were passed between the hospital staff in whispered calm. Jane understood little of it. She watched Sofia to gauge what was occurring. Sofia's face seemed to change from pink to gray.

Everyone looked at Fred, then at the box.

"What takes place, Sofia?" Jane asked her.

"Oh," Sofia replied, and said nothing more.

Footsteps thundered down the hall and a man pushed a chest of steel drawers on wheels into the room, which rattled as it entered. More steel boxes painted white and blue sat atop the chest. The cart pusher handed out items to the group. The group sprang into action. One person placed a clear mask over Fred's mouth and pumped a balloon into his throat. Another removed Fred's gown.

Next, a man with gray hair entered. He wore a suit. More people entered after him. Each new person seemed older than the last. In less than thirty seconds, a dozen people had entered the room.

Dr. Marks entered last. The cart man handed him two black paddles, shaped like irons. The boxes buzzed and beeped. "Charging to two hundred," the cart man announced. "Clear."

Dr. Marks placed the irons on Fred's chest. They buzzed. The sound sickened with its volume and flatness. Fred's body lifted half an inch from the bed, then flopped back onto it like a rag doll dropped by a child.

The group all looked to the box. It must not have given them the answer they wanted, for they chatted and muttered again. Dr. Marks shook his head. He looked at the irons as if to check that they worked.

"What has happened, Sofia?" Jane asked.

"His heart has stopped," she replied. Jane nodded. She knew little, but she knew a heart was made for beating. Sofia seemed to have ceased blinking and breathing.

Jane clutched the chair beside her, then cursed herself for the display. This person was but a friend. She had known him less than two weeks. It was silly to get swept up in the affairs of persons she hardly knew, but she hoped he survived, for Sofia's sake.

Sofia took Jane's hand. Jane held it, if only to bring Sofia comfort. She did not need comforting herself.

"Charging two hundred," the cart man announced. "Clear."

Dr. Marks placed the irons on Fred again. They buzzed, and he rose from the bed once more, then flopped.

They all watched the box. "Damn," said Dr. Marks.

After Sofia had banned Jane from observing the advancements of the twenty-first century, Jane made her peace with shutting her mind to the wonders of the new world. Now, as words rushed past her ears like *cardiac arrest* and *ten thousand volts,* she yearned to have disobeyed Sofia and learned every detail of the medical endeavors of the past two hundred years.

The strawberry-haired matron bowed her head. The cart man exhaled.

Jane sensed the group begin to tire. Not in their physical action, which remained crisp and practiced, but in their mood. The strawberry-haired woman's voice grew less sure. Dr. Marks's commands were less vital. A vapor seemed to descend upon the room, some sort of malaise, or wobble of faith. She saw that the longer this process went on, the less likely it stood to succeed. These doctors and nurses completed not the steps of some infallible sequence, which, when followed correctly, would lead to their patient's recuperation. Instead they made a series of attempts, with each subsequent shot wilder than the last. The more boxes and tubes and people added to the gamble, the more diminished the chance of return.

Earlier, when she was presented with the option of leaving him on her own terms, Jane had resigned herself to the notion with sadness but determination. Now the choice was taken from her—Fred threatened to depart from her life with the audacity to not even check with her first. She found it an unacceptable proposition.

"What are they doing, Sofia?" Jane asked.

"Giving him electricity," Sofia said.

"But the electricity is what did this! He does not need more of it!" Jane announced so loud Sofia jumped. "Is it working, at least?" she asked then.

Sofia shook her head.

"Charging three hundred," the cart man called. "Clear."

Dr. Marks placed the irons down once more. Fred lifted and flopped. His eyes remained closed.

Dr. Marks lowered his irons. He scratched his face.

Jane then had the grim notion, the one afflicting fools throughout the ages, of only realizing the worth of something once it was gone. Throughout almost the entirety of her acquaintance with Fred, Jane had been preoccupied with the issue of returning home, concerning herself primarily with reversing a spell she considered to be faulty. But Mrs. Sinclair had made no error, she realized now. Jane had not come to the twenty-first century by mistake. The witch had promised to take Jane to her one true love, and she had delivered.

Jane's legacy in this time, her books and her authorial reputation, were indeed disappearing in front of her eyes, because a return to her own time to create them was growing less likely by the day. But her unlikelihood of returning home was not due to her being so enamored by this era that she felt obliged to stay in it; it was not the horseless steel carriages, the tube trains, and the abundance of food that compelled Jane to remain. It was a person. He had bought Jane sea-bathing clothes and danced with her. As a child, he had tried to walk across England to save his dying mother and almost managed the task. Now he verged on departing the earth without ever knowing how much Jane loved him.

Was it always supposed to end this way? Mrs. Sinclair's promise had mentioned nothing of electricity or destroyed heart muscle. She had said nothing about him surviving once Jane got there. Perhaps this stood as her lot, to meet him briefly before he departed. What a cruel thing. How should she act now? Should she thank the gods for the short time they'd had together? Speak wistfully in hushed tones? She wished it were not so. But then who was she in the scheme of these things?

As he died there before her on that splendid twenty-first-century hospital bed, surrounded by experts and wizards who could not make him well, Jane wondered if she would go on breathing in a world without him in it.

Then the box beeped.

The group all snapped their heads toward it. It beeped once more, and then again.

"A-fib," announced the strawberry-haired woman, in more twenty-first-century medical jargon. Someone else nodded. Another smiled.

"Is he alive?" Jane demanded.

"Yes," Sofia cried. "I think!"

Dr. Marks nodded. "Let's get him to theater." The group moved in balletic coordination, bundling blankets up, separating tubes from the wall and placing boxes on Fred's bed.

"Where are you taking him?" Sofia bellowed.

"There's more work to be done on his heart," Dr. Marks told her. "He needs surgery."

Six people took hold of the bed and wheeled Fred from the room, past Jane and Sofia. His eyes stayed closed and his head rocked as they moved him. A tube protruded from his mouth.

"Take care with his head," Jane whispered, pulling Sofia out of the way.

They rolled him down the hall. He disappeared through swinging doors.

Sofia screamed to a woman in green who sat behind a desk to explain what was happening.

Jane stood in the doorway and watched the place where he went. There was more work to be done on his heart. Now she carried around something in her own heart, too. She wondered how its weight could be borne in her one little chest.

Chapter Forty-Two

$\mathcal{J}$ane returned to the room where they had waited before. Sofia joined her.

"I'm a selfish woman, Jane. I'm afraid if I lose my brother, I might do something stupid like be sad for the rest of my days."

Jane touched her hand. "You must be calm, Sofia. The physician said the operation will take one hour. It has only been three minutes."

"If he leaves me, I will have no one left. I will die alone naked in bed like Marilyn Monroe after a barbiturate supper."

Jane had long stopped asking Sofia what she meant with her references to people and places Jane could not possibly know anything of, so she simply nodded and smiled and offered what best encouragement she could. "I am still here, Sofia. I will not leave you." Sofia sat down next to her.

"You say that now," she said. She paused. "Probably not the time to tell you this, but Mrs. Sinclair writes you a letter in 1810. Make of that what you will."

Jane shifted in her seat. "Mrs. Sinclair? She writes me a letter?"

Sofia nodded. "The letter still exists. We found a book about it."

Jane considered this. "What says the letter?"

"We don't know. But I could hazard a guess."

"You think the letter explains how to reverse the spell?"

"I can't think what else she'd write to you about, can you? You two weren't pen pals."

Jane nodded, stunned. Her mind raced. "Thank you, Sofia. You did everything you said you would."

"You doubted me?"

"Not for a second. But how can I ever repay you?"

"No repayment necessary." They sat in silence. Jane knew she should feel happy: she now had the means to return home. She would see Mama and Papa again, and she would write her books. "Unless you don't *want* me to find the letter," Sofia said after a time, staring straight ahead.

Jane stared ahead also. "Might you delay your location of Mrs. Sinclair's correspondence, for a week, perhaps? I only ask, as I feel it would be impolite of me to leave you at this juncture, with a family member in the hospital and all."

"Okay." Sofia touched her arm. "For politeness' sake."

Jane sensed Sofia wanted to say more but was thankful she did not.

THE OPERATION DID not require one hour. Dr. Marks came to them four hours later. Jane and Sofia both jumped to their feet.

"What's the prognosis, Doc?" Sofia asked. "Don't dumb it down. I did a three-episode special-guest run on *ER* where I played a beautiful but troubled neurosurgeon."

Dr. Marks squinted at her. "We performed an ablation on his heart."

Sofia paused. "Refresh my memory?" she asked. "What is a fla-bation?"

"The electric shock damaged the circuits in his heart. We conducted an electrical physiological study. The SA node was not firing." Dr. Marks rubbed his eye.

Sofia nodded. "Perhaps break it down for my friend, doctor."

Dr. Marks turned to Jane. "A piece of his heart was damaged in the accident. It was stopping his heart from beating properly. We inserted a catheter and ablated the damaged tissue with an electrical impulse. We destroyed it."

Jane understood only a few words, but it was enough. "You destroyed a part of his heart, doctor?" she asked.

"Spit it out, Doc. Is he alive?" Sofia begged.

"He is alive," Dr. Marks replied. "There was more damage than we thought. We put a pacemaker in."

"Can we see him?"

The doctor led the women down a corridor to a different room. A small waxen man lay in a bed, his skin gray, his eyes closed. A tube sprouted from his mouth to a steel box that pumped. Another tube grew from the bandage at his wrist and three sprang from his chest. Jane felt confusion as to why the doctor showed them some random, pitiable fellow.

"Fred!" Sofia cried. She ran to him and kissed his hand. "When will he wake up?"

"I was hoping by now," Dr. Marks said. He rubbed his eye once more.

"What is his condition, sir?" Jane asked.

"I've seen worse," Dr. Marks said. "I've seen better. We've done all we can."

"Fred's father hit him, a few times," Sofia said. She cleared her throat. "The old man would go after our mother, see." She forced a laugh. "So Fred would provoke him, and Dad would wallop him instead. He ended up in this place once. Could that have made it worse?"

The doctor looked at her. "Unlikely," he said.

Sofia nodded and wiped a tear. Jane watched the interaction with astonishment. "What do we do now?" Sofia asked.

Dr. Marks gave a nod. "We wait."

SOFIA SAT BY Fred's bedside; Jane stood behind her. He did not awaken. Rob, the young man with the red shirt who had accompanied Jane to the hospital, appeared at the door. Sofia went to him. They spoke, and she returned to Jane.

"They're asking when I can come back to the set. I need to rehearse a scene. Rob's kindly reminded me there are fifty people waiting for me, and if there's nothing I can do here, perhaps I could go, do the scene, and come back. He also was good enough to mention that my contract does not allow me time off for sick relatives." Sofia looked stricken. "I told him to bugger off. There's nothing I can do here, but I can't leave him on his own."

"I will stay," Jane said.

"Are you sure?" Sofia asked.

"Go. Do your work. If he wakes, I . . . you shall know the second it occurs. I shall sit here until you return."

"Thank you." Sofia kissed Fred's forehead and departed with the red-shirted boy.

JANE SAT ON the chair by the bedside; night fell outside.

The boxes continued to buzz and whir. Fred wore a bandage on his head. Bags filled with strange fluids entered his arm through tubes.

The woman with the strawberry hair entered the room. She inspected the boxes and made notes with a self-inking quill. She smiled at Jane.

"You were here before," said Jane.

"I was," she replied.

"I am a stranger here. Where I come from, I consider myself a woman of intelligence and sense. But here in this place with all of these boxes and tubes, I am ignorant."

The woman smiled again. "I am Sister Elizabeth. I am the matron here." She spoke in a Leicestershire accent like Margaret the housemaid's, thick, warm, and salty like a good beef stew. She walked to one of the boxes. One glass box had an accordion inside. It depressed with a whoosh and Fred's chest rose up. "This breathes for him," Sister Elizabeth said.

Jane nodded in astonishment. Sister Elizabeth moved behind her. She pointed to another box. "This one here? This monitors his heart."

Jane watched the box. "What is that line?" she asked.

"His heart beating," Sister Elizabeth replied.

Jane smiled. A symphony score of arches and valleys rose and fell across the frame. Fred's heart beat before her.

"You must be truthful with me," Jane said to her. "You walk in, note the boxes with your papers, and say nothing. I must know. Will he die?"

"We are doing everything we can," Sister Elizabeth replied.

"Of that I am in no doubt. Madam, I know it is your protocol to promise nothing. But I do not come from this place. You have cut him open and sewn him back together again. You have seen the inside of his heart. I have never witnessed such genius and wonder. Surely, with all this magic, he is going to be well. Tell me the truth, good lady, or I shall run mad."

Sister Elizabeth's face softened. She nodded. "It doesn't look good. Even if he does wake, there's no promise he has not suffered brain damage. There's nothing more they can do."

"How can it be these magical boxes and tubes are no good? I feel useless. I wish there was something I could do."

"You could hold his hand," Sister Elizabeth said.

Jane laughed. "What am I compared to these glorious machines? How could that help?"

"I don't know, but it does," Sister Elizabeth said. "I can name every chamber and artery. I can explain the pumping mechanism, the movement of the sinus rhythm, the fibrillation. I can tell you every muscle and valve. But I cannot tell you how the heart works. I do know this. I've seen a cancer patient riddled with tumors keep himself alive to see his brother at Christmas. I've seen a woman with MS wait until her new granddaughter was born before dying. I've seen a man with a C4 spinal cord rupture stand from a wheelchair to walk his daughter down the aisle. Every doctor and nurse knows this in their heart. The greatest patient vital signs are recorded during visiting hours. More patients die at three and four A.M. than any other time, in the dark, when everyone's gone home. Machines can only start your heart. They can't keep it going. Only love can do that."

Jane held Fred's hand.

"See that?" Sister Elizabeth said. She pointed to the box. "His heart rate went up."

Jane smiled. "Truly?"

Sister Elizabeth nodded and pointed to the box. The number in the corner that had read 65 now read 72. "It's what happens when loved ones are around."

"I am not a loved one," Jane said. "I am a new friend. I upset him."

"That's not what the machine says."

Jane did not let go of Fred's hand for the next eight hours.

Chapter Forty-Three

*F*red remained asleep when Jane woke the next morning. Sofia slept in an armchair in the corner of the room; she opened her eyes and wished Jane good morning.

"I got in at midnight," Sofia told her. "You'd fallen asleep. You slept like that, at his side, holding his hand. You can let go of it now, Jane," Sofia said.

"Not until I am instructed," Jane replied.

"I checked with Sister Elizabeth. You can let go. Surely you need to use the toilet? I will hold his hand until you get back."

Jane released her hand and excused herself to visit the bathroom, where she momentarily tore herself away from thoughts of Fred to be astounded by the dozen gleaming white privies. She washed her hands under the powerful taps and returned to Fred's hospital room. She paused in the doorway as she arrived there, for Sofia was whispering something in Fred's ear and wiping a tear from her face. Jane waited until Sofia sat back in the chair, then cleared her throat to announce her approach. Sofia smiled and wiped her face and offered Jane the chair. Jane resumed her place at Fred's side. She put her hand back where it was before.

Three hours passed and Fred did not stir. With nothing to

do and no sign of Fred waking, Sofia returned to set once more, promising to be back as soon as she could.

The day wore on and the defeated looks returned to the faces of those who worked at the hospital. Sister Elizabeth and Dr. Marks visited often. Fred did not wake. His eyes remained closed.

Jane spoke to him. "Fred. I do not know if you can hear me. I am sorry to have upset you," she said. The boxes beeped and whirred.

"I understand if you are unable. But if you could find it in yourself to wake, I would be most appreciative."

She should have run from him the first day they met. She preferred ignorance to knowing this pain. She slapped her leg and told herself to take charge. She had lived without this person for twenty-eight years; she could learn to do it again. Then she said three words that she had never said to anyone—not her sister or her dear papa or any man. Three words so riddled with cliché as to be laughable, and so laden with meaning it was safest to tell them to another person while they slept. "I love you," she said.

She imagined it for certain; he squeezed her palm.

Jane fell asleep. She did not let go of his hand.

JANE WOKE TO the feeling again. This time it became obvious. Someone was squeezing her hand. Grasping it, even. She looked over. Fred opened his eyes. He stared at the ceiling.

Sofia entered the room and saw him. "Sister Elizabeth!" she called down the hall.

Fred shook and pointed at nothing. His eyes bulged.

"He can't breathe!" Sofia said. Sister Elizabeth entered the room and moved to Fred.

"He can breathe, hush now," Sister Elizabeth said. "This is a good thing. He is trying to breathe on his own." She turned to Fred. "Mr. Wentworth, I want to remove this tube. Will you help me?"

Fred nodded to her with wet eyes, trying to sit up. She eased him back down onto his pillow. Jane watched him struggle in confusion and agony. His face bore a look of terror.

"I am going to pull the tube; I need you to cough." Fred nodded. Sister Elizabeth pulled the tube quickly from his mouth. Fred choked and gurgled and let out a horrid groan. A tear seeped from each eye. Jane sighed; she could not stand much more of this. A length of slimed tube emerged from his throat.

"Good job," Sister Elizabeth said. "Keep coughing."

She pulled once more, and Fred coughed again. The tube came free, and Fred relaxed back onto the bed. Sweat plastered his hair to his face. His eyes darted around the room, but he said nothing.

"Fred?" Jane called to him. He made no answer. Jane turned to Sofia. "Is he a simpleton?" she asked her.

Sofia shrugged. "Fred. If you're in there, say something," she said.

"Is my hair spiky?" he choked out in a hoarse voice, and grinned.

Sofia slapped him across the arm. The slap grew to an embrace. "You said that already."

"Careful. You will crush him," Jane said. Sofia loosened her grip on her brother.

"It is good to see you again, Mr. Wentworth," Sister Elizabeth said. She touched his arm.

"Please. After that, call me Fred."

She laughed, then checked his boxes and papers and left the room. As she left, she winked at Jane.

Fred turned his eyes to Jane. "Hello," he said.

"Hello, Fred. Are you in pain?" Jane asked him.

"No," he said. "Thank you."

Jane waited for him to say something about her sitting by his side. Had he heard what she had said to him? Did he know? Did he believe she was Miss Jane Austen of Hampshire, daughter of George and Cassandra Austen? Or did he still think she was a woman of his own time who made up stories to injure him? Did he feel as she did? But instead of answering any of these questions, he said nothing. She cursed herself for her selfish concerns. This man had been through an ordeal; what had happened between them would be the last thing on his mind. He smiled at her and turned back to Sofia.

"How do you feel?" Sofia said. "Are you cold? Do you recall feeling cold while you were on the other side?"

"I do feel a little cold, Sofe," Fred said.

"Leave it with me," Sofia said and left the room.

Fred turned to Jane. "You held my hand," he said.

She looked to him. An excited feeling welled up inside her.

"Why did you say such things to me?" he asked.

She was unsure as to which things he referred. Did he mean the things in the pool, or the things in the hospital bed? Did he refer to the declaration of her identity, or the declaration of her love? He had heard the first; she was unsure if he had heard the second.

"Do you mean in the baths?"

"Of course," he replied. Those things were easier to speak of.

"I could not lie to you," she said. "I am who I am." Jane swallowed at the memory of it. "It does not matter if you believe me," she insisted. "I am who I say I am. It is the truth."

"I never said I didn't believe you."

Jane commanded her heart to stop its thumping.

"You are Jane Austen."

Jane nodded and cleared her throat. She shifted in her chair.

"On some level, I've always known," he said.

"You have?"

"Something was strange, at least," he said. He smiled.

"You will not have to worry about it too much longer, in any case, for I shall be leaving soon." She said it lightly, but she searched his face for his reaction. "Your sister has secured the means to return me to 1803. She has been a valiant helper, quite the heroine."

"She's good like that."

"So I shall be on my way. I have books to write."

"Of course. As you should," Fred replied with a nod. He paused. "Or do you think you might stay for a little while? I know you need to get back, but Sofia will leave me to fend for myself with a bottle of sherry and a pile of blankets. Just a week."

Jane considered this. "I suppose I could stay one week. To help you get back on your feet."

They stared at each other. An excited, terrified feeling moved through Jane at the way he looked at her.

"I have one more request," he said.

"Goodness. You are a demanding person, sir," she replied, trying to sound calm.

"I'm quite the dictator when I want to be."

"Name your demand, then," she said. She coughed.

"I should like to do the thing I wanted to, before." He moved his eyes to her mouth, then back to her eyes.

She cleared her throat. "I'm afraid your demand is more of a request, sir," she said in a voice gone hoarse. "You are not much of a despot." She reminded herself to breathe.

"True. I can't demand this, in fairness. Unfortunately, this is one of those things I can only do if you want me to. Do you want me to?"

She breathed out finally; their eyes met. She looked away. "Promise me your heart won't stop again? From the exertion?"

He laughed. "I promise."

Jane swallowed. "Very well, then."

He leaned forward, slowly, and placed his lips on hers. If Jane lived another thousand years, if she wrote a hundred novels, she already knew she would never know another feeling like it.

Chapter Forty-Four

Sofia returned with the blankets, and Jane left Fred's bedside. He waved her goodbye as she left the room, grinning with a wide smile.

Sofia looked around the room. Flowers, cards, and balloons from the kids at Fred's school festooned the area. "You're so cool, Mr. Dub," she said to Fred in a juvenile voice, slapping his arm. He shrugged and smiled and looked out the door. "I see you two made up." She nodded in the direction Jane was walking down the hospital corridor.

Fred wiped the smile from his face and scoffed. "What are you on about?" he said, forcing a laugh she only heard him make when he'd been caught.

"Don't play coy with me," Sofia replied. "You must think I'm pretty stupid."

"I don't think you're stupid at all," he replied. "But I don't know what you're talking about."

"You like Jane. That's what I'm talking about."

"As if," he said. He folded his arms across his chest, like a teenager. The machine wires connected to his forearms twisted in a bundle and an alarm went off. He uncrossed his arms and apologized to a nurse who rushed in.

Sofia laughed and shook her head. "You also do that thing with your shoelaces whenever I mention her name."

"What thing?" Fred said, scoffing a second time.

"I mention Jane's name and you tie your shoelaces. Even if they are already tied. You bend down and untie them, then tie them back up again. You used to do that whenever you liked a girl at school. Like Molly Parson! You tied your shoelaces every time someone said 'Molly.'"

"You come out with some whoppers, Sofia, but this takes the cake." He placed his hands on his hips. If he intended to look serious, he did not pull it off, dressed as he was in a backless cotton gown, lying on a hospital bed.

"That whole year, you had perfectly tied shoelaces, double knots, triple knots."

"Complete rubbish."

Sofia raised both eyebrows and rested her chin on her hand, like a professor posing a philosophical question. "Where is Jane now?"

Fred bowed his head and gazed at the end of the hospital bed.

"See! You looked at your feet! Ha. You're thinking about tying them. You're not even wearing any shoes. You should get it checked out, your shoe-tying, love-concealing compulsion."

"Sofia, shut up."

"You also smile more. It's nice. I don't blame you, Fred. She's quite the woman."

He swallowed.

"You two had a fight, didn't you? But now you've made up. I'm glad. She must have said something pretty terrible to upset you." She raised an eyebrow.

"She told me she was Jane Austen," Fred said, looking down at his hands.

"She is Jane Austen," Sofia replied. She waited for him to react.

Fred snapped his head back up. He moved to cross his arms once more.

"Don't cross your arms. The alarms will go off again," Sofia said.

Fred rested his arms by his sides and shifted in the bed. "What do you know about it?"

"She appeared to me in a pile of curtains." Sofia laughed ruefully. "It was a big to-do. You missed the whole thing."

"You're crazy" Fred said.

"Undeniably," Sofia replied. "Doesn't make it any less true."

"What curtains?" Fred said.

"Jane appeared out of thin air in the wings of the Bath community hall while I was rehearsing for *Northanger Abbey*. You were there. You danced with her afterward."

Fred nodded and paused. "How much had you had to drink?"

"Nothing," Sofia answered. "Aside from a few puffs of a brown paper bag, I was stone-cold sober. I did not dream it, nor did I hallucinate. I wish I had. I'd prefer not to have to help a time-travelling nineteenth-century author return home. I've got enough on my plate already, trying to get my estranged husband back and my brother seducing live electricity."

"You realize the absurdity of what you're saying?" Fred said.

"Utterly and completely. But here's the thing. I believe you've thought a great deal more about this whole Jane caper than you're letting on. And while you're pretending I'm crazy, you already know she's Jane Austen. It's just taken some time to sink in."

Fred nodded. "Why didn't you tell me?" he asked.

"Not really the type of thing you tell people, is it—'Jane Austen appeared to me from a pile of curtains'—unless you want to be taken away in a straitjacket. I'm only telling you about it now because you've clearly gone gaga for her." Fred opened his mouth to protest once more, then seemed to think better of it.

"Let me know when you have made your peace with everything discussed so far," Sofia said. "For there is more to tell you."

Fred turned back to her. "Okay?"

"Putting aside the whole Jane Austen thing for a moment. Do you have feelings for her?"

Fred shifted in the bed. "Oh, I . . ." He inhaled but said no more.

"I know something's already happened between you two. But what I'm really asking is, how deep do those feelings go?"

"Um," he said. He gazed out the window.

"I know this is a bit of a thing to lump on you, after you've been electrocuted and all, and I don't want to burst the early romance bubble, but unfortunately, time is short."

He scowled at her. "What do you mean?"

"You don't have to answer right now. But whether you believe Jane is Jane Austen or not, she is going back. To the year 1803. She is going to fulfill her destiny as a writer, and she will go soon."

"What? I don't . . . okay, when?" he stammered.

"As soon as she instructs me. I discovered the way to get her home. I had help from a nice young man in a cardigan, but I led the mission. Anyway, bottom line, she will go home. Unless . . ."

"Unless what?" Fred said.

"Unless she is given a reason to stay."

Fred sighed.

"I think you've been your charming self, daft boy, and made her grow feelings for you. I have the means to return her home, and if you don't get your act together, she will go. She won't wait forever. She can't. While I loathe the idea of rushing a budding romance in its fragile early stages, I'm afraid in this case, a push may be required."

"What kind of a push?" Fred asked her.

"You need to give her a reason to stay," Sofia replied.

"But we hardly know each other," Fred said.

"I understand. And in normal circumstances, I'd counsel against large, fast, declarative gestures of affection. They almost always end in disaster, embarrassment, and legal paperwork—I should know. But these aren't normal circumstances. And she is not a normal woman. And so, if your feelings are moving in that direction, toward love, houses, babies, all the happily-ever-after stuff, may I suggest that, as soon as humanly possible, you tell her how you feel."

Chapter Forty-Five

$\mathcal{S}$ofia returned to set. She felt like she walked on a cloud. Fred had woken up; she had flowers from her director. It could not get any better than this. She'd thank Jack for the roses one day. Let him sweat a little first. She walked to the sound stage and waved hello to Derek. He looked surprised to see her.

"Back so soon? Why not spend the afternoon at the hospital?"

"All good—Fred is well and has a friend there. I felt like a third wheel, actually, so I headed back. Are you annoyed to see me?"

"Of course not," Derek said. "Let's go to the truck." He tried to move her away from the sound stage. She caught him looking over her shoulder.

"What is it, Derek? What's going on?"

"Nothing," he replied. But he glanced past Sofia again as he said it, then quickly looked back to her. Sofia turned to see what he was looking at. Jack and Courtney stood by the coffee machine. Jack had his hand on Courtney's bottom. Not mistakenly, or to move her out of the path of an oncoming vehicle; he patted her behind for no reason in particular, except his own comfort. Courtney whispered something in his ear, and he smiled. Then they kissed. On the lips. Sofia blinked and fiddled with an earring.

It wasn't a first kiss between them. Courtney lifted her heels the perfect amount and Jack bowed his neck the requisite balance, so their lips met in an exact, casual point of intersection, practiced and known. They had done this before, but they were not tired of it, either. It was one of those kisses that come right in the middle of things. Sofia blinked three times, bit her lip, and hoped no one noticed.

"I'm so sorry, Ms. Wentworth," said Derek.

Jack kissed Courtney the same way he used to kiss Sofia. He cupped her bottom with his right hand and tipped his temple to the left. These moves were not reserved for Sofia, she realized. They were generic moves of tendon and bone dictated by his DNA; he performed the same for all women. She paused for a moment to consider the unique vista afforded her—to see the man she had kissed for ten years kissing someone else. Most people never got such a view; she should feel lucky. He looked good when kissing—great, even.

She became aware of many sets of eyes on her—the camera crew, the catering people. They stared with looks she'd never received before: of pity.

"My makeup is still not right, Derek," she stated in a cool voice. She strolled to the truck with a blank expression. Derek followed her.

"How long have they been seeing each other?" she asked him once they were inside.

"I don't know. A while."

Sofia felt like dying. "A while is not long. They could still break up," she said. Then her blood ran cold.

She recalled a moment six months earlier. Coming home after the film in Prague, she had discovered a message on Jack's phone from an unknown number. A graphic message, sexual. She left it for three days without bringing it up. When she asked him about it, he accused her of snooping. They fought horribly, and a week later, he moved out.

"They've been together six months, at least," Sofia said. She bowed her head.

"I'm so sorry," Derek said. "There's more. Courtney's trying to get you fired."

Sofia snapped her head up. "What? Impossible. She can't fire me."

Derek shook his head. "It's all over set. Courtney is telling everyone it's not working, there's no chemistry between the two of you, you don't gel."

"We *don't* gel. It isn't working. But what can she do about it? That's how it goes sometimes—your cast mate is a better actor. But she can't just get rid of me. I'll get rid of her! I'm the star." Sofia's face fell. "Oh."

"She's the star."

Sofia scratched her face. "She's the star." She felt exhausted again. "I've had enough of this," she said. She stormed out of the makeup truck and walked over to Jack's trailer.

On the way over there, she lined up her speech. She'd dress him down, tell him to pull his mistress up, bring her back into line. She'd lecture him on how unprofessional this all was. But as she stormed into his trailer and saw him sitting there, the grand cries for professionalism and the good of the production went out of her head. Instead, she vomited out words of neediness and scorn. "How could you do this, Jack?" she heard herself say. "You're making a fool of me."

"I'm sorry, Sofe, it just happened. You know how it goes. We fell in love."

She rolled her eyes at the cliché. "But what about the flowers?" she asked then, hating herself instantly for saying it.

"What flowers? Oh, right. I don't know." He shrugged and gave a little chuckle, triumphant and smug.

Sofia looked him in the face. There it was. She would have missed it if she hadn't looked up right then. A flash of something that danced across his face as he smiled. What was it? Oh, yes. Victory and contempt. He could still turn any woman's head, and he knew it. He was required to give nothing of himself for this head-turning, not his time or his affection. He killed some plants and Sofia came running. Why had he sent her the flowers? He probably did not know himself. To get a rise out of her? Ah, she realized then, silly her. Because of the librarian who'd put his arm around her.

She shook her head. "And you're happy to throw away a decade of marriage?"

"No," he replied. "Not happy. But it's serious with Courtney," he insisted.

Sofia scoffed. "How serious could it be? She's an adolescent."

"She's pregnant."

Sofia felt her lunch loosen in her stomach. She stumbled and fell onto his leg a little. He leaned down and caught her. His clothes smelled like expensive laundry powder; the maid would have washed them. She found a chair and sat down.

"Sofe? Say something." He touched her shoulder. She flinched and shook his hand off her. A numbness crept over her.

"How many weeks is she?" she asked in a friendly tone, like a work colleague inquiring about an acquaintance.

"What?" Jack said. He looked confused.

"How many weeks pregnant."

"Oh. I don't know. Twelve, I think." He smiled a little into the distance. She tormented herself with what might have caused the smile. Perhaps he recalled some prenatal moment, attendance at a recent ultrasound, perhaps, or Courtney surprising him with baby clothes.

He had told her, long ago, that he did not want children, though she'd expected him to come around. She'd thought he would see how wonderful she was and realize he'd be a fool to pass up a little family. Every year went by and it became another year gone. It went on for too long to start afresh with someone else; she'd invested too much time.

"Sofe? Are you okay?" he said.

She wiped her nose. She looked him in the eye. "Is it because she is younger?" she asked. "Because I don't look like I once did?"

"Sofe. You're still gorgeous. Of course not."

"I know I am, but that wasn't the question. Is it because I got older?"

"Don't do this to yourself," he said.

"I'd appreciate an honest answer," she said. "I deserve that."

He nodded. "Okay. You are older. You don't look like you once did. But that's not the reason," he said.

She bristled at the honesty, both grateful and horrified. "Wow, okay. What's the reason, then?" She leaned forward in her chair, fascinated now.

He sighed. "Everything with you became so difficult."

She had to laugh; while the relationship might have punished her, he seemed to enjoy no end of success. He was more famous, richer, and more sought after now than ever. "And with her?" she asked.

"Everything with Courtney," he said, "it feels so easy." She stared at him and scowled. His face turned to a look of worry then, and he seemed to wince, as though bracing for a scolding. "Do you hate me?" he asked.

Sofia sat back in her chair and went quiet. She studied his face, noting how handsome he was, how attractive she still found him. She was about to shout, "Yes, of course I hate you, and who could blame me?" She prepared some words to that effect, recounting a list of all the times he'd disappointed her, all the hurt she felt, all the reasons why he deserved the hate. She opened her mouth to say them, paused, then closed it again.

Finally, she sighed, exhausted, and shook her head. "No, I don't hate you," she replied. It was the truth. She stood and left the trailer. She walked across the set, her face bathed in tears. She felt too tired to care who saw.

If they were Mr. and Mrs. Butterworth of Hockessin, Delaware, they might have stuck it out. If she taught kindergarten and he ran a vinyl record store, and they kept bees in their spare time, they might have stood a chance. If their parents had taught them good lessons about the ups and downs of marriage, taught them to muddle through when the going got tough, to push through the lean years when the sex waned, when everyone felt tired all the time, when work sucked the life out of them, they might have survived, emerging out the other side in their fifties, with a marriage bruised but intact. But they weren't Mr. and Mrs. B of Hockessin, they were Jack Travers, Directors Guild of America member, and Sofia Wentworth, movie star. They were not people, they were gods, above doing the dishes and arguing about whose family to go to for Christmas. And when the going got tough for gods, they didn't muddle through; they packed it in and moved on and searched for perfection somewhere else. And while she was keen to give it another shot, Jack evidently thought it easier to start afresh with someone new.

Sofia could not blame him. In time, he'd tire of Courtney, too, when sleep deprivation and disappointment took the easiness of now and turned it to dust.

There had been some glory days, especially in the beginning, when fireworks rained down on them. But in truth, she realized now with pain, the passion and ecstasy she felt with him had come from accepting a compliment or a kind touch after days of neither. The marriage had ended years ago.

This realization made nothing easier.

Chapter Forty-Six

Sofia collected Jane from the hospital and brought her home for the night. She relayed the day's stories to her, and when she'd finished, she sat down on the kitchen floor. "Say something," Sofia said when Jane remained silent.

Jane shook her head, and instead of speaking, she sat down on the floor next to Sofia. Sofia felt gratified to have the power to render speechless a woman who normally had things to say on a range of topics. Sofia told herself not to give any more tears to him but found she could not prevent their flow any longer and began weeping on the floor like an idiot. Jane touched her shoulder, which made her cry more.

After a time, Jane finally spoke. "Your pocket buzzes once more," she said.

Sofia sifted her phone from her pocket and squinted at the screen through one teary eye. Dave's name appeared. Her heart sank. She rejected the call and sighed. "I thought it was Jack," she said with a bitter scoff. "I hoped he was calling to see if I was all right. I'm an idiot." She wiped her face.

"You are the furthest thing from that," Jane said to her.

"I cannot show my face at rehearsal, Jane. I could take it before, when we were only separated. But this?" She shook her head. "I won't turn up tomorrow. I won't give them the satisfaction of sacking me. I'll quit."

"This man has ruined your marriage," Jane said. "Must he ruin your career, too?"

Sofia laughed and raised an eyebrow. "What do you propose I do instead? Go out there, and what . . . act?"

"Something like that."

Sofia laughed ruefully. "Even if I showed up, I look absurd in this role. I fostered a fantasy of looking fabulous in this film, of breaking hearts."

"That is your goal? To break hearts?"

Sofia shrugged. "It's all I know how to play. I play sexpots, ingenues, manic pixie dream girls," she said.

"I don't know what those are, but they sound horrid," Jane said.

"Either way, I am too old to play them now. I know I'm still a decent looking woman. I know I'm still a . . . MILF"—she cringed—"but I'm no longer a comic book character, do you see? I can't pull off the perky young love interest anymore. But it's all I know how to do, so I keep doing it, and I'm making a fool of myself. There's nothing more tragic than a woman who tries to pretend she is still young."

"Stop pretending, then," Jane replied.

Sofia turned to her. "And do what?" she asked.

"You've always played your characters a certain way, yes? You've always played the pretty young object of men's affections."

"Correct." Sofia shrugged.

"But this character is different?"

Sofia nodded.

"So, play her differently."

"I don't know how. I usually have sweet, cute things to say. Now

I have inane, ridiculous words to speak. And I don't know how to deliver them. I don't have it in me."

"Tell me of the happiest moment in your profession," Jane said.

Sofia went quiet. She thought back through all of the red carpets, the press events, the limousines, and the screaming fans. "Ever been to a town called Barrow?" she asked.

Jane shook her head.

"Horrid place. Up north. It was a tiny theater; I was nineteen. I was Cordelia in a regional production of *King Lear*. The audience comprised senior citizens and a group of miners who'd got the day wrong and thought it was poker night. One man asked for his money back before we'd even started." Sofia paused to wipe her tears. "I thought about how to say my lines. I had little training at that point, but I tried to put myself in Cordelia's shoes. My own father had left us, so there was that boring news to draw on, but that's not where the feeling came from. Her voice and her walk came from something inside me. It was deeper than missed recitals and birthday cards. It came from my imagination."

"The best always does," Jane said.

"I delivered her final soliloquy, then died in Lear's arms. I stole a glance to the crowd. They stared back at me, rapt. You could hear a pin drop. It was as though another dimension had opened up. We'd entered a new plane. I wore a costume of rags, and I was barefoot. I looked up again. The rough man who'd wanted his money back was still in the audience. He was crying. He sought me out afterward and told me he was going to call his daughter, whom he hadn't spoken to in twenty years."

Jane smiled. "Brava." She touched Sofia's shoulder. "You already have all the tools you need to play this character."

"But how?" Sofia asked.

"What kinds of things does Mrs. Allen say?" Jane asked.

"My first line is 'We neither of us have a stitch to wear!' They put me in ridiculous outfits. One day I wore an actual ship in my hair."

"What ship? A frigate? Schooner?"

"Not sure. A tugboat, maybe. Every time Mrs. Allen misses a stich in embroidery, she announces it to everyone. Why?"

"Women are notorious for apologizing," Jane said with a shrug. "An illness afflicting us from birth."

"She is the punch line to her own jokes," Sofia continued. "She recites a three-minute monologue about muslin."

Jane scratched her head. "Who is this character I have created?" She spoke to herself, more than to Sofia. "Perhaps she is based on someone I have met."

"Like who?" Sofia said. "Is it a thinly veiled takedown of some enemy of yours? Spill, Jane."

Jane paused. "I'm thinking back over all the women of my acquaintance. There is a woman who is my neighbor, Lady Johnstone. She is a vicious person. Perhaps that is who I have based her on. Is Mrs. Allen cruel?"

Sofia tilted her head. "Actually, no. She's not cruel at all. She's sort of . . . sad."

"Ah," Jane replied. "A sad one." She offered a rueful smile. "I know this character."

"Who is she?"

Jane stared at the floor. Sofia normally viewed the top of Jane's head when they talked—she towered over Jane—but now as they sat at eye level, Sofia took a good look at her face. She was smaller and prettier than her portrait at the Jane Austen Experience. Her doe eyes stared into the middle distance and seemed to pierce the space between the door and the wall. What was she thinking about all the time? Lord only knows, but she stared this way often.

"Who is she, Jane?" Sofia said again.

"She is no one," Jane said. "Just a woman." She smiled. "I've observed in this place not how things change, but how they stay the same. Women speak more but expose more flesh. Mothers and washerwomen alike, chambermaids and duchesses. While they darn socks and knead dough, their minds wander and their hearts sing. How deep the waters run behind the masks we wear. I cannot say for sure, but I wager this character lives a second life inside her heart, and she hides some sadness behind her chatter of expensive fabric."

Sofia nodded and sat up. "So how do I play those ridiculous lines?"

"Those lines are ridiculous because women of a certain age are ridiculous. Men of sense and intelligence have deemed it so. Where I come from, her fertility and her dowry comprise a woman's value. Now, her worth seems to lie in her looks. Never has anyone mentioned the brain—occasionally the heart, but never the brain. To grow old is a privilege denied to many, yet women bear it as a curse. She is a woman who has aged. So play her like one. With all the dignity and humiliation that entails. With all the happiness to have survived, and the sadness youth is gone. The dishonor that looks have faded, and the grace that you know this to be true." Jane turned her head to Sofia. "When I first met you, I stood in awe. You strolled around this new Bath with zest and splendor."

"I'm sorry to disappoint you now," Sofia said.

"You sit more magnificent now on the floor of this kitchen, with your heart laid bare. Could this pass not as a tragedy, but a liberation? With your ornamentation gone, the opportunity presents itself."

"The opportunity to what?"

"To tell the truth. You once hung as a bauble. You played the handmaiden for others' desires. Now you can set yourself free."

Sofia wiped a tear and shook her head. "To do what?"

Jane smiled. "To do the thing you were put on this earth to do."

Chapter Forty-Seven

Sofia waited alone on set in her green dress costume. "What is the holdup?" she asked Derek. "I've been standing here for thirty minutes. I'm sweating my no-makeup makeup off."

Derek shrugged and promised to find out.

Rehearsals had entered their final week. Sofia waited for them to fire her. Today's schedule called for a pivotal conversation between Mrs. Allen and Catherine Morland before they entered the evening assembly. Twenty extras gathered in the square behind the Pump Room; they'd grow to four hundred on the day of filming.

Derek returned and whispered to Sofia, "It's Courtney. She won't come out."

Sofia smiled. "She's in her trailer? Is she throwing a tantrum?" She called over to Jack, "Mr. Travers. You'd better go see what's going on with your star."

Jack shook his head. "She'll be out when she's ready."

"We're all standing here. I know filmmaking can't be taught, but I do know an awful lot of people are waiting, and that big light up there in the sky?" She pointed to the sun. "I know how you like big lights. Once it's gone, you can't switch it back on again."

Derek and some of the extras chuckled. Jack rolled his eyes and walked to the dressing rooms. He returned without Courtney. "She won't come out," he whispered to Sofia.

Sofia stifled a grin. "Tell her she's under contract. We can't rehearse the scene without her."

"She said she doesn't care."

"Use your charm, then."

"We had a fight," he blurted out.

Sofia bit her lip and grinned. "Forgive me if I do not shed a tear."

"You have to go and talk to her," Jack said.

"Me?" Sofia exclaimed. "She hates me more than carbohydrates. I won't be any help."

"Just go talk to her. Like a woman."

"Are there any sharp objects in her trailer?"

"Please, Sofe." Jack looked miserable.

Sofia sighed, handed her parasol to Derek, and lifted her skirts. "I will talk to her for the good of the production." She trudged to Courtney's trailer and knocked on the door. There was no reply. Sofia peered through the window. "Courtney?"

"Go away," called Courtney from inside. Her voice sounded muffled and hoarse.

Sofia sighed. "Are you ill?" she shouted, trying to see inside. The curtains remained drawn.

Courtney spoke through the door. "I'm peachy, thank you. Please go away."

"It's time to start rehearsal. The extras are all in position," Sofia replied.

"I'm not coming."

"Fine. What excuse shall I give everyone? You're practicing your baton twirling? You're writing a speech for the United Nations?"

"You'd love that."

"I'd prefer you come out and act."

There was no reply, just sobbing. Sofia winced. "Is that you or is a cat being tortured?"

"Leave me alone!"

"I'd love to more than anything, dear. Unfortunately, I have been tasked with your retrieval. Either let me in and tell me what's going on, or I shall continue to shout insults through the door. I have many of them, and I can talk for hours. The choice is yours."

The door opened and Sofia fell inside. The trailer was decked in orange and red silks, gold statues, and candles. "It looks like Gandhi threw up in here," she said. Courtney sat huddled in the corner, her eyes red.

"You know these are different religions? That's Ganesh; that's Buddha," Sofia said, pointing to two gold statues. "I don't think you should put them together. It might bring forth the apocalypse."

"Shut up. Just because I didn't go to Oxford, you don't need to make fun of me."

"I didn't go to Oxford either, dear. I went to a reform school for the children of alcoholic dreamers. Still, I know the difference between Indian food and Chinese. I admire your pragmatic approach, though. Best place your bets on a few deities; you never know who might come through in the end." Sofia picked up an incense stick. "I can see Jack all over this place. He was confused by religious idolatry, too."

"Does he always do this?" The floor was strewn with tissues

screwed up into little balls. Courtney picked one up and blew her nose into it.

"Does he always do what? I'm not sure that was clean," Sofia added, pointing at the ball of sodden tissue pulp in Courtney's hand.

"Last night, my agent sent me a rough cut of *Bone Dry*."

Sofia shrugged. "Never heard of it."

"It's this new picture I'm in. It's a biopic about a comedian who died of an eating disorder. Sounds stupid, I know." She discarded the tissue, now used to the point that it disintegrated into fibers, and wiped her nose on her sleeve.

"As much as I want to agree with you, it sounds cool, actually," Sofia said.

"I thought so. The script felt great. I enjoyed acting in it."

"What's the problem, then?"

"I showed the cut to Jack. He watched fifteen minutes. Afterward, he said nothing. I was so excited to show it to him! I've never done anything like this role. It was highbrow, you know? I had to remember a bunch of lines. The whole afternoon he was silent, just working at his computer. I thought he was looking for something for me, acting techniques or film references. But he was buying a Rolex on eBay, like Warren Beatty wore in the seventies. I demanded he tell me what he thought of the film. He said, 'I think you should get a nose job.'"

Sofia snuck a glance at Courtney's nose.

"You're looking at my nose. Stop it!"

"I've never taken much notice of it before," Sofia replied.

"You think he's right." Courtney sniffed.

"Truth be told, dear, it is quite large. There's a bump at the top which I'd never observed. Fascinating."

"You're loving this."

"Let me finish. Your nose is big and bumpy. It is also long and elegant. In the olden days, they called noses like yours 'patrician.' It frames your face well. It gives you personality and character. It's quite beautiful. Careers snuff out after nose jobs."

"You say that because you want me to fail."

"I do want you to fail. But I am telling the truth about your nose. Change it and you'll resemble every other starlet. You are no starlet, my dear. You are a star."

"Why did he say it, then?"

Sofia sighed. "He's a director. They're visual people. It's his job to point out physical flaws."

Courtney nodded, still sobbing. "But he's my boyfriend. It wasn't a nice thing to say."

"No. It wasn't." Sofia rose and headed for the door. She could not blame Courtney for wanting to protect the inch of leverage she had. Sofia had done the same once and would do so again if she still could. She reached the doorway and hesitated.

"What is it?" said Courtney.

"He said something similar to me once," Sofia said.

"He did?"

Sofia nodded. "Before the first *Batman* was released. We went to a preview screening and he told me I could improve if I lost weight."

"That was a great film," said Courtney. "And you looked good in it. I feel terrible about *Bone Dry* now. I thought it was great, but now I think it sucks."

"On the contrary, dear. If this conversation is anything to go by, it's likely a hit. Will you come and do acting now?"

Courtney shook her head. "Everyone will laugh at me. I'll be the difficult actress."

Sofia turned to her. "You are a difficult actress. This is a difficult job. They can't do what we do. So tell them all to bugger off."

With a deep breath and one final tissue, Courtney gathered her things and they headed to set. It was a big scene between Catherine Morland and Mrs. Allen—a bigger scene for Courtney's character, but Sofia's character stood next to her for the duration. Sofia spent no energy tripping up Courtney, she did not add in extra lines or ad lib, she did not roll her eyes. She fed Courtney the lines and played the straight man. It was a cracking scene. The older foil and the young heroine made a fabulous duo. When Jack called cut, a strange thing happened: the crew applauded. Courtney took a bow, looking thrilled. Sofia rolled her eyes, but then she bowed, too.

It was all Jane's fault. She had turned Sofia into a nice person.

As THE DAY drew to a close, Courtney had another scene to rehearse. Sofia ducked out of Courtney's eyeline and headed for the makeup truck.

"No, it's okay. Please stay," Courtney called to her.

Sofia shrugged and stayed.

Afterward, the rehearsal ended. The crew packed up. The camera and lighting trucks drove away; everyone went back to London. They would return in a few weeks for the first day of shooting. Sofia did not expect to join them—one truce with Courtney did not mean she'd be sticking around—but then a runner found her and gave Sofia her call time for day one.

She thanked him and agreed to see him then. She stared at the piece of paper in shock. It was a call time, all right. She would be playing Mrs. Allen after all. Not only that, but she knew how to play her now, and she had a great costar, a hilarious costume, and a half-decent director leading the show. This film might not actually be the bomb she had earlier predicted.

Almost as soon as she entertained these thoughts, she realized, with a small horror dawning, that this posed something of a concern for other things.

She had encouraged her brother to make some sort of grand declaration to Jane, to profess his feelings for her to make her stay. This was what Sofia wanted, and what Jane and Fred deserved, but if Jane were to stay with Fred, the novels that had been disappearing one by one from the liquor cabinet would continue on their present course and disappear entirely.

If Jane's novels ceased to exist, then *Northanger Abbey,* Sofia's film, would disappear, too.

That little gem of a movie she had started to see potential in would vanish. She stiffened at the predicament. She kicked herself for all the sanctimonious demands she had made on Jane: commanding her to remain inside the house, warning her that if she did not return to her own time she would never write her books. Now Sofia had ordered Fred to manifest the situation she had cautioned against.

She shuddered at her own stupidity. Not only might she have single-handedly halted the writing career of the most celebrated, pioneering, bad-ass female writer in history, she might have destroyed her own career, too.

She tried not to panic. Maybe Fred would make no declaration. Maybe Jane would refuse him. Sofia knew a day might come when Jane would ask her advice on that subject. She hoped rather than knew that she would have the strength to say the right thing.

Chapter Forty-Eight

After a week in the hospital, Fred was allowed to go home. A lunch of soup went down into his stomach, then came back up again. Jane cleaned it from the floor.

"I'm sorry, I'm embarrassed," he said.

"Do not feel so, sir. You are human, and you are ill. Let us get you to the privy and we can worry for the rest later."

He needed help with everything. Sofia's work had held her captive, so Jane cared for Fred. He was correct in his assertion that he might need help. A trip to the privy required three handkerchiefs to mop the sweat from his brow. The smallest move required the largest effort. Jane walked back and forth from the sofa. She brought him tea. She helped him eat and wash his hands and face. He had stood tall and strong before. Now his spine protruded under the skin of his back, and his shoulders sloped forward.

Six days passed, and he did not say a word on the event in the hospital. Jane wondered if he thought about it. She thought of it constantly. Barely a thought had ever occupied more space in her brain. His own neglect of the topic was understandable, having recently suffered a near-fatal accident and requiring machines to breathe for him, but this did not stop Jane from feeling aware of the topic herself, and his seeming total amnesia on the score terrorized her. She tormented herself with speculations on the reasons for his silence. Perhaps her performance was so terrible and amateurish he was trying to forget it. Yes, probably. He made no signal of regard beyond appreciation for Jane as nurse and seemed to have resigned her to the role of perfunctory helper, not even friend; rather, someone who administered meals and attended to bodily functions.

"I've a confession to make," he said with a grave face one morning.

"Do you need the privy?" she said. She stood up.

"No, thank you. I need to tell you: I've never read any of your books."

Jane sat down once more. She stared at him and took a moment to realize what he meant. "Do you mean to tell me you've never read a Jane Austen novel?" she said.

He nodded. "Correct," he said. "I'm a terrible person."

"How dare you," she said. She spoke in a tone of mock outrage, though she also secretly felt a small piece of real outrage, too. She added this to the outrage she already felt about him not acknowledging what had passed between them in the hospital and found herself wrapped up in a ball of agitation, full of real emotions and fake ones.

"I was supposed to read *Emma* in secondary college, but I watched the film instead," he said. He winced, as if preparing for her to slap him.

"I'd hit you if you were not moments from death's door. Are you not a teacher of English literature?"

"I am."

"Someone led me to believe my books sat on the school syllabus for English."

"They do." He flinched.

"Well, then? You don't teach them?"

He shrugged. "I don't teach every book on the syllabus. I've never had to teach your books, so I've never read them."

"And you never picked one up, to read for pleasure?"

He laughed. "I'm sorry, no. I feel terrible."

Jane crossed her arms. "You should read them. I'm told they are masterpieces."

"I don't doubt it," he said. "I want to."

She pushed her shoulders back. "You can do so anytime you wish. They are locked in the liquor cabinet."

"How about now?" he said. "There is a spare key in the drawer. Don't tell Sofia."

Jane went to fetch one of her novels. She was excited to get a book for him. Not to read it, as this led to erasing self and universe, as Sofia had warned, but she could at least smell its pages.

Jane stopped at the glass cabinet. Six of her books were once there. Then five. Before Fred went to the hospital, there were four. Now there were just three. Another of her books had joined the others in disappearing.

Jane returned to the sitting room. "No book?" Fred asked her.

"No time; we must get on with your exercises," she replied, and said no more on the subject.

Jane fumed. She continued to erase her novels, and for what? There was no declaration from him. There was no sign of any regard at all, except his thanks for her being his servant. And now with another book gone, Jane found her position in this place increasingly foolish. Mrs. Sinclair had brought Jane to her one true love, but that did not mean she had brought Fred to his. Jane had given her heart to someone who did not return the affection, and the price she paid was removing her life's work from the world.

Jane wondered what she was doing there. She was in limbo. It was beneath her dignity to linger so. She was conducting a love affair with herself, playing both parts. The longer she remained like this, waiting for a declaration that would not come, the longer she made herself ridiculous.

She would tell Sofia to fetch the letter. It was time.

"PLACE THE LETTERS on the board, please, or you shall get the cane." Jane spoke in a stern voice.

"I'm being taught words by Jane Austen," Fred said with a grin. "I should feel privileged, but I feel annoyed." They had moved to the kitchen table. Between them was a board with a white surface. Letters of the alphabet painted in shiny colors were spread across the table. A blue *L*, a red *M*. They were a teaching aid for children, with a magnet on the back of each letter.

They were engaged in a rehabilitation exercise that was the result of a conversation Jane and Sofia had had with the medical staff before they had left the hospital. "The electricity has fried parts of his body," one of the nurses had explained. "His memory has been damaged. There will be a list of exercises which he will need to do every day."

"That sounds like a lot of work." Sofia grimaced.

"The occupational therapist is booked up for the next month."

"I will pay them double," Sofia said.

The nurse scoffed. "You can't bribe a healthcare professional!"

"I can do whatever I want," Sofia countered. "I am a celebrity!" She pointed to her chest, as if the title were branded there.

Jane lowered Sofia's arm, which had been raised dangerously

close to the nurse's face. "That won't be necessary," Jane said. "What are the exercises? I will be happy to do them until the language teacher is available."

"It's a lot of work," the nurse protested. "Are you any good at English?"

"My skills should suffice," Jane said.

The nurse had given Jane a list of the exercises and since Fred had arrived home they had done one lesson every day. She regretted accepting the commission now that it was obvious Fred did not return her affection. She would continue the lessons, as his recovery was important, but she insisted on doing so with a governess-like frostiness.

"Recall the associated word I told you earlier and spell it out on the board," she commanded. He did not move. "Do you not recall it?"

"Remind me of the rules again?"

Jane rolled her eyes. "Earlier I provided you with a list of word pairs. Do you not remember?"

"I don't know. My memory is broken, after all." He chuckled.

Jane scowled. "I provided you with pairs of words: 'ball' and 'tree,' for example, and 'triangle' and 'candlestick.' Your task is to remember which words paired with which in the list. So, when I say 'ball,' you must recall that its word pair is 'tree' and spell it out on the board."

"You never said 'candlestick,'" Fred said.

"I most certainly did," she countered.

She saw him laughing. "Perhaps I forgot," he said. Clearly, he did not share her determination for cold, professional instruction.

"Have you forgotten the next one also? What word goes with 'bottle'?"

"Actually, I remember that one."

"Good. Then why do you not write it down?"

"I don't know how to spell it. The word is 'descant,' right? I don't even know what that means." He grinned and scratched his cheek.

"'Descant'? A melody over the top of another melody. It is a wonder you have survived thus far."

"You remind me of a grumpy schoolmistress," he said.

"I am a grumpy schoolmistress. You are an insolent student. I make allowances for your memory loss, but I cannot tolerate poor spelling."

Fred chose some letters and placed them on the board.

Jane observed the letters—d-e-s-c-a-n-t—and offered a begrudging nod. "Correct. Next word: 'stone.'"

The accompanying word was *terrific*.

Fred took out the letters and placed them on the board.

"No. 'Terrific' has two *r*'s."

"You should pick easier words," Fred said. "I couldn't spell 'terrific' before the accident." He grinned again, to show Jane he was joking. A teacher of literature could obviously spell these words.

Jane was outraged. Why was he grinning, when she was dying inside? She ignored the remark. "Next word: 'bauble.'"

The word paired with it on her list was *masterpiece*.

"Could I have a glass of water? My throat is dry."

"Spell the correct word and the water shall be fetched for you. Like magic."

"I was burned to a crisp. Cooked from the inside! Please, I beg you. Get me some water."

Fred placed a magnetic *m* on the whiteboard, by way of encouragement.

Jane fetched the water, returning with a pitcher to look over his shoulder. Fred placed the next letters on the board. Jane grimaced. "No. That's incorrect," she said. "You've put an *r* there." She narrowed her eyes at him. "You vex me for sport."

Fred added more letters to the board with glee.

"You've put an *r* there; it should be an *s*," she said. "It's m-a-s, not m-a-r."

But Fred ignored her and added a second *r*. Jane stared at the words as they formed on the board. Fred's hands shook as he placed the child's letters down. Jane held her breath, watching his trembling hands. Another *m*, then an *e*, formed the second word: "me."

m a r r y   m e   j a n e

Jane swallowed. She turned her head, but Fred had vanished from his chair. She swung around and found him kneeling on the floor before her.

"Could you reach into my pocket?" he asked.

Jane did as she was told.

"The other one."

Jane obliged and removed a box from his trouser pocket.

"Open it," he said.

She snapped open the lid. A ring lay inside, one she had seen before. She stepped back in shock. A blue stone of creamy turquoise shone from a band forged from warm gold. It gripped her with the same sensation she had felt when she beheld it in the painting, only now the feeling was a thousandfold.

"It was my mother's," Fred said. Jane nodded. "Do you like it?"

"It is beautiful." It was all she could manage to say. For a reason she could not place, Jane thought of her own mother. Astonishment gripped her, surprise at the about-face, but as she looked at his face, she saw he had been thinking about this, planning and preparing all morning. Her mind raced at the speed of the declaration; her heart thumped in her chest.

"This is all so sudden," she said to him. Although she had wanted it, the shock of it and the haste forced her to protest. "We've only been acquainted with each other a short time. I hardly know you. You hardly know me," she said.

"What more do you want to know?" he asked.

She remained silent. The effort of kneeling down had made him break out in a sweat and his hair lay across his forehead in clumps. Jane brushed it to the side. "Do you only give me this ring to prevent me from leaving? I can stay and look after you as long as you need. I will care for you, help you recover. You don't need to give me a ring to stay for that reason."

"I don't need you to stay and help me. I'm not giving you a ring for that. I want you to stay. Not as my helper, but as my wife. I love you."

Jane breathed. "I love you too," she said.

He smiled. Then the smile left his face; he seemed to wait for her to say more.

Jane felt the back of her neck prickle. Water filled her eyes. "Are you sure?" she asked him.

His knee trembled. "I feel like I've known you my whole life," he said. "You pierce my soul. Yes, I am sure. Will you marry me?"

The words were so beautiful and honest, she could give only one reply. "I will," Jane said. Fred beamed at her, and she embraced him and helped him up from the floor.

Part
Three

Chapter Forty-Nine

*T*he day of Maggie's christening had arrived. Fred was to be god-father. Jane and Sofia got to St. Swithin's early, carrying flowers for the service. Jane wore a yellow dress that Sofia had bought her as an engagement present. Fred told her she looked beautiful and kissed her on the cheek.

"I must show you something," Jane said to Sofia as they placed the flowers on the altar. She led Sofia over to the transept. "I almost forgot it was here. You will enjoy this."

They rounded the corner and Jane pointed at the white-and-gray marble wall.

Sofia stared at the marble and squinted. "Not sure what I'm supposed to be looking at," she said. "Good masonry? Jane?"

Jane stared at the wall in horrified silence.

"Can I go now, love?" Sofia said. "We're staring at a blank wall."

"A plaque stood here before," Jane said.

"There are loads of plaques," Sofia replied. She pointed around to the brass and bronze plates that littered the rest of the wall. "Catching dust everywhere."

"No. A plaque stood right here," Jane said. She pointed to a clear space of marble.

Sofia, listening now, turned to Jane. "What did it say?"

"It said, 'Here worshipped Jane Austen.'"

SOFIA AND JANE departed the church just as the other guests were arriving. Sofia made an excuse about wanting to change to a bigger hat, which Fred mercifully believed, even though her present head covering was roughly the size of a wagon wheel. They made their way home, promising to return before the service started.

"Perhaps I imagined the plaque," Jane offered in a futile voice as they walked from the churchyard. She hoped rather than knew this to be true.

"Perhaps," Sofia said. They spoke few other words to each other on the way. Sofia seemed to know why Jane wanted to return to the house; she needed to survey the contents of a certain glass cabinet.

They turned down Gay Street and, now out of sight of the rest of the christening party, they ran. With each passing step, Jane's feeling of dread grew. They arrived at the house, both puffing, starved of breath. Sofia fumbled with the keys in the door. Jane, calmer, took them from her and unlocked it. They raced inside to the sitting room and the glass liquor cabinet.

Where there once sat a stack of six novels, then five, then three, there was now an empty space.

Sofia sat on the floor and placed her head in her hands. "Jane. Your books have disappeared."

Jane joined Sofia on the floor. "Because I do not write them anymore."

Sofia searched her bedroom for another hat and Jane stared at the wall. Sofia returned. "I'm beyond sorry, Jane."

Jane shrugged. "What did I expect? I could both stay here and return home to write? Jane Austen can hardly write novels in that world if she stays in this one. Your prediction has proven half-correct, Sofia. While I have not destroyed the universe, I have destroyed myself."

WITH NO PLAN for anything better to do, and people expecting their return, Jane and Sofia made their way back to the christening. They stopped at the Bath library on the way, just to check. The same librarian as the first time addressed them.

"Do you have anything by Jane Austen?" Sofia asked her.

The librarian turned to her machine. "How do you spell it?"

"A-u-s-t-e-n," Jane spelled out in a pitiful voice.

The librarian typed the name into the box. "There's no writer by that name."

Sofia bit her lip. "Oh, Jane." Jane merely nodded. They thanked the woman and left.

They passed the building where they'd visited the Jane Austen Experience. It now housed a patisserie.

To make triply sure they both did not hallucinate some perverse nightmare, Sofia spoke to her theatrical agent using her steel box, her telephone.

"Max, may I confirm my call time for *Northanger Abbey* next week?" she spoke into the device.

"Northanger what?" the telephone voice replied. Sofia bowed her head.

"The Austen film? The one shooting in Bath," she said in a feeble voice.

"Never heard of it," the voice replied. "What are you talking about?" He paused. "Are you okay, Sofia?"

She nodded and said nothing.

"Sofia?" the voice continued. "Who is this Austen person? Is he a writer? Does he need representation?" Sofia replaced the telephone in her pocket. They walked on down the road.

"I think it's clear," Jane said. "We can feel satisfied. Jane Austen is gone."

"What shall you do?" Sofia said to her.

"I don't know," Jane said. She spoke the truth.

"What about Fred?"

Jane nodded. What about him? "What do you think I should do?"

"There are two options. You either return to your world and write those books, or you stay here with Fred and be happy, yes? First, full disclosure—if you never return home and write those books, disaster for me. By deciding to stay, everything has gone: your books, your museums, your legacy." She laughed in a grim tone. "The films based on your books, too, which means my career is likely kaput as well. In short, for me, a catastrophe."

Jane inhaled. "Good God, Sofia. Your part vanishes, too. I am so sorry."

Sofia shrugged. "It's okay. There are more important things." She smiled at Jane.

"A woman excelling at her profession? There are few more important things to me," Jane replied. She pushed out her chin.

Sofia held her arm and cleared her throat. "On the other hand, if you do return home, you will write your books, but you will break Fred's heart. And your own. So yes, quite the dilemma. Helpful, aren't I?"

Jane bowed her head.

"Jane. Do you love him?"

Jane gazed at the floor. "I have never felt like this."

Sofia sighed.

Jane shrugged. She could not choose. "May I have more time to decide?"

"If you decide to stay here, you can have the rest of your life."

They walked toward the church. "I shall know what to do when I see him," Jane said with confidence. She immediately felt gripped with dread and cursed herself for saying it. Suddenly she did not want to see him, to be forced to decide; she felt rushed. But then, she reminded herself, she had been prepared to leave him before. It would not be so bad; she could do so again.

They arrived at the church, faster than she had hoped, and walked through the doors and down the aisle. Fred stood by the altar. He held the baby. He waved to Jane but his face bore a look of pain. He knew something had changed; he possessed too much intelligence for anything else.

"What's happened?" he asked her when she reached him. He rocked the child in his arms. Maggie touched his face and cooed; she liked him. He would make a wonderful father.

An odd feeling overcame Jane, one that disarmed her with its rareness. What was it? Oh. Happiness. As one world closed for her, another opened up. She was no longer the voyeur, writing of other people. She had put down the pen and was living instead.

"Nothing at all," Jane said at last, and took her place by Fred's side.

"Are you going to leave me?" he said. His voice shook.

Jane looked up at him and inhaled. "I go nowhere," she said. She did not tell him about the books disappearing, and she had asked Sofia to say nothing. Little reason existed to get into it now; she had made her decision. She turned instead to the future, and the new joys it held, here in the twenty-first century, with the man she was going to marry.

Chapter Fifty

The vicar arrived and welcomed everyone, and the service began. Jane and Sofia took their seats in the front pew. Fred, in a blue suit, stood at the baptismal font and held Maggie in his arms. Sofia sobbed as the curate began. Jane wiped a tear also.

The vicar performed the benediction over Maggie. "I hereby baptize you in the name of the Father, and of the Son, and of the Holy Spirit." Jane smiled; her father had said the same words many times.

"Amen," Fred replied.

The vicar poured water over Maggie's forehead. A boy soprano sang "Amazing Grace," as they did in Jane's time. Afterward, the vicar invited the party to the altar to pose for what Jane now knew were called photographs. Fred asked Jane to join him, and she took her place by his side.

Maggie awoke from her slumber at the shock of the talking and fussing. She grizzled like a baby bear, then threatened to cry. The congregation tensed. The sacred mood so carefully engineered by the singing, the chants, the words threatened to crack with the unscheduled wail of tears. Fred looked panicked. Jane took the baby from him, held her, and rocked her on instinct.

The child sensed the motion and waited. Jane played her best hand, smiling down at the child. Jane had a round and pink-cheeked face babies loved. She could elicit a smile from the fussiest, most colicky child. She was Naughty Aunt Jane, beloved by infants. This twenty-first-century specimen reacted no differently.

The child played her hand back. She looked up at Jane and gurgled and smiled, suddenly entranced by Jane and perched on the verge of laughing. Jane heard herself inhale as the baby offered up little smiling gasps of chubby breath, the sweetest sound she ever heard.

Something stirred deep within Jane. A pang of love in the depths of her soul, an unstoppable force beyond cognition. Did a trick in Nature exist more beguiling than this?

Jane had often felt a pang of jealousy when her mother wrote her recipes in verse. Mrs. Austen wrote lines that delighted all with their wit. Her mother loved to read but did so late at night and only if all the socks were darned and the letters replied to. Most nights it didn't happen. Mama had read half the books Jane had, despite owning twice the age. This made sense, as Jane had quadruple the time. Jane shook her head at her mother's obsession with her children's concerns. Mrs. Austen slaved to help Henry find the right curtains for his bank and listened for hours to James's terrible sermons. Jane saw now the reason: a smile from one's child becomes the only thing.

She imagined having one of her own, and the child gorgeously sucking Jane dry. She would feed it, wake when it woke, and feel pride in being the only one able to soothe it. This pride would hypnotize her and occupy her time. The little life would swallow up everything, murdering the whim to nurture anything but itself.

"You're a natural," Fred said to her. She nodded.

Jane handed the baby back to Fred. He gave her a quizzical look, seeming unsure why she returned the child when they enjoyed such a time together. The congregation smiled and cooed at how Jane had calmed the child, and Fred gazed upon her with love and awe. The perfume of church incense, at first spiced and mystical, now turned Jane's stomach. She forced her face into a smile and swallowed to push back down the bile that crept into her throat.

THE NEXT MORNING, Sofia greeted Jane with an excited declaration. "Today, we're trying on wedding dresses."

Jane protested and shook her head, laughing. "No, thank you," she said.

"Why not, Jane? It will be fun!" Sofia said. "This is the best thing about getting engaged."

"Sofia. I was only engaged two days ago," Jane said. "I don't need wedding clothes just yet."

"That's where you're wrong, Jane. This is exactly the time. Wedding dresses take months, and these women are the gatekeepers to our dreams. You have to get in early with these people or you will be left behind." She drained her coffee and grabbed her giant reticule. "This is going to happen, Jane. It's better if you don't resist." She pulled Jane out the front door and they walked into town.

An agreeable-looking man waved to them as they arrived in the center of the village. "This is Derek, my consigliere," Sofia said. "He will help us find the best gowns on the planet."

The man held out his hand with a smile. Jane shook it.

"Now, Derek, when we get inside and try things on, if we look hideous, do not hold back your commentary," Sofia commanded him.

"Yes, Ms. Wentworth. Though I am sure you will look beautiful."

They toured five dress shops in six hours and emerged empty-handed. Jane felt exhausted. Jane tried on dozens of gowns, all beautiful, but none of them met Sofia's standards. "We've been to every rag shop in Bath," Sofia said with dismay. "I say we jump on the Eurostar and hit Paris. I have friends there."

Jane begged instead to be allowed to return home to rest her feet, but Sofia remembered one final shop in the village. "An older place." She dragged Jane and Derek down the lane, ignoring their protests and rounding a corner onto Westgate Street. Sofia halted and pointed at the shop's facade. "Here it is."

Jane gasped at the sight of the shopfront. "I have been here before." The sign had changed but the name remained the same: Maison Du Bois, the shop in which Mrs. Austen had bought Jane her dress. The Royal Warrant still sat on a brass crest by the door.

"Shall we go inside?"

Jane nodded earnestly and they went in.

It looked as it did before. The white plaster roses still lined the ceiling, the brass cornices still gilded every surface, the glass cabinets still sparkled with a recent polish. The gowns had changed, but the room of two hundred years ago remained as Jane remembered. The attendants still wore red cravats, though they were women now. Sofia ordered one to bring her their finest gown. A woman nodded and ran for a measuring tape.

The woman measured Jane and presented them all with flutes of champagne. Another brought Jane a dress on a silk hanger to try on.

One of the women helped Jane into the dress. "Made in the art deco style. We've cut the silk crepe on the bias." They returned to Sofia and Derek, and Jane peered at her reflection in the mirror. A white angel peered back at her.

"What is this wet stuff coming out of my eyes?" Sofia was smiling at Jane.

"What color is this?" Jane asked, gazing at her reflection. The wedding dresses from her own world abounded in shades of blue, striped with gold, cream, lemon.

"Ivory. Perfect for a May wedding," the shop assistant said.

"You've made all the dresses in white," Jane said.

"Yes. They are wedding dresses, miss," the woman replied.

"Jane, wedding dresses are white now," Sofia said. "White means purity. It symbolizes that the bride is a virgin."

"Oh, I see," Jane said, blushing.

"We like to pretend."

"Yes," Jane said. She bowed her head.

"How do you feel?" one of the women asked Jane.

Jane shrugged and checked her reflection once more. How did she feel? The beautiful white dress seemed to float across her body. Although her life up until this point had been preoccupied with procuring and acquiring a husband, she had never imagined what it involved once she achieved the elusive prize. She had never before pictured herself in wedding clothes, nor as a wife.

"How should one feel?" she said.

"Triumphant?" Sofia said. "You look stunning. Fred will love it." She winked at Jane and turned to the shop assistant. "Now that's sorted, I shall be trying on bridesmaids' dresses. If we're going art deco, then I want *Gatsby*—the seventies one. I want classy. I want diamond brooches, I want pearl earrings, I want *Bonnie and Clyde*. Show this to me."

The woman rushed off and Sofia followed her with more directions.

Jane stared at her image in the mirror.

"You do look beautiful," Derek said to her. "No lies." He smiled and nodded his head toward Sofia on the other side of the room.

"Thank you," Jane replied. "Are you married, Derek?"

"Four years," he said with a smile. He held up his hand. A gold wedding band graced his finger.

"Congratulations," Jane said. "And your wife. Did she wear something similar to this on your wedding day?" She pointed to her dress.

"My husband, actually."

"Oh," Jane said. She inhaled, staring at him.

"And he did want to wear something similar, but luckily I talked him out of it." He chuckled with a kind voice.

Jane's head whirred. "You married . . . a man?"

"Yes. Are you okay?"

"Uncle Anthony," Jane replied. She found herself overcome with such a feeling she heard herself make a little gasp.

"I'm sorry?"

"I had a godfather named Anthony. A friend of the family. My favorite. He practiced the law and was an adroit man. He wrote great letters. Everyone feted him at parties; he entertained all with his warmth and good humor and his generous gifts. He had a friend, a gentleman named Matthew. One day, a neighbor . . . discovered him and Matthew. His business went under. They went abroad. I was told not to write to him. His name was never mentioned again by any of us."

"I'm so sorry," Derek said. His face bore a surprised look, and he seemed to study Jane with new eyes.

Jane smiled at him. "Have you known such things, Derek?"

He shrugged. "My father has not spoken to me since I told him."

"Goodness."

"But I do live with the man I love." He smiled.

Jane looked at her reflection once more. The attendants placed her on a pedestal, so all could view the full length of the dress. She felt like a statue.

"Uncle Anthony stayed with his friend," she said. "I believe they were happy." She forced her face into a bright smile. "I wish you agency and joy in your life, sir. You are living the life you choose, regardless of what other people think. May the rest of us possess half your courage."

"Oh," Derek replied. "Thank you." He smiled.

Sofia and the others returned. "Well, what do you think?"

Jane wiped a tear. Derek did also. The shop people cooed. "Look at her! She is so happy," they sang.

"Would the mother of the bride approve?" one of them asked.

"I don't know. What do you think, Jane?" Sofia asked in a soft voice.

"I think she would smile," Jane said.

"Where is she?" one attendant asked.

"She is not here," Sofia answered in a stern voice, halting any further questions on the subject. Jane did not meet her eye.

"Let's take a picture for your mum." They placed a veil on Jane's head and gave her a flower. She posed for the picture. Derek took her hand as she did so and squeezed it, and she found herself wiping another tear.

Chapter Fifty-One

The next morning, Fred bundled through the front door with a pile of envelopes.

"What is this?" he said. He held an envelope up to Jane's face.

"It appears to be the post," Jane said. She read the address on the front of the envelope. "It's a letter. Addressed to you."

"It's from Blackheath James," Fred said.

"If you say so," Jane replied.

"Why am I getting a letter from a publisher?" Fred asked her, his eyes wide. "I've never sent them anything."

"And yet here we are," Jane said. She raised her chin and said nothing more.

Fred looked at the envelope once more. "How dare you," Fred said, his voice filled with outrage, though he stared at the envelope longingly.

"Will you open it?" Jane asked.

"I'm going to throw it in the bin," he replied. He did as such, though his action resembled more a careful placing in the receptacle, away from food scraps.

"You feel no curiosity as to its contents?" Jane asked.

"Nope." He looked at the rubbish pile with a mournful stare.

"It looks foolish, lying there in the refuse, unopened," Jane said.

Fred paced about the room. He snatched the envelope up, har-rumphed at Jane, and tore it open.

"Read it aloud," Jane said. She inhaled and chewed her lip. She hoped she had showed wisdom in sending it.

"*Dear sir, thank you for your recent submission of* Land's End. *I would be delighted to read the whole manuscript. Please call my office via the details below to arrange a meeting at your convenience.*" Fred sat down. "They liked it."

"They are but human," Jane said. She wiped a line of sweat from her brow and thanked whatever god might be listening for such an extension of mercy. Publishers were likely as capricious now as they had been in her own time.

"I don't believe it," Fred replied. His face wore a suitable look of confusion and disbelief.

Jane shook her head. "Can you not see what I see?" she asked. "You are brilliant. The book is wonderful."

Fred embraced her. "Thank you," he whispered. Then he broke the embrace. "But I haven't written the whole manuscript!" he said, panicked.

"Oh dear," Jane replied. "Yes, that poses a problem." She pan-icked a little herself. She had overlooked that part when sending half a manuscript.

"This is a disaster," Fred exclaimed. "What am I going to do?"

"You shall have to finish it," Jane said.

"But when? How? I have a job." He paused. "I do have school holidays next week. But only for two weeks."

"How many words do you need to write to finish?" Jane asked him.

He swallowed. "About fifty thousand."

"*Fifty thousand words,*" Jane repeated in a concerned voice. She checked herself when she saw his expression. "Not to worry," she said in a bright tone. "How many days is the school break, did you say?"

"Fourteen days, if you count weekends."

"Very well. Fifty thousand words in fourteen days? That's"—she tilted her head—"about three and a half thousand words a day."

He laughed. "I'll take your word for it."

"Do you think you can manage it? Write three and half thousand words a day, for two weeks?"

"No." He laughed again.

"Do you think you can try?" Jane paused. "I offer my help," she said. "If you want it."

Fred chuckled.

"What is it?" Jane asked.

"Jane Austen is going to help me write a novel."

THE FORTNIGHT OF writing began. Ironically, Jane's greatest help to Fred would not come from advising him on character or assisting with dialogue. She did not help him with structure, or where to put the chapters. Instead, Jane cooked and cleaned for him.

She made him breakfast, lunch, and dinner; she brought him his daily coffee, his clothes, breakfast. The never-ending tasks of drudgery—dusting, sweeping, washing clothes—she took them on. She taught herself how to use the contrivances of the kitchen. She filled her days like never before. This amused her; she never laid claim to being a goddess of the hearth in her old life, but she did so now. It might seem the obvious choice for one writer to help another by counselling on word choice and sentences, but Jane knew better.

In her previous life, Jane's singular task in the domestic sphere had been to prepare the breakfast items. It required but ten minutes every morning. Jane was obliged to place the foodstuffs and crockery on the table. She was not even required to clear the things away afterward; Margaret the housemaid did that.

Between breakfast and lunch, Jane spent every day pleasing only herself, walking the fields for hours, writing, thinking, and editing. In the afternoons, she met Cassandra and Mama for afternoon tea, then walked in the village. Time for supper arrived, and afterward, her sister and parents attended a play or assembly. Jane was rarely invited. Cassandra bore the gloss of agreeableness and good manners, an asset at balls and parties. Jane remained insolent and refused to entertain fools. She felt more than happy to be left at home, and her family agreed. She would write some more in the silence of the house.

First Impressions, her novel, took four years to write and revise. She worked on it consistently, every day. She came to rely on the time alone and felt annoyed when company or politeness denied her some seclusion. She embroidered no cushions and darned no socks. She cared for no husband and raised no children. She spent the majority of her time alone. Her mind made its greatest leaps in these stretches, when silence and solitude freed it to roam.

These were the conditions necessary for great writing: hours of time alone to oneself. No time spent on washing, chores, domestic tasks, no space of brain wasted on menial things. So she took on all this labor herself, to unburden Fred. Every great writer had a great woman behind them, she recalled. She had read the biographies of many authors and knew this to be true.

Fred was not as fast as she at writing. She had never witnessed another writer at work, but she observed he took longer than she did. He had not the knack for knowing exactly where words should just go. He also lacked some drive, which had always come easily for her. She pushed through terror and doubt. She knew she would never stop writing, despite rejection, despite censure. He frequently took breaks and chopped wood, tried to help with the chores. That was fine; other writers worked differently. A few times she asked to see what he had written, and he admonished her and told her to go away. She laughed and left him to it and took care of the house.

At the end of the two weeks, they reconvened for the unveiling. Sofia had travelled to London to attend auditions for other films to perform in, now that *Northanger Abbey* had vanished. Jane waited patiently in the kitchen for Fred to emerge from his bedroom. He finally showed his face, an hour later than the agreed time. Jane did not mind; genius required patience. He shuffled toward the table, looking exhausted, and presented her with the pages. She sifted through them eagerly. He scratched his head and said nothing.

"There's only fifty pages more here," Jane said. She turned them over to check if they contained writing on both sides. They did not.

He made no remark.

"How many more words did you write?" she said.

"Another ten thousand," he said. "Give or take."

"But you need fifty thousand more."

"I know."

"Well, what happened?"

"I didn't write them," he said angrily. He crossed his arms.

Jane shook her head. "I don't understand. Why not?"

He said nothing.

"Fred?" She began to panic. She couldn't understand it. "Why did you not tell me, when you were struggling? Before it reached this stage?"

"Because I knew you'd be mad," he said.

"I'm not mad," she said with a laugh.

"Yes, you are! You're mad and you're judging me. You pushed me to do this."

"I object to that. I did not push you." She could not believe what she heard.

He scoffed. "You sent the letter to the publisher! I never asked you to."

"I thought you'd be grateful. Instead, you've squandered this opportunity."

He glared at her. "I didn't want to do anything else with this. It's not working."

She softened. "I know it's difficult, but this is merely a blip in the road. This is the time—"

"The darkest before the dawn, I know." His voice was cruel.

She squinted at him and began thinking cruel things herself. She recalled his time as a child when he walked two hundred of the eight hundred miles required to cross England. She admired his bravery, but she also thought, *I'd keep going. I'd let naught and no one stop me until I walked the eight.* "Don't be angry at me because you failed," Jane said. She realized she may have gone too far.

"I'm getting out of here," he said. He stood and grabbed his coat.

"Wait, Fred. I'm sorry," she said.

"I don't know what you want from me," he said, putting his coat on. "I don't know if I can give you what you want."

She gasped, horrified at the words and his tone. "I don't want anything from you," she replied meekly.

"I don't believe that. I think you want many things I can't give you."

"Where are you going?" Jane said, her voice growing desperate.

"Anywhere but here." He left.

IT TOOK SEVERAL hours for Jane's anger to subside. When it did, Fred had still not come home. She stood in the kitchen, inert, and watched the door. She began to worry he might never return at all. Pain gripped her, a feeling like she had never felt before. She had never quarreled with someone like this; she had never quarreled with a man she loved. She felt torn to pieces and could focus on nothing except wanting him home. Another hour passed and still there was no sign of him.

She worried that he had gone for good. She collapsed onto the floor; her body seemed to fold into a neat pile of bones and skin. She stared at the pages on the table, the new ones he'd written, and felt ashamed. It was just a book and she had pushed him. She regretted this now. What were words on a page compared to him going?

So, this was love, then: a horrid, tremendous quickening, something terrible and sweet, painful and fierce. Nothing mattered but him coming back.

She was his slave, happily, she realized. A picture of her life stretched out before her. She would spend large parts of her time in a state of flux, wondering where she stood with him, wondering if he would leave, if he would do what she said, if he would hurt her. He would come first; she would set herself on fire to keep him warm. She would spend a part of her life trying to make him happy, and her success on that score depended entirely on him. She was signing her heart over to another human being. If he could only return, she promised to love him every day. She would do nothing else of value in that time.

THEN THE DOOR opened, and he walked inside. Fred pulled off his coat and lay it on the hook. He turned to face Jane. Relief and joy washed over her. She had never beheld a sight so wondrous as him walking through that door. He looked at her and smiled. "I'm so sorry," he said.

"Oh, Fred," she replied. "I'm sorry too."

She ran to him and they embraced. "I thought I would never see you again." He held her. She found herself lingering in the warm hold. He seemed to respond to this; she felt his arms tighten around her. A new feeling swelled in her. She buried her head in his shoulder.

Fred broke away first. His breath was ragged. He cast his gaze at the floor; he seemed unable to look at her.

"What are you thinking?" Jane asked him. She searched his face.

He looked up and met her eye, then shook his head. "You don't want to know what I am thinking," he replied.

She stared at him. She took his hand and led him to his room.

Once inside, she raised her fingers to a button. He moved and stopped her with his hand. "Are you sure?" he asked her.

Jane had been advised from her cradle about society banishing her if she came to know certain things outside marriage. A living death awaited. Those women who indulged in the unsanctified union were nonpeople, punished with disease and scorn. It was some terrible thing, for certain. She looked at his face, so glad to have him back.

"Never ask me that again," she replied.

The next hour passed in seconds. A series of moments burned in her head.

The way he said "Jane" with a furrowed brow.

Him bending to untie her boots. His knuckles brushing the bone at the floor of her throat. The scent at his ear, which she knew was put there with her in mind. The weight of him.

Toward the end, there was a moment when he looked at her. It was the same look he gave her when they'd first danced together. Jane knew not what it meant then, and she was no wiser to its meaning now. It was something alien and masculine, full of shame and desire, and she felt sure she would live her whole life never understanding it.

"What is it?" he asked her. He swallowed.

"The way you look at me now. I will remember it forever," she replied.

AFTERWARD, SHE LAY beside him and he held her.

"Are you okay?" he asked her.

She nodded and smiled. "We should not have done that."

"We should do that, and only that, for the rest of our lives," he said. He wrapped his arm around her. She heard herself choke and laid her head back.

IT CAME TO a head on a Sunday evening, as things usually do. Jane went quiet for a time.

"Are you all right?" he asked her.

She insisted she felt fine, never better.

"That's the third time you've said that," Fred replied. "Tell me what's wrong." She walked away from him with a smile, not wanting to delve into it. This tug-of-war had persisted for several days already, her insisting her felicity and calmness, him asking with increasing worry toward his suspicions of the opposite. Finally, she served him a lunch of roast beef and potatoes, which she had burnt a little, and her placing of the plate in front of him may have been more of a drop than a place, for the dish fell and cracked as it hit the table.

"Enough," he said, sweeping up the food that had spilled onto the tablecloth. "What's the matter, Jane? I'm not leaving the room until you tell me."

"I don't want to make your meals!" she cried. "Why are you laughing?"

"I don't want it, either," he replied. "You're a terrible cook." He laughed again.

"All my books disappeared," she said glumly, without looking at him.

"Oh, Jane." He took her hand and nodded, as though it all made sense to him now. "I'm so sorry." He pulled up a chair. She sat on it. He knelt down in front of her. "Jane. I've been making my own food, washing my own clothes, for about twenty years now. You don't need to do anything around this house."

"What shall I do then?"

"Write," he said. "Write new stories."

She laughed and admitted she had never considered such a thing. "Yes. Why couldn't I?" she said. "I could write here." They embraced again and a warm feeling radiated through her.

Fred provided her with some paper and a self-inking quill. "Or will you prefer my laptop?" he asked her.

She scowled at him and he explained to her what it was. She inhaled with wonder at his description, but then shook her head, thanking him. "Clean white paper and a pen will suffice as more than enough modern tools at this point," she said. She would try the other object later.

"When shall you return?" she asked him as he headed out the door.

"I won't be back for hours," he said. She thanked him and he left. She felt a little leap of pride. Her turn now. She would show him how one did it.

Jane sat forward in her chair and perched the pen over the paper. She smiled. What new things could she write about? The possibilities remained endless. She laughed. She looked up into her head and found it empty of ideas. No matter. Inspiration took time. She sat until she thought of something.

An hour later, she remained perched in the same position as before. The blank page of pristine white mocked her. What occurred? New words always came slowly, but after an hour she had usually written at least something. She could not even think of a line, a droll thing to say.

Another hour passed, and she confirmed the new truth. The buzzing ideas that once filled her mind had departed. No stories remained.

She heard Fred's footsteps approaching the front door. She panicked; hours had passed, and she had written nothing. She had admonished him heartily for the same crime. She felt wrapped in a ball of agitation. Fred opened the door and she plastered a smile onto her face.

He looked at her hopefully. "How did you go?" he asked her. He removed his coat and hung it on the hook.

"Very well," she said. She found the lie easier to say than the truth. "Thank you, Fred," she added, in genuine appreciation. Guilt gripped her at not having made use of the time. She felt lazy and horrid, but she embraced him. He excused himself and told her to keep writing, promising he would not disturb her for the rest of the afternoon. She thanked him and watched him go.

The fact that he struggled to write was bad enough. But the fact that she could not write was intolerable. When she had lain with him, she recalled having felt given over to two opposites of feeling. The first was warmth, the greatest relief and calm. The second was a random terror she could not put away. The act had failed to still a growing demon inside her; rather, it performed the opposite. It created a new yearning within her, another hunger to compete with all the others. The act did nothing to inspire her either, she had noted with curiosity and horror at the time. Now afterward, she could confirm this fact. Her head remained empty. Her communion with the dream of the world had ended. In this condition, she was no writer. Would it always be like this? Would she never be able to write? Surely things would change.

The realization crept inward as the memory now returned. The concern that had gathered in recent days, the small wave of confusing dread that built, in the dress shop, at the christening, and in his bed, now became realized. She had brushed aside the warning Mrs. Sinclair gave her in Cheapside. She wrote off those words as theater, a portentous statement the woman made to make things seem deep. Now it hit Jane: the deal she had signed, the bargain she had struck. The fate she had sealed for herself. *You cannot have both.* Jane comprehended now the choice those words had offered and blinked at the selection she had made. She closed her eyes.

She derived pleasure in life from doing something well, an affliction perhaps she shared with many. She wondered if she could deny herself the thing that came to her most naturally, that lit her up, for the rest of her time. She recalled the white heat moving through her after what had happened with Mr. Withers, the writing that came. Terror and glory had gripped her. She would feel happiness with Fred, but she would never feel *that*. And another thought struck, from the cunning and nasty part of her, which she hated herself for having but couldn't resist admiring the honesty of: not only did separating from Fred allow her to be her true self, but she could put the pain it would cause to good use.

No question existed of their love for each other. They were two good people. But she could not live here, and he could not live there. Jane could not be a writer and be someone's wife.

That night she went to his bed again. If possible, this time was more lovely than the first. Afterward, he held her close and said nothing. It was over, and she knew he knew it, too, because he held her tight and desperate, like one did when one knew the holding was for the last time. In the morning, she expressed a desire for some fresh air and, dressing quickly, departed the house.

Chapter Fifty-Two

She wandered Bath, going nowhere in particular. She sought the time and panicked; hours had passed. Fred would come looking for her soon. She walked into a clearing of green grass. She turned and found to her surprise not Fred but Sofia, walking toward her with a smile.

"What are you doing here?" Jane asked. "How did you find me?"

Sofia shrugged and smiled. "I thought you could use this. It's turning cold." She handed Jane a coat. Jane put it on, and they walked in silence. They arrived at the edge of a forest. It was up here in the woods, around the trees, that this world smelled closest to her own.

"I never marry, do I?" Jane said after a time.

"I beg your pardon?" Sofia said. "You have a wedding dress. You have a ring."

"If I return to 1803, I mean. I never marry." Jane stopped walking and waited for a reply.

Sofia sighed. "How should I know?" she said. "What a ridiculous inquiry." Though from the way she laughed and moved her hand, Jane sensed Sofia had expected the question.

"You owned all my books, before they disappeared," Jane said.

"You told me yourself you learned of me during your education. Are you saying you have no idea of Jane Austen's biography?"

Sofia did not speak.

"Tell me what happens to me, if I go back," Jane said.

"Everything has changed now that you've stayed here, so what's the point of telling you?" Sofia said. "Why torture yourself, and everyone?"

"I cannot help myself," Jane said. "I've asked the question. Please tell me. Tell me what happens to the Jane Austen you once learned of."

Sofia sat down on a park bench. Jane joined her and waited.

"Okay." Sofia looked up to the sky. "Like I said, everything has changed now that you've decided to stay here, in this time. But I will tell you what I know."

"Thank you."

"The Jane Austen I learned of? Whose books I read as a child. No, she never marries."

Jane bowed her head. It was as she expected. That did not dull its feeling.

"She also never has any children," Sofia added. Her voice wobbled.

"I see," Jane said. She forced a smile.

"But she does become one of the greatest writers in the English language."

Sofia and Jane both stared straight ahead. Sofia touched Jane's arm and seemed to sense where the conversation was headed.

"Jane. You won't be famous in your lifetime. You will receive some small recognition, but you will never know the reception that celebrates you now. You will never know what you become."

Jane nodded and gazed at the ground. "But I will write?"

Sofia sighed and fixed her face in a sad smile. "You will write."

TWILIGHT FELL. AFTER much staring and sighing, Sofia spoke. "You have to go back."

"But I could write books here?" Jane said.

"Could you?" Sofia replied.

Jane already knew the answer. She sighed. "I must be unhappy to write? That's no life."

"Could you be happy the other way?"

Jane frowned. "But I hate it there," she said. She cringed at the memory of how happy everyone had been when marriage with Mr. Withers seemed imminent. How would she tell them that she wouldn't marry, but write instead? She could not face such a conversation. In hearing that she chose spinsterhood, they would disown her, like they had Uncle Anthony. "I do not fit in my world," she protested.

"There's something exquisite about the way you don't fit," Sofia told her. "You are responsible for more than books."

"I do not see how. I do not see a path." Though she had seen her books in print, felt their fabric, she could not see how she could return to that place and make such things happen. That role belonged to some other Jane.

"There is no path," Sofia replied. "You make the path. Then you leave a trail. You protest now, but I see it in your face. You're already thinking of all the things you want to write."

"I will be miserable," Jane declared.

"Yes," Sofia said. "You will rise at three A.M. in terror and write until dawn to chase the demons away. You will write so that happy, boring people can buy your books and escape for a time. You will write about it, so they feel like they live it. They will consume your pain and pay you for it. That's the transaction. And you will be more alive than most people combined."

"But I will be without love."

Sofia shook her head. "You will be the furthest thing from that," she whispered. She smiled and wiped her eye. "You will carry this love with you for the rest of your life. It will tear your heart in two. You will use it to write symphonies."

The singular ray of English sun dropped behind the horizon. A breeze blew and made Jane shiver; she buttoned the coat Sofia had given her. "All right," she said.

"All right?" Sofia turned to her.

"Take me home," Jane said.

"Truly?" Sofia said. She took Jane's hand and kissed it, then wiped a tear. "You could take Fred with you?"

Jane sat back into the bench. She thought of Fred. He had not come looking for her, despite her being gone for hours. Sofia must have said something to him to make him stay away. She wondered what Sofia had told him: a kind lie to keep him in ignorance, at least for a little while longer, or the truth, perhaps.

"I could not," Jane said.

"No," replied her friend. They walked home as the gray sun set over the hills of Bath.

RETURNING TO THE old rules made the best tactic. Jane stayed indoors as before and risked no further contamination by the modern-day world. She felt awkward remaining under Fred's roof, but there was no remedy for that. She avoided him as much as was possible without seeming rude. It broke her heart to conceal her plans from him, to act like all was well when secretly she intended to leave him, but she and Sofia had agreed that telling him anything would only hamper their plans; he might try to stop them. Everything was done to ensure the chance of her returning home.

"You need to accept that the damage might already be done," Sofia told her. "It may already be too late to get you back to 1803." She collected her bag and walked to the door.

Jane nodded. "What are you going to do?" Jane asked.

"Impose on a person who deserves better," Sofia said.

Chapter Fifty-Three

Sofia waited in front of the University of Bristol's main library. "Hi, Dave," she said as he walked past her to enter the building.

Dave swung around. "What are you doing here?" He didn't smile.

"I need your help," Sofia said.

"Sorry, no can do," he replied, and ran inside.

"I need your help, Dave. Please!" She ran after him.

"No way. I called you about a hundred times and you never answered. You can't do that to people."

"It was not a hundred times," Sofia called. "It was a significant number. I'm sorry."

"You are a rude person!"

He went into an area with a sign that read *Library Staff Only*. Sofia waited. He didn't come out. Sofia walked into the staff-only area and hit Dave with the door on the way through. He seemed to have been standing there watching but pretending not to. He now pretended to make a cup of tea.

"Dave. I behaved poorly."

"I believed you when no one did. When you told me Jane Austen was living with you—no proof, no nothing. Makes me some kind of idiot. But I believed you."

"I know."

"Do you know how many phone calls I made to Sotheby's to try to get that letter for you? I spoke to a man in a bow tie."

"I'm sorry. Can you call him again?" Sofia looked at him beseechingly. Dave blustered and fumed and spilled the tea all over the laminate counter. "You did not deserve it. But now Jane needs your help."

He harrumphed and shook his head. "Sorry, no can do."

"Okay, answer me one question, and I'll leave."

"Go ahead," he said, a little too quickly.

"If Jane Austen had to choose between the heart and the pen, what would she do?"

He sighed. "You are a cunning woman. I go weak for literary hypotheticals."

"I thought you might. How do you answer?"

He put the tea down. "I think, for a time, she chooses the heart," Dave said, crossing his arms. "But then, with great sadness, I think the pen." Sofia bowed her head. "What's happened?" he asked.

"As you have said," Sofia replied in a sad voice. "She chooses the pen."

Dave leaned back on the counter, nodding thoughtfully.

"She wants to return to 1803," Sofia said. "I only hope it's not too late to help her. You said Mrs. Sinclair wrote Jane a letter in 1810. Where is it?"

They returned to the stacks. They sought out the Sotheby's book once more. Dave turned to the page and gasped. "It's gone." He pointed for Sofia. He told the truth. The entry detailing Mrs. Sinclair's letter was no longer on the page. "I can't believe it! This is the correct page."

"Welcome to my world," Sofia said.

"Why is it gone?" he asked.

"Returned any Jane Austen books to the shelves lately, Dave?"

He looked upward, as though trying to remember. "Come to think of it, no."

"Do you know anything about time travel?"

"I may have read one or two things on the subject." He coughed and shifted his feet. Sofia waited for him to think, to catch up. His face fell. "Oh no."

"Oh yes. Jane has fallen in love with my brother. She has accepted his marriage proposal."

"If she marries your brother and stays here, she never goes back to write her books. They've vanished."

"Yup. And the letters?"

"She's not Jane Austen anymore. She's not famous. Her letters, her personal correspondence, they're not valued or of historical importance. No one has collected them. They're gone."

Sofia sat down next to him. "What can we do? Does any chance exist we can still get her back?"

"I don't know." He scratched his head.

"Is this bad?" Sofia asked.

"It's not good," he said. "Wait a minute. How come I still remember Jane Austen if no one else does? Her books are gone, the films adapted from her books are gone."

"Even the woman at the library didn't remember her," Sofia added.

"Right. No one else remembers her. But we do. Why?"

Sofia nodded. "We're exempt, somehow. Because we know her."

Dave stood up. "Maybe I can help. But I need more information."

"About Jane?" Sofia asked. He nodded. Sofia grabbed his arm. "Come on."

"Where are we going?"

"There's someone I want you to meet."

SOFIA RETURNED TO Fred's house with Dave.

"You must be Dave," Jane said to him. She held out her hand for him to shake.

"It's you," Dave replied with a gasp. "It's her," he said to Sofia.

"Dave. Meet Jane Austen."

He shook Jane's hand. "I need to sit down." Sofia fetched him a chair before he fainted. "Extraordinary," he said when he finally regained the power of speech. "You are the spitting image of her."

"Yes," Jane said. She smiled. "Can you assist me to return home, Dave?"

"I don't know," he said.

"Are you a detective?" she asked.

"No," he replied. He puffed out his chest. "I'm a librarian."

"Do you have questions to ask me?"

He nodded. "Absolutely. What do you love most about writing?" Jane smiled.

"She meant about time travel, Dave," Sofia barked.

"It's quite all right, Sofia," Jane said. She smiled again at Dave. "What do I love most about writing? It takes a chair and gives it a soul. It tells the truth with a lie. It adds one's voice to the dream of the world."

He smiled back at her and looked like he might slip down to the floor, then touched her hand.

Jane's eyes filled with tears. "Can you help me return, sir?"

"I wish I could say yes."

"Wherein lies the issue?"

"Your books are gone. Jane Austen, the writer, is gone. Public record of you is gone. Our one hope was the letter Mrs. Sinclair wrote to you. No more."

Jane frowned. "This is less than ideal news."

"Can we not simply find Mrs. Sinclair's letter somewhere else?" Sofia asked.

"We can't," said Dave. "Jane Austen no longer exists as a famous person, so the letter is lost to history."

"She still wrote it, though? Mrs. Sinclair still contacted Jane."

Dave paused. "I suppose so." He shrugged.

"Might anyone else have kept the letter?" Sofia asked.

"If there was even the slightest chance the letter survived, there's only one way." He gave a grim laugh. "It happens in such an unlikely set of circumstances you will laugh when I say it."

"Try us," Sofia said.

"Jane Austen the writer has disappeared, yes. But Jane Austen the parson's daughter hasn't. People used to write each other letters. Loads of them. Certain families used to keep these letters as heirlooms. Someone might have kept Jane's letters as part of a family collection. But even if by some miracle they did so, to find the letter, you must track down every Austen in the country—many won't even carry the surname Austen. One of those families might have preserved their letters. As the Austen name is no longer famous, those families will have no idea why you're calling on them. It's a one-in-a-million shot, needle-in-a-haystack stuff. Where are we going?" he said to Sofia, who had stood while he talked and now dragged him to the front door.

"Stay here, Jane," she said on her way out the door. Jane nodded.

"Where are we going?" Dave asked again as she pulled him toward his car.

"To London."

"What's there?"

"A one-in-a-million shot."

DAVE TURNED OUT of the street onto the A36 in his Volkswagen Beetle.

"You're a terrible driver," Sofia said.

"Sorry. Too fast?" said Dave.

"Too slow." A man in a station wagon hurled abuse out the window as he overtook them. They moved onto the M4 and drove in silence for a while. Sofia turned her face to the window and willed the ancient car to go faster. Two hours and twenty-seven minutes later they arrived in Notting Hill. Dave pulled up to a white Georgian town house.

"That looks expensive," said Dave, pointing to the grand facade.

"It is," Sofia said, realizing she might be about to lose it. She rolled her eyes.

"Do you want me to come with you?"

"I'd better go by myself," Sofia said. "Back in a few." She exited the car and knocked on the front door.

"WHAT DO YOU want?" Jack Travers, in a designer tracksuit, stood in the doorway of the house bought with Sofia's earnings.

"I will sign your divorce papers," Sofia said, "on two conditions."

Jack rolled his shoulders back, the way he always did when try-ing to listen. "Name them."

"One. If there is ever a role you think I'd be great in, offer it to me."

"Done," said Jack. "You're a talented actress, Sofe."

"Yes, I am."

"Two?" said Jack.

"There is a box of letters in the attic. I want them."

Jack squinted. "Why?"

"Do you still have them, or not?"

"That bunch of dusty old letters in the shoebox? I still have them."

"The ones your mother left you," Sofia pressed.

Jack nodded, irritated. "I know them. What's the catch?"

"No catch," Sofia said.

"You're giving me half your money, plus alimony, for some let-ters? This is a trick. They must be worth something." He scratched his head.

"They're worthless."

"Why do you want them, then?"

Sofia scowled and searched for an answer. "I always liked them," she said. "They reminded me of us. Old love letters . . . who knows what's inside? It's romantic. It will make the separa-tion from you easier." She tried not to gag.

Jack sighed and looked at her with wistful eyes. "Fine." They shook hands.

"Can I have them?" Sofia said.

Jack's eyes widened. "You want them now?"

"Why not?"

Jack shrugged. "Be my guest."

Sofia darted upstairs to the attic. She found the shoebox, kissed it, and returned downstairs.

Jack waited in the doorway. "Find them? Good. Did we do okay, Sofe? By each other, I mean?" He shifted his feet.

Sofia smiled. "We did okay," she said.

Jack nodded. "We had some good times," he said.

"That time with the fruit," Sofia said.

He laughed. "Or the time we were three days down on *Batman* and that Turkish gymnast walked off set."

"I strapped a wig on, and we got the cutaway."

"You saved the film."

"We saved it," she said.

He flashed her a smile. "God, you look good. Stay for a drink? We can reminisce."

"Another time," she said.

"I guess this is goodbye, then," he said.

"Take care, Jack. See you around." She touched his arm, took one deep, indulgent breath, and left.

Chapter Fifty-Four

She joined Dave in the car. "Everything okay?" he asked in a nervous voice.

"Great," Sofia said. She handed him the shoebox. "I hope it's in here. I just agreed to a divorce for these." Dave stared at her and inhaled sharply. He nodded and seemed to require a minute or two to compose himself.

"Dave, are you still with us?" Sofia asked finally.

"Yep," he said. He exhaled. He turned to the shoebox. He threw the lid open and peered inside. The contents smelled of vanilla and almonds. He gasped. "What a stupid man. The lignin and cellulose have broken down. These should have been preserved."

"Jack doesn't know these are Jane Austen's letters, remember," Sofia said.

"Even still. They are hundreds of years old. Letters from his own flesh and blood. They're in a shoebox."

Inside the cardboard box lay thirty dried yellow pages of various sizes and shapes. Dave lifted out the top one with great care.

"Is it Jane's?" asked Sofia.

Every inch of the square page was covered in a brown cursive hand.

Dave nodded. "This is Austen's handwriting; I'd know it anywhere. See the long curlicues and the sloped—"

"Dave," Sofia interrupted. "Sorry to interrupt, but can we move on?"

"Right you are. Sorry. It is beautiful handwriting."

"Praising Jane Austen for her handwriting is like praising Sylvia Plath for her baking," Sofia said. "What does it say?"

"It is a letter to her sister. It reads, 'My dear Cass, another stupid party last night . . . Miss Langley was like any other short girl with a broad nose and wide mouth, fashionable dress, and exposed bosom.'"

Sofia smiled. "Witty. Go on."

"'Bath is vapor, shadow, smoke, and confusion. I cannot continue to find people agreeable.'" He read the next lines to himself.

"What is it, something juicy?" Sofia said. She craned her head to read.

"The opposite," said Dave. He put the letter down.

"What is the matter, Dave? Why have you gone all misty-eyed? Get a grip, man. Time is of the essence."

"These are so sad," Dave said. "She hates Bath. Are you sure we want to send this woman back to a place that makes her feel like this, just so she can write some books?"

Sofia sat back in the car seat. She knew what fate awaited Jane in 1803. Derision and solitude. "We do," she replied. "She will be sad. It will be the making of her."

Dave nodded and sifted through the next pages with gentle hands. He read the first line of each only before handing it to Sofia.

"What if it's not here?" Sofia asked in a low voice.

"Jane Austen will be gone," he replied, bowing his head. He read on. In the next letter, Jane wrote to her brother James, declining an invitation to attend his anniversary party. In the next, she wrote to her younger brother Frank, thanking him for a pair of silk stockings.

"Only two letters left," said Dave. He surveyed the next page. "Jane's mother writes the first. She's not happy about something." He handed the letter to Sofia. She read it and agreed.

"And the last?" Sofia said, anxious.

Dave snatched the letter up. "Written in a new hand." He read aloud.

June 18th, 1810

Dear Miss Austen,

How is your health? How are your parents? I enclose a recipe for cabbage soup which may assist with your stomach complaint.

Life in the capital is full of drudgery but if you ever desired a laugh at my expense, it may please you to hear I had a recent excursion to the Old Bailey. An ongoing dispute with a pugilistic neighbor reared its head and I found myself in the dock. The court erupted into laughter when my neighbor from nowhere accused me of witchcraft. The magistrate and everyone laughed. I noted their laughter and decided to run forward. I asserted I was a witch. I said this all in the voice of a lunatic. When the lawyer for my complainant then asked me for examples of my warlock creed, I decided to continue the farce and proceeded through a list of my daily maleficent business. I composed spells for the judge and even gave advice on casting them; for instance, to reverse any spell, repeat the incantation, then to the blood of the talisman add the blood of the subject.

In any case, the tactic worked, for the judge seemed to take pity on me for my gross insanity. He handed down a sentence leaner than I expected, and I spent the afternoon in celebration. My penalty involves a journey to a faraway land. I shall write again when I arrive, but in the meantime, you may wish to read this letter again for diversion if you ever find yourself stranded indoors on a rainy afternoon. But the cabbages are boiled, and my house begins to smell.

Yours sincerely,
Emmaline Sinclair

Sofia smiled. Dave put the letter down, turned over the Beetle's engine, and commanded it to return to Bath as quickly as its bald tires could spin.

"IF YOU NEED me to help get any other stranded authors back to their own time, let me know," Dave said as they trundled back down the M4.

"I don't know any other authors, sorry," Sofia replied.

"Or maybe we could get a drink sometime," he said.

Sofia scoffed and turned her head to him. "Why have you never told me I am beautiful?" she asked accusingly.

"What?" His eyebrows shot up.

She swallowed, aware she may have sounded a tad strange. She had good reason; she still felt a little raw from giving away her house and her marriage to Jack for a shoebox of letters. She decided to express her anger by irrationally taking things out on the man next to her, who had been nothing but annoyingly kind and helpful. "Why have you never told me I have a 'banging body'?"

Dave changed lanes. "You do have a banging body. You are beautiful."

"Why have you never said these things before?"

"Because those are the least interesting things about you."

Sofia stared at the road. "Oh."

The car made some sort of clanking sound. Dave checked the gauges. "It does this sometimes," he explained. "It's quite an old car."

"You don't say," she replied.

"If I jiggle this a bit, it usually stops," he said. He jiggled one of the ancient-looking sticks that sprouted from the steering wheel. The clanking, as promised, ceased.

Sofia gathered the words in her head to turn him down. She'd be gentle, but also tell it to him straight—he deserved that much.

"Look, Dave, you're a really great guy," she began.

He nodded with what seemed like resignation. He exhaled a huge puff of held breath. "I understand, all good," he replied. "No explanation required." He drove on.

Could she be with someone who was nice to her? It sounded unglamorous and dull.

"Okay, fine," she said.

"Fine?"

"Yes, fine, let's get a drink," she said.

Dave kept his eyes on the road. An elderly woman drove past in a Morris Minor and overtook them, shouting hints out her window at ways Dave could improve his driving. Dave waved to her in return, with the biggest grin Sofia had ever seen. They arrived back in Bath and Dave dropped Sofia at Fred's house, wishing her luck with the letter and hoping for Jane's safe return to 1803. They made a plan to go out the following week.

Chapter Fifty-Five

Sofia showed Jane Mrs. Sinclair's letter. Jane read it and sighed.

"Sofia. You are a wonder. I think you paid a fortune for this." She touched Sofia's arm.

Sofia coughed. "Never mind that now. We have work to do. I'll get your dress."

Jane stiffened. "You want me to go back right now?"

"Did you have another time in mind? Jane, I thought we were on the clock here."

"I suppose. Of course, yes." Jane turned her head and looked into the house.

"Where's Fred?" Sofia asked. "Is he at work?"

Jane nodded. "If I leave now, I won't say goodbye."

Sofia nodded. "Do you want to wait?"

Jane gazed at the floor. "No."

"I'll fetch your dress."

AN HOUR LATER, Jane had put on her white muslin dress. She changed to her brown boots and donned her brown gloves, bonnet, and pelisse. She tied her hair in a Grecian knot. She curled the short pieces around her face.

Sofia inhaled when she saw her. "My God," she said.

"Do I look different?" Jane said, worried.

"You look exactly the same as when I met you," Sofia said.

"Good."

"A little taller, maybe." Sofia took a deep breath. "Are you ready?"

"I am ready," Jane said. They turned to the door.

"It's Fred!" Sofia cried, pointing out the window. "What's he doing here?" Fred walked up the garden path. Jane froze. "Quick, run!" But it was too late.

Fred shuffled up the path with a confused look on his face.

"Fred," Sofia said in a cheerful tone. "What are you doing here?" Sofia and Jane both nodded an awkward hello.

Fred looked at Jane's ensemble, her bonnet, boots, and pelisse, and the smile drained from his face. "Why are you dressed like that?" he asked. Jane turned away and made no reply. "Jane. What's going on?" He stared at her. "Is someone going to tell me what's going on?"

Jane shook her head. Finally, she turned to him. "I am going home, Fred."

He stepped backward and stumbled over a kitchen chair. He turned and walked out the door.

"Fred," Jane called after him. "Come back."

He walked down the path.

Sofia grabbed Jane's arm. "It's better this way."

Jane nodded.

THEY ARRIVED AT the hall and walked to the area behind the stage. Jane took her place among the pile of black curtains, the place she had first appeared. The sight of Fred walking toward her, the look on his face, still haunted her. She turned to Sofia.

"I have no words," Jane said. "A rare occurrence for me."

"There are no words for this situation, Austen."

They embraced. Sofia read aloud. "To reverse any spell, repeat the incantation, then to the blood of the talisman add the blood of the subject." She shrugged. Sofia gave Jane a pin. "Here goes nothing."

Jane pricked her finger with it, then removed the scrap of manuscript from her pocket. She dropped her blood onto the page and swallowed. "Take me to my one true love," she chanted.

"Goodbye, Jane," Sofia said.

"Goodbye, Sofia." Jane shut her eyes and waited for the dust to come as before.

Nothing happened.

Jane opened her eyes. "I'm still here."

Sofia scanned the letter. "What? You repeated the incantation; you added a drop of blood. I don't understand." She handed Jane the paper. "Why is there always some complication?"

"To the blood of the talisman add the blood of the subject," Jane read aloud. She frowned. "This is the talisman, yes?" She held up the scrap of manuscript where Mrs. Sinclair had first scrawled the spell.

"Correct," Sofia said.

"And I am the subject," Jane said. She pointed to herself.

"That's right," Sofia said.

They stood in silence. Jane ran back in her mind through everything. *Take me to my one true love.* "No," she said. "I am not the subject."

"You aren't?" Sofia said. "Who is, then?"

"Jane," said a voice behind them. A figure walked toward them in the darkness.

"He is," Jane said.

"How did you know we would be here?" Jane asked Fred. She felt relief and sadness to see him.

"I worked it out," Fred said. He saw the smile on her face and looked at her with hopeful eyes.

"I have little right," Jane said to him, "but if you would be so kind as to give me a drop of your blood."

His face fell; he shook his head. "No. I came to stop you. What happens if I do not give you my blood?" Fred asked.

"I cannot return to 1803," Jane said.

"Good," Fred said. "I will see you at home." He walked out.

"No, Fred. Come back!" Sofia shouted. But he had gone.

Jane sat on the floor of the hall with her arms crossed over her chest. Sofia paced the floorboards and hatched a succession of schemes.

"I could offer to give him a hot shave," Sofia suggested. "Then I could accidentally on purpose nick his throat and collect whatever blood happened to spurt forth."

"You do not think holding a hot blade to his neck is a touch dangerous?" Jane said. "I have witnessed you cut an orange. Your dexterity left something to be desired."

"True. And knife throwing is on my CV. Go figure." Sofia tapped the wall. "I say we go back to the plan where I drain his blood in his sleep," she said. "I will take an online course in blood collection. Once I am trained up, I will wait until he's in the middle of an REM cycle, pop the needle in, and grab a few drops. He won't even miss it."

"And how do you suppose you will open a vein in his arm without him noticing?" Jane asked.

"I will make him a hearty dinner of turkey and quaaludes."

"Do you know how to cook a turkey?" Jane asked.

"Not exactly. But he won't notice with all the quaaludes."

"No," Jane said. "None of these ideas have merit."

"Why not? The turkey idea is solid."

"Because they all involve stealing your brother's blood. I cannot take it from him. Let us return home, Sofia. If he will not give it to me, then perhaps I do the wrong thing by leaving." They stood and walked to the door.

"Jane," Fred said. He reappeared in the doorway.

"Fred!" Jane exclaimed. She went to him. Relief washed over her again. The sight of him made everything clear. "I do not care about this," she said, pointing to the paper. "Each time you go, it tears my heart out. I do not want to leave you ever again. I will stay." She smiled.

He took the pin from her and nicked his finger. A bead of crimson formed on his fingertip.

"No, Fred. Did you not hear me? I said I will stay. With you."

"It's not what I want," he said. He held up his hand and offered it to Jane.

Jane hesitated. The drop of blood bloomed outward, eventually turning to a trickle that threatened to spill to the floor. She held out the manuscript scrap and caught the blood on the page. The fresh red drop merged with the old brown spot of her own and became one.

"Thank you, Fred," Jane said in a voice gone hoarse. She looked down at her hands. She removed the ring with the turquoise stone and held it out to Fred. "Give it to someone who deserves it."

Fred shook his head. "That ring belongs to my wife."

Jane nodded. She wiped her eyes. "How does one say goodbye in the year two thousand and twenty?"

"The same way you always say it," Fred said. "You hug them. You tell them you will see them again soon. Even if it's not true." His voice cracked.

"A true English goodbye," she said, her voice breaking.

Jane hugged him. Little sounds exited her body, howling gasps, sounds she had never heard herself make. She destroyed them both by staying. It did not make it easier. "See you again soon," she managed to say. The words came out in a croak. Sofia sobbed.

"It was good, wasn't it?" Fred whispered in her ear.

"It was," she whispered back.

Jane broke away and stepped onto the pile of theater curtains. She held up the manuscript. "Take me to my one true love," she said. She closed her eyes. Nothing happened.

Fred smiled and wiped his eye.

The room grew dark and something like snow began to fall.

"Fred," she called out. He snapped his head up to her. Tears bathed his eyes. "If you ever want to see me, look for me, and you will find me. Do you understand? I will always be with you."

He nodded.

The snow fell harder; the room spun.

"Say you will look for me," Jane said. "Promise me."

"I promise," he replied, shaking his head in some confusion. "I will look for you."

She transformed into an outline of dust and disappeared.

Chapter Fifty-Six

*J*ane opened her eyes. She sat in the woodsman's cottage.

Outside in the forest, darkness fell. Moonlight lit her path back to town. Jane walked through the trees over a path of pine needles, and when she reached the edge of the forest, she looked up ahead. The Bath skyline rose in the distance. The roofs of the Crescent and the Circus punctured the sky. The Pump Room dome sat by the Avon. Smoke pumped from chimneys.

It rained. Jane's curls plastered themselves to her forehead. Her pelisse was soaked. She reached Bath Abbey in the center of town, crossed Pulteney Bridge, and walked to Sydney Place. She stopped on the corner and watched.

The front of Sydney House hosted a crowd. Lady Johnstone waltzed around the gathered people, smiling and whispering to everyone. Mrs. Austen had a tear-stained face and spoke to a policeman. Jane heard herself gasp at the sight. No time had passed at all.

Jane took several deep breaths and hoped she inhaled sufficient air for what she was about to do, then she turned to the crowd and walked through it. Whispers and snickers rose from the throng. People pointed and stared at her. The policeman stopped writing in his notebook. "And where have you been, miss?" he said. The crowd hushed one another and seemed to wait with bated breath for Jane's answer. Instead Jane ignored him and everyone else and walked inside the building. Mrs. Austen followed her.

Jane braced for an attack from her mother once inside the house. But one did not come. Mrs. Austen kneeled. "Stupid girl," she whispered through sobs. She held Jane.

"I am sorry, Mama."

Mrs. Austen walked Jane into the parlor. "You are soaked through," she said. She called for the housemaid to fetch a cloth to dry Jane's hair.

"I am glad you've come back safe, Jane," a man's voice said. Jane looked up. Reverend Austen leaned on the doorframe. His white hair hung loose and wet around his neck. He had lost the sole from his left boot. For once, he looked older than his more than seventy years.

Jane ran to him. "Papa," she cried and sobbed into his shoulder. She almost tipped him over.

"Easy, girl," he said with a wince. "All is well." He patted her head.

Jane was racked with guilt. "Papa, I am sorry. You have been out in the wet and cold."

"Hush now, Jane. I am well." His hand shook as he held the chair to sit down.

"You should not have been out looking for me. Let others go."

"I do not leave that task to others." He smiled at the floor.

"Oh, Papa." She held him.

Jane's mother sighed. "Jane, my girl. You did not need to run away. Mr. Withers hurt us all. I have put in a serious complaint with that matchmaker. But all is not lost. There are other men out there. We will help you find a husband."

"I do not want one, Mama."

"I know, but when the time comes, when you feel better, you will want one."

Jane nodded. "Mama, I am not going to marry."

"You will, Jane."

"I will not. Do listen, Mama. I've decided. I am sorry."

Mrs. Austen whimpered and clutched her breast. "Good God, George. She's turned mad." Margaret, the housemaid, entered the room with a cloth. "Never mind, Margaret," Mrs. Austen said, pointing at the towel for Jane's hair. Margaret nodded and crept backward. Mrs. Austen glared at Jane. "Please clarify your remarks, child. Your last words were a nonsense."

"I am not going to marry. Not now, nor ever."

Mrs. Austen stood up and sat down. She stood up again. "And how do you intend to survive without a husband?" she asked.

"I will be a writer."

"A writer! Fetch the physician. Our child is insane. And who shall support you, Jane?"

"I expect nothing. I am happy to starve until I can earn my own wage."

"Earn a wage? What is this stupidity? Jane, you cannot. Need I remind you, you are a woman?"

"I can, Mama. I have seen it done."

Mrs. Austen squinted at her daughter's tone and studied Jane's face. "Something about you is different," she declared. Jane panicked. She had taken pains to make her hair and dress identical to before. "Look, George."

Reverend Austen peered at his daughter. "I see no difference," he said.

"I do," said Mrs. Austen. "She has changed."

"I am still your daughter, Mama," Jane said.

Mrs. Austen scratched her brow. "I have always said you are too clever for your own good."

"I inherited many traits from my mother."

"It was a shame you were born a woman," she muttered. "But there it is. You must deal with it."

Jane took her mother's hand. "Will you not be happier knowing you have a fulfilled child, rather than one who is simply married?"

"Fulfillment! What is this talk? You have not thought this through, Jane."

"On the contrary, madam. I have thought on this more than once. I shall ask Henry for a small investment of funds to cover my room and board while I rewrite my manuscript."

Mrs. Austen scoffed. "Preposterous! Henry will never give you money for such a foolish scheme."

"Henry delights in foolish schemes, Mama. And he will do this because he knows as well as you, this is a sound investment."

"I know nothing of the sort," her mother scoffed. "We sent the book to Cadell. He gave his answer."

"Before you threw my manuscript on the fire, you read it, did you not?"

"I do not recall," she replied. She took a long pause. She shrugged. "So what if I did?"

"Place your eyes on mine and tell me I cannot do this. I shall marry whomever you choose, and I shan't write another word."

Sounds of chatter rose up from the street below, where a small crowd still lingered outside, muttering and speculating. Lady Johnstone's voice remained among them. Jane's mother walked over and shut the window; silence filled the room. Finally, her father spoke. "Jane, my darling girl. I know the writing is all to you. But to never marry, to be alone, to live without someone—Jane, it is a sad thing. You do not know what you give up."

She inhaled, then turned to him. "Papa, I know it may not seem so, but I know in the pit of my heart what I give up," she said.

Her father stared at her with sad eyes. Mrs. Austen frowned and sat down. "It is too much of a risk, Jane."

"As is everything great in this world, Mama."

Mrs. Austen stared at her daughter. The room fell silent again.

Margaret walked back in. "Ma'am. Oh. Goodness. Beg pardon." She looked about the room at the silent faces and seemed to figure she had disturbed a great discussion. She curtsied in apology and turned to hurry back out again.

"No. What is it, Margaret?" said Mrs. Austen.

Margaret stopped and addressed her in a gentle voice. "Cook asked now that Miss Jane is back, will Mrs. Lindell be coming around tomorrow? If yes, should she purchase spatchcocks from Stall Street, which are pricey, but Mrs. Lindell was put out by the standard we served last time, which were gamy and full of buckshot."

"I thought they were all right," Reverend Austen muttered.

The room fell silent again. Mrs. Austen continued to stare at her daughter. Margaret went to leave once more but paused when Mrs. Austen began to speak. "Tell Cook that the birds Reverend Austen shoots will be sufficient." Mrs. Austen spoke, pushing her shoulders back. "If Jane is to be a spinster, we can't be keeping the matchmaker in store-bought spatchcocks."

Margaret nodded and exited with a smile. Jane's eyes filled with tears.

"Mrs. Austen? Truly?" said the Reverend.

"I love you, Mama," Jane whispered, for the first time.

Mrs. Austen wiped a tear from her own eye. "What now then?" she asked.

Jane smiled and shrugged.

JANE STARED AT the wall. Six weeks had passed since she had returned to her own time. Insomnia took her. Every night she pleaded with herself, "Tonight we shall sleep, for we are so tired." The clock struck eleven, then twelve, then one, all without slumber. By two o'clock, she resolved to get up, drink tea, walk. By three , she was back in bed, as wide-eyed and awake as if she had rested for a week. By four, the problems of the world rested on her shoulders. By five, she accepted there would be no sleep tonight. By six, she dozed off, only to be woken at seven by the house stirring, to endure the day, a walking ghoul.

She cried for hours on end, soft weeps on the floor in her room and angry wailings by tree trunks in the forest. Items slipped from her mind. She forgot Fred's breath. She misplaced the bend of his fingers. A pain in her chest refused to go. In the darkness, while the house slept, Jane stared at the ceiling and thought of him. The enormity of what she had done gripped her.

What business did her inexperienced heart have mixing itself up in love for another human? Before she knew Fred, she existed on a tolerable plane. She was lonely, but it was paradise compared to this. The love she had read about was all summer's days, crackling fires, and honeyed almonds. Now that she had experienced it for herself, she knew this to be a falsehood, written by men to sell volumes of poetry. Love was not spring buds and fluffy meadows. Love was laudanum. The first dram of it flooded into the blood and took away a pain one never knew one had. Then it exited and left a hole deeper than the one it had been sent in to fill.

She walked to the Black Prince to buy a ticket to London. She would visit Mrs. Sinclair once more. She would procure a new spell, then hold him again.

"Return to London, please," she told the driver.

"Six shillings," he said and held out his hand. "Welcome back, miss."

"I beg your pardon?" Jane said. She eyed him curiously.

"You have been in my carriage before," he explained.

Jane stepped back and wiped her eyes. She asked the driver for a moment and never went back. Instead, she walked to the Pump Room and stood outside. She stared at the honey-colored facade and returned to the night Fred had taken her there. She sat down on a stone bench and cried until her eyes formed two red welts. People passed her and no one inquired of her well-being. A woman weeping in front of the Pump Room surprised no one.

When her eyes ran dry of tears, she picked herself up and walked to the house. She climbed into bed and went to sleep.

When she woke at three A.M., the blackness returned. She did not run this time. She rose out of bed and sat at her desk. She picked up her quill. She gripped its spine until her knuckles turned white and began a new story.

Chapter Fifty-Seven

Sofia burst into Fred's bedroom and kicked him in the foot.

"Ouch," Fred said. He was lying on the floor, the duvet covering his head.

"It smells like a brewery in here," Sofia said. She kicked an empty beer bottle along the floorboards.

"Is there something I can help you with?" he asked.

This is how he had been when their mother died. Sofia knew how it went. He collapsed in a heap, then took years to recover.

"Why did you give Jane your blood?" Sofia kicked him again.

"Ow. I don't know." He pulled the duvet away from his face.

"You could have refused and kept her here. She'd be okay, too. Relieved, even. But you sent her back. Why?"

"I don't know."

"Because you knew she could only be happy doing the thing she loved. You loved her so much you gave her up."

Fred shrugged. "Whatever."

"This is not what Jane wanted."

"Shush," Fred grumbled.

"Okay, so she's gone. I miss her, too. You can drink yourself to death—I can see the appeal. I could give you pointers on how to do it. You could pick up a hobby to pass the time, like trolling or collecting your fingernails in a jar, and you could rant about how Jane Austen did you wrong. Living like half a person. Not living—just breathing. A great option. Do you choose it?"

Fred rolled his eyes. "No."

"Okay, good. We won't shut the door on that option, we'll shelve it for now. There is a second option."

"What's that?" Fred muttered.

Sofia sat on the windowsill. "It's sappy and gross and mushy. You don't want to hear it."

Fred groaned. "I do want to hear it," he said in an unwilling tone.

She cleared her throat. "Okay, here goes. You could honor her." Fred met eyes with his sister.

"Say, 'I saw the sun once and it was beautiful,'" Sofia said. "'But it's gone now and that's sad, but some people go their whole lives never seeing such a thing. I'm going to thank the universe for showing me that and do the same service to myself I did to her. I'm going to stop scowling that she's gone and smile that she was here at all.'" Sofia grimaced. "Mushy, huh?"

"Disgusting," Fred replied.

"So those are your two options. Sad, drunken hobo, or smiling and living. Which option will you go for?"

"Probably the second," he mumbled.

"Good choice." Sofia gave him a thumbs-up.

"It hurts," he said then, in a soft voice.

Sofia frowned. She sat down on the floor next to him. "It's going to hurt tomorrow," she said. "And the next day. Then one morning, you'll wake up, and it will hurt less than it did the day before. Hang on for that day."

Fred nodded. He got up off the floor and walked to the door.

"Where are you going?" said Sofia.

"To do option two," he replied.

"Are you going to give me a hug? After that epic speech?" Sofia said.

Fred rolled his eyes and embraced his sister. "Thank you, Sofe."

"You did a noble thing letting her go," she whispered into his ear.

THE FIRST DAY of shooting arrived. *Northanger Abbey* returned to the production listings, with no one the wiser except Sofia. She stepped into the makeup truck and greeted her old friend. "No makeup today, Derek," Sofia announced as she hugged him hello. "Put away the concealers. Jettison the potions and unguents. Today I shall be wearing my own face."

"Ms. Wentworth, do you feel okay?" Derek asked.

"I am well, Derek."

"Are you sure I can't give the crow's-feet a touch-up?"

"Leave them be, Derek. Strip down the plaster. Let's show the ruined castle within."

Derek grimaced. "But the no-makeup makeup," he whispered in a reverential tone. "We had such good times."

"Yes. Those are gone now. Pour yourself a drink. You'll be needing it."

Afterward, when Derek had stripped her existing makeup away, Sofia dressed in the lime-green velvet gown. Lines covered her bare face. Dark half circles hung below her eyes. Her skin, once soft and even, bloomed with splotches of red.

"There, Derek. What say you now?"

Derek's face bore a strange look. Like he felt both happy and sad. Happy-sad. "It's possible you look lovelier now than before." He wiped a tear.

"We both know that's not possible, Derek, but I accept the compliment anyway."

She walked onto set. Jack looked at her. "I almost didn't recognize you," he said.

"Well, this is what I look like," she said. "Will this be a problem for you?"

"No," he replied and said no more. He escorted her to her mark.

Sofia waited for Jack to call action, then delivered a three-minute monologue about muslin. Every line written big, she played small. Every line that felt small, she played big. The words she thought to shout before, she now whispered with a grand smile. Her lime-green dress, rather than evoking mocking—though it did that too—added a Shakespearean-fool, tragic wisdom to her virtuoso, a grand irony, a pit of sadness. When the time came for her immortal line, "we none of us have a stitch to wear," she said it with resignation, as though the character had said it for years, in places not shown in the film, and saying it once more now placed her on the brink of polite despair.

She did not say it morosely or bitterly, or go for the crotch and deliver it in cheap parody or schtick; she did not sneer or cackle as she spoke. Sofia said the line with kind, knowing eyes, as tears wetted them. She might have been a woman having a nervous breakdown, or she might have been bored with it all. Who knew for sure? But with a little help from some eye bags, divorce papers, and advice from the book's author, that day Sofia took Mrs. Allen from one dimension to three.

She returned home that night and poured herself a drink.

She toasted farewell to her career; it had brought her millions and served her well. She wiped a tear from her lined eyes, for her friend. No one treated her like a star now. No magazine crowned her hottest woman. She raised her glass and went to bed.

SOME MONTHS LATER, Sofia was enjoying a quiet afternoon of sprawling on her sofa when the telephone rang. Max Milson was calling. "Are you sitting down?" her agent said.

"I'm lying down. Does that count?"

"You are up for Best Supporting Actress," said Max.

"Up for what?"

"For an Oscar! For Mrs. Allen in *Northanger Abbey*. Break open the champagne!"

Sofia choked on her drink. She was already nursing a bottle of Prosecco—close enough. "How?" she spluttered into the phone.

"Well, I'm not sure of the exact process but I believe the Academy creates a long list, then consults with its members."

"No," she interrupted him, "how did *I* get nominated? I played an old bag! I've done scores of films where I was beautiful, sexy, promiscuous—none of them got me anything. Now I get the nod for wearing a lime-green sack? This is bad."

"It is not bad," said Max. "It's good. You played her well, Sofia. You played her true."

"I do not accept the nomination," Sofia huffed.

"Yes you do," said Max. "People will suck up to you and you'll get loads of free stuff."

"Fine. I accept the nomination." Sofia hung up the phone and smiled.

The next few weeks passed in a blur of congratulatory texts, phone calls, and visits from the industry. The texts came from people she'd prefer a phone call from, the phone calls from those she'd prefer a text from, and the visits came from people she hoped never to see again. Sofia had practiced her Oscar acceptance speech every night in the bath since the age of four. Sometimes she chose a gushing and tearful exhibition, thanking everyone who had ever helped her, including her Barbie dolls and her hairbrush. As she'd grown older, the sentiments evolved into a spiteful hate speech, naming the people who pushed her down and thanking them all for sweet nothing. But in the end, when she stood at the podium that February and collected her trophy for Best Supporting Actress in *Northanger Abbey*, her thank-you speech consisted of five words only.

"This is for you, Jane," she said, then walked offstage. The crowd seemed so hushed with shock, their faces so fixed in unedifying stares, they had no choice but to give her a standing ovation.

Chapter Fifty-Eight

Fred walked up Praed Street in Paddington to board a train back to Bath. He was heading into the station when something caught his eye. Piles of books lined the dusty window of a secondhand bookshop. Fred chuckled; Jane had teased him about never reading any of her books. He stepped inside. It was a ramshackle room, filled floor to ceiling with books. A rumpled man approached him. His name tag read *George*. "Something to read on the train home?" he said.

"Do you have anything by Jane Austen?" Fred asked.

George smiled. "Indeed." He escorted Fred to a shelf of classics.

Fred scanned the book spines. Jane was the author of many of the titles. "What do you recommend? Sorry if that's a stupid question."

"Not at all. I get asked about her often. Delighted to help." George rolled up his sleeves. He selected a title and skimmed through its pages, taking his time. He furrowed his brow, then picked up another and tapped the cover. "This."

Fred took the book. "*Persuasion,*" he read aloud.

"It's not as flashy as *P and P* or *Emma,* with the zingers and wit. Those are Jane showing off. Showing why she is the best that ever was," George said. "This one she wrote as she got older. It's quieter. It's the last book she wrote before she died." Fred frowned and went quiet. "Are you all right, sir?" George said then.

"Yes," Fred said. "It's . . . she's dead."

"Oh yes," said George. "Austen died long ago." He tapped the cover. "Give this one a go. This is the real Jane."

Fred flipped through the pages. "What's the book about?" he asked.

"It's about regret," George replied. He offered him a sad smile.

Fred nodded. "I'll take it."

"Good," said George. He led Fred to the register. "If you're an Austen fan, perhaps join our mailing list. We often have Jane Austen nights, book clubs."

Fred smirked. "Sure."

"Splendid. What is your name, sir?"

"Wentworth," Fred said.

George typed the name on a dusty keyboard. "And your first name?"

"Fred."

George stopped typing and stared at Fred. "Your name is Frederick Wentworth?"

"Is there a problem?" Fred said.

George smiled and handed Fred the book. "No. Enjoy your book, sir."

FRED RODE THE three P.M. train back to Bath. At first, he stood among crowds of schoolchildren and tourists, but by Maidenhead they'd alighted and the train car grew empty. He found a place by the window and sat. He pulled out *Persuasion* from his bag and turned to the first page.

Afternoon light streamed in from the window. The countryside whirred past outside.

Sir Walter Elliot, of Kellynch Hall, in Somersetshire, was
a man who, for his own amusement, never took up any
book but the Baronetage . . .

Fred winced. It was a slow, old-fashioned novel, a tome from
the canon they forced you to read at school. The students always
rolled their eyes when he assigned a text like this. He stumbled
over the archaic words and long sentences. He googled *baronetage*.
He read a few more paragraphs and found his mind wandering
over the drawn-out passages, taking nothing in. He put the book
down and stared out the window. The fields whizzed past him in a
blur of emerald green.

He picked the book back up again and forced himself to persist. Read ten pages. He read through the next page with gritted teeth and breathed a sigh of relief when he reached the final
word. He exhaled and nodded; he could do this. He was determined to get through it, for Jane. He arrived at the top of the next
page. The first sentence was easier to get through now he knew
what to expect with the semicolons and clauses. Her sentences
were passive, with the meaning end-loaded. She waited until
the final moment to reveal her intention. It was a frowned-upon
technique these days. Every guru taught to put the point up front,
for all to see. But as Fred's comfort grew with the style, the point
emerged. Each sentence came with a punch line. He read on
about Sir Walter Elliot.

He smiled. A handsome arrangement of words, clever and
droll, showed themselves at last. She set up a character in a few

lines. Fred had never met Sir Walter, yet he had met someone like him a hundred times before. He read the second chapter in half the time. By the third chapter, a transformation had occurred: reaching ten pages was forgotten; instead of forcing himself to plow through Jane's work, which he endured only because he loved her, he now forgot Jane had authored the book at all and read simply to discover what happened next. Fred smiled. Damn. Something he'd long suspected was now confirmed. He had stood in the presence of greatness. How he must have bored her.

He felt a pair of eyes on him and looked up. A familiar woman about his age sat in the opposite seat. She held up her book. She was reading *Persuasion* also.

"Simone, right?" he said. "St. Margaret's. Goal attack."

"That's me," she said. He shook her hand. "Do you like it?" she asked. She pointed to the book.

"It's good, isn't it?" Fred said. "Witty."

"She's the master," Simone said. She smiled.

The train pulled up to Reading station.

"Enjoy," Simone said. "This is my stop." She alighted the train and waved at Fred as it pulled away from the station. He waved back.

The train continued its way to Bath and Fred read on.

The next part contained a description of the middle daughter, Anne Elliot. She was an intelligent and dutiful spinster, at the financial mercy of an extravagant father. Further chapters revealed her to be a devoted aunt and a good listener. She had rejected a young man in her youth who loved her and now, older, she regretted it. Fred reached the end of the chapter and looked out the window. A sea of green fields rushed by. This was a sad book.

Fred turned the page. A new character was introduced, a naval captain. His gaze drifted out the window and he thought of Jane's love for her seafaring brothers. His eyes darted back to the page and locked onto two words.

The book hit the floor with a crack, which echoed through the carriage and startled awake a laborer who dozed in the vestibule. Fred apologized with a nod. He picked up the book once more and double-checked.

The naval captain's name was Frederick Wentworth.

Fred exhaled. He raced through the page, then turned it over. The next page contained no text. Instead, a line drawing illustrated Captain Wentworth. He wore a uniform of King George's navy, and a ribbon held back shoulder-length tresses. He wore no beard but sideburns. Beneath the Georgian epaulets and long hair, Fred's own face stared back at him.

Fred wiped his eye. The picture's likeness to his own features startled him. He saw how it would have been achieved. The woman with the photographic memory would have related every curve of his skin and bump of his nose to a beloved sister, and Cassandra would have nodded and sketched each detail faithfully, with a steady hand. Beyond the accuracy of the features, though, something else lurked to disarm him. In the picture, Fred smiled. A huge grin with bared teeth did not describe the expression; instead, his mouth remained closed, his lips touching, and the smile came more from his eyes, which shone from the page in a warm gaze. A look of utter love might describe it best, and he had given it to just one person. She had promised him at the time to remember that look forever, and she had kept her word.

Chapter Fifty-Nine

Jane walked into Forsyth's, a general shop that sold stamps and stationery on Stall Street. Forsyth himself sat at the counter and read from the newspaper. Jane dumped the bag of sugar on the counter. It had survived the journey from the twenty-first century, to her delight, alongside one ballpoint pen she had stuffed in her pocket at the last minute and which had enjoyed such prolific use over the past few days Jane had almost drained it of ink.

"How much will you give me?" Jane asked.

Forsyth looked up from his paper. He dipped a finger into the bag and tasted the white crystals. He scoffed. "Ten shillings."

"I see you have perfected the art of the swindle," Jane said.

Forsyth crossed his arms. "Fifteen."

Jane huffed. "Perhaps Buxton's prefers to purchase this."

"Perhaps they do," Forsyth said with a shrug.

Jane picked up the bag and began to walk from the shop.

"Very well. Twenty shillings," he called after her.

"Eighty," Jane said, turning.

"Sixty," said Forsyth.

Jane smiled. "Deal."

She exited Forsyth's and pocketed her banknotes. Forsyth had paid her, relatively speaking, more than three hundred times what she had paid for the sugar in the twenty-first century. She puffed out her chest, proud of her first business deal. Sixty shillings would buy a year's worth of ink and paper.

She stretched her right hand. She had written for four hours that morning and felt anxious to get home. Her mother had done her a service with her pyromancy. Jane remembered what she had written before word for word. But when it came to the task of rewriting, she hesitated to write the same. Since a young age, she had bit and scowled at the world through her prose; her characters always met with violent and farcical ends, saying crude and clever things. But now she found herself writing with sympathy for her heroines. Their triumphs came not at the expense of stupid companions but through curious items such as their own talents and dignity. The jokes remained; she still made fun—the world provided her with too much material to do otherwise. But she made fun of everything except love. What a soft head she was turning out to be.

Two young women stood in the street and snickered at Jane behind lace-gloved hands. In the wake of the Withers event and Jane's temporary exit from the village, the concerned women of Bath fixed Jane as a hysteric. Their assertions, considering Jane's behavior, probably held water. Every assembly shunned her; people pointed in the streets. Jane waved at the two women, which seemed to cause them great confusion, and walked on.

Jane turned the corner and smiled to herself. She dipped her hand into her pocket. She slipped the gold and turquoise ring off her middle finger and slid it onto the other one. She cradled her hand in a ball.

Had she made the right decision? Of course she had. She bent to tie her bootlace and wiped her eyes with a shaky hand.

And when, fourteen years later, she died on a settee in the sitting room of a rented house in Winchester, the last thing to go through her mind was Fred taking her hand the first time he danced with her.

But for now, Jane turned into Bennett Street and crossed the piazza. A crowd filed into Wood's Rooms for the evening assembly. Married couples waited by the main doors, arm in arm. A trio of old men discussed France. A gaggle of young ladies gossiped with hope about their latest beaux. Jane weaved her way through them and turned for Pulteney Bridge, her face warmed by the sun of a pink and yellow sky.

About the Author

RACHEL GIVNEY is a writer and filmmaker originally from Sydney, currently based in Melbourne. She has worked on *Offspring*, *The Warriors*, *McLeod's Daughters*, *Rescue: Special Ops*, and *All Saints*. Her films have been official selections at the Sydney Film Festival, Flickerfest, and many more. *Jane in Love* is her first book.